THE SERPENT & THE WINGS OF NIGHT

THE SERPENT & THE WINGS OF NIGHT

A CROWNS OF NYAXIA NOVEL

The Nightborn Duet

BOOK ONE

CARISSA BROADBENT

BRAMBLE

TOR PUBLISHING GROUP · NEW YORK

THE SERPENT & THE WINGS OF NIGHT

Copyright © 2022 by Carissa Broadbent

Interior design by Carissa Broadbent

A Bramble Book
Published by Tom Doherty Associates / Tor Publishing Group
120 Broadway
New York, NY 10271

www.torpublishinggroup.com

Bramble™ is a trademark of Macmillan Publishing Group, LLC.

The Library of Congress has cataloged the hardcover edition as follows:

Names: Broadbent, Carissa, author.
Title: The serpent & the wings of night : a Crowns of Nyaxia novel / Carissa Broadbent.
Other titles: Serpent and the wings of night
Description: First Bramble edition. | New York : Bramble, Tor Publishing Group, 2023. |
    Series: The Nightborn duet ; book one
Identifiers: LCCN 2023045861 | ISBN 9781250343178 (hardcover)
Subjects: LCGFT: Fantasy fiction. | Vampire fiction. | Romance fiction. | Novels.
Classification: LCC PS3602.R5396 S47 2023 | DDC 813/.6—dc23/eng/20231004
LC record available at https://lccn.loc.gov/2023045861

ISBN 978-1-250-34318-5 (trade paperback)

Our books may be purchased in bulk for promotional, educational, or business use. Please contact your local bookseller or the Macmillan Corporate and Premium Sales Department at 1-800-221-7945, extension 5442, or by email at MacmillanSpecialMarkets@macmillan.com.

Previously self-published by the author in August 2022
First Bramble Paperback Edition: 2024

Printed in the United States of America

0 9 8 7 6 5 4 3 2 1

For all the underdogs
who don't let fear stop them from fighting

The king did not know then that his greatest love would also be his ruination—nor that either would come in the form of a tiny, helpless human child.

She was a lone flutter of life in an endless expanse of decay, the only living mortal for a hundred miles. The child was perhaps four, perhaps eight—it was hard to tell, because she was so, so small, even by human standards. Just a frail little creature with slick black hair that curtained wide gray eyes.

Somewhere, buried beneath charred beams and crumbled stone, the girl's family likely lay crushed beyond recognition. Or perhaps their ravaged bodies had been left out in the night, taken by predators just like the ones that stalked the child now, looking down at her with the interest that a hawk afforded a rabbit.

The humans, of course, were nothing more than that in this world—prey, pests, or often both.

The three winged men landed before her, smiling at their luck. Immediately, the little girl struggled against the debris that pinned her. She recognized what they were—recognized their pointed teeth and black, featherless wings, and perhaps she even recognized the uniforms they wore, the deep purple of the Hiaj Nightborn King. Perhaps the men who had burned her home had worn uniforms just like these.

But she could not run. Her clothing was torn and hopelessly tangled in the ruins around her. She was too small to shift the stones.

"Look at this. A little lamb." The men approached. As one of them reached out for her, she snarled at him, catching his fingertips between small, blunt teeth.

The soldier hissed and yanked his hand away, while his companions laughed.

"A lamb? More like a viper."

"Or a garden snake," another scoffed.

The bitten soldier rubbed his hand, wiping away a few droplets of crimson-black. He started for the child. "Doesn't matter," he grumbled. "They taste the same. And I don't know about you bastards, but I'm hungry after such a long night."

But then a shadow fell over them all.

The men stilled. They lowered heads in reverent bows. The cool air shivered, the darkness twisting around their faces and wings like a blade caressing a throat.

The Hiaj king did not utter a single word. He did not need to. The moment he made his presence known, all of his warriors fell into silence.

He was not the physically strongest vampire. He was not the fiercest warrior nor the wisest sage. But they said he was blessed by the goddess Nyaxia herself, and anyone who had ever met him would swear it to be true. Power seeped from his every pore, and death stained his every breath.

His soldiers said nothing as he stepped over the wreckage of the little home.

"The Rishan have been eradicated from the area," one of them chanced, after several long moments. "The rest of our men have traveled north and—"

The king lifted his hand, and the warrior went quiet.

He kneeled down before the little girl, who glowered at him. So young, he thought. Her life, a mere handful of years, was nothing compared to his centuries of existence. And yet, she drew upon such intense hatred as she glared at him, her eyes as bright and silver as the moon.

"She was found here?" the king asked.

"Yes, sire."

"Is she the reason for the blood on your hand?"

A wave of poorly suppressed snickers from the other soldiers.

"Yes, sire." The answer was slightly bashful.

They thought he was mocking them. No. This had nothing to do with them.

He reached for the girl, and she snapped at him. He let her bite—did not move his hand, even as her teeth, tiny as they were, sank deep into his bony index finger.

She looked him straight in the eye, unblinking, and he returned that stare with mounting interest.

This was not the stare of a panicked child who didn't know what she was doing.

This was the stare of a creature who understood she was confronting death itself, and still chose to spit in its face.

"A little serpent," he murmured.

The men behind him laughed. He ignored them. It was not a joke.

"Are you all alone?" he said softly.

The girl did not answer. She could not speak with her teeth clamped around his flesh.

"If you release me," he said, "I will not hurt you."

The girl did no such thing, still glaring at him as black blood dribbled down her chin.

The corner of the king's lips curled. "Good. You should not trust me."

He pried his finger free, then carefully extracted the girl from the wreckage as she thrashed. Even in the throes of her violent resistance, she was utterly silent. And it was only once he picked her up—Goddess, she was so light, he could have held her with a single hand—that he realized how injured she was, her torn clothing soaked with blood. The sweet scent of it permeated his nostrils as he tucked her against his chest. She teetered on the precipice of unconsciousness, but she resisted it, her entire body tense.

"Rest, little serpent. No harm will come to you."

He stroked her cheek, and she tried to bite again, but a spark of magic trailed his fingertips. With that whisper of night came a dreamless sleep too heavy for even this vicious little thing to fight.

"What do you want us to do with her?" one of the soldiers asked.

The king strode past them. "Nothing. I will take her."

A beat of silence. Though he could not see them, the king knew they were exchanging confused glances.

"Where?" one asked, at last.

"Home," the king replied.

The child slept, one hand clenched tight around the silk fabric of the king's shirt—fighting still, in this small way, even in sleep.

Home. He would take her home.

Because the king of the Hiaj vampires—conqueror of the House of Night, blessed of the goddess Nyaxia, and one of the most powerful men to have walked this realm or the next—saw a fragment of himself in this child. And there, right beneath the clenched fist of her palm, something warm and bittersweet stirred in his chest at the sight of her. Something more dangerous than hunger.

Hundreds of years later, historians and scholars would look back upon this moment. This decision that, one day, would topple an empire.

What a strange choice, they would whisper. *Why would he do this?*

Why, indeed.

After all, vampires know better than anyone how important it is to protect their hearts.

And love, understand, is sharper than any stake.

PART ONE

DUSK

CHAPTER ONE

It started as practice. Just a little game, a little exercise. Something I needed to prove to myself. I wasn't sure when it had evolved into sport—my shameful, secret rebellion.

Some might find it stupid for me, a human, to hunt at night, when I was at a considerable disadvantage compared to my prey. But the night was when they acted, and so it was when I did, too.

I pressed to the wall, the dagger clenched tight in my hands. The night was warm, the kind when the sun's heat clung to the steamy humidity of the air long after sunset. The smell hung in a thick, rotten cloud—rancid food from the trash in the alleys, yes, but also decaying meat and sour blood. The vampires didn't care to clean up after themselves here, in the human districts of the House of Night.

Humans were supposed to be safe here, within the walls of the kingdom—citizens, if inferior ones, weaker than the Nightborn in every way. But that second truth too often rendered the first irrelevant.

The man was a Hiaj, his wings tucked in close to his back. Apparently he wasn't much of a magic user, because he didn't spirit them away for easier hunting. Or maybe he just enjoyed the effect that they had on his prey. Some of them were showy like that. They liked to be feared.

From the rooftop, I watched the man stalk his target—a little boy, perhaps ten, though small from obvious malnourishment. The boy was in the fenced-in dirt yard of a clay house, bouncing a ball against the dust over and over again, oblivious to death creeping up on him.

It was so, so stupid for this boy to be out at night alone. But then again, I knew better than anyone how growing up in constant danger could wear upon a person. Maybe this family had kept their children inside after dark every single day of the last ten years. It only took one lapse, one distracted mother who forgot to call him back, one grumpy child who wasn't ready to come inside for dinner. Just one night in a lifetime.

It happened so often.

But it wouldn't happen tonight.

When the vampire moved, so did I.

I dropped from the rooftop down to the cobblestones. I was quiet, but vampire hearing was impeccable. The man turned, greeting me with icy eyes and a curled lip that revealed a glint of sharp ivory.

Did he recognize me? Sometimes they did. I didn't give this one the chance.

It was practically routine, by now. A system I'd honed to perfection on hundreds of nights just like this one.

Wings first. Two slashes, one through each—enough to keep him from flying. With Hiaj vampires, that was easy. The membranous skin was delicate as paper. Sometimes I would catch Rishan vampires instead, and that was a bit more challenging—their feathered wings were harder to puncture—but I had refined the technique. This step was important, and that was why it came first. I needed to keep them here on the ground with me. I made the mistake of skipping it once, and almost didn't survive to learn the lesson.

I couldn't be stronger than them, so I had to be more precise. No time for mistakes.

The vampire let out a sound between a gasp of pain and a snarl of rage. My heartbeat had become a rapid thrum, blood close to the surface of my skin. I wondered if he smelled it. I had spent my entire life trying to hide the flush of my blood, but right now, I was glad for it. It made them stupid. This fool wasn't even armed, yet he still threw himself at me without a care in the world.

I loved it—really, truly loved it—when they underestimated me.

A blade to the side, beneath the ribs. Another to the throat. Not enough to kill. Enough to make him falter.

I pushed him against the wall, one blade skewering him to keep him still. I'd coated the edges with Dhaivinth—a fast-acting paralytic, potent though short-lived. It would only work for a few minutes, but that was all I needed.

He only managed a couple scratches across my cheek with razor-tipped fingers before his movements began to weaken. And just when I saw his eyes blink fast, like he was trying to wake himself up, I struck.

You have to push hard to make it through the breastbone.

I did—hard enough to crack the bone, to open the passage to his heart. Vampires were stronger than me in every way—their bodies more muscular, movements swifter, teeth sharper.

But their hearts were just as soft.

The moment my blade punctured their chests, I always heard my father's voice.

Don't look away, little serpent, Vincent whispered in my ear.

I didn't. Not then, and not now. Because I knew what I'd see there in the darkness. I knew I'd see the beautiful face of a boy I once loved very much, and exactly how it looked when my knife slid into his chest.

Vampires were the children of the goddess of death. So it was a bit funny to me that they feared it just as much as humans did. I watched them every time, and I saw the terror settle over their faces as they realized it was coming for them.

At least in this, we were the same. At least we're all fucking cowards in the end.

Vampire blood was darker than human blood. Almost black, as if darkened layer over layer by human and animal blood consumed over the course of centuries. Once I let the vampire fall, I was covered in it.

I stepped back from the body. It was only then that I saw the family staring at me—I was quiet, but not quiet enough to avoid notice when I was practically on their doorstep. The boy was now clutched tight in his mother's arms. A man was with them, too, and another child, a younger girl. They were thin, their clothes plain and threadbare, stained from long days of work. All four of them stood in the doorway, eyes locked on me.

I froze, like a stag caught by a tracker in the forest.

Strange, that it was these starving humans, not the vampire, that turned me from the hunter to the hunted.

Maybe it was because when I was with vampires, I knew what I was. But when I looked at these humans, the lines grew blurry and ill-defined—like I was observing a twisted reflection of myself.

Or maybe I was the reflection.

They were like me. And yet, I could find nothing in common between us. I imagined that if I opened my mouth to speak to them, we wouldn't even understand the noises each other made. They looked like animals to me.

The ugly truth was that perhaps a part of me was disgusted by them, the same way I was disgusted by all my own human flaws. And yet another part of me—maybe the part that remembered I had once lived in a house just like this one—longed to venture closer.

I wouldn't, of course.

No, I wasn't a vampire. That much was abundantly clear, every second of every day. But I wasn't one of them, either.

A shock of cold struck my cheek. I touched it and my fingers came back wet. Rain.

The drops disrupted our breathless silence. The woman stepped forward, as if to say something, but I had already slipped back into the shadows.

I COULDN'T RESIST the detour. Normally, I would have scaled the castle directly to my room in the western towers. Instead, I climbed east, jumping the garden walls and heading to the servants' quarters. I slipped in through the window, which overlooked an overgrown bush of indigo blue blossoms that flushed silver in the moonlight. As soon as my feet touched the floor, I cursed, nearly toppling over as what felt like a pile of liquid fabric slid beneath my boots over the smooth wood.

The laugh sounded like the caw of a crow, devolving quickly into a cacophony of coughs.

"Silk," the old woman croaked. "The best trap for little burglars."

"This place is a fucking disaster, Ilana."

"Bah." She rounded the corner and peered at me through narrowed eyes, drawing in a deep, rattling inhale of her cigar and letting the smoke out through her nose. She was dressed in cascading chiffon dyed in waves of color. Black-and-gray-streaked hair piled atop her head with admirable volume. Gold pendants dangled from each earlobe, and her wrinkled eyes were painted with shades of gray-blue and a generous lining of kohl.

Her apartment was just as colorful and chaotic as she was— clothing and jewels and bright paint strewn about every surface. I had come in through her living room window, which I now pulled closed against the rain. The place was tiny, but far nicer than the clay, crumbling slums in the human district.

She looked me up and down, rubbing her neck. "I take no criticisms from a drowned rat like you."

I glanced down at myself and blanched. Only now, in the warm lantern light, did I realize what a mess I was.

"You'd never guess you were pretty under all of that, Oraya," she went on. "Dead set on making yourself look as unappealing as possible. Which reminds me! I have something for you. Here."

With knobby, arthritic hands, she fished through a crumpled pile beside her, then tossed a fistful of fabric across the room to me. "Catch."

I caught it in my fist, then unfolded it. The band of silk was nearly as long as I was tall, and a stunning deep violet with edges embroidered in gold.

"Made me think of you." Ilana leaned against the doorframe and took another puff of her cigar.

I didn't ask where she had gotten something like this. Age had not made her fingers any less deft—or sticky.

"You should keep it. I don't wear this sort of stuff. You know that."

Day to day, I wore only black, plain clothing that attracted little attention and allowed me free range of movement. I didn't ever wear anything bright (as it would draw unwanted eyes), flowing (as it would allow someone to grab me), or restrictive (as it would impede my ability to fight, or flee). I wore my leathers most of the time, even in the oppressive heat of the summer. They were protective and unobtrusive.

Sure, maybe I admired pretty things just as much as any other. But I was surrounded by predators. Vanity came second to survival.

Ilana scoffed. "I know that you love the fineries too, rat. Even if you're too afraid to wear 'em. Damned shame. Youth is wasted on the young. Beauty, too. It's a good color for you. Dance around naked in your bedroom with it for all I care."

My brow quirked as I eyed her hoard of colors. "Is that what you do with yours?"

She winked. "All that and more. And don't pretend you don't, too."

Ilana had never been to my room, and yet she knew me well enough to know that I did, indeed, have a single drawer stuffed with little, colorful trinkets that I had collected over the years. Things that were too pointlessly ostentatious to wear in this life, but that, perhaps, I could dream of wearing in another.

No matter how much I tried to explain it to her, Ilana didn't understand my caution. She'd made it clear many times over that she was done—"*Done!*" she proclaimed—with caution.

I honestly didn't know how the old bat had survived this long, but I was grateful for it. The humans I had seen in the slums this morning were nothing like me, and the vampires that surrounded me even less so. Only Ilana lingered somewhere in between, just like I did.

Albeit for very different reasons.

I had been raised in this world, but Ilana had joined it of her own volition ten years ago. As a young teenager, I had been fascinated by her. I had met few other humans. I didn't realize then that Ilana was, even among humans, somewhat . . . unique.

Ilana touched her neck again. I realized the cloth clenched in her fist wasn't red, or at least, it hadn't started that way. I stepped closer and noticed the wounds on her throat—three sets of two. Then the bandage on her wrist, which covered up Nyaxia knew how many more.

My face must have changed, because she hacked another laugh.

"A big dinner tonight," she said. "I was paid well for it. Paid, to have handsome men suck on my neck all night. My younger self would be thrilled."

I couldn't bring myself to even crack a smile.

Yes, I had no idea how Ilana had survived this long. Most voluntary human blood vendors—of which there were few—were killed within a year of starting work. I knew too well exactly how little self-control vampires had when hunger was involved.

Some things Ilana and I would never agree on.

"I won't be around for a while," I said, changing the subject. "I just wanted to let you know, so you don't worry."

Ilana's face went still. Even in the dim light, I saw her pale two shades. "That bastard. You're doing it."

I didn't want to have this conversation, even though I knew it was coming.

"You should think about leaving the inner city temporarily," I went on. "Going to the districts. I know you hate it, but at least there—"

"Fuck that."

"It's the Kejari, Ilana. It's not safe here for you. For any human outside the protected district."

"'*Protected district.*' Those *slums*. There's a reason why I left. They reek of misery." Her nose wrinkled. "Misery and piss."

"It's safe."

I didn't miss the irony of saying this when I was covered in blood after returning from that place.

"Bah. Safety is overrated. What kind of life is that? You want me to leave when the most exciting event in two centuries is about to happen on my doorstep? No, sweetheart. I'm not doing that."

I had told myself that I would stay calm—had known that Ilana would probably not listen to me. Still, I couldn't keep the frustration from my voice.

"You're being foolish. It's just a few months. Or even a few days! If you were to leave just for the opening—"

"*Foolish!*" she spat. "Is that *him* talking? Is that what he calls you, whenever you want to do anything outside his control?"

I let out a breath through clenched teeth. Yes, Vincent *would* call me foolish if I was refusing to protect myself for no good reason. And he'd be right for it, too.

The human district may be a slum, but at least humans there had the veneer of protection. Here? I didn't know what would happen to Ilana, or any human within the inner city, once the Kejari began. Especially one that had already signed away their blood.

I'd heard stories about how humans had been used in these tournaments. I didn't know what was true and what was exaggeration, but they made my stomach turn. Sometimes I wanted to ask Vincent, but I knew he'd think I was concerned for myself. I didn't want him to worry over me any more than he already did. And . . . he didn't quite know exactly how close Ilana and I had gotten over these last few years.

There were a lot of things Vincent didn't know. Parts of myself that didn't line up with his vision for who I was. Just as there were things about me that Ilana would never understand.

Still, I didn't know what I would do without either of them. I had no family here. Whoever was in that house with me when Vincent found me had been killed. If any distant relatives remained, they were trapped somewhere I couldn't reach; at least, not until I won the Kejari. But I had Vincent, and I had Ilana, and they had become everything that I imagined a family to be, even if neither of them could understand every contradictory part of me.

Now, as the possibility of losing Ilana seemed suddenly far too tangible, fear clenched my heart and refused to relinquish it.

"Ilana, please." My voice was oddly choked. "*Please,* just go."

Ilana's face softened. She stuffed her cigar into an overflowing ashtray and came close enough that I could count the wrinkles around her eyes. Her leathery hand caressed my cheek. She smelled like smoke and too-pungent rose perfume—and blood.

"You're sweet," she said. "Prickly, but sweet. In an acidic sort of way. Like . . . like a pineapple."

Despite myself, the corner of my mouth twisted. "A *pineapple*?" What a ridiculous word. Knowing her, she probably made it up.

"But I'm tired, sweetheart. Tired of being afraid. I left the district because I wanted to see what it was like here, and it has been exactly as much of an adventure as I thought it would be. I risk my life every day to be here. As do you."

"You don't have to be stupid about it."

"It becomes a rebellion not to care. I know you know that as well as I do. Even if you stuff the colors into the back of your dresser." She shot a pointed look at my bloodstained clothes. "Even if you hide it in the shadows of the district's alleyways."

"Please, Ilana. Just for a week, even if it isn't for the full Kejari. Here." I thrust out the scarf. "Take this garish thing and give it to me when you come back, and I even promise I'll wear it."

She was silent for a long moment, then took the silk and tucked it into her pocket. "Fine. I'll leave in the morning."

I let out a sigh of relief.

"But you. *You,* stubborn rat . . ." Her hands came to my face, squishing my cheeks between them. "You be careful. I won't lecture you about what he's making you do—"

I pulled away from her shockingly strong grip. "He's not *making* me do anything."

"*Bah!*" I had moved just in time, because the scoff was so vicious it sent flecks of spittle flying. "I don't want to watch you become one of them. It would be—" Her jaw snapped shut, and her eyes searched my face, a wave of unnervingly intense emotion passing over her expression. "It would be fucking *boring.*"

It wasn't what she wanted to say, and I knew it. But Ilana and I had that sort of relationship. All the raw honesty, all the unpleasant tenderness, hid in the things we didn't say. Just as I would not say aloud that I was competing in the Kejari, she would not say aloud that she was scared for me.

Still, it startled me to see her on the verge of tears. Only now did I really realize that she only had me. I, at least, had Vincent, but she was alone.

My gaze drifted up to the clock, and I spat a curse.

"I have to go," I blurted out, retreating to the window. "Don't drink yourself to death, you old hag."

"Don't skewer yourself with that stick up your ass," she retorted, wiping her eyes, all hints of her earlier vulnerability gone.

Crazy old bitch, I thought, affectionately.

I threw open the window and let the steam of the summer rain hit my face. I didn't mean to pause—something heavier sat on the tip of my tongue, words I'd only said out loud once before to someone who deserved it less.

But Ilana had already disappeared back into her bedroom. I swallowed whatever I was going to say, and fell back into the night.

CHAPTER TWO

Once the rain started, it came on fast. Typical of the House of Night. Vincent joked often, in his dry, sardonic way, that this country never did anything halfway. The sun either assaulted us with unrelenting heat, or it retreated completely beneath many layers of dusky, red-gray clouds. The air was arid and so hot you swore it would bake you alive, or cold enough to make your joints crack. Half the time, the moon hid within the haze, but when it was visible, it gleamed like polished silver, its light so intense it made the dips and hills of the sand resemble the waves of the ocean—or what I'd imagined such a thing would look like.

It did not rain often in the Nightborn kingdom, but when it did, it was a downpour.

By the time I made it back to the Palace, I was soaked. My path up the side of the building was treacherous, each grip of stone slippery and water-slicked, but it wasn't the first time I'd made the journey in the rain and it wouldn't be the last. When I finally vaulted into my bedchamber, many stories above the ground, my muscles burned with the effort.

My hair was dripping wet. I wrung it out, sending a symphony of droplets spattering to the velvet bench beneath the window, and turned to the horizon. It was so hot that the rain summoned a silver cloud of steam over the city. The view from up here was very different from the one from the rooftop in the human quarter of the city. That had been an expanse of clay blocks, a painting of varying shades of brown squares beneath the moonlight. In the heart of Sivrinaj, though—in royal Nightborn territory—every glance overflowed with sumptuous elegance.

The view from my window was a symmetrical sea of undulating curves. The Nightborn drew their architectural inspiration from the sky and moon—metal-capped domes, polished granite, silver that cradled indigo stained glass. From up here, the moonlight and rain caressed an expanse of platinum. The ground was so flat that even though Sivrinaj was a massive city, I could still glimpse the dunes in the distance beyond its walls.

Eternity gave vampires so many years to perfect the art of dark, dangerous beauty. I'd heard that the House of Shadow, across the Ivory Sea, crafted their buildings the way they crafted blades, each castle an intricate set of pointed spires sprawling with blood-kissed ivy. Some claimed theirs was the most exquisite architecture in the world—but I didn't know how anyone could say that if they saw the House of Night as I did, from this room. It was even stunning in daylight, when no one here but me could witness it.

I carefully closed the window, and I had barely finished latching it when the knock sounded at my door. Two raps, quiet but demanding.

Fuck.

I was lucky I hadn't gotten here just a few minutes later. It had been risky to go out tonight, but I couldn't help myself. My nerves were too strained. My hands had to do something.

I hastily removed my coat and tossed it into a discarded pile of clothes in the corner, then grabbed my robe and wrapped it around myself. It would be enough to cover the blood, at least.

I rushed across the room and opened the door, and Vincent didn't hesitate before striding in.

He gave my room a cold, judgmental once-over. "It's a mess in here."

Now I knew how Ilana felt. "I've had bigger things to worry about than cleaning."

"Keeping a tidy space is important for mental clarity, Oraya."

I was twenty-three, and he still lectured me that way.

I touched my forehead, as if he had just bestowed upon me information that rearranged my universe. "Fuck. It *is?*"

Vincent's moon-silver eyes narrowed at me. "You're an insolent brat, little serpent."

He never sounded more affectionate than when he was insulting me. Maybe it meant something that both Ilana and Vincent cradled their tenderness in harsh words. They were so different from each other in every other sense. But maybe this place made all of us that way. Taught us to hide love in sharp edges.

Now, for some reason, that rebuke made my chest clench. Funny, the things that make the fear finally bubble to the surface. I *was* scared, even if I knew better than to give voice to it. And I knew Vincent was, too. I saw it in the way his smirk slipped away as he looked at me.

Some might think that Vincent was not frightened of anything. I did for a long time. I grew up watching him rule—watching him seize absolute respect from a society that respected nothing.

He was my father in name alone. Perhaps I didn't have his blood, or his magic, or his immortality. But I had that ruthlessness. He had cultivated it in me, one thorn at a time.

Yet as I grew older, I learned that being ruthless was not the same thing as being fearless. I was afraid constantly, and so was Vincent. The man who was afraid of nothing was afraid for me— his human daughter raised in a world designed to kill her.

Until the Kejari. A tournament with the ability to change everything.

Until I won, and it freed me.

Or I lost, and it damned me.

Vincent blinked, and we both made the mutual, silent decision not to voice such thoughts. He looked me up and down, as if noticing my appearance for the first time. "You're wet."

"I took a bath."

"*Before* training?"

"I needed to relax."

Well, that was true. I just decided to do it in a very different way than soaking in a lavender bath.

Even that statement came a little too close to acknowledging the reality of our situation for Vincent's comfort. His mouth slanted, and he ran a hand through pale blond hair.

His tell. His only one. Something was weighing on him. It could be about me and the impending trials, or . . .

I couldn't help but ask.

"What?" I asked, quietly. "Trouble with the Rishan?"

He was silent.

My stomach dropped. "Or the House of Blood?"

Or both?

His throat bobbed, and he shook his head. Yet that little movement was enough to confirm my suspicion.

I wanted to ask more, but Vincent's hand fell to his hip, and I realized he had brought his rapier.

"Our work is more important than such boring things. There will always be another enemy to worry about, but you only have tonight. Come."

VINCENT WAS AS ruthless an instructor as he was a ruler, meticulous and thorough. I'd gotten used to this, but still, the intensity of it caught me off guard tonight. He didn't give me time to think or hesitate between strikes. He used his weapon, his wings, the full force of his strength—even his magic, which he rarely employed in our training sessions. It was as if he was trying to show me exactly what it would be like if the king of the Nightborn vampires wanted me dead.

But then again, Vincent had never held back with me. Even when I was a child, he never let me forget how close death lingered. Every falter was met with his hand at my throat—two fingertips pressed to my skin, mimicking fangs.

"You're dead now," he would say. "Try again."

I didn't let him get those fingers to my throat this time. My muscles screamed, already tired from my last encounter, but I dodged every blow, slipped every grip, met every strike with my own. And finally, after countless exhausting minutes, I had him against the wall, one finger to his chest—the point of my blade.

"You're dead here," I panted.

And thank the Mother for it, because I wouldn't have survived another fucking second of this match.

The corner of Vincent's lip curled in pride for only a moment. "I could use Asteris."

Asteris—among the most powerful of the Nightborn vampires' magical gifts, and the rarest. Pure energy said to be derived from stars, manifested as blinding black light capable of killing instantly at full force. Vincent's mastery of it was peerless. I'd once witnessed him use it to level an entire building of Rishan rebels.

Vincent had tried, over the years, to teach me how to wield magic. I could make a few little sparks. Pathetic compared to the lethal skill of a vampire magic user—from the House of Night or any other.

For a moment, the thought of this—a fresh reminder of all the ways I was inferior to the warriors I was about to face—made me dizzy. But I pushed this uncertainty away quickly. "Asteris wouldn't matter if I'd already killed you."

"Would you be fast enough? You always struggled to get to the heart."

You have to push hard to make it through the breastbone.

I blinked back the unwelcome memory. "Not anymore."

My finger was still pressed to his chest. I was never entirely sure when our sparring sessions ended, so I never let up before the match was called. He was only a few inches from me—a few inches from my throat. I never, ever allowed any other vampire this close. The smell of my blood was overwhelming to them. Even if a vampire *wanted* to resist it—and they so rarely did—they might not be able to control themselves.

Vincent had carved these lessons into me. Never trust. Never yield. Always guard your heart.

And when I had disobeyed, I had paid for it dearly.

But not with him. Never him. He had packed my bleeding wounds countless times without revealing even a hint of temptation. Had guarded me when I slept. Had cared for me at my weakest.

That made it easier. I spent my entire life afraid, forever conscious of my weakness and inferiority, but at least I had a single safe harbor.

Vincent's eyes searched my face.

"Very well." He pushed my hand away. I went to the edge of the ring, wincing as I rubbed a wound he'd opened on my arm. He barely glanced at the blood.

"You have to be careful of that when you're in there," he said. "Bleeding."

I wrinkled my nose. Goddess, he *must* be worried. Telling me such basic things. "I know."

"More than usual, Oraya."

"I know."

I took a swig of water from my canteen, my back to him. My eyes instead traced the fresco on the wall—beautiful and terrible paintings depicting razor-teethed vampires writhing in a sea of blood beneath silver stars. The arrangement stretched the entire room. This private training ring was reserved for Vincent and his highest-ranking warriors, and it was more disgustingly ornate than any place meant for spit, blood, and sweat should be. The floor was soft ivory sand replaced from the dunes every week. The fresco covered the circular, windowless walls—a single, panoramic tableau of death and conquering.

The figures depicted in it were Hiaj vampires, with bat-like wings ranging in shade from milky pale to ash-black. Two hundred years ago, those wings would have been the feathered wings of the Rishan, the rival Nightborn clan perpetually battling for the throne of the House of Night. Since the goddess Nyaxia created vampires more than two thousand years ago—since before then, some even claimed—the two sects had waged constant war. And with every turn in the tide, every new bloodline on the throne, this fresco would change—wings painted and erased, painted and erased, dozens of times over thousands of years.

I glanced over my shoulder at Vincent. He had left his wings out, which was rare. Usually he spirited them away with his magic, unless it was some diplomatic event that required him to flaunt his Hiaj power. They were long enough that the tips nearly brushed the floor, and black—so black it defied nature, as if the light seeped into his skin and died there. But even more striking were the streaks of red. Crimson ran down his wings like rivulets of water, collecting at the edges and at each pointed tip. When Vincent's wings were spread, they looked as if they were outlined in blood, vivid enough to cut through even the most unforgiving darkness.

The black was unusual, but not unheard of. The red, though, was unique. Each Hiaj or Rishan Heir bore two Marks—red on their wings, and another on their body—which appeared when the previous Heir died. Vincent's Mark was at the base of his throat, just above his clavicle. It was a mesmerizing, ornate design that resembled a full moon and wings, wrapping around the front of his neck in crimson as vibrant as a bleeding wound. I had only seen it a couple of times. He usually covered it beneath high-collared jackets or black silk wrapped tight and neat around his neck.

When I was younger, I had once asked him why he didn't leave it visible more often. He'd just given me a serious stare and blandly remarked that it was unwise to leave one's throat exposed.

That answer shouldn't have surprised me. Vincent was well aware that usurpers lurked around every corner, both outside his walls and within them. Every new king, Hiaj or Rishan, was crowned upon a mountain of corpses. He had been no exception.

I turned away from the painting, just as he said softly, "It's nearing a full moon. You should have a few more days, but it could begin any time. You need to be ready."

I swallowed another gulp of water. Still, my mouth tasted ashy. "I know."

"The start could be anything. She likes it to be . . . unexpected."

She. Mother of night, shadow, blood—mother of all vampires. The goddess Nyaxia.

At any moment, she could trigger the start of the once-in-a-century tribute that the House of Night staged in her honor. A savage tournament of five trials over four months, resulting in only one winner, and granting the most precious prize the world has ever known: a single gift from the Goddess herself.

Vampires from across Obitraes would travel to participate in the Kejari, drawn by the promise of wealth or honor. Dozens of the most powerful warriors from all three houses—the House of Night, the House of Shadow, and the House of Blood—would die in pursuit of this title.

And, most likely, so would I.

But they were fighting for power. I was fighting for survival.

Vincent and I turned to each other at the same time. He was always pale, his skin nearly matching his silver eyes, but now he seemed a downright sickly shade.

His fear made my own unbearable, but I fought it down with a promise. No. I had trained my entire life for this. I would survive the Kejari. I would win it.

Just like Vincent had before me, two hundred years ago.

He cleared his throat, straightening. "Go change into something decent. We're going to look at your competition."

CHAPTER THREE

Vincent had said this was a feast to welcome travelers to the House of Night ahead of the start of the Kejari. But that was an understatement. The event wasn't a "feast" so much as it was a display of shameless, exuberant gluttony.

Well, that was fitting, wasn't it? The Kejari only happened once every hundred years, and hosting it was the House of Night's greatest honor. During the tournament, Sivrinaj welcomed guests from every corner of Obitraes, including all three Houses. It was an important diplomatic event, especially for nobles from the House of Night and House of Shadow. No one was *quite* as eager for a visit from the House of Blood—there was a reason why none of the Bloodborn had been invited to this event—but Vincent would never pass on the opportunity to peacock before the rest of vampire high society.

I came to this part of the castle so rarely that I had forgotten just how striking it was. The ceiling was a high dome of stained glass, gold-dyed stars scattered across cerulean blue. The moonlight spilling through it danced over the crowd in whorls. Half a dozen long tables had been set, now holding only the remnants of what had certainly, hours ago, been an incredible banquet. Vampires enjoyed all forms of food for pleasure, though blood—human, vampire, or animal—was necessary for their survival. The food still sat, long cold, on the tables, while the blood dotted plates and tablecloths in dribbles and spatters of drying crimson.

I thought of the wounds on Ilana's throat and wrist and wondered which stains were hers.

"Everyone already ate." Vincent offered me his arm, and I took it. He put me between himself and the wall. Everything about his demeanor was coolly casual, but I knew this was a very intentional decision—the arm, and my placement. The former reminded the rest of the room that I was his daughter. The latter physically protected me from anyone who might, in bloodlust, make an impulsive decision they'd regret.

Vincent didn't usually allow me to these types of events—for obvious reasons. He and I both understood that a human in a ballroom of hungry vampires was a bad idea for everyone involved. On the rare occasions that I did go out into vampiric society, I attracted flagrant attention. Today was no exception. All stares fell to him as he entered. And then they shifted to me.

My jaw locked and muscles stiffened.

Everything about that felt *wrong*. To be so visible. To have so many potential threats to watch.

With dinner done, most had moved to the dance floor, a hundred or so guests milling about dancing or gossiping as they sipped glasses of red wine—or blood. I recognized the familiar faces of Vincent's court, but there were also plenty of foreigners. Those from the House of Shadow wore heavy, tight-fitting clothing, the women adorned in corsets and clingy, velvety gowns, the men clad in stiff, minimalist jackets—all very different from the House of Night's flowing silks. I also saw a few unfamiliar faces from the House of Night's outer reaches, people who lived not in the inner city but perhaps lorded over districts far to the west of the deserts, or in the House of Night's island territories in the Bone Seas.

"I've been watching for bandages." Vincent ducked his head and spoke quietly to me, low enough that no one else could hear. "Some have already made their blood gift."

To Nyaxia—to signal their entry into the Kejari. My opponents.

"Lord Ravinthe." He nodded to an ashy-haired man locked in enthusiastic conversation across the ballroom. During one of his gesticulations, I caught a flash of white on his hand—black-red soaked fabric, covering a wound.

"I fought with him long ago," Vincent said. "His right knee is bad. He hides it well, but it pains him greatly."

I nodded and carefully filed this information away as Vincent continued to take me around the room. Maybe to someone who wasn't paying attention, we might have looked like we were just taking a leisurely walk, but with every step, he pointed out other contestants, telling me all he knew about their background or weaknesses.

A slight, fair-haired Shadowborn woman with sharp features.

"Kiretta Thann. I met her long ago. She's a weak swordswoman but a strong magician. Guard your thoughts around her."

A thick, tall man whose eyes had immediately found me the moment we entered the room.

"Biron Imanti. The worst bloodlust I've ever seen." Vincent's lip curled in disgust. "He'll go after you, but he will be so stupid about it that it should be easy for you to use that against him."

We finished one lap about the ballroom and started another. "I saw a few others. Ibrihim Cain. And—"

"*Ibrihim?*"

Vincent's brow twitched. "Many will enter the Kejari solely because they feel they have no other option."

I found Ibrihim across the room. He was a young vampire, barely older than I, with an unusually meek demeanor. As if he could feel my stare, his gaze flicked to me from beneath a mop of curly black hair. He gave me a weak smile, revealing mutilated gums jarringly absent of canine teeth. Beside him was his mother, a woman as brutally aggressive as her son was quiet—and the source of his wounds.

It was a story too common to be tragic. About ten years ago, when Ibrihim was on the cusp of adulthood, his parents had pinned him down, removed his teeth, and hobbled his left leg. I had been thirteen or so when it happened. Ibrihim's face had been a mess of swollen, bruised flesh. Unrecognizable. I had been horrified, and I didn't understand why Vincent wasn't.

What I didn't realize then was that vampires lived in constant fear of their own family. Immortality made succession a bloody, bloody business. Even Vincent had murdered his parents—and three siblings—to gain his title. Vampires killed their parents for power, then maimed their own children to keep them from doing the same. It satisfied their egos in the present and secured the future. Their line would continue . . . but not a moment before they were ready for it.

At least the Kejari would give Ibrihim a chance to regain his dignity or die trying. Still . . .

"He can't possibly think he could win," I muttered.

Vincent gave me a sidelong glance. "Everyone here probably thinks the same of you."

He wasn't wrong.

An overwhelming cloud of lilac scent wafted over us.

"There you are, sire. You had disappeared. I had been starting to get concerned."

Vincent and I turned. Jesmine approached us, carefully tossing a wave of smooth ash-brown hair over a bare shoulder. She wore a rich red gown that, while simple, clung to the lush shape of her body. She, unlike most of the Hiaj here, left her wings visible—they were slate gray, and her gown dipped low enough in the back to frame them with painterly drapes of crimson. The dress was deeply cut to reveal generous cleavage and a mottled white scar that ran up the center of her sternum.

She was never shy about displaying either—her cleavage, or the scar. Not that I could blame her. Her cleavage was objectively impressive, and as for the scar . . . rumor had it she'd survived a staking. If I'd done that, I'd flaunt that mark every damned day.

The corner of Vincent's mouth quirked. "The work never ends. As you know."

Jesmine raised her crimson glass. "I do indeed," she purred.

Oh, sun fucking take me.

I didn't know how I felt about Vincent's newly promoted head of the guard. It was rare for a woman to achieve such a rank in the House of Night—only three women had served in that position in the last thousand years—and I approved of that on principle alone. But I had also been trained my entire life to be distrustful. Vincent's previous head of the guard had been a scraggly, scar-riddled man named Thion, who had served for two hundred years. I didn't like him, but at least I knew he was loyal.

But when Thion grew ill and eventually died, his top general, Jesmine, had been the natural choice to replace him. I didn't have anything against her, but I didn't know her, and I certainly didn't trust her.

Maybe I was just territorial. Vincent seemed to like her.

He leaned a bit closer. "You look lovely," he murmured.

Really like her.

Despite myself, a hint of my scoff slipped from my lips. At the sound, Jesmine's amethyst eyes slipped to me. She was new enough that she still regarded me with blatant curiosity rather than the somewhat long-suffering annoyance of the other members of Vincent's tiny inner circle.

Her gaze slowly moved up my body, taking in my stature and my leathers, drinking in each feature of my face. If I didn't know better, I'd think she was being lecherous. Which would be . . . well, flattering, if it wasn't so often a precursor to an attempt on my throat.

"Good evening, Oraya."

"Hello, Jesmine."

Her nostrils flared—a subtle movement, but I saw it immediately. I stepped back, my hand moving to my dagger. Vincent noticed too, and ever-so-slightly shifted to put his body between mine and hers.

"Give me an update on the House of Blood," Vincent said to her, shooting me a look that commanded me to go. I drifted back toward the door, away from the rest of the crowd.

It was almost enough distance from the party guests to let me breathe a little easier. Almost.

When you're young, fear is debilitating. Its presence clouds your mind and senses. Now, I had been afraid for so long, so ceaselessly, that it was just another bodily function to regulate—heartbeat, breath, sweat, muscles. Over the years, I'd learned how to hack the physicality of it away from the emotion.

The bitter taste of jealousy coated my tongue as I leaned against the doorframe, watching the partygoers. I paid special attention to those Vincent had pointed out as Kejari contestants. With the exception of Ibrihim, who sat quietly at the table, most seemed carefree, dancing and drinking and flirting the night away. When dawn came, would they fall asleep entangled with one or three partners, sleep soundly, and not give a single thought to whether they would survive long enough to wake again?

Or would they finally know what it was like to lie awake staring at the ceiling, feeling their deathly goddess over their skin?

My eyes fell to the other side of the room.

The figure was so still that my gaze nearly passed right by. But something strange about them made me pause, even if at first, I didn't quite know why. After several seconds of observation, I realized it wasn't any single thing, but a collection of little ones.

He stood at the opposite side of the ballroom, far beyond all the debauchery of the dance floor, his back to me. He stared at one of the many paintings that adorned the wall. I couldn't see the details from this distance, but I knew the painting well. It was the smallest in the ballroom, the canvas narrow and long, star-dotted indigo blue at the top that gradually darkened to deep red. It depicted a lone figure: a Rishan vampire, falling, frozen halfway to his death in the center of the frame. His nude body was mostly covered by dark feathered wings splayed out around him, save for a single outstretched hand, reaching desperately for something that he could see but we could not.

Few pieces of Rishan artwork remained in the castle after the rise of the Hiaj. Most of it had been either destroyed or repainted to depict Hiaj vampires. I didn't know why this one survived. Perhaps it was deemed appropriate to keep because it portrayed a Rishan doomed, falling to the depths of hell even as he grasped for the sky.

This piece got little attention compared to the majestic epics around it, celebrations of bloody justice or triumphant victory. It was quiet. Sad. The first time I saw it, when I was only a child, my chest had tightened. I knew what it felt like to be powerless. And this single fallen Rishan, cradled by wings that could not fly, reaching for a savior who would not reach back . . . it was the only indication I'd ever seen that vampires could know what it was like to be powerless, too.

Maybe that was why I found myself intrigued by this figure—because he was looking at *this* painting, when no one else ever did. He was tall—taller than even most other vampires—and broad. He wore a deep purple jacket cut tight against his frame, a bronze sash wrapped around his waist. That, too, was a little off. The style was similar to the bright silks that all the other Nightborn wore, but the cut was a bit too sharp, the contrast a bit too bold. His hair was dark red—nearly black—and fell across his shoulders in rough waves. An unusual length, neither the flowing nor cropped styles favored by the House of Night's court.

I could count on one hand the number of Nightborn vampires from beyond Sivrinaj that I'd met. Maybe the styles were different in the outer reaches of the kingdom. Still . . .

He glanced over his shoulder, directly at me. His eyes were rust red, a striking enough color to be visible even from across the room. His gaze was casually curious. Still, the intensity of it skewered me.

Something was strange here, too. Something—

"Have you tried these?"

"Fuck."

I jolted.

I hadn't heard the woman approach, which was both embarrassing and dangerous. She was tall and willowy, with freckles scattered over bronze skin, wide dark eyes, and a halo of cropped black curls around her head. She grinned, a meat pastry dripping pink juices onto her fingertips as she held it out to me.

"This is *delicious.*"

I didn't much like vampires saying the word "delicious" while standing that close to me. I took two smooth steps away.

"I'm fine."

"Oh, you're missing out. It's—"

"Oraya."

Vincent never shouted. His voice was strong enough to cut across any room. I looked over my shoulder to see him at the arched entryway to the ballroom, nodding down the hall in an unmistakable message: *Let's go.*

He didn't have to tell me twice. I didn't bother bidding the woman a goodbye as I strode after him, more than grateful to leave this pit of claws and teeth.

Still, I found myself casting one more glance back to that painting. The man was gone. The fallen Rishan just grasped at open air, abandoned once again.

CHAPTER FOUR

I never drank. Vampire alcohol was incredibly strong for humans, and that aside, it was dangerous for me to dull my senses. Vincent rarely did, either—probably for the same reasons as me. So I was surprised when he brought the wine to my chambers. We took tiny sips and then set it aside, leaving it untouched as we sat in silence, listening to the crackling of the fire.

Finally, he spoke. "I think you are as prepared as you possibly could be."

He sounded like he was mostly trying to convince himself.

"The others will underestimate you," he went on. "Use that. It's a powerful weapon."

He was right. I had learned long ago that the best weapon I had was my own weakness. I used it to kill almost every night in the slums. Right now, it didn't feel like enough.

I swallowed past the lump in my throat. I watched my father as he looked to the fire, red light playing over the pale, hard angles of his face. Had he been this nervous the night he offered himself to his own Kejari?

"Is that what you did?" I asked. "Let them underestimate you?"

He blinked, taken aback. I rarely asked him about his time in the Kejari. I rarely asked him about his past at all. Maybe that sip of wine, or my nearly inevitable impending death, made me a little bold.

"Yes," he said, after a moment. "And it was likely why I won."

It seemed laughable now that Vincent was ever someone who could be underestimated. But two hundred years ago, he had just been a young, lesser Hiaj noble. The House of Night was under Rishan control then and seemed like it would remain that way for centuries more.

"Were you nervous?"

"No. I knew what I had to do."

At my visible skepticism, he lifted one shoulder in an almost-shrug. "Fine," he admitted. "I was nervous. But I knew the Kejari was my only path to a life worth remembering. Death isn't frightening when weighed against an insignificant existence."

An insignificant existence.

Those words hit me unexpectedly hard. Because what existence was more insignificant than this? Living in constant fear, hobbled by my own blood and my own human weakness? I could never be anything this way, fighting so hard to survive that I could never *do* anything. Could never *be* anything of worth to . . . to the people who had nothing but me.

My jaw clenched so hard it trembled. I grabbed my glass and took another sip of wine, mostly because I was desperate to do something with my hands. I could feel Vincent's eyes on me. Could feel the softening of his gaze.

"You do not have to do this, my little serpent," he said softly. "I realize only now that perhaps I never told you that."

It would be a lie to say that I wasn't tempted to run away—tempted to hide in the space between the dresser and the wall, just as I had when I was a small child. A part of me still always was hiding, because I was never going to be anything other than prey.

No, that was not a life of significance. It wasn't even a life at all.

"I'm not backing out," I said.

I looked down to my hand—to the delicate silver ring on my right little finger. A simple band with a black diamond so small it was no bigger than the band itself.

I'd had it in my pocket when Vincent found me as a child. I liked to think it belonged to my mother. Maybe it was just some worthless trinket. I would probably never know.

Absentmindedly, I rubbed it. Not even that tiny movement escaped Vincent's attention.

"I would have found them for you, if I could," he said. "I hope you understand that."

A pang rang out in my chest. I didn't like to openly acknowledge my own hopes. It made me feel . . . stupid. Childish. Even more so to hear Vincent reference them aloud.

"I know."

"If I had ever had an excuse, if there was ever a rebellion—"

"Vincent. *I know.* I know you can't go there." I stood and frowned at him, and his eyes fell to the fire, avoiding mine.

Fuck, it was strange, to see Vincent look something close to—to *guilty.*

Sixteen years ago, Vincent pulled me from the wreckage in the wake of a horrible Rishan rebellion. The city I left behind, or what remained of it, was deep within Rishan territory. The only reason why Vincent had entered it at all decades ago was because the uprising had given him license to, but now? That territory was protected by Nyaxia. A Hiaj king could not breach it outside of wartime between the clans, and though it was ridiculous to call this eternal tension "peace," my father had no reasonable excuse to invade and find my family.

If any of them had survived. Likely not. Whoever had been in that house when Vincent found me had not survived. But had there been others? Did I have anyone out there searching for me?

I knew the logical answer. Human lives were so fragile. Yet it still didn't stop the dark corners of my mind from wandering. Wondering where they were. Wondering how they had suffered. Wondering if any of them remembered me.

I didn't remember them. Maybe that was why I missed them so much. A dream could be whatever you needed it to be, and maybe the twelve-year-old version of myself needed saving them to be the missing piece that would finally make me feel whole.

"Soon," Vincent murmured. "Soon you'll be strong enough to go."

Soon.

No, Vincent couldn't act, but I could—if I was something stronger than human. I would need to be stronger, even, than most vampires.

I could do it if I was as strong as Vincent himself.

This would be my wish from Nyaxia, if I won the Kejari: to become Vincent's Coriatae. His heart-bound. A Coriatis bond was a powerful thing—verging on legendary—only granted a handful of times in history, and only forged by Nyaxia herself. It would strip away my humanity, making me a vampire without the risks of Turning, which most often ended in death. And it would bind my soul to Vincent's, his power becoming mine, and mine becoming his. Not that I had much to offer him, of course. It was a testament to his love for me that he was willing to offer me such a gift at all.

As his Coriatae, I would be powerful enough to save the family that had birthed me and to become a true daughter to the man that raised me. I would be one of the most powerful people in the House of Night. One of the most powerful people in the world.

And no one would ever underestimate me, ever again.

"Soon," I agreed.

He gave me a faint smile, then rose. "Are you ready?"

"Yes." But the word was ash in my mouth.

I had attempted to pray to Nyaxia many times over the years. I never felt much of anything—maybe because, as a human, I wasn't truly one of her children. But as Vincent brought the bowl and the jeweled dagger, as he slit my hand and let my weak, human blood roll into the hammered gold, the hair prickled at the back of my neck. Vincent whispered prayers in the ancient tongue of the gods, his thumb pressed to my wound to squeeze drop after drop into the offering.

His eyes flicked up to meet mine.

"Nyaxia, Mother of Ravenous Dark, Womb of Night, of Shadow, of Blood. I give you Oraya of the Nightborn. She is the daughter my heart gave me, just as my heart made me your son. Her presence in the Kejari is the greatest gift I will ever offer you." Maybe I imagined that his voice had thickened, ever-so-slightly. "Save, perhaps, for her victory."

Fuck. I was not expecting that this would be so difficult.

No, I wasn't much of a devotee. But now I felt the Goddess here, taking the offering of my blood and promising me only more blood in return. I wondered if she might just keep taking, and taking, and taking, until my poor mortal veins had nothing left to give.

The words that would bind my fate hung thick as smoke in the air.

"I offer myself to you, Nyaxia. I offer you my blood, my blade, my flesh. I will compete in the Kejari. I will give you my victory, or I will give you my death."

And then the final, sealing words:

"*Aja saraeta.*"

Take my truth.

"*Aja saraeta,*" Vincent echoed, his gaze never leaving mine.

Drip, drip, drip, as my blood slowly drained away.

IT WAS PROBABLY only the work of those tiny sips of wine that I was able to sleep at all. Eventually, dawn loomed, and Vincent retired. I lay in bed, staring at the stars painted on my ceiling. The wound on my hand throbbed. It would likely be another few days before the Kejari began, but my offering made it feel suddenly *real* in a way it never had before.

It was nearly sundown again by the time sheer exhaustion forced my eyes to close, my blades tucked beside me. Just in case.

When sleep took me, restless and anxious, I dreamed of safety.

I barely remembered my old life. But dreams were so good at filling in memories moth-eaten by time. It was a smear of sensations, like paints too watered down. A little clay house with cracked floors. An embrace in strong arms, a scraggly cheek, and the scent of dirt and sweat. Bloodless food—sickeningly sweet, absent of the iron tang—crumbling over my tongue.

I dreamed of a tired voice reading me a story and taking for granted that there would be a happy ending because I did not know of any other kind.

I hated these dreams. It was easier not to remember these things, and the fact that they always ended the same.

The moonlight streamed through windows locked tight. When the vampires came, wings upon wings upon wings blotted out those streaks of silver.

The two other little bodies scrambled out of bed to look at the sky. I was too afraid. I pulled the blankets over my head.

Put out the fire, quick, the woman hissed. *Before—*

Crack. Crack. CRACK.

I squeezed my eyes shut as the screams started, far away, rising closer and closer.

As the clay around me began to tremble and shake—as the floors split and the walls collapsed and the woman screamed, and screamed, and screamed—

CRACK.

CRACK.

The screaming followed me as I woke—so much of it that my ears couldn't separate the voices, couldn't make sense of where my dream ended and reality began.

My eyes opened, and met only an impenetrable wall of black. Complete, utter darkness, so thick it choked me. My hands flew out, grasping at nothing.

My first disoriented thought was, *Why did my lantern go out? I never let my lantern go out.*

And then, too slowly, I realized I was not in my room. The scent of must and blood burned my nostrils. My palms pressed to the ground. Hard, dusty tile.

The painful reminder of the fresh wound of my offering cut through my addled mind. Dread rose as I pieced it together.

No. It was too early. I should have had a few more days, I should have had—

The memory of Vincent's voice unfurled in my mind:

It could happen at any moment. She likes to do something unexpected.

I pushed myself upright. Panic spiked, but I forced it into submission. No, I could not afford to panic. Because this was it.

This was it.

The Kejari had begun.

Part Two
Full Moon

INTERLUDE

The little girl did not speak for days. The king of the House of Night gave her a room right next to his, on the most secluded, well-protected floor of his castle. Everything about this place overwhelmed her. Her bedroom at home had been shared with a brother and a sister, her bed just a tiny cot stored beneath the stacked frames of her siblings'. Here, the floors were not made of warm, rough clay but hard mosaic tile that froze her toes. Everything was so big. The bed alone was nearly the size of her entire room back home.

And, of course, there were monsters everywhere.

She tucked herself into the corner, wedging her tiny body between the dresser and the wall, and refused to move.

The king of the House of Night sat in the armchair at the opposite side of the chamber, reading. He rarely left, and never acknowledged her. The little girl would only leave her hiding spot in the rare moments he was gone—to relieve herself or scarf down a few bites of the food left for her. As soon as she heard his footsteps down the hall, she would return to her corner.

A week passed.

And another.

And another.

And at last, when the moon was full in the sky again, the child, fighting hunger pangs, crept from her spot toward the plate of bread on the table. Her silver-coin stare never left him, even as her little fingers closed around the bread and she nibbled it in slow, tentative bites, backing away.

Not a muscle moved save for his eyes, which flicked to her and remained there. Even that was enough to make her back farther into the shadows.

He laughed softly.

"Do you feel unsafe here, little serpent?"

The girl stopped chewing and said nothing.

The king set his book down gently.

"Good. You are not safe. Not in this castle. Not in this room. You are prey in a world of predators."

He leaned closer.

"I will never hurt you," he said softly. "But I am the only one who will make that promise, and keep it. I will never give you false safety or kind lies. But I will teach you how to wield those teeth of yours." He smiled, revealing for the first time the full length of his sharp canines—the death blow, surely, of hundreds.

The girl should have found this sight terrifying. And yet, for the first time in a month, she felt . . . safe.

"Perhaps they are not as sharp as mine," he went on, "but they can still kill, with the right bite."

Even so young, the girl understood what he was offering her. Living in a world like this, one had to learn such things early.

"Will you do me the honor of offering me your name?"

At last, the child spoke.

"Oraya."

"It's a pleasure to meet you, Oraya." He rose, and this time, she didn't back away. He reached out his hand. "I'm Vincent."

CHAPTER FIVE

I forced myself to steady my breaths. Panic quickened the heart. A quickening heartbeat meant rushing blood. Rushing blood meant I became even more of a target than I already was.

Nyaxia's magic was powerful and inexplicable. She could spirit us away wherever she pleased. My head was still fuzzy, every sensation hazy. I struggled to get my bearings. It felt like I had been drugged.

Take stock of your senses, Oraya.

The voice in my head was Vincent's.

Smell—blood and must. If the tournament had begun, then I had to be in the Moon Palace. I pressed my hands to the floor. A fine layer of dirt and dust stuck to my palms. The Moon Palace existed solely for this competition. It wouldn't have been touched for a hundred years.

No one was allowed within these walls outside of a Kejari, but I had studied it many times from the outside. I needed to go up. The tallest spire was covered in windows. No vampire would be caught there once dawn broke. The light would be extremely uncomfortable, if not deadly.

Sound. My ears strained. Screams of pain echoed from all directions—screams that didn't sound like they belonged to vampires. My stomach turned. Had humans been dropped into the Palace, too? As . . . prey? Distraction? I didn't know whether to be horrified or secretly grateful that they would draw the vampires' bloodlust. And I could hear that happening, too. The snarls. The distant, graceful beat of footsteps against the floor.

The others were awake. Maybe my humanness had meant I was the last to rise from whatever magic had been cast over us. It may have lowered inhibitions—the vampires sounded abnormally animalistic, even by the standards of a bloodlust frenzy.

I was very, very lucky I was alive right now.

I blinked into the darkness. Unlike vampires, I had no night sight. I couldn't see anything. Just a wall of black. I tried to call light to my fingertips and failed miserably, releasing only a single spark that quickly dissipated into smoke.

I bit back a silent curse for my useless magic and groped around for my blades, praying they had made the journey with me. If I had been dumped in here unarmed, I was dead.

Searing pain sliced across my hand.

FUCK.

I clamped my lips down on the cry.

I'd found my blade. By the sharp end. *Fucking idiot.*

Warm blood filled my palm. The dull *drip, drip, drip* of it hitting the tile floor was deafening, even over the distant screams.

Bleeding was bad. Very bad.

I had to move fast to find safety before someone scented me. I grabbed the dagger—by the hilt this time—and found the other not far from it. Then I rose and carefully stepped back until my shoulder met stone. I followed the wall, keeping my arm against it, blades poised and ready in each hand. My steps were silent and deliberate. When my toe hit a cold, hard block, my heart leapt.

A step. A way up. I had to pray this staircase would take me where I needed to go. I had no other option—not this blinded.

I started climbing, clinging to a dusty metal rail sideways, so my back wasn't left unguarded.

I'd heard stories that the Moon Palace was a magical, mysterious place, blessed—or cursed—by Nyaxia herself. Even Vincent believed it. He told me that hallways moved and rooms shifted. That it had a way of putting you exactly where you did or didn't want to be, depending on your luck that day.

I promise that if you let me survive this, Nyaxia, I will make this Kejari the most interesting and glorious performance for you in a millennium, I told the Goddess, silently. *You are going to be so fucking impressed. I swear it.*

The screams faded slowly into the distance, to my relief. I was moving away from them. Good. I continued climbing—one flight, two, three.

But the Moon Palace wasn't about to let me go that easily.

At first, I thought I was imagining it. My ears strained so much; it became easy to doubt my own senses. But as my steps continued, the ball of dread in my stomach swelled. No. I was right: the screams were getting closer again. Even though minutes ago they had been fading far behind me. Like I'd been climbing a never-ending spiral staircase that went nowhere.

I nearly stumbled as my feet met flat tile where I expected another step. The sounds of carnage echoed directly above me. I couldn't keep ascending. I was trapped.

I pressed to the wall. My eyes still stared uselessly into a vat of pitch black. What now? What could I—

One voice in that distant cacophony cut through all the others.

I no longer had to regulate my heartbeat, because it simply stopped.

The scream was cut short, buried beneath so many other distant voices. But I recognized it, even in that split second. I recognized it as the voice that affectionately called me a little brat, punctuated by a husky cough from years of incessant cigar smoking.

My mind emptied except for one name:

Ilana.

You never know—not truly—what it takes to make you discard caution until it's happening. And Ilana was enough. I left a lifetime of vigilance piled on the ground like a forgotten coat.

Ilana. Ilana was in this Palace. Ilana was *in that frenzy.*

Another scream, this time louder, closer, right down the hall, as if the fucking place was taunting me with it. And I didn't think, couldn't think, I just *ran*—

—Until a powerful force stopped me. A strong grip folded around my shoulders, pulling me back against a firm wall of a body.

"They're dead."

The man's whisper was low and gravelly, so close that his exhale tickled my skin. Stubble scratched my ear, a brush of hair grazing the dip where my neck met my shoulder. Every instinct revolted at this person's proximity, at their nearness to my throat—a place that no one but Vincent was allowed to go.

"They're dead, little human," the voice said again. "And if you go after them, so are you."

He's right, the Moon Palace seemed to hum, the darkness shivering in delight.

And I knew it. *I knew it,* even as another ragged shout of agony rang out, closer than ever.

I knew it and didn't give a fuck.

I didn't bother fighting against the grasp that held me. It wouldn't work. He was too strong.

So I stabbed the bastard.

Apparently he wasn't expecting that, because he hissed, *"Ix's fucking tits!"* and staggered away from me. I had buried my knife deep enough in his thigh that I had to yank hard to pull it out, and then I was sprinting down the hall, fingertips to the wall to guide myself.

Another scream. Louder. More desperate. Mother, it was awful, how vampires sounded when they were well and truly in a bloodlust. You could *hear* them ripping apart the flesh. It wasn't quiet, it wasn't elegant, it wasn't graceful. It was loud and messy and horrible.

I wanted to call out to her, wanted to tell her I was coming for her, but I couldn't—it would only attract attention to my position. I settled instead for quickened steps. As fast as I could move.

Ilana's wails did not grow farther away. But they did not grow closer, either. They just remained forever beyond me, just outside the reach of my blade, as I ran down hallway after hallway after hallway.

The truth dawned on me with every footstep. Her proximity was an illusion. I would never reach her. Her voice was growing weaker, her cries fewer and farther between.

Still, I pushed one more step, one more step.

One more step, as the shrieks rose to a crescendo.

One more step, as they lowered to a wet gargle.

As the gargle became a weak moan.

As that familiar voice disappeared beneath the sounds of feeding vampires, looking for something new to occupy them.

Eventually, I stopped, my ribs aching and eyes straining. I pressed myself against the wall. Squeezed my eyes shut, darkness falling deeper into darkness. My heartbeat, my precious blood, rushed deafeningly in my ears.

They're dead, the voice had whispered. *And if you go, so are you.*

He was right. And I had never hated anything so much. I lived a life of ugly truths, had gotten used to them—but this one—Mother, *this one*, it just—

The hairs rose on the back of my neck as I felt a presence behind me. The footsteps were nearly silent. I turned just in time.

"What do we have here?" a low, smooth female voice whispered.

I didn't wait this time. I struck—hard, and in the exact direction of the voice. I wouldn't win in a fight. I didn't wait for her to retaliate. I sprinted, fingertips touching the wall just enough to keep me from running into it. Some skirmish broke out behind me—I wasn't about to stop and think about what it could be, or, Goddess forbid, join it. The more they fought with each other, the less they would come after me.

At first, I thought I was imagining the faint silver outline before me. Maybe my straining eyes were just inventing what I so desperately wanted to see.

But no, it was no illusion. A wall of humid air hit me as I stumbled through a threshold. My hand bled so heavily that I struggled to grip the hilt of my blade. My muscles screamed at me. I could barely, barely make out the faint outline of—of—

Leaves.

I lifted my eyes to see stars. It was an overcast night, black-gray clouds covering most of the sky. But as the wind shifted, slivers of light peered through. The moon, nearly full, stood in mournful watch. Wrought-iron whorls cradled glass walls, rising into a dome that culminated in a silver crescent.

The earthy scent of damp soil washed over me.

A greenhouse. This was a greenhouse.

I pushed my way through the dense foliage until I hit the far-thest wall. I could see a little, now, with the help of the moonlight. Sivrinaj's skyline towered in the distance to my right, and to my left, dunes rolled in elegant swells and dips. And there, where the sand kissed the horizon line, was a faint streak of purple.

Dawn.

I would need to survive here for another hour, yes, but the mo-ment it arrived, this greenhouse would become the safest place I could possibly be. No one could hide from the sun in here for long.

I gripped my weapons tight as I sank into the shadows between the leaves. I would be able to hear the movement of whoever came in, even if I couldn't see them. The sounds of feeding had quieted, as if the Palace had decided that it had tired of my horror. Or per-haps the vampires had simply tired of gorging themselves.

I barely blinked, staring at the single door into the greenhouse, as the sun—my savior—rose to meet me.

CHAPTER SIX

I waited until the sun was so strong beads of sweat gathered on the back of my neck before I crept from my hiding place. In daylight, the greenhouse looked like a relic from a past world—fittingly, maybe, because in a way it was. The plants had long ago broken free from their elegant containments. Bright, spiky, red leaves burst from between crumbling cracks of stone. Vines strangled faceless worn statues. Ivy crawled up the patinaed metalwork all the way up to the curved glass overhead, encircling a single missing panel—as if demanding release.

I stared up at that one gaping glimpse of the sky for a long moment. It was unreachable, at the very top of the highest point of the dome. Not that it mattered. The walls weren't what kept us here—our oath to Nyaxia did, and she would kill us if we tried to evade it.

It was silent in the Moon Palace. After the chaos of the night before, whoever survived appeared to have holed up, resting and preparing before the official start of the trials. Still, I kept my blades ready. Vampires would probably not come into the greenhouse during daylight hours, but they would have no problem moving about so long as they didn't sun themselves in the windows.

Either I had been hallucinating last night or the legends about the Moon Palace were indeed true, because the layout of the building was now very different. The door to the greenhouse revealed a long hallway that led to a great room, which opened up all the way to the top of the Palace—countless stories. I looked up to see balcony after balcony after balcony rising above me, climbing so high and growing so small that they resembled little decorative wisps of silver near the distant domed ceiling. Grand mosaics covered the floor. The tiles were sharp, as if they had been shattered rather than cut. Some were bleached shades of ivory. But most were red . . . bloodstained. Burned brown a century old, and deep black even older. The stains from last night were sickeningly bright in contrast, even as they now dried down to a rusty crimson.

I didn't know how I knew where to go. Perhaps once again, the Palace led me where it pleased. I traveled up the stairs, not down, even though I could have sworn I had been climbing the night before. When I hit the third floor, the smell hit me—rotting flesh and death. A pool of congealing blood seeped from around the corner.

I followed the smell and the blood.

Some of the doors up here had been barred. Perhaps these rooms had been claimed by my fellow contestants. I was careful not to wake anyone as I moved past lifeless carcasses.

I found the one I was looking for on the balcony, where the maze of hallways gave way to a great open space that overlooked the drop to the first floor below and the dizzying height of the full tower above. She was not the only human there. Three other corpses were strewn over the tile, some missing limbs or defaced far beyond recognition.

And Ilana . . .

She didn't even look human anymore. Didn't even look like a corpse. She just looked like meat. I recognized her only because I had known her so well. They had mostly left her bright clothing on, tattered and torn, the blue now purple with her blood. Not that any blood was left in her mutilated body at all, at this point. They had made sure of that. They didn't let any of it go to waste.

Once, as a child, I watched a pack of wolves rip apart a deer. They were starving—everyone and everything was starving, back then. They didn't even wait until the poor thing was dead before they tore it to pieces. That was how vampires acted in bloodlust. That was what they had done to my friend.

I kneeled beside her. Her face was mostly missing, but I cradled it anyway.

You were supposed to leave. You were supposed to leave, you stupid, stubborn old bitch.

But then again, Ilana had never done what she was supposed to. Had never done what this world told her she needed to. It was what had drawn me to her from the beginning.

I had been fourteen. I had at last settled into my unsteady place in the world, but had also begun to feel the chafe of its boundaries. Vincent never allowed me anywhere near his parties, but that night, while he was off entertaining at some diplomatic event, I slipped downstairs even though I knew it was foolish. I went outside, keeping walls between me and the guests, and stole glances through the windows at the party within. It was from such a distance that I could only glimpse moving bodies, but I was too cautious to go any closer.

"What are you so afraid of, creeping around like a rat over there?"

Ilana's voice—already rough and hoarse, even all those years ago—had made me jump. She watched me, a cigar in her fingers and amused grin at her lips.

Right away, I had known she wasn't a vampire. Ilana had always been so brightly, vividly human. I had seen it from that very first moment, and it was what had transfixed me.

I had shied away into the shadows, and she scoffed.

"You're too young and pretty to be so frightened of the world. It's so rare I meet an interesting human around here. Come, come."

I'd hesitated, knowing that I shouldn't, that Vincent would not approve. But I had not so much as spoken to another human since coming to Sivrinaj, and the few blood vendors I'd seen in the halls were silent wraiths with empty faces. Nothing like the woman before me now.

I was too curious. I went to her that night, and then many others. Ilana became my little rebellion. I cultivated a friendship with her, finding comfort in all the ways she was like me and all the ways I wished I could be more like her. She had made a tiny, tiny part of me believe that there was another version of a human life than the one I lived.

Now, as I stared down at her corpse, all her vivacious tenacity snuffed out, the fragile remnants of that belief shattered.

There was no other version of humanity. Ilana should have been more afraid. She was human, and that meant she was worth nothing here. The Kejari had started early. The moon had been almost full, but not quite. Twelve hours were the difference between her safety and her death.

A fucking animal's death. Because that was all she had been to them.

A tiny, muffled sound made my head snap up. Silently, I rose and peered around the corner to see a figure slumped against the wall. The vampire was so listless that at first I thought he was dead, but no—he was sleeping. Red dribbled down his chin and the front of his once-blue shirt. He hadn't bothered to hide his wings. He was Rishan, his dark-brown feathers surrounding him like a blanket.

The others, apparently, had fled. Or perhaps this one gorged himself on his own, and that was why he slept so unnaturally soundly. His gluttony was stupid. Overeating made vampires sluggish.

He didn't even stir when I approached. Nor did he move when I took my dagger and plunged it into his chest—pushing hard until the cartilage cracked, pushing until the blade pierced his heart.

Then, his eyes finally snapped open.

Good.

I liked to watch it when they realized death was coming for them. This one pissed himself when he went. I pulled him close, caressed his face with my red-stained hands, and made sure Ilana's blood marked him as I let him slump down in a puddle of his own cowardice.

I had never despised my humanity so much. The weakness had been Ilana's death sentence. We were so fragile, so weak, that even this piece of shit vampire wiped out a whole life as if it meant nothing.

My hands shook. My heartbeat pounded in my ears, numb and distant, as if my rage and grief bubbled beneath a sheet of ice on the brink of shattering.

I returned to Ilana and fished through her pockets. First, I pulled out a familiar balled-up scarf of purple silk. I stared at it, fighting a lump in my throat, before tucking it into my own pack. Then I returned for her box of matches. She never went anywhere without them.

Her body was so dry, skin so papery. She burned easily, accepting the flame like another brightly colored silk.

I left her on that balcony and went back downstairs to the greenhouse. The Moon Palace was dark, the open air of the great room rising all the way up to the top. The fire lit all of it. In the greenhouse, I drew my knees to my chest and watched that glow flicker beyond the double doors, as my friend burned and burned and burned.

CHAPTER SEVEN

Come nightfall, a call rang out through the halls of the Moon Palace—three melancholy notes of Nyaxia's hymn. At the sound, I peered through the foliage to see a single, smoky thread of shadow leading through the greenhouse to the door and into the hallway beyond.

The message was obvious: I was being summoned.

My eyes were sandy and my joints aching when I rose and followed. Ilana's bloodless, torn-up face still lingered behind every blink. I had clutched that purple scarf all night, the blood from my wounded hand soaking the silk.

I didn't cry. No. I was fucking *furious*. Sadness was a futile, weak emotion. At least anger was useful—a sharp edge to cut another's heart, or a hard shell to protect your own.

The thread of shadow grew thicker as more streaks joined the main corridor. The summons had been sent, it seemed, to every contestant who had survived the previous night. The Moon Palace was not as pitch-dark as it had been before. Now, warm light rippled over the hall, emanating from the torches lining the walls and the candles that floated above us in the vaulted ceilings. As I walked, I watched that light shiver over the not-quite-smooth mosaic tile and felt foolish when I realized what I hadn't during the day: the floors were made of shattered bone and teeth.

The group of us grew larger as we moved down the hallway, more and more joining with each turn or doorway we passed.

We sized each other up silently. By the time we reached our destination—the great room—there were, by my rough estimation, about fifty contestants. Most were clearly members of the House of Night—an even split between Hiaj and Rishan, based on those who had their wings out—but I counted about ten members of the House of Blood, and fifteen or so members of the House of Shadow. Some looked around anxiously. Sizing up their competition? Or searching for someone who was missing?

How many of us had died last night?

Most ignored each other, though the Bloodborn vampires remained close together in one tight pack. That made sense, I supposed. No one else would have them. I eyed the woman at the center of their group. She was taller than all the others. Her armor left her shoulders bare, revealing impressively cut muscles. Her hair hung in a long silver braid down her back. She had to be their leader, judging by how the others deferred to her.

I hung back, watching my competition with a lump in my throat. I'd spent my entire life trying to avoid being in this situation: trapped with powerful vampire warriors twice my size.

Across the room, Ibrihim caught my gaze. He gave me a grim, humorless almost-smile, as if maybe he knew we were both thinking the same thing.

On the balcony, a tall, thin man with a bald head and wan skin stretched tight over his skull regarded us. He wore simple black robes and a sash across his body that bore three sigils: a moon, a mask, and a weeping woman—the symbols of the three kingdoms of Nyaxia. The church was independent of the three vampire houses, operating across all Nyaxia's subjects as a nebulously powerful and mysterious force. Most powerful and mysterious of all was the Ministaer himself, who was said to not even be a living being anymore, but merely a flesh-vessel for Nyaxia's will.

This, to me, sounded like bullshit.

It was impossible to follow the Ministaer's gaze—his eyes were solid milky white, with no iris or pupil—but his chin lowered, and I couldn't shake the skin-crawling sense that he looked directly at me.

I met that stare without flinching, even though I wanted to shudder and look away.

The Ministaer didn't especially seem like the embodiment of a god. He mostly seemed like a lecherous old man. I'd met him a few times at various religious feasts. No matter how big the crowd, he was always far, far too interested in me. After one night when he practically trapped me in a corner when I was thirteen years old, Vincent never left my side when he was in my presence ever again.

If Nyaxia needed a flesh-vessel—which she probably didn't— this one didn't seem like a wise choice.

Several other acolytes joined the Ministaer on the balcony to his right, and to his left was the leadership of the House of Night— Vincent and his cabinet. He wore a long, dark cloak embroidered with silver stars. His wings were on display, the threads of red stark against the black, and he even exposed his Heir Mark, leaving several buttons at the top of his jacket undone to reveal the swirls of red ink on his throat.

The intent would not be lost on anyone here. Simply revealing his wings and his Mark served as a warning: *I am stronger than any of you. I stood where you stood, and I won.*

It was odd to see Vincent flaunting his power so brazenly, but maybe it shouldn't have been surprising. Rulers of the House of Night often killed the Kejari's victors. Anyone that strong was inherently a threat. And as I looked around the room, so many of these bloodthirsty warriors stared at Vincent with such lustful hate.

I felt a bit naive for not realizing earlier Vincent's other selfish reason for encouraging me to enter the Kejari: if I won, it meant these people wouldn't. And there was absolutely no one in this world—not a single soul—that Vincent trusted, except for me.

The Ministaer cleared his throat, and an eerie hush fell over the room.

"Welcome," the Ministaer said, "to the Kejari, the greatest honor in the name of our lady Nyaxia, Mother of the Ravenous Dark, Womb of Night, of Shadow, of Blood. In her name, I thank you for the offering of your presence. *Aja saraeta.*"

"Aja saraeta." The echoing prayer rose from the contestants in a misty murmur.

"I have overseen twenty-one Kejaris, now," he went on. "Two thousand years of tribute to our Mother of the Ravenous Dark. And every time, this eve is the one that is the most meaningful. Such possibility. Such potential."

A too-long silence as he surveyed us. Then: "You have survived the initial call, and the initial cull. At sundown tomorrow, the Kejari officially begins. It will continue for the next four months. When you made your oaths, you gave our Dark Mother your lives. You gave her your blood. You gave her your soul. And she shall keep all three. Even if you survive the trials, a part of you shall always belong to her. *Aja saraeta.*"

"Aja saraeta," we all repeated.

"There will be five trials, each designed to pay tribute to the story of our goddess's escape from the clutches of the White Pantheon and rise to power. The Full Moon Trial. The Waning Trial. The Halfmoon Trial. The Crescent Trial. The New Moon Trial. Each trial will take place three weeks after the prior. The details of each test shall be revealed as it begins and not before. For the entire length of the Kejari, you shall reside here, in the Moon Palace. You may leave its walls between sundown and sunrise, if it pleases Nyaxia, but you must always be within its doors come dawn. Countless worshippers have lived here before you. Countless others will come long after your blood has dried from the floors. Through the Moon Palace, Nyaxia shall provide for you as she sees fit."

As she sees fit. That sounded appropriately ominous. The Moon Palace provided shelter, food, water—until it didn't. It provided safety—until it didn't. The Moon Palace was not a place of rest. It was a trial all its own.

"Regarding the spilling of blood within the Moon Palace . . ."

I didn't know it was possible for the room to get even more breathlessly silent. We had all, it seemed, been waiting for this. Sometimes, Kejari contestants were forbidden from killing each other outside of trials. Other years, no such restriction existed.

That was the thing about the Kejari. It had its rules and conventions, yes, but it was a little different every year, subject, like so many things, to Nyaxia's whims.

"You may defend yourself against aggressors," the Ministaer said. "However, the Goddess appreciates the gift of blood within her trials."

What the hell did that mean?

I wasn't the only one wondering. Bodies shifted uncomfortably— eyes scanned the room in confusion. This wording was . . . unhelpful.

The Goddess appreciates the gift of blood within her trials.

Did that mean, *Try to wait to kill each other until there's an audience, if you can? If not, oh well!*

Or did that mean, *Save it for the trials and face Nyaxia's wrath if you don't?*

I couldn't decide which I preferred. If killing was outlawed this year, it might allow me at least a little bit of peace within the Moon Palace's walls—*maybe,* given the lure of my human blood. Then again, it might be easier for me to pick off my opponents when they weren't expecting it than it would be in the ring.

"You bind yourself to these rules when you offer your soul to Nyaxia in service of the Kejari," the Ministaer said. "And you shall abide by them until the moment the tournament concludes, or until the moment she releases you from your oath. *Aja saraeta.*"

"*Aja saraeta,*" we murmured.

"You will be summoned at sundown tomorrow for the Full Moon Trial. May the Mother guide you."

The Ministaer lifted his hand, as if casting some great invisible blessing over us all, and turned away without another word. There was no final speech, no inspiring goodbye, no wrought-out prayer.

With eerie silence, the double doors beneath the balcony swung open, revealing what appeared to be a dining room. Above us, the priests and priestesses filed away. Vincent caught my gaze just before he went with them. An unspoken agreement passed between us. He inclined his chin, and I nodded in response before following the others through the double doors.

THE FEAST IN the dining hall put the one at Vincent's party to shame. I'd spent many of the daylight hours combing through the greenhouse trying to identify edible plants, just in case—I wasn't sure whether we would be given food at all, and if so, whether any of it would be safe for humans. But despite my shaky nerves and exhaustion, my mouth watered at the sight of the spread before me. Two long tables had been laid out with platters, each seating perhaps twenty-five or thirty chairs. We all filed into the room and lingered near the walls, as if we all feared that the feast might explode if we got too close to it.

Finally, a tall Hiaj man muttered, "Fuck it," sat down, and seized a goblet of blood. That was enough to break the tension. The crowd descended upon the feast. I grabbed a plate, hastily piled it with food that at least appeared to be human-edible, and backed away, instead choosing to sit at one of the small end tables scattered around the outskirts of the room. A better spot for watching.

Some contestants gulped down blood like they thought they might never eat again—a fair concern. Others, though, seemed uninterested, instead stuffing provisions into their pockets or packs.

My lips thinned. My fingers curled tight enough to leave nail marks in my palm.

Of course they weren't hungry. They had gorged themselves last night.

Only one ignored the feast completely. A dark-haired man moved about the room frenetically, circling the tables. I recognized him— I'd seen him looking around, a bit panicked, before the Ministaer's speech. Now, my suspicion from earlier became a certainty. He was clearly looking for someone, and growing increasingly frantic when he couldn't find them. After three quickening laps around the table, he ran out the door, pushing roughly through two Shadow-born who scowled after him.

A few minutes later, a feral, animalistic roar sliced through the air like shattering glass.

Every head snapped up. Hands went to weapons. My own gripped the hilts of my blades.

My first thought was that it was some sort of monster. That they'd lulled us into a false sense of security with this meal and figured they'd pick off a few more of us before the trial tomorrow.

But no, it wasn't a monster that came barreling back into the dining hall—it was the dark-haired man, howling, face mottled with sheer rage. I realized that his screeching actually formed words: "My brother! *They killed my fucking brother!*"

His wings were out now, outstretched, the feathers many different shades of brown-black.

. . . Just like the wings of the Rishan man who'd been covered in Ilana's blood.

And when this man spun around, his eyes wild, I realized they looked just like the ones that had stared into mine last night as I slowly sank my knife into his heart.

I stiffened.

"Who fucking did it?" the man howled. "You think you can kill an Ajmai and get away with it? Which one of you bastards did it? *I'll fucking kill you!*"

No, you certainly will not.

I almost—almost—wanted to confess to it.

To my surprise, Ibrihim was the first to move, rising from his chair with his palms up. "Easy, brother. We don't need any more death before—"

"*Brother?*" the man snarled. "You're not my fucking *brother*. My brother is *dead.*"

The group of Bloodborn sniggered amongst themselves, and I thought surely that would be the thing to send this man on a mur-derous rampage. His mouth contorted into a sharp-toothed snarl, his fists quaking. But just as he was about to lunge—at whom, or

what, even he didn't seem to know—a deep, smooth voice came from
the far corner of the room.

"Oh, please. It isn't any of our fault that your brother was such
a fucking idiot he got himself killed before the tournament even
started, Klyn."

The voice was oddly familiar.

The man—Klyn, apparently—whirled. Heads swiveled. The
source of the voice took a long, long drink of blood. It was difficult
to see him—we were seated at opposite corners of the room, with
four rows of people between us—but I glimpsed a broad form and
wavy, dark hair with a red sheen, which rustled slightly as he threw
back his head to drink, unperturbed by the fuss.

When Klyn's gaze fell to the man, he seemed to forget the rest of
the room existed.

"*You*," he breathed. "Raihn fucking Ashraj. *You* hadn't gotten
over that thing in the outer city. I should have known we shouldn't
have trusted—"

The man—Raihn—set down his goblet and laughed. It was a
low sound that slithered through the air like a snake.

Klyn turned *purple*. Perhaps he was senseless with his own rage,
but he was still a vampire, and that meant he was strong and fast.
He crossed the room in several graceful strides.

"*You* did this!"

And just as quickly, Raihn was on his feet, meeting him halfway.

I drew in a sharp inhale.

The man I had seen at the feast. I recognized him right away,
because here, just as he had at the ball, he stood out as markedly *different* than any other vampire. Everything about him seemed rough
and unfinished, right down to the way he held himself—with an untamed, threatening ease, stark in contrast to elegant vampire beauty.

And when he stood, I realized all at once why his voice had
sounded so familiar. There it was: the bloody bandage wrapped
around his thigh. Right where, say, a short human girl might have
plunged a dagger when trying to break out of his grasp.

Fuck.

Even across the room, I could see that his knuckles were white as he gripped Klyn's wrist, seizing the sword mid-strike.

"You think I killed your brother?" Raihn said. "Me?"

"Don't fucking toy with me, Raihn. I know you did it."

"Oh, *I* didn't kill your brother."

Raihn's eyes—rust red—slipped right across the room. Landed right on me.

And he smirked.

Goddess fucking damn it. I didn't expect to have to fight my way out of a pack of vampires before the tournament even started, but I would do it if I had to.

I started to rise, my hands going to my swords.

"This is ridiculous, isn't it?"

I nearly jumped halfway across the room. I spun around to see a slender, curly-haired woman leaning against the wall beside me, rolling her eyes.

The very same woman I'd seen at Vincent's party the other night.

"We should be saving our energy," she sighed. She glanced at me like she expected an answer.

I said nothing. Mostly, I wanted to ask her what she was doing here. She didn't exactly seem like the tournament-to-the-death type. But I could barely tear my gaze from the scene across the room.

Now, Klyn was inches from Raihn's face. "Yes, you did! I know you did!"

"No," Raihn said calmly, "I did not. Wish I had, though, because he was a repulsive asshole."

"He was," the girl agreed, beside me. "The worst." She leaned close and whispered, "You did it, didn't you?"

"I—what?"

"You did it. Right?"

"I—"

Across the room, Raihn said, "And I'm warning you, right now, not to go for that sword again, Klyn."

"Oh, no," the girl muttered.

Klyn went for his sword.

SMASH.

Klyn's body hit the wall with enough force to send two of the grand antique paintings crashing to the ground, their wood frames splintering under the force of the impact. Raihn pinned him against arabesque wallpaper now dotted with spatters of black-red blood. Klyn's sword arm dangled from his body at an odd angle, clearly broken. His head lolled.

Half the people in the hall had now gotten to their feet, watching wide-eyed. Everyone held their breath, waiting for the answer to the question no one was voicing: *Would he do it?*

Klyn's attitude had changed dramatically in the last five seconds. "You can't kill here," he croaked. "You heard the Ministaer. He said you can't kill until the trials."

"Oh no," the girl said again, not seeming all that distressed.

We were all thinking the same thing. Thinking of the Ministaer's cryptic words. I knew someone would test the boundary. I just didn't know it would happen so soon.

Raihn smiled.

"Oh, I can't?"

The blast shook the room. I gasped, the air yanked from my lungs in one dramatic pulse. Pitch blackness consumed me, followed by blinding white, followed by a coughing fit as I found myself blinking hard, shaking away goose bumps.

Sun fucking take me.

Everyone gaped at the rust-eyed man, jaws hanging, questioning what we'd just seen.

Raihn let Klyn's very, very dead body slide down the wall into a wobbly, boneless heap on the ground.

Silence. No one blinked. Raihn looked up, as if waiting for Nyaxia to strike him down. Five seconds passed, then ten, then thirty.

"Hm," he said, at last. "Well, I suppose that answers that."

He sat down and resumed eating.

The girl sighed. "So dramatic."

I couldn't bring myself to speak. That was fucking Asteris.

CHAPTER EIGHT

Vincent was exactly where we had agreed. I snuck out of the Moon Palace just before dawn, waiting as long as I could for the other contestants to retreat back to their rooms. After the feast was over, we had started to somewhat warily explore the rest of the Moon Palace and discovered hundreds of fully furnished and stocked suites throughout it. Most had claimed rooms as their own, some by themselves and some in partnerships or groups for protection.

Still, I remained in my greenhouse. No walls or locks would protect me as well as those windows could. Besides, I found something oddly comforting in the way the greenery wrapped me in an embrace. The plants were fragile and alive and impermanent—just like me—and yet, they'd still managed to reclaim the ancient structure. It was a little inspiring.

When the sky was tinted red, I made my journey. The Ministaer had been honest. The Moon Palace did not lock us in. Vincent met me beyond the gates, beneath the steps where the slab paths gave way to the silty mud of the riverbank. Stone bridges arced overhead, leading to the city.

Vincent had described this spot to me before the Kejari began. "It's private," he had told me. "It will be our meeting place."

Here, under the shadow of the bridge, I felt like I stood upon the boundary between two worlds. To my right, the Moon Palace loomed, ancient and foreboding. To my left, Sivrinaj rose into the sky, silhouetted by the near-full moon. No one cared what happened here, in this little shadowy crevice that was a part of neither.

How did Vincent know about this place? Had he met someone here when he was a contestant in his own Kejari, two hundred years ago? Did he have . . . well, a Vincent? Someone who had trained him, guided him? A member of the family he had killed in his rise to power?

Or another mentor who told him to do it?

I knew better than to ask those sorts of questions. Maybe when I became Vincent's equal—his Coriatae—I finally would.

"Oraya."

I wasn't expecting the sound of Vincent's voice to hurt as it did—an ache right in the center of my chest. I turned to see him approaching from beneath the shadow of the bridge. When the moonlight fell across his face, my throat grew suddenly thick.

I'd been strong before this. There was no time to grieve, no time to be frightened, when I had to focus singularly on survival. But now the sight of him, the sheer familiarity of his face, took me back sixteen years. I was a child again, hiding in the space between the wall and the dresser, and Vincent was the only safe person in the world.

Ilana was gone. Dead. I had only him.

He looked me up and down. His face was stone-still.

"Are you injured?"

"No."

He lifted his chin to my hand. "That?"

I'd forgotten about it. "Nothing. Just a little cut."

"You need your hands."

He beckoned, and I rested my hand in his palm. He gently removed the bandage—purple silk. I had to fight the sting in my eyes as I watched it shimmer beneath the moonlight, now covered in blood. The rest of Ilana's scarf was in my pocket. I'd tried to salvage as much of it as I could, though so much of it was now stained and torn.

Vincent frowned at it—not at my wound, but the fabric. "Where did you get this?"

"I found it. In the Moon Palace."

I didn't even have to try to lie anymore. It came so easily.

"Hm." He withdrew a bottle from his pocket, then dripped a few drops of the shimmery, silver-blue liquid onto my palm. A puff of smoke unfurled from the cut, the sound echoing the hiss I drew through my teeth.

"Don't whine."

I did not miss the hint of affection in the chastisement.

"I never whine."

And he probably did not miss the slight crack in my voice.

The wound on my hand was now just a puffy pink-white scar. He replaced the bandage and handed me the bottle. "Take care of that. I don't know when I will be able to get you more. I'll try."

Medicine that was safe for humans was, understandably, difficult to come by in the House of Night. Vincent needed to trade for it from the human kingdoms in the south and the east. The stuff was precious as gold. More, actually—gold did nothing to stop bleeding.

"It was earlier than I thought," Vincent said. "My year, we started the night before the full moon. Not two. I suppose they like to keep things interesting. It makes no difference."

It made a difference to Ilana. One more night, and she would have been out of the city, safe—if unhappy—in the human districts.

If I allowed my grief to show, he didn't seem to notice it. He unhooked two sheathed weapons from his belt.

"Here."

He tossed them into my arms. I caught them deftly, then slid one from the black leather scabbard—blinking in stunned awe at what was revealed.

The swords were—they were—

I couldn't speak. Couldn't find words.

They were short and delicate, designed for dual wielding, as I preferred. They were impossibly light for their size. The blades curved gracefully, polished black steel with red marks etched into the flat—long swirls of decorative smoke and stark, staccato glyphs locked in a dance. The hilts—silver, topped with two interlocking moons—welcomed my hands as if they had been waiting for me my entire life.

And yet, it felt wrong to even touch them.

"They should serve you well," Vincent said. "Light. The right size. I gave the smith all your measurements. They're designed specifically for you."

"These are . . ."

Perfect. Stunning. Eye-wateringly expensive, yes, but it wasn't just about the money. The weapons were the epitome of the deadly artistry the Nightborn were known for, wielded only by the most esteemed House of Night warriors. Hundreds and hundreds of hours of craftsmanship had gone into creating these. Centuries of expertise in blacksmithing and magic. An entire civilization's skill, right here in my hands.

No doubt several generations of Nightborn kings rolled in their graves to think of such a weapon wielded by an adopted human girl. I felt as if I was tainting these simply by touching them.

"These are . . ." I started again.

"They are *yours*," Vincent said quietly.

As if he heard everything I didn't say.

I swallowed my wave of emotion—*Mother, Oraya, get a fucking hold on yourself*—and affixed the sheaths to my belt. Perhaps I didn't deserve these yet. But I would, one day. Once I won.

"Thank you," I said.

Vincent glanced again to the sky. "You should go. The sun is coming."

He was right. The last thing I needed was to get disqualified for being late back to the Moon Palace. I nodded. But before I could turn, he caught my arm, gripping so hard his fingernails dug into my flesh.

"I won't tell you to be careful, Oraya. I won't tell you because I know you are. I taught you to be. Resilient. Clever. Fast. Focused. Vicious. You must be all of it now. You have no room for weakness or missteps."

Emotions rarely showed on Vincent's face. But now I caught a glimpse—only a glimpse—of some strange tenderness shivering across the cold muscles of his expression, gone before either of us could or would acknowledge it.

"I will," I said.

"You must be better than they are."

And just as Vincent heard what I didn't say, I heard his unspoken words here, too: *To make up for what you are not.*

There was no room for weakness in the Kejari, but mine was entwined in my own human flesh. I blinked and saw Ilana's body, so easily destroyed. I fought back the wave of nausea, the stab of pain. Those were weaknesses, too.

Instead, I made my grief into anger. I made it steel.

"I know," I said. "I am."

He was still for a long moment, then released me.

"The blades hold poison," he said. "There's enough in them to last you awhile. You can refill it through the hilt."

This, I knew, was Vincent telling me that he loved me. No one had ever said those words to me—at least, not that I could ever remember. But he communicated it a thousand ways over the years, most of them coated in death. *I love you. Here's how you stay alive. Here's how you make sure that no one can hurt you.*

For vampires, that was the ultimate gift.

I nodded, lifted my hand in a silent goodbye, and we parted without another word.

I CUT MY return closer than I should have, but at least it meant that the Palace was quiet when I got back. I was trying to figure out whether I was hallucinating or if the layout of the place had changed—again—when I rounded a corner and nearly ran into a wall.

No—not a wall. A *person.*

I reacted fast, putting several strides between me and the figure before I even looked at their face. My blades were out in seconds. Mother, these things were light.

I lifted my gaze to see dark red eyes drinking me in.

At the feast, even from across the room, I'd thought this man seemed unlike most other vampires I'd met. Up close, there was no doubt about it. Raihn's features were strong—almost unpleasantly so, like each held too much personality to be combined in such a way. While time left marks on humans, in vampires it simply sanded away imperfections, leaving them with beauty as finely honed as a Nightborn blade. But this man's face certainly seemed to hold evidence of the life he had lived—a scar marking his left cheek in two lines arranged in an upside-down V, one eyebrow that seemed a little higher than the other, hair that was left in unruly waves.

That stare now casually moved down my body, then to my blades, which were poised and ready to strike. His left eyebrow, the one that seemed permanently, ever-so-slightly raised, quirked even higher.

"Are those new? Thank the Mother you didn't have those last night. I wouldn't have a leg anymore."

"Get out of my way."

"Where were you?"

I tried to walk past him, but he placed his hand on the opposite wall, blocking my path with a thick, muscled arm clad in leather, right at face-height.

"I know where you were. You were visiting the Nightborn King. That's you, isn't it? His human?" He cocked his head. "You're very famous, you know. Even in the borderlands. A real curiosity."

I tried to duck under his arm to continue to the greenhouse, but he moved it down to block my path. Then he nodded down to his leg.

"You stabbed me."

"You grabbed me."

"I was trying to save your life."

I shouldn't even engage. I could practically hear Vincent's voice in my ear: *Think about what you have to gain from an interaction. The answer is usually nothing.*

But my ego spoke first. I made a show of looking myself up and down.

"I don't think so. I escaped, and I look alive to me."

That eyebrow twitched again. "For now."

He said this as if it was very amusing.

But only now, a moment too late, did my mind circle back to what he had said—*I was trying to save your life.*

That night, I'd been so distraught, I hadn't even given myself time to think about who had grabbed me—or why. It only sank in now that he *had* been trying to help me, or at least, appeared to be.

That was . . . strange. So strange, it did nothing to endear him to me. Far from it. I was certain he hadn't done it out of the kindness of his benevolent heart.

"What do you want?" I demanded.

"I want an apology. For stabbing me. Especially given that I could have turned you over to your victim's brother, and didn't." He leaned a bit closer, and I matched the movement by stepping back. "Because you *did* kill that bastard, didn't you?"

I scoffed.

He frowned. "What?"

"I'm not a fool."

"Oh?"

"You wanted him to give you an excuse. You just wanted to swing your cock around."

Because in the House of Night, everything was a power game. His spectacle at the feast? That was a performance.

Well, fine. I'd rather have my enemies looking at him than looking at me. But that didn't mean I had to put up with it. Maybe he was curious about me. Maybe he just liked to toy with his food. I didn't need to know why he was playing the game to know I had nothing to win.

I raised my blade. "Now let me pass."

He arched his brows. "I ask for an apology, and I get threats."

"I'm sorry I didn't aim higher."

He looked pointedly down at himself. "A little higher, or a lot higher?"

That was almost funny. It caught me a bit off guard. It was rare that vampires made jokes. Hundreds of years withered away a sense of humor. When I was fifteen or so, I gave up on trying to make Vincent understand. I was lucky I'd had Ilana to—

The casual thought of her triggered a stab of pain so intense it took my breath away.

"Let me pass," I snapped.

He gave me a strange look. "What was that?"

That caught me a bit off guard, too. That he noticed the brief emotion I had allowed to flinch over my face.

"Let me pass."

"Or what?"

"Or I'll stab you again."

"How much higher?"

For a moment, I actually considered doing it. Maybe this was the best opportunity I'd get, right now, when he was acting like it was all a big fucking joke. What a luxury that must be.

It was only the thought of that flash of black, then white—Asteris, I was sure of it—that stilled my hand.

Instead, I made a dramatic show of looking him up and down—lingering at his thigh and trailing up to the crotch of his leather pants, and said, "A little."

I ducked under his arm. This time, he chuckled softly and didn't try to stop me.

THE MOON GLEAMED bright and full, hanging heavy with challenge. The minutes since it rose had been tense and still. From my place in the greenhouse, I couldn't hear a single sound from the Moon Palace halls.

It was nearly midnight when the ghostly thread of shadow appeared again, summoning us from our rooms. I followed it to the great hall, where the Ministaer had addressed us all the night before. The room slowly filled with people as more and more threads of shadow joined mine, until no more arrived and the shadows dissipated, leaving us all standing in awkward silence.

Everyone had taken the last day to prepare. Contestants were armed with new, freshly cleaned weapons, leather armor strapped tight to their bodies. Some wore protective sigils at their throats or etched into the armor itself. I noted those carefully—it didn't necessarily mark them as magic wielders, but it did make the possibility more likely. Magic would be an ugly surprise in the ring.

The House of Blood contestants stayed together in a tightly packed group. Now, there was little doubt that the tall, muscular woman was their leader, as I'd suspected. The others listened, rapt, as she whispered to them in hushed command. Her mostly silver hair was now bound up in a long braid, the tight pull of it emphasizing her sharp cheekbones and strong brow. As she turned to speak to one of her companions, I noticed a faint crimson crawling up from beneath the collar of her white leather armor.

Her curse. I'd never met a Bloodborn vampire before, but I'd heard that red marks on their skin signaled the end stages of it. If that was true, this woman was far along. The next step would be insanity. And beyond that . . .

Well, people murmured about what the House of Blood's curse did to them. Turned them into little more than animals in the end.

I shuddered and looked away.

Some of the other contestants had formed alliances overnight, too—probably seeing the temporary value of strength in numbers. Almost certainly, too, thinking ahead to the Halfmoon Trial. It was the only trial structure that was the same every year: in which contestants would need to fight in teams or as partners, and half the field would be eliminated.

My eyes found Raihn at the other side of the room. Beside him was the cheerful woman with the short hair. She leaned close, whispering excitedly, while he surveyed the room.

What an odd pair.

Only a few now remained notably set back from the rest of the group: me, several members of the House of Shadows—known for their staunch independence—and Ibrihim, who was one of the last to reach the great room, visibly limping on his mangled foot.

The Kejari was no place for pity. Still, I felt it anyway as I watched him hobble down the hall. I knew better than anyone that no one should be dismissed out of hand. But it was hard to imagine any version of today's events that wouldn't end in Ibrihim's death.

The minutes passed. We waited in tense silence.

I unsheathed my blades, adjusting my grip around the hilts.

I'd studied each of the twenty Kejaris that came before this, and I had thought long and hard about what this trial could be. The first trial usually represented Nyaxia's departure from her home in the White Pantheon. She had ventured out beyond the borders of her land and was attacked by beasts during her midnight walk. They pursued her for miles, and in her panic, she grew impossibly lost. Sometimes, the trial involved blinding contestants, as Nyaxia was blinded during her attack. Sometimes, it required contestants to run and fight over treacherous terrain. But most often, it involved beasts—sometimes many, sometimes one.

The long silence gave way to uncomfortable whispers of confusion. Eventually, one of the Hiaj contestants asked what we were all wondering:

"So what now? Are we supposed to—"

The Moon Palace simply disappeared.

CHAPTER NINE

The screaming of the crowd shook the ground. Light blinded me—so bright that at first I questioned whether it was somehow sunlight.

But no. Torches. Thousands. Lining the rounded rim of the colosseum, floating hundreds of feet above our heads, clutched in the thousands upon thousands of hands of the thousands upon thousands of spectators—all of whom were screaming, screaming, screaming—

Screaming like Ilana had screamed—

For a moment, nothing existed but the sky and the light and the roar of the spectators. I craned my neck up to the stars that were barely visible over the flare of the lanterns. They smeared in a circular blur, punctuated by rails of silver metal—like the top of the greenhouse. A glass ceiling.

Move, Oraya! a voice roared in the back of my head—Vincent's voice, it was always Vincent's voice—and I did, just in time.

Massive claws shredded the packed sand where I had been standing seconds ago.

The world snapped into violently harsh focus.

Another shriek rang out, much closer, as a Hiaj contestant was torn to pieces—one shattered wing clenched in a dripping maw, his body clutched in claws, black-red blood pouring onto the dirt.

Not just a beast. A fucking demon.

I'd only seen a demon in real life once, and I had been so injured that I barely remembered it. Even that horror had been nothing compared to these. They moved on all fours, hairless and dark-gray, with blackened veins that pulsed beneath their skin. Serrated black claws capped too-long fingers on hands made for grabbing and killing. Their faces—flat, with sharp cheekbones, slit noses, and white, mucus-coated eyes—were mostly mouth, which extended from pointed ear to pointed ear, dripping with blackened saliva over layers of jagged teeth. They were, at once, chillingly animalistic and sickeningly . . . humanoid.

They moved so fast I couldn't count them—so fast that they crossed the arena in the time it took me to blink. More than five. Fewer than ten.

I pressed my back to the glass. It shook as something slammed violently against the wall in the next enclosure. The colosseum had been split into many smaller rings, separated by glass domes. I was trapped here with several Hiaj vampires. One Rishan. One Bloodborn. Kiretta, the Shadowborn magic wielder Vincent had warned me about. And—I let out a rough laugh, because it fucking figured—Raihn.

As the demons tangled in the center of the ring, momentarily distracted by the still-twitching body of the vampire they'd just ripped apart, the rest of us looked around warily. We were all thinking the same thing: Was the objective to kill the demons, or each other?

Or both?

I had no time to think about it as one of the demons lunged for me. I rolled out of the path of those razored hands—but then my body seized up. My muscles railed against me, as if they wanted to keep me in the demon's path, wanted to—

Fuck. Blood magic.

I glanced up just in time to see the Bloodborn contestant meet my eyes, red mist around his raised hands, his magic in my blood. He could only maintain his focus for a moment, but that was enough to send me tumbling under the demon's claws.

Move move move—

Pain skewered me. The moment I broke free of the magic hold,

I grabbed one of my swords and plunged it into the roof of the demon's mouth, just as those teeth were coming down upon me.

A horrific burning smell filled my nostrils—the poison in action. The demon let out a high-pitched, hollow wail. Puffs of black surrounded us as I yanked my sword from its flesh. When its jaw snapped closed, the skin was melting, top jaw dripping into bottom.

Mother, this shit was strong. I thanked Vincent silently and scrambled from my attacker's grasp as it staggered back into the pack.

On the opposite side of the enclosure, Raihn went after a demon with sweeping strikes of his sword. An impressive weapon, even from a distant glimpse. It was Nightborn steel, like my blades, with streaks of red-tinted darkness following every swing.

To my right, the Bloodborn man dodged as one of the demons leapt for him, sinking its teeth into his leg. His lips twisted into a grim smile, hands raised and ready.

But then he froze. Horror fell across his face that had nothing to do with pain—as if he had just made a terrible realization. It distracted him long enough for the beast to yank him closer. A sheen of black-red beaded over its skin, followed by a fog of crimson.

Unnatural goose bumps rose on my arms, a burning sensation ghosting over my flesh as I leapt away from its swinging tail. Strange. Unsettling. Familiar. I couldn't pinpoint it, but—

The Bloodborn man tried to fight now, but it was too late. His body crumpled like moist paper beneath the demon's claws.

Puffs of shadow filled the enclosure as Kiretta unleashed the full force of her magic, fragments of darkness wrapping around demon limbs and throats to little effect. One of the Rishan had risen to the top of the glass dome and now shot arrows at the monsters below, lurching and dipping to avoid their barbed tails, but they barely reacted to the blows. Blood spurted across my cheek as another Hiaj contestant fell.

Four. Four of us remained.

I fought until I couldn't feel my own body anymore. Kiretta was slowly being worn down. The Rishan with the arrows had more and more difficulty dodging. Even Raihn's seemingly unstoppable blows appeared to be slowing. My hands were so slick with putrid black blood that I struggled to grip my swords, drips of poison leaving my skin raw.

We hadn't managed to kill a single demon. Even the one I'd injured had torn its mouth back open and was acting like it had never been hurt at all.

Across the ring, a demon lunged for Raihn, and he leapt smoothly out of the way . . . majestic, feathered wings unfurling from his back. He stretched them wide as he rose to the top of the enclosure, red-black feathers tinted purple beneath strokes of silvery moonlight.

So he was Nightborn. A Rishan, of course. I should have fucking known.

I rolled out of the way of another attack, one eye still on him. I watched him plunge, watched him thrust his sword into the ribs of a demon—

And the beast diving for me—the one I hadn't even struck yet—flinched.

Everything faded except for that single twitch. That one little seize of muscle. My attacker recovered fast, leaving me scurrying across the sand, but in my mind I replayed that moment, over and over.

No, I hadn't imagined it. The demon had flinched, and *exactly* where Raihn had hit the other one.

I thought of the look of horror on the Bloodborn vampire's face as the demon drank from him. Of the red sheen that covered their bodies now, the mist, the strange burning sensation of my skin—

Realization shook me.

It was blood magic. Sloppy and unrefined, yes, but blood magic all the same. And if the demons were using gifts exclusive to the vampires of the House of Blood . . .

I stabbed the hand of a monster that came for me and found fresh horror in its terrible wail of agony. Mother, it did almost sound like . . . like a voice.

These were not just demons. These were demons that had once been vampires—Bloodborn, cursed vampires.

Think, Oraya.

Transfiguration. I knew the curse made Bloodborn vampires something terrible in their final days, but nothing like this. So these had been changed. Created. Were they linked, somehow? I watched their movements with the split seconds I could spare between dodges or strikes—watched their dynamics.

A pack. They moved together, as if connected. And maybe that meant there was a leader. A heart at the core of the rotten flesh. If these were transfigured vampires, perhaps one was the original, and the others its spawn.

"Do that again!" I screamed to Raihn, who had risen back into the air. He cocked his head in confusion. The din of the crowd swallowed my words.

I jabbed my finger to the demon, then tapped my forehead— where it bore a single white mark between its eyes. *"THAT ONE, YOU FUCKING IDIOT!"*

I didn't know if he'd understand what I was trying to tell him, or if he would help me even if he did.

I cut through the pack of beasts. I was betting everything on this theory. There was no way I'd survive this if I wasn't right. Getting into the pack was difficult—getting out of it would be impossible. I levied strike after strike with my poisoned blades, making the demons falter, but had no time to make them fall. Precise. Fast.

The red mist, which had grown thicker with the demons' every kill, burned my skin. The writhing bodies blended into each other, slick gray against slick gray, but I refused to take my eyes off my target, refused to blink—

My mark let out a sickening scream, its limbs flailing in all directions. Black blood spattered over my face as a massive blade plunged into its side. Raihn's body trembled with exertion as he pinned the beast, barely dodging its tail and claws. His gaze met mine through the chaos and red smoke—and he nodded.

I couldn't even believe these words crossed my mind, but I thought, *Nyaxia bless him.*

If this demon had once been a vampire, that meant we needed its heart. And that meant I had to slide under this thing. I dropped to my knees, poised my blade, and—

Pain exploded through my hip.

My vision blurred. A *POP* rang out in my ears as the sound of the crowd and the demons faded to a distant din.

I didn't realize I'd hit the ground until I saw my hands braced against the dirt. I looked down at myself. An arrow protruded from my thigh.

Fuck, I thought, just before all the demons were on me.

CHAPTER TEN

I couldn't move. I stabbed wildly, hitting flesh here, bone there, an eye here. I could see nothing but slithering masses of gray flesh. My pathetic magic sparked at my fingertips, useless fragments of blue-white light. Blood and blood and blood rained on me. The thrashing bodies of the demons parted enough for me to glimpse the sky above me through a haze of toxic red smoke—glimpse the moon, taunting me from beyond the glass.

Then it was blotted out beneath the powerful spread of massive wings. Silhouetted by the light of the moon and the lanterns, the feathers were rich, deep shades of red and purple.

Time slowed to a crawl as Raihn plunged his sword into the demon on top of me. The monster hissed and flailed. A slice opened across my cheek as I narrowly missed one of its thrashing claws.

I couldn't hear anything, but I saw his lips move—saw them form the word, *"Now!"*

As my consciousness faded, I gathered my final strength and rammed my sword into the demon's heart.

Push hard, little serpent, Vincent whispered in my ear.

The world had gone silent. Raindrops of blood became a waterfall. I kept pushing and pushing, until my hands were within the wound and I felt the demon's slippery flesh around my knuckles.

I was going to die. I thought I'd come close to it before. But this was different. When the demon's head lowered, when its cataract-ridden eyes met mine, I knew we were united in that—in the terror of our own mortality.

If this wasn't the key to victory, I was fucked. Completely fucked. Locked up in hell with this thing. For a moment and an eternity, the demon and I balanced together, dancing on the blade's edge of death.

And then the sudden absence of the weight left me gasping.

Raihn let out a ragged roar as he yanked the demon off me, gripping it by the throat and hurling it to the blood-soaked sand. The screaming from the crowd was now deafening. I couldn't catch my breath. Couldn't move. Pain paralyzed me.

I cringed, waiting for another demon to leap on me. Seconds passed. It didn't happen. Instead, Raihn stood over me, one hand on his hip, wings spirited away but sword still drawn and dripping. His lips moved, but I couldn't hear the words they formed.

"What?" I tried to say.

He leaned closer, mouth twisting into a grin. "I said, *good idea.*"

He stretched out his hand for me, but I rolled away and pushed myself to my feet. That earned an explosion of agony up my thigh.

The demons were now motionless husks, just boneless sacks of meat on the ground. Four of the seven of us remained alive. We stared at each other, weapons still poised. I struggled to grab hold of my slippery, pain-and-poison-addled thoughts.

Had we won? Or did we still need to kill each other?

The Hiaj—the fucker who had shot me—looked pointedly to the ground. Not at the corpses, but at the lines of shadow that led us to the edge of our enclosure. There, an archway had appeared. Within it was the cold, silent halls of the Moon Palace, standing in laughable contrast to the bloody chaos in the ring.

That was it. As much of a victory celebration as we would get, apparently.

Kiretta and the remaining Hiaj both limped to the door with only momentary pauses of confusion, eager to leave with their lives. But I didn't move. I wouldn't show it, but I wasn't even sure if I *could* walk.

I glanced back over my shoulder. For the first time since arriving, I took in the stands, where thousands of screaming spectators watched. They were so far above us that individual faces were lost in the crowd, but I still found myself looking for Vincent, anyway.

Raihn, too, had not moved. He was looking to his left, at the enclosure beside ours, whose occupants were still locked in a brutal battle—including Ibrihim, who was, remarkably, still alive and fighting. A faint wrinkle flitted across Raihn's brow in an expression that oddly resembled concern, and I realized why when I followed his gaze to his friend. She leapt around with all the erratic grace of a butterfly, wielding—

My brows lurched.

She was wielding *fire*. Not the white, dark power of Nightfire, either, a uniquely Nightborn gift. No, this was *fire*.

My lips parted in shock. Fire magic was the domain of Atroxus, the sun god—a member of the White Pantheon. I'd never seen a vampire wielding magic that was not born of Nyaxia's dark arts, let alone magic in the domain of her greatest enemy. I didn't know such a thing was possible.

Raihn pounded on the glass wall of our enclosure, loud enough to attract her attention. She glanced at him, and he tapped his forehead right between his eyebrows. Then he pointed to the demon in her cage that had the white mark on its face.

With that, he casually turned back to me, looked me up and down, and motioned to the door.

"After you."

There was absolutely no way in hell I was letting him walk behind me—especially not with my leg bleeding this much. I could only imagine how I smelled to him.

"After you," I said sweetly.

He shrugged, walked ahead, and I hobbled after him. My leg trembled violently.

The first trial ended with little fanfare. We all skulked away to our hideaways in the silent embrace of the Moon Palace. I went for the greenhouse immediately, desperate to hide before anyone else scented my blood and decided I was an easy meal. From my hiding place, I listened to the echoes of the other returning contestants.

One trial done. Four remained.

I thought I'd feel some sort of relief. But as I crouched among the leaves and tried to quell my bleeding—tried and failed—I fought back only rising dread.

No, relief was for the safe. And as I piled bloody rags higher and higher, safety was far, far from my reach.

CHAPTER ELEVEN

My wounds were even deeper than I'd feared, the one in my thigh continuing to bleed despite many tight bandages. The arrow must have been cursed, and who knew whatever venom the demons' claws held. Both of my injuries were so severe that Vincent's potion would only heal one. After a long internal debate, I used it on the cut in my side, which seemed at most risk for infection.

That still left me in rough shape, though. I needed to see Vincent. Surely, he'd meet me tonight—he was protective, and after seeing me in the ring, he'd want to know I was alright. I prayed he had been able to get his hands on more medicine, though I knew it was unlikely. Fuck. If he hadn't, I didn't know what I—

"Beautiful place you've claimed for yourself."

I stiffened so abruptly at the sound of the voice that I was greeted with a wave of pain. Grabbing my blades, I rose and turned. It was hard to get to my feet. Dawn was still hours away. And I was in no shape to fight. Not that I wouldn't try.

"How fitting. Every living thing in this depressing, dead castle, all in one place." Raihn wandered to the center of the greenhouse, pausing at the long-dry fountain at its center. He gazed up at the faceless statue, then out the windows, and then at last his eyes fell to me—the corner of his mouth twisting into an almost-smile.

"Get out," I snarled.

"I brought you something."

"*Get out.*"

"That's rude." He sat down on the edge of the fountain. I half expected the ancient stone to crumble under his weight—he was truly a wall of a creature, big enough to even look it when surrounded by gods-damned demons. And yet, he moved with surprising grace, like he knew his body well. He lounged with one foot propped up on the stone, elbow braced against it, while the other leg stretched out before him. He looked utterly casual—so casual I knew it was calculated.

Then he glanced up to the star-scattered sky, and something momentarily shifted in his face. I knew how to read expressions well. Those of vampires were always muted, frozen by centuries of dull immortality, and my survival depended on my ability to find meaning in every twitch. But that brief expression struck me—both because it was a glimpse of something unusually raw, and because I could not even begin to decipher it.

Then his stare fell back to me, the smirk returned, and once again I was looking at a vampire, toying with me in terms I was innately familiar with.

A performance. This was someone who cared very much about what people thought of him. I knew that much already from his little outburst at the feast, goading that poor bastard into attacking him so he had an excuse to be the first to draw blood.

He swung his legs down and leaned forward. With that movement, I twitched backward, drawing a step closer to the wall.

"What?" he said. "Do I smell?"

"I told you to get out."

"You think I came here for a meal? That's my grand intention?"

His intention was worth shit. Vampires had notoriously poor self-control when confronted with human blood. My life would be a lot safer if protecting me was just a matter of Vincent threatening painful and horrible death upon anyone who hurt me. Coming after me was a logically unwise decision. They all knew it would result in their execution . . . or worse. But they might not even *decide* to do it, they might just be overcome by—

The memory was as sharp as ever—lips on my throat, a kiss deepening to a nip deepening to a vicious stab of pain—

"What was that?"

I jerked back to reality. Mother, the blood loss must be getting to me, to let my mind wander off like that. Raihn still wore that little smirk, but now a wrinkle of curiosity deepened between his dark brows.

"Where did you go?"

That unnerved me more than I'd ever admit aloud—the fact that he'd seen whatever had just changed on my face.

"I told you," I spat, "to get—"

"What are you going to do? Stab me?"

He looked pointedly at my blades. Daring me. Mocking me, because we both knew I couldn't, not in this state.

"That thigh looks bad. It's a little poetic, isn't it?" He touched his thigh—still bandaged.

Sure. Fucking poetic.

"I brought you something for that."

He reached into his pack and pulled out a blue crystal bottle, contents thrumming with a light shimmer.

Mother. At the sight, I almost leapt for it just on impulse. How had he found that, if even Vincent was struggling to get his hands on it?

Raihn placed the potion on the stone beside him, then rested his forearms on his knees and watched me.

"You know," he said casually, "I heard some of the others talking before the first round. Betting on who would survive. Your name was worth shit, because everyone was so sure you'd be the first to die."

He paused, waiting for a reaction, and I refused to give him one.

"But I thought better," he went on. "I knew you were one to watch. That you weren't just some ordinary human. The great Nightborn King's human pet."

It wasn't the first time I'd been referred to that way, and it wouldn't be the last, but I still bristled. I was in so much pain that it was more difficult than usual to keep my temper at bay.

Calm down, Oraya. Anger means an accelerated heart rate. A higher heart rate means your scent is stronger. Give them nothing.

It wasn't as if I didn't know exactly what he was doing. Baiting me, just like he had baited that man at the feast. If I was the serpent, he was poking me with a stick to see when I'd snap it in two.

"Did he teach you how to fight like that? He must have, right?" He nodded to my weapons, still braced in front of me. "He gave you those, obviously. Nightborn craftsmanship. The good shit."

"Are you deaf, or just stupid?"

"You're unfriendly."

What did he think he was accomplishing here? Did he think I was so easy to manipulate? Did he think I didn't know what this was?

"Why are you here?" I snapped. By now, I struggled to hide the labor of my breathing and maintain the strength in my voice. "For entertainment? I'm boring as shit, I promise you."

"I can see that."

"Stop playing with me. I don't have the patience."

Again, the corner of his mouth lifted in a grim, satisfied smirk. "Or time," he said flatly, his eyes falling to my wounded thigh.

My jaw snapped closed. His gaze flicked back to mine, and for a long moment we just stared at each other, locked in a wordless conversation.

I knew it was the truth. He knew I knew it. I hated that he knew I knew it.

"Then stop wasting it," I spat out, at last. "What do you want?"

"Who will you ally with for the Halfmoon Trial?"

I blinked. I wasn't sure what I was expecting—more games, maybe—but it wasn't that.

It was a good question. An important question. The choice of ally for the Halfmoon Trial was a critical strategic decision. It needed to be someone strong enough to keep you in the top fifty percent of contestants during the Halfmoon, but not *too* strong, because they then became your greatest competition in the final two trials.

While the exact nature of the trial changed in every Kejari, those three important elements remained constant: the fact that it

required cooperation, that it resulted in the death of half the partic-
ipants . . . and that many, many contestants would be killed in their
sleep immediately after it, most often by former allies who decided
they were more risk than reward.

Despite my best efforts, I couldn't keep the wince from flitting
across my nose.

Raihn let out a low chuckle. "I thought so." Then he said, with no
hesitation, "Ally with me."

My eyebrows shot up.

Vincent had often chided me for my poor control over my facial
expressions, and at this one, Raihn laughed again.

"Ally with . . . you," I said.

"Me and Mische."

Mische. Was that the name of the short-haired girl? The one
with the fire?

"We claimed a room near the top of the towers," he went on. "It's
secure. Big—a whole apartment. Safe. Or safer than this place, at
least."

This didn't feel right. "Why?"

"Because you impressed me."

"Bullshit."

His brows twitched in the faintest hint of surprise, like he was
genuinely not expecting this answer.

"Excuse me?"

"You haven't said a single true thing since you strode in here,
so I'll be honest for both of us. I'm a human. We both know that
makes me the weakest one here. You have your pick of fifty stronger vampires you could ally with. And you expect me to believe
you want me?"

He examined a cut on his ring finger. "Only forty, now, actually.
Look, you beat warriors that outclassed you many times over tonight. You and I . . ." His gaze raised back to me. "We worked well
together, didn't we? And I like an underdog."

"Bull. Shit." I jabbed one of my blades at him for emphasis with
each word. "Do other people fall for this? Give me one honest
thing, or get out, like I've been telling you to since you showed up."

I didn't trust anyone in this place. But I *especially* didn't trust someone who pursued me under such blatantly false pretenses. The very fact that he wanted to ally with me made him the least trustworthy one here, because no sane person would want to do such a thing. And I could handle selfish motivations—I expected them— but not when I didn't know what they were.

He blinked twice, biting the inside of his cheek. I couldn't tell if he was insulted or if he was fighting back laughter.

Finally, he said, "All the other decent fighters that are people I could actually tolerate are already allied."

"And?"

"And?"

"Not enough. Keep going. You already have your friend. Why invite another?"

"I'm curious about you. Can you blame me? Everyone is. Vincent's little human princess, kept in a glass palace where everyone could look but never touch." He glanced around, smiling wryly at the greenhouse's crystal walls. "Are you missing your glass castle, princess?"

I wouldn't let him bait me, not even if I did find myself shifting in irritation at that characterization.

But the mention of Vincent triggered a wave of understanding. This, at least, made sense. Maybe it was the first thing out of Raihn's mouth that I actually believed.

"Vincent can't help me in here."

"I doubt that very much."

Ah.

Vincent. It was about Vincent. The offer of alliance had nothing to do with me. Raihn thought that if he allied with the king's *little human princess*, it would earn him advantages afforded to no one else in here . . . and prevent other contestants from getting them first.

I didn't like it, and it wasn't true, but at least it made sense.

I scoffed but didn't argue. Instead I said, "And?"

He looked confused. "And?"

"Why else?"

Another long stare. Another wordless conversation. I'd forgotten what it was like to talk to someone whose face communicated so much.

There was one more thing—one more key reason why I was the ideal ally. We both knew it. He knew I knew it. He hated that I knew he knew it.

But I'd asked for honesty, and I wanted him to say it.

He was clearly weighing this, deciding which answer was the right one to pass the test. At last, he said, "And you'll be easy to kill, when the Halfmoon is over."

It was legitimately satisfying to just hear someone say it out loud.

"But until then," he added, quickly, "no harm will come to you. I can promise you that."

I heard Vincent's voice in a sixteen-year-old memory:

I am the only person who will ever make that promise and keep it.

"What makes you think I need your protection?"

To his credit, he didn't laugh at me.

"You're a skilled fighter. Better than I thought you'd be." He rose from the fountain and took a few slow steps closer, never breaking eye contact, his large, scar-nicked hand open on one side, the other clutched tight around the healing potion. With each step, I drew backward.

"But you are still human," he said quietly. "And that means that in here, you are prey. You'll always be prey. No matter how good you are with those fancy weapons."

The truth, of course. But maybe he didn't realize that I knew how to be prey. I'd been doing it my entire life.

He was right. I would need to ally with someone for the Halfmoon, and then I would need to kill them afterward. Maybe I could ally with him, allow him to prot·ct me, and spend that time learning his fighting styles and weaknesses—preparing myself to kill him as soon as it was over. He could underestimate me, and I could use that against him.

But allying now? This was early. The Halfmoon Trial, the mid-point of the tournament, was six weeks away. That was a long time to stay in close proximity to not one, but two vampires, without

THE SERPENT & THE WINGS OF NIGHT

getting killed. A long time to allow him to learn my strengths and weaknesses, too.

"No," I said. "Tempting offer, though."

He took another step closer, and again, I matched the distance back.

"What was it that you asked of me? An honest thing? I was honest with you, so now you be honest with me. Do you *really* think you'll survive another night here? It's almost dawn now, but after that? Your scent is all over the Moon Palace right now. I could smell you even from the east tower. And let me tell you, you smell fucking *delicious*. You need to stop that bleeding, fast."

My eyes fell to the potion tightly gripped in his hand. Hearing it all acknowledged out loud made me uneasy. But so did having him this close to me. I did not like that he was pushing me into this so forcefully. The reasons he had given me didn't warrant that, which made the ones he didn't far more concerning.

"No," I said.

"You'll bleed to death, or they'll kill you."

He started to step closer, and I ignored the horrific rip of pain as I leapt away, blades raised anew.

"I will stab you again if you come even a single step closer to me," I snarled. "*Get out.*"

He raised his hands.

"As you wish, princess. Suit yourself."

He made sure I watched as he slipped the potion back into his pack, then gave me one last smile and turned to the door.

"Top of the eastern tower. If you change your mind."

CHAPTER TWELVE

I left an hour before dawn broke. It was a gamble to go at all—my wound was so bad that I struggled to move. If I passed out half-way between our meeting spot and the gates of the Moon Palace, I was fucked. But I gritted my teeth through it, replaced my dressings, and made the trek. It took me twice as long as it had the night before. I hid beneath the bridge and waited.

And waited and waited.

Please, Vincent. Come on. Please.

At first, I was in denial. He was just a little late. Something had kept him. There was no way that he *wouldn't* be here, not when he had witnessed that battle and seen my injuries. He would appear any second now.

But the minutes ticked by, and Vincent did not come.

Fuck.

I knew my father, and I knew that there was no explanation for this that could possibly be good, but I had no time to worry about that. When sunrise was far too close, I gave up and dragged myself back to the Moon Palace. By then I was moving even slower. Bleeding heavier. I had been betting on Vincent's help, and losing that gamble had cost me dearly.

I barely made it back before dawn broke. As early-morning light streamed through the floor-to-ceiling windows, I crept into the feast hall. It was, thankfully, empty. The table overflowed with fresh food that looked as if it had hardly been touched. But the carafes? The ones that had once held blood?

Those were ominously empty.

I was in so much pain that the thought of eating made my stomach churn, but I stuffed some food into my mouth and into my pack anyway. I had to keep my strength up somehow, and I had to move fast. Days prior, the Moon Palace had been near-silent during daylight. But now, I could hear activity echoing through the halls—muffled voices, dull thumps, and light footsteps. Raihn had been right. The greenhouse was safe in the day, but the rest of the Palace wouldn't be.

I moved as swiftly as my injuries would allow from the feast hall to the great room. My eyes locked on the smear of light at the end of the hallway—the greenhouse entrance. It was a bright, clear day, not a cloud in the sky. Sunlight flooded it.

I was two steps away—so fucking close—when I heard the footsteps.

I dropped the food. Grabbed the hilt of my weapons. Turned just in time.

One of my blades slid into the taut muscle of my attacker's side, and the other blocked his strike to my face. The sudden force of the movement left me breathless with pain as my wounds tore open anew, the fresh flow of blood driving my attacker into a frenzy.

It happened so fast. I didn't even get a good look at my assailant, only glimpsed little details—the white of his wild stare, the gray of his hair, the overall wiry shape of his form—before we were tangled together. He was half-feral, moving in jagged lurches, mouth twisted into a snarl and claws digging deep into my shoulders as I fought him back. He wielded a rapier, which opened another wound in my side.

I flung myself against him and together we tumbled into the greenhouse. The vegetation was so thick that it did little more than make my attacker hiss in mild discomfort.

But he was savage with bloodlust. Sloppy. Wasn't paying attention to his surroundings. When he lunged for me, I used the force of his own movement to slam him against the glass wall.

The morning beat down over us both, the heat beading perspiration on my skin in seconds. His back pressed against the glass, taking the full intensity of the sun. The scent of sweat and burnt flesh filled my nostrils.

It would be enough to jar him from bloodlust. Surely.

But no. He let out a grunt of pain and kept thrashing against me. I could block his teeth, or his sharpened nails, or his weapon, but not all three—at least, not while keeping him pinned. The burning smell grew more pungent.

I stumbled. He lunged. I had one chance. I flung him back against the glass. Seized the moment of his hesitation as the sun scalded one side of his face.

And before he could recover, I plunged my dagger into his chest.

. . . Not hard enough. The blade didn't make it through.

Fuck.

I was so, so weak. I drew back again, and nearly collapsed as the world went sideways.

My blurring vision sharpened around the vampire's eyes—yellow, with threads of red. He turned to me, a slow smile spreading over his lips.

I threw everything I had into one final thrust, *hard hard hard,* until I heard a crack, until my dagger went through his chest.

A horrific burning pain skewered me.

My attacker went limp. The dead weight of him nearly toppled me over. He wasn't dead. His fingers still twitched. I hadn't gotten deep enough. But my hands didn't obey when I tried to push again.

I staggered back. Looked down. My abdomen was covered with blood. I couldn't feel where the cut was.

Couldn't feel much of anything, actually.

You're in shock, Oraya. Vincent's voice was urgent in my head. *You are going to bleed out. You need to get out of here,* right now. *They'll smell you.*

My mind was a muddy mess, but I could make out a single thought: *I am not going to survive this way for four months. No chance.*

I clutched my stomach and lifted my head. And there, right before me, as if presented to me as a gift from the Moon Palace itself, was the spiral staircase.

I looked back. The greenhouse door was suddenly far behind me. Had I walked this much? I didn't remember doing that. But then again, there was little I *did* remember as I dragged myself up that staircase. Flight after flight after flight, seemingly endless, just as it had been that first night, the first time I'd run up these stairs desperate to make it to the top with my life.

Probably wouldn't be the last, either.

By the time I made it to the top, I was crawling on my hands and knees. Blood dripped down the stairs and rolled through the gaps in the banister, landing on the distant great room floor like little flower petals.

When there were no more stairs, I lifted my head. A single door stood before me.

I fought to my feet. One step, and I collapsed. Tried to rise. Slipped on my own blood. I didn't feel it when I hit the ground. The world spun. Faded.

After what felt like an age, someone flipped me onto my back. My throat released a strangled sound of pain.

Raihn leaned over me.

"Well," he said, crossing his arms, "*that* didn't take long."

Fucking prick.

Aloud, I gurgled.

The last thing I saw before I lost consciousness was his broad grin, revealing two very long, very sharp canines.

"Oh, you're very welcome, Oraya."

And the last thing I heard was Vincent's voice in my head, saying, *What the hell did you just do?*

Part Three

Waning Moon

INTERLUDE

Let me tell you about the first time the child wishes to be something she is not.

Five years is a blink to a vampire. A half a lifetime to a little human. The king keeps his new adopted daughter carefully sequestered from the rest of his bloody world. He gives her everything she could possibly wish for within the confines of four walls.

The girl is eleven years old before her wishes venture beyond those walls. The king tried to be everything to her, but for all his affection and protection, he was still several hundred years older than her, and an entirely different species aside.

The girl remembered the life she had before she came here—even if those images were fleeting, eaten away by time. Years are long to a child so young, and memories so short.

Still, she remembered that she had a life before this. A life with people who were like her.

One night, when the king came to visit her, she asked him about her family. It was not the first time. She recognized the look on his face as he prepared to give her the same answer he always had, for the thousandth time.

"I know my parents are gone," she said quickly, before he spoke. "But there must be others."

"Others?"

"Others like me."

"Humans."

The girl nodded. The king was silent.

The girl went to her bookcase and pulled out a tome that weighed almost as much as she did. She had to battle it to make it to the table. It hit the wood with a thud, and she flipped through the book of maps.

"You found me in the western regions of the House of Night."

The king blinked in surprise. He had never told her the details of where she had been found.

The girl beamed a little, pleased to impress her father.

"I figured it out," she said. "Rishan territory. Right?"

She could not read her father's face. He nodded.

"Then where?" Her finger trailed over fading lines—cities and townships that only existed to her as ink on a map.

"It doesn't matter."

The girl paused. It did matter. It mattered very much.

She had learned to choose her words carefully.

"Maybe someone is still there. Looking for me."

"But you have a home here, little serpent." The king gave her a small, warm smile. "A home that suits you. Maybe your blood runs red, but you belong here."

He didn't understand. She did have a home here, but the life within its walls was one of constant fear.

"I don't," she said. "Everyone wants to kill me here."

The king did not argue with her. He had told her this was true many times over.

Finally, he sighed.

"I found you in a place called Salinae. A faraway district on the other side of the House of Night's borders. But even if you had family still living there, Oraya, I could not find them for you."

The girl didn't realize just how tightly she held onto this hope—this fragile, invented reality—until it shattered in her chest.

"Why?" she choked out.

"That is Rishan territory. As the Hiaj king, and leader of the House of Night, I can't go there unprovoked."

"Then I can." She did not hesitate. "I'll go."

He laughed, but she snapped, "It isn't a joke!"

The king's smile faded. He looked at his daughter for a long moment. "You are a human," he said. "It's too dangerous for you to do this."

"Then Turn me," she shot back. "Make me like you. I read all about it."

"I can't do that, either, Oraya."

Another hope fractured. Her eyes burned. "Why not?"

"Because you are far too precious." He stroked her hair. "Two in three Turnings end in death. That's more than half. I will not take that risk with your life."

Her throat was thick. Her eyes stung. She had to hold back her tears with all her strength. She was on the cusp of the age when children begin to understand the future. And in this moment, the little girl understood that this truth—that the prison of her own human flesh—damned her to a life within these four walls.

She whirled to her father, her little hands balled into fists. "There has to be something," she said. "There has to be some way. There has to."

The king chuckled, though his eyes were distant and sad. "Such teeth."

He was silent for a long moment, his smile fading to serious thought. He was quiet for such a long time that it seemed like his mind had traversed to a whole other world. The little girl knew better than to interrupt, so she watched him and waited.

She had already learned how to read his expressions, but this one was foreign. More than a decade later, she would think back to this conversation and know that what she had been seeing in him then was conflict—an expression so rare that she had not known how to identify it. She would think countless times about this night and about what her father would say to her next. The unanswered question of what he had been considering in that silence would haunt her.

But the little girl knew none of this now. She simply waited. At last, the king leaned forward in his chair, arms braced on his knees.

"There is one way you could, one day, become just as powerful as me."

Hope flooded her.

"How?" she breathed.

The king's mouth twisted into a rueful smile. "With a gift from a goddess."

CHAPTER THIRTEEN

The laugh was low and deep, rough and smooth at the same time—quiet, and yet it commanded the room. It was the first thing to seep through my addled mind; the first thing to cut through my hazy consciousness.

I rolled over. My body protested with a symphony of aches, but that was nothing compared to before. The absence of pain was jarring.

As I blinked away sleep, the first thing I saw was wings—deep black, the gloss of the feathers reflecting warm strokes of lantern light. I hadn't had the time in the ring to properly admire Raihn's wings, but they were—as much as I hated to admit it—quite beautiful. I saw Rishan wings much less often than I saw Hiaj ones, and never any as uniquely colored as these—deep black, with that oil-slick sheen of reds and purples and blues.

Raihn crouched before Mische, who sat atop a coffee table. He held her foot, which he leaned over with what seemed like intense concentration, a roll of bandages in his other hand.

"I told you to stop moving, Mische," he muttered.

"It's taking too long."

"You can stay still for two fucking minutes."

His words were rough. And yet, the tone of them was so much softer—tender, even.

Mische heaved a long-suffering sigh and squirmed like an impatient child.

I blinked again and the rest of the room came into focus. We were in what looked to be the common space of an apartment—a very, very nice one, albeit a couple of centuries out of date. Lanterns lined the walls, lit with a mix of fire and blue-white light that flickered over brocade wallpaper in a strange contrast of warmth and coolness. A wall of thick velvet curtains covered the eastern half of the room—all windows, if I had to guess. Grand furniture was arranged artfully throughout, crafted of deep mahogany wood or generously marbled black stone and upholstered with silky brocade. All of it appeared to be a relic from another age in style, but looked as pristine as if it had been made yesterday.

"I told you, it's fine! It won't slow me down a—oh! *Oh!*"

Mische leapt to her feet with such excited verve that she came delightfully close to kicking Raihn in the face.

"What did we *just* talk about?" he muttered as he dodged, and Mische paid him no mind as she darted across the room to me. My head was still spinning, but I lurched away from her nonetheless.

She froze, raising her hands.

"Oh. I'm sorry! I know—he told me. Slow." She shrugged, letting out an awkward laugh.

He told me. I bristled at that. What might that have looked like? *She's a weak little human, terrified of everything, so treat her like a wounded animal.*

Raihn looked away, muttering a curse.

"How are you feeling?" Mische asked. She settled down on the floor, folding her legs beneath her and resting her palms on her knees—like she needed to physically restrain herself from running over to me. Her eyes were too large for her face, almost comically out of proportion with her small nose and forever-upturned mouth. Yet, somehow, she was still strikingly beautiful. Then again, vampires always were.

"Better," I answered, after a long moment.

Mische grinned. "Oh, good! I'm Mische. So excited to finally meet you."

"We have met. At the feast."

"Well, I mean, *really* meet. Raihn told me all about the trial. And how it was your idea to find the pack leader. That saved my ass, so thank you." She laughed and shook her head, as if the recent near-death experience was a fond distant memory.

I'd never met another vampire who behaved anything like this. Even at their most outgoing, they were reserved. And yet, I couldn't shake the sense that she did remind me of someone. Not a vampire, I realized after a moment, but a human. She reminded me of Ilana.

Sure, Mische had none of Ilana's biting edge. But she had that same loud, unapologetic flair. She was . . . unabashedly colorful. What was the relationship, I wondered, between her and Raihn? They were both odd by vampire standards, but in ways that could not possibly be more different from each other.

She rose and spread her arms, gesturing to the room. "Welcome to our home. Isn't it stunning? Well . . . maybe you don't think so. I'm sure it's nothing compared to the Nightborn castle. But we've never been anywhere like this before. Or—well, I suppose *Raihn* has, but *I—*"

"Give her a sun-damned minute before you talk her to death, Mische."

Raihn slid his hands into the pockets of his jacket—long, black, simple, and slightly too small at the shoulders—and approached me, a smug smile that made me bristle spreading over his lips.

"You changed your mind quickly, didn't you?"

"I didn't have a choice."

"So we saw."

"And thank the gods you did come here," Mische breathed. "You would've died." Her face hardened. "Those Bloodborn shits. He tried to rip you to pieces, didn't he?"

Thank the gods, she had said. Not the Goddess. Interesting.

"I have a gift for you," Raihn said, very casually, "to welcome you to our little family."

Mische grinned. It was jarring to see such a sunny and cheerful expression punctuated by those sharp canines.

"Oh, yes!" She reached into one of the chests pushed against the far wall, and when she turned back around, I had to stop myself from recoiling.

It was a head.

A man's head, the skin pale and wan, the hair mostly gray and streaked with some ash-brown. His ears were pointed, as were his teeth, visible through the perpetual snarl that graced his lips even in death.

I'd hardly gotten a good look at the vampire that attacked me, but I had to assume this was him.

My stomach lurched with sudden nausea. The memory came, as it always did, in brief, all-consuming flashes.

I have a gift for you.

I blinked hard, shaking away the past. Then carefully ironed my expression back into one of cold disinterest.

"And what the hell am I supposed to do with that?"

Raihn shrugged. "I don't know. Gloat?"

"How satisfying," I said dryly. "He certainly looks like he can now appreciate my superiority."

Mische's grin faded. Raihn's lips thinned in wry disapproval.

"I've saved your life twice now and presented you with the head of your enemy, and this isn't enough? You're a demanding little thing, aren't you?"

"All of those 'gifts' have been self-serving. I helped you survive in that ring, too. And I'm sure you loved killing this one."

An odd expression twitched over his face, quickly discarded in favor of an easy smile.

"That's why we're allies. Because our interests are mutually beneficial."

"Hm."

I tried not to show that the word "allies" chilled me down to my bones. Only now did the full consequences of my actions hit me. I had been forced to make a decision out of base desperation, and now, I was trapped here with these two.

Mische still held the head, though she now looked down at it with a slight pout.

"He really was an ass." She sighed. "Even before. He would have died eventually, anyway. You practically gutted him."

"Must've been quite a fight," Raihn added, "judging by the state of both of you."

I chanced a couple of steps closer to Mische, examining the head. Even for vampires, the pale gray tinge to his skin was unusual, as was the vibrant red that rimmed his sightless eyes. A spiderweb of black-crimson veins crawled up his throat. They were visible on his neck, his jaw, at the corners of his mouth and eyes. And even in death, they seemed to . . . pulse.

"What?" Raihn said. "You've never seen a Bloodborn curse up close before?"

I disliked that he found it so easy to read my face.

"It was bloodlust," I said.

"It was a hell of a lot more than that."

He sounded strangely serious. Perhaps even grim. When I tore my eyes away from the head to look at him, the smirk had faded from his lips.

Then he noticed my stare, and just like that, it returned.

"His days were numbered either way. A mercy. This was the least painful way he could've gone. *Anyway*." The smirk became a crooked grin. "I'm glad you came to your senses. Mische, you want to get rid of that thing now?"

Mische nodded and tucked the head under her arm as she headed for one of the doors in the back of the room. "I'll be right back. Then I'll give you a tour, Oraya."

RAIHN AND MISCHE really had managed to find a prime location. The apartment was huge, featuring a study, a kitchen, an office, four bedrooms (each with their own adjoining washrooms), and, of course, that grand sitting room—all of which were luxuriously ornate, even compared to the Nightborn castle. All citizens of the inner city were accustomed to seeing the Moon Palace stand watch over Sivrinaj in blessed monument to Nyaxia, but it was only now that I actually stopped to think about how it had gotten there or why. Had people lived here once? If so, why was it abandoned in favor of the Nightborn castle? This place was almost as big and every bit as grand.

Mische showed me to my room—"We gave you the one with the most windows!" she announced. "For, you know, obvious reasons!"—and left me to my own devices to clean up and get some rest. My bedchamber, like all the rooms in this place, was beautifully ornate in an ancient, outdated sort of way—even if, strangely, there wasn't a speck of dust anywhere.

The curtains were a heavy, deep blue velvet, with silver braided pulls. I hauled them open with considerable effort. The window revealed a near-perfect mirror of the view from my room in the Nightborn castle. In the distance, its silhouette was reduced to a series of vicious peaks and moon-silver domes. I couldn't remember the last time I'd seen it from so far away. Buildings that were small in the distance from my bedroom window were now so close I could see every imperfection . . . of which there were many. Yes, the architecture was grand, but gold paint flaked and carvings crumbled. Stress fractures crawled like ivy over stone walls and cracks severed stained-glass windows. All marks of decay that were invisible from my room in Vincent's castle.

I had always assumed that the ugliness of Sivrinaj was confined to the human districts. It had never occurred to me that perhaps the inner city was rotting in its own way, too.

My eyes settled on a little flash of blocky darkness against the horizon. From my room at Vincent's Palace, I saw the dunes in the distance, graceful and silent. But from this one, that far-off view was instead of the human slums, partially hidden beyond the silhouetted grandiosity of the Nightborn castle.

I didn't know why the sight of those two things, so stark in contrast, made me so uncomfortable.

I pulled the curtains closed again.

"You got this from the feast hall?"

"Uh-huh!"

Mische threw a cherry in her mouth and chewed, clearly savoring it, before swallowing—pit and all. She and Raihn picked at food, but mostly drank two large goblets of blood. The plate of food Mische presented me was far more than I could ever eat, artfully arranged by color—berries and meats and cheeses, piled high.

I eyed them both as they sipped their blood. Mische had clearly wanted me to sit across the table from her, but I moved to the end of the table instead. It just felt more comfortable to put some distance between us. Give myself time to react if either of them made a move.

I lifted my chin to their glasses. "What kind is that?"

Raihn took a sip and smacked his lips. "Deer. I think."

I couldn't tell if I was relieved or not that it wasn't human. I didn't like to think about where it might be coming from, but at least if the others were getting it from the decanters, they wouldn't be quite as tempted to get it from me. There was, after all, nothing quite like human blood for them.

It wasn't the only kind that sufficed. Deer, horse, cow, or pig's blood was the most common. Chicken or crow blood was the cheapest, though it was nutritionally poor and apparently tasted horrible. In Vincent's court, horse blood was often cured and flavored into delicacies. But even the finest of substitutions didn't compare to human blood. The upper class had it often, harvested or consumed straight from blood vendors like Ilana had been.

"There wasn't any left," I said. "When I went down there earlier."

"We know," Raihn replied.

We were silent for a long, awkward moment, all very aware of what that could mean. At least for now, contestants could leave the Moon Palace in search of more. But I had a feeling that the leash would tighten, sooner or later.

"We have plenty for us, though!" Mische said brightly, breaking the tension and holding up a very full decanter, sloshing the red, thick liquid within. "Took as much of it as we could carry before the others got to it."

"And food, too," Raihn added. "For you."

I could be grateful for that, at least, on both counts. Though their kindness made me uncomfortable.

One of the candles in the candelabra at the center of the table remained unlit. Mische frowned at it, then snapped her fingers. A little fragment of flame sparked at her fingertip, which she used to light the candle with a satisfied smile.

I watched in fascination. It was just as surprising here, up close, as it had been to see in the ring. My curiosity won out. "That isn't Nyaxia's magic."

"Nope. Atroxus."

Just like I'd thought. And yet the confirmation didn't make it any less unbelievable. While each of the thirteen gods could be called on for various forms of magic, none of the twelve deities of the White Pantheon allowed their powers to be drawn upon by vampires. Vampires, after all, were Nyaxia's children, and the White Pantheon despised Nyaxia.

Mische read my face.

"It is perfectly possible for a vampire to wield magic from beyond Nyaxia's domain," she said, in a tone that implied she'd given this explanation many times before. "It just takes the right talents, that's all."

She seemed proud of herself. But I didn't miss the disapproval on Raihn's face as he sipped his blood at this exact moment—as if to stop himself from saying something he'd regret.

"What about you?" she asked. "Do you wield magic?"

I hesitated before answering. Maybe I didn't want them to know that I did, even if my magic was basically worthless anyway. An advantage was an advantage. But I was silent for a moment too long. Mische grinned and leaned closer. "You do! I can feel it. It's shy though, huh?"

Shy. That was rich. I considered calling it that next time Vincent made a disparaging comment about the weakness of my magic. *Don't judge it. It's just shy!*

He'd love that.

"Only a little," I said. "Useless things. It's never done anything for me." My gaze slid to Raihn. "And what about you?"

"Oh, same," he said, taking another sip of blood. "Useless things."

As if we hadn't all seen him use it to kill a man mere days ago.

Mische giggled, clearly finding Raihn more amusing than I did.

My eyes narrowed. "Useless things like Asteris?"

The corner of his mouth quirked. "Exactly like that."

BANG BANG.

I jumped. My gaze snapped to the front door, which shook with the force of each knock.

BANGBANGBANGBANGBANG.

Raihn barely glanced at it. "Now *that* sounds like something we shouldn't answer."

"Raihn Ashraj, *OPEN. THIS. FUCKING. DOOR.*"

The deep female voice boomed from beyond the door, so loud it might as well have been coming from inside the apartment. If the banging kept up, surely it would be in a matter of minutes.

Mische glanced to Raihn. He narrowed his eyes at her. They had an unspoken conversation.

He groaned. "Why is it always *me*? Why is it never *your* name they're screaming through the sun-cursed door?"

She smiled sweetly. "Because I'm nice and pretty."

"I'm nice and pretty," he grumbled. He rose, grabbed his sword from where it lay haphazardly on the coffee table, and unsheathed it in one smooth movement. Then he stalked to the door and threw it open, giving whoever was on the other side no time to react before the sword was in their face.

"Hello, Angelika."

And immediately, that sword was met with the cold metal edge of an axe. Bearing it was the woman who led the House of Blood contestants . . . and she was *furious*.

Up close, she might've been the most muscular woman I'd ever seen, nearly as tall as Raihn and broad enough to fill the doorway. The defined cut of her arms, exposed in her sleeveless armor, flexed as she deflected the full force of Raihn's blow—and if the strain of his was any indication, he wasn't holding back, either.

"Where is he?" Angelika snarled.

"I don't know what you're talking about."

"I'm not like that Rishan piece of shit you killed during the feast. I'm not falling for your games. *Where is he?*"

I hovered near the door, my own weapons out, but I wasn't about to jump into that unless I had to. Mische seemed shockingly blasé, watching with obvious interest but little concern.

Apparently, Angelika didn't especially want or need an answer from Raihn, because instead of waiting for one, she struck. And Raihn was ready for it. He deflected her blow and used the force of it to push both of them out into the hallway, away from the entrance to the apartment.

When they fought, it was like watching two forces of nature collide. Angelika was vicious, every movement woven with sheer power. The light of the hall illuminated the scars up and down her arms—she was a blood magic wielder.

If she used such magic against Raihn, though, it didn't seem to affect him—save, perhaps, for a minuscule lurch when her weapon met his. He was a breathtakingly skilled warrior. Damn near an artist. In the trial, I'd been too distracted to notice just how good he was. He moved with incredible grace for such a large person. Each strike or dodge or step blended into each other like steps to a dance. The puffs of darkness around his sword intensified with every swing, leaving streaks of night behind every blow and wrapping the two of them in ribbons of shadow.

Yet Angelika was just as good, just as strong, just as fast. They were evenly matched, both trembling under the force of each other's power. By the nature of my position in life, I'd gotten very good at sizing up predators—at recognizing killers. And right now, I was watching two ruthlessly efficient ones toy with each other.

With one forceful thrust against her axe, Raihn pushed her away. "It's his own damned fault. And you know it, too."

"It was the human," she shot back. "I know it was."

"He was out of his mind. Went after her in the greenhouse, of all places."

Angelika had been ready to strike again, but at this, she paused. Lowered her axe, just a fraction of an inch.

Raihn did not lower his. But he didn't strike, either. "*In daylight,* Angelika."

"The greenhouse," she repeated.

"He was long gone," Raihn said. "He got himself killed. Hell, you should be thanking us. We saved you from a very unpleasant task."

"Watch yourself," she hissed.

"What? Would you rather he lived long enough to get used by this place? Like those poor bastards we fought in the ring?"

Angelika flinched. Her fingers lifted—paused, briefly, at her throat. She didn't speak for a long moment, and I tensed, waiting to see if she would move again.

"I'd rather kill her in the trials than kill her here," she said, at last, voice low and thick with promise—and at this, her eyes fell to me, hard with hatred. Her nostrils flared. I became very conscious of the rapid pace of my heartbeat.

"And as for you." That glare settled on Raihn. "*You* . . . you're lucky it's not your time yet. Remember right now exactly how lucky you are."

Then she simply lowered her axe and stalked away.

We waited until she was long gone before any of us moved. Raihn was the first to speak.

"I probably should've killed her."

"You say that like you would have won," I said.

He let out a low chuckle. "Oh, I would have won."

His rose-colored gaze slid to me, and I became aware all at once of how close he was standing—close enough that I could smell him, a scent that reminded me of saffron and heat beating down over the desert, and something else, something I couldn't quite place.

Goose bumps rose at my skin, instincts rebelling against allowing someone this close. I took several casual steps back, and Raihn's stare drifted back to where Angelika had disappeared down the stairs.

"Still. Her? She's a problem. She's the one to watch."

"I feel sorry for her," Mische said softly, and offered nothing more.

CHAPTER FOURTEEN

That was a foolish decision. I taught you better than to serve yourself to your enemies that way."

I hadn't seen Vincent this appalled by my actions in nearly a decade.

I had no choice, I wanted to say, but I swallowed those words before they made it to my lips. I knew better. Vincent believed that you always had a choice, and if you found yourself in a position where you didn't, you'd made a very poor one earlier that put you there. Either way, you had no one to blame but yourself.

"I need an ally for the Halfmoon, and he's a good one," I said instead.

"He is a Rishan."

"So are nearly a third of the contestants in there."

"Think about why a Rishan would want to get close to you, Oraya. *You.*"

He paced. Vincent only paced when he was nervous, but even that was a smooth, deliberate movement. Three long steps, and a sharp turn, exactly the same length, exactly the same rhythm.

He was tense. I was tense. It was a bad combination, and I knew it from the moment I saw him. He had worked hard over the years to grind my emotional impulsivity out of me. But the stress of the competition, my injury, and the choice I'd been forced to make brought my nerves to the surface. Beneath all of it lay my grief over Ilana's death; never acknowledged but still raw and bleeding, amplifying every negative emotion.

All of that meant I had to watch my voice and my words very carefully.

"I have," I said. "He thinks that allying with me will mean advantages from you. As far as selfish motivations go, I can accept that one. Better that than him keeping me around for a quick meal if food gets scarce."

Step, step, step, *turn*, as Vincent pivoted sharply to me. "And it will."

I almost shivered at that thought. "At least when that happens, I have protection."

"*Protection.*" His lips curled into a sneer—he threw the word at me as if I'd just said something revolting.

My teeth clenched, biting down on my response. Did he think I wasn't well aware of all the caveats and weaknesses of that word in this place? There was no such thing as protection—not in the Kejari, not in the House of Night, and not in all of Obitraes. There was no such thing as safety, and there was certainly no such thing as trust, not for anyone other than the person who stood before me.

But my irritation faded under a rising tide of concern as I watched my father pace. Watched his hand run through his hair in his only forever-clear tell.

"What happened?" I asked, quietly.

Rebel activity from the Rishan? That might explain why Vincent was so sensitive to the thought of me allying with a Rishan, no matter who it was. Or . . . maybe more threats from the House of Blood. That would be even more disturbing.

I didn't know why I even bothered to ask. Predictably, Vincent looked away and said nothing. A single muscle twitched in his cheek, signaling his annoyance.

Concern knotted in my stomach as I thought of Angelika's sneer and the way she had looked at me, and as I thought of Raihn, a Rishan vampire. In theory, the Kejari was an isolated tournament, in which each contestant stood on equal footing. But in practice? It was just an extension of the tensions and conflicts of the outside world.

"If things are happening out here that could affect what's happening in there, I need to know about it," I said.

"You need to focus on staying alive. Nothing else."

"I am focusing on staying alive."

"By throwing yourself into the grip of a Rishan? I taught you better."

Before I could stop myself, I spat, "Would you rather I have let myself bleed to death? I needed to act, and I tried to come to you for help and *you weren't there.*"

The words shot from my lips too quickly to stop, sharp as the blades he had given me the last time we met. His eyes snapped to me, revealing a momentary glimmer of hurt that quickly hardened to ice.

I regretted my words right away. I had pushed too hard. The change in him was stark and immediate, as if the same features were now a mask worn by an entirely different person.

Vincent, my father, loved me above all. But Vincent, the Nightborn King, was too ruthless to allow the slightest challenge, love or no.

"You think I haven't been doing everything I can to help you?" he said coldly.

"I do," I said. "Of course I do."

"I gave you those blades to help you become someone who deserves to wield them. If you don't want that—"

"I do."

The last time he sounded this way, he left my room and did not speak to me again for a week. I was a little ashamed of the sudden, desperate panic that seized me at the idea of him withdrawing like that now.

That foreign hardness in his expression did not soften. He turned away, silhouetted against Sivrinaj's skyline.

"I apologize," I said, past a lump in my throat. "I know you're doing everything that you can. I shouldn't have implied otherwise."

And I meant it. I had overreacted to his protective grumbling. I owed everything that I was to Vincent, and I never forgot that.

Several long, tense seconds passed. I let out an involuntary exhale when he turned back to me and his expression was no longer that of a disrespected king, but of my concerned, tired father.

"I would have been there," he said, "if I could."

It was the closest I'd ever get to an apology. I had never seen Vincent apologize to anyone for anything, ever. But one had to learn how to hear what lingered in between the words. Just like he never told me he loved me, but I heard it in every stern instruction. And now, even though he did not say he was sorry, I heard it in the slightly lower cadence of his voice in that single sentence.

You had to bend, with people like Vincent. Reach for what they wouldn't give you themselves.

"I know," I murmured.

He gave me a long, searching look. "You need to win this."

He said it not with tenderness, but straightforward firmness. A directive.

"I know."

He reached out and touched my cheek.

I flinched, just because it was so unexpected. I could barely remember the last time that Vincent had touched me other than to strike me in the sparring ring. And yet, a part of me wanted to lean into that small caress.

When I was very young, he used to hug me, sometimes. One of my earliest memories was laying my head against Vincent's shoulder and experiencing the sudden jolt of realization that I felt *safe*. Even so young, I knew how rare it was—I felt it then like a sigh of relief, as if I'd been unknowingly holding my breath since the day my house had collapsed around me.

It had been a long, long time since I'd felt that way. One day love became not an offering of safety, but a reminder of everything cruel and dangerous in the world.

He pulled his hand away and stepped back. "Keep your ally," he said. "But keep those teeth ready, little serpent. Watch his back, but don't let him see yours. Because the minute you turn it, he will kill you. Use him. But *never* allow him to use you."

All things I was acutely aware of. I nodded.

He reached into his pocket, then handed me another little vial of healing potion.

"Guard it," he said. "I don't know when I'll be able to get more."

I slipped the potion into my pack and slipped off into the night.

It was much more useful than a hug, anyway.

I ENCOUNTERED NO one else on my way back to the Moon Palace. The hours this close to dawn were often quiet—most vampires had retreated to their homes by now, preparing for sleep, and the route I took was secluded.

Still, just as I was preparing to scale the walls of the Palace grounds, I paused.

I peered over my shoulder to see nothing but silent cobblestone paths and the murky, untamed outline of overgrown rose vines. Not a hint of movement. Not a single sound.

Yet, the hairs rose on the back of my neck, as if coaxed to attention by the touch of watchful eyes.

I shuddered, turned back to the wall, and hoisted myself over it.

BY THE TIME I made it up all the stairs, dawn peeked over the horizon. When I opened the apartment door, I was surprised to see that the curtains had been parted, and Raihn's considerable form filled the space between them. He leaned against the window, one arm braced to the glass.

"Where were you?" he asked, without turning.

"That's not your concern." I closed the door and crossed the sitting room.

"It's a little my concern, isn't it? Allies and all."

Mother, I hated that word and all he seemed to think it implied.

I said, pointedly, nothing as I went to the hall. His face tilted just enough to watch me. The silver of the moonlight had started to flush with the pink promise of the sun, outlining the strong angle of his cheekbone to his jaw, bleeding down to the muscle of his throat.

Those muscles tightened slightly as he gave me a rueful almost-smile.

"You don't give an inch, do you?"

My eyes flicked coldly up his body.

"Do you? Or is an inch all you have to offer?"

Petty. Stupid. I didn't even know why I said it, except that when he let out a low laugh, I found it oddly satisfying.

"Sleep well," he said. "I hope the knife under your pillow doesn't give you a crick in your neck."

"I'm used to it."

"Good. We'll start training tomorrow. Need to prepare for the next trial."

Fuck. The next trial. I had barely recovered from the last one, and I'd lost precious days to my recovery. We had only two weeks to prepare. And the thought of training with Raihn—and somehow managing to do that without inadvertently showing him too much—made me a little ill.

"I'm thrilled," I said flatly, and began to return to my room. But at the last moment, I looked back over my shoulder. It was right on the cusp of daybreak. The cast on Raihn's face was now golden—the definitive light of the sun. And still, he didn't move, face to the horizon.

I couldn't stop myself from asking. "Doesn't that hurt?"

He didn't so much as look at me. "Not too bad yet."

Bizarre.

It was all I could do to bother myself with this vampire's stupid self-destructive habits. I went back to my room. I threw open the curtains to let the light flood in, then dragged the desk chair to the door and wedged it firmly beneath the handle.

Sleep took me fast. I dreamed of goddesses and trials and sharpened teeth, and exactly how Nightborn steel might feel sliding deep into my back.

CHAPTER FIFTEEN

We began training right away. The next trial, Waning Moon, likely wouldn't require allies, as the Halfmoon was the only one that typically demanded teamwork. Still, Raihn and Mische seemed certain that we had an opportunity to help each other—and that five weeks of training was better than three to see if we could work well together.

I really did consider refusing. But I understood, too, that I was in no position to turn down help, even help riddled with dangerous caveats . . . nor the opportunity to study my enemy, even if I didn't love that it meant they got to study me, too.

So, we trained together. It went . . . differently than I expected.

"What in the seven fucking hells is *wrong* with you?"

Worse.

So much worse.

Raihn threw his sword to the ground in an utterly childish fit of frustration. The metal hit the carpet with a forceful, deafening *THUD*, even against the soft surface.

Me? What the hell was wrong with *me*? I wasn't the one throwing my weapons around. I drew back to the edge of the living room, glowering at him. Mische pulled her legs up onto the armchair, cringing as her eyes darted between us.

Raihn jabbed his finger at me. "We can't cooperate if you won't let me get close to you."

"What do you want me to do? Crawl into your lap?"

"I won't even dignify that with a response," he spat. "How many times are we going to do this? We have less than a day until the trial. *A day.* And you're wasting our fucking time."

Mische heaved a sigh and rubbed her temples.

Thirteen nights of this. Night after night after night.

I was beginning to think that our cooperation in the first trial had been some sort of twisted stroke of luck. Vincent was a ruthless teacher, and I'd still take his harshest instruction—sessions that sometimes pushed me to the point of losing consciousness—over this.

I'd take it ten times over. Twenty times.

At least Vincent's training was straightforward. I knew what he wanted from me. This? This was an exercise in choosing between two losing scenarios. We needed to learn how to cooperate, at least if this alliance thing was going to work. But I also needed to protect myself. I needed to watch Raihn as he worked and learn his strategies—in only a handful of weeks, I would need to exploit them. And at the same time, I needed to shield myself from his prying eyes.

You'll be easy to kill later, he had told me.

Like hell I would.

But as the nights passed, I learned that these two objectives— being a strong ally and protecting myself—were in direct conflict. Each goal compromised the other, and I couldn't afford that.

So we trained, and we bickered, and we ended each session more frustrated than the one before. But I knew the minute we began that tonight would be the night it finally exploded. Raihn woke up itching for a fight, barely grunting a greeting before grabbing his sword and launching into an especially brutal drill. No hesitation, no pleasantries, no smiles at Mische's cheerful quips, not even any biting jokes at my expense. He came after me hard during sparring, like a man with a grudge. And later, when we switched tasks and practiced our cooperative fighting against Mische's opposition, his annoyance at last erupted in an outburst of rage.

"Do you think I don't know what you're doing?" he snapped. "You're working against me, not with me."

This was a mistake. All of it. I should've just bled out in the greenhouse. I'd prefer to do that than wait for Raihn to rip my throat out, which seemed increasingly inevitable.

"Working *with* you? What does *working with you* look like, by your standards? Following you?" At his hesitation, I scoffed bitterly. "You don't even know."

This was someone who was used to working alone, and when he wasn't, he was the leader. Mische was talented, especially with magic, but she was content to support. The two of them were clearly close, though I still wasn't sure in what capacity—though by now, I gathered it wasn't romantic. Regardless, they knew how to complement each other, Mische falling to the back while Raihn took up the forefront.

Me? That wasn't my style. I was used to fighting alone. Two decades of training from Vincent had taught me how to do that well: survive, *alone.*

"What do you not understand about this, Oraya? We are going to be thrown back into that ring in one day. One day." His lips twisted into a cruel, humorless smile. "We've trained together for more than a week, and I'm still not totally convinced you're not going to stab me again the minute we're in there."

I wasn't either.

"Maybe I will. Maybe it'll be more satisfying this time." I cocked my head, frowned. "Do women say that to you often?"

He barked a laugh. "I'm sure you're proud of yourself for that one."

I was, actually.

"Oraya, look—"

He took two steps forward, and just as quickly, I matched the distance away.

He paused, eyes narrowing. "What?" he said. "You're afraid of me?"

The cocky smile had left my face. I said nothing.

"What, no smart-ass retort for that?"

He took another step forward, and again, I took one back.

"Get away from me," I hissed.

And he said quietly, "No."

Another step.

I hit the wall.

"Raihn," Mische whispered, "maybe don't . . ."

My palms began to sweat. Raihn was now two strides away from me. My back pressed against the wood paneling, wedged to the corner.

Even during training, I never let him get this close. He was only three strides away—two of his. That was how much larger than me he was. He wore a linen shirt that clung to his body, sweaty with the exertion of the last six hours of exercise, highlighting each swell and dip of his muscular form. His hair was bound, but over the hours, strands of it had escaped and now plastered themselves to his face and neck. I couldn't decide if he looked more or less intimidating this way—more, because he looked a bit unhinged, or less, because I appreciated all of these unpolished things more than I appreciated any other aspect of him.

His eyes now seemed especially red, and he didn't break them from mine for even a moment as he took another step.

"We're allies," he said firmly. "You need to let me get close to you."

My heart beat faster. Faster. Faster. My throat was thick, my skin slick.

"No," I said, as calmly as I could manage. "I don't."

The realization shifted in his face. "You *are* afraid of me."

No, I wasn't, I told myself. Fear did not exist. *Fear is just a collection of physical responses.*

But I wasn't fooling anyone. Of course he could feel my heartbeat. Of course he could smell the rush of my blood.

"Raihn . . ." Mische said from the other side of the room.

"Back up," I commanded.

"I am not going to hurt you. How close do I have to get without splitting you open to make you believe that?"

Don't trust anyone, Vincent whispered in my ear.

Raihn took another step. "This close?"

I didn't blink. Couldn't. Couldn't take my gaze off a predator this near to me. Less than one stride. So close I could count the beads of sweat on his collarbone. So close I could see the flutter of his pulse beneath the angle of his jaw.

"Stop."

"*This* close?"

"Back. Up. Raihn."

He looked me dead in the eye.

"No," he said.

And took one more step.

"*BACK THE FUCK UP.*" I slammed my palm against the hard muscle of his chest.

The burst of magic blinded me. Deafened me. White-blue consumed my vision. My back smashed against the wall.

Raihn went flying across the room.

And the flare of light faded just in time for me to see the window shatter, as he went careening through the glass.

CHAPTER SIXTEEN

shit!" Mische gasped. "How did you *do* that?"

I barely heard her over the rushing blood in my ears, and even if I had, it might as well have been my own voice in my head—because all I could think as I dove across the room was, *Ix's tits, how* did *I do that?*

We were at the top of one of the Moon Palace's tallest spires, hundreds of feet above the ground. *Fuck*, did I just kill him? I didn't mean to. At least, not yet.

My heart in my throat, I ran to the window, thrust my head through the open frame, and—

—nearly toppled backward as a streak of tan and black soared up from below with enough force to send my hair whipping around my face.

Raihn's wings were spread, looking as if they were made of the night itself, a million variations of purple and red and black and rust. Almost pretty enough to distract from the sheer *fury* on his face.

"You," he breathed, "are being a shit about trusting *me*, and yet you've been hiding *that*?"

The words sat on the tip of my tongue—*I didn't know, I don't know how the hell I just did that*—but I swallowed them down. I didn't need them to know that I wasn't even aware of my own abilities. Give them yet another weakness to take advantage of.

Let them be a little afraid of me, for once.

So I tucked my trembling hands into my pockets and simply shrugged. "I'm sure you're hiding all sorts of things from me."

"I don't know how I ever thought this was going to work." He landed back in the apartment. The movement was effortlessly smooth, the boundary between the sky and the ground nothing but a single graceful step. "You don't know how to give a fuck about a single person other than yourself. Just like all the rest of them. The Nightborn princess, living up in Vincent's castle, probably taught that the whole fucking world belonged to her. Is that what he promised you? Become just like him, learn how to double-cross all the right people, and this whole shitty dead world will be yours. Is that what you think you have waiting for you?"

"Don't talk about my family that way," I snarled.

He scoffed—a sound of pure hatred. "*Family.* What a sad life you must have."

My fists trembled, white-knuckled at my sides. "What the hell have you done to earn my trust? Am I supposed to be so *honored* that you chose me that I fall into a little pile of gelatin at your feet? Typical Rishan trash. Look at where that kind of entitlement got *your* people before you speak that way about my father."

The room brightened, the orange of the flames turning white in fits and bursts. A well-timed gust of wind whipped my hair and Raihn's about our faces. His entire body was rigid, his wings still out, his eyes spearing me while mine skewered him to the wall.

Mische darted between us. "Alright. Alright. Everyone is angry. That's enough."

I wasn't going to be the first one to break the stare.

"*That's enough,*" she repeated, voice high and nervous.

At last, Raihn turned away.

"Fine," I said, doing the same. "I'm done."

"Me too."

He simply stepped from the open window and into the night sky. I threw open the door, setting off down the hallway. Both of us left Mische standing there among the broken glass, looking hopeless.

I NEEDED VINCENT to be at our meeting spot, and yet I wasn't all that surprised when he wasn't. I went every night. He met me less than half of those times, and when he did, he was distracted. Something big was happening, even though he refused to tell me what it was. And similarly, maybe he sensed my mounting annoyance with my situation with Raihn, even though I never uttered a word about it. I knew well by now which things were better kept from Vincent.

But tonight I was so angry—so *confused*—that I would have told him everything if he had been there. He, at least, would have answers about what my magic had just done, and I needed those desperately. The force I had used to throw Raihn across the room was so wildly disproportionate to anything I'd ever managed before, and I didn't even know how I had done it. Now, as I walked alone through the darkened streets, I tried to summon that power and was greeted with only a few familiar weak sparks at my fingertips.

Still, maybe a small part of me was grateful for my father's absence. As much as I wanted answers, I hated to reveal emotions that I couldn't control. And I'd already done that more than enough today. Lost control. Of my magic. Of my temper.

I had been too raw. And I had been petulant. I knew it. I had allowed Raihn to goad me and bowed to my own worst impulses. He was wrong about a lot of things—a *lot* of things—but maybe he was right that I needed to either choose to be an ally or properly become an enemy.

When it became clear Vincent wasn't coming, I wandered through the deserted grounds of the Moon Palace. I longed to go to the human districts and bury this sense of helplessness with a blade in some vampire piece of shit's chest. It had been years since I'd gone so long without it. I hadn't even realized how reliant I was upon that release.

The first time I killed there, it had been an accident, and now, I could barely function without it.

It was only a few days after . . . after. My own grief and loneliness had been eating me alive. It had been years since I had been so obsessed with my own flesh, but those awful days, I had gone back to old bad habits, opening little paths of blood over my skin and watching how easily it tore, how slow it healed. I hated that my body was so weak. That it attracted in all the ways I didn't want it to. That it bore the marks from every bad memory, like the ones that now marked my throat, then two barely scabbed wounds.

I wasn't sure what I had been looking for that night when I went to the human districts, but I hadn't been looking to kill. I had never felt like less of a vampire than I did in those awful days—maybe I had been searching for whatever connection I couldn't get in the Nightborn castle. Maybe I had hoped I would find some missing piece of myself, when I had never felt more painfully incomplete.

Instead, I had found a district full of humans who seemed like foreign creatures, and a vampire who intended to prey on them. When I saw the vampire stalking a young woman washing laundry behind her crumbling little house, I didn't think. I just acted. It was easier than I thought it would be. I was well-trained. The vampire was not prepared for a fight.

After, I'd panicked and run back to the Nightborn castle. I spent the day in my washroom, vomiting. I couldn't wash the blood from my hands, couldn't scrub the sight of my victim's face from the insides of my eyelids. I'd been certain that the minute Vincent showed up at my door, I would confess everything to him. He would lock me up for the next decade, and in that moment, I would have been grateful for it.

But the hours had passed. I lay on my bed and watched the sunlight filter through the curtains as guilt settled in my stomach like a disagreeable meal. I realized that killing that vampire—saving those humans—had made me feel powerful. And the guilt was fading, but the strength was not.

Was my guilt worth more than the life of the human woman I'd

saved? Were Vincent's arbitrary rules worth more than the countless other humans that monster would have killed, if he hadn't been
stopped? No. I hadn't felt guilty about killing that man. I felt guilty
about lying to my father.

But Vincent had made me this way, and a lie was a petty sin.

I realized that day, as I stared at the sunlight-speckled ceiling,
that I'd gone a full twenty-four hours without thinking about the
face that haunted me.

I wish I could say it was my noble intentions that brought me
back to the slums the next night. But it wasn't. It was my own self-
ishness. I'd rather dream of these dying faces than the other one. At
least this made me stronger instead of weaker.

Now, I felt nothing when I killed but the satisfaction of a job
well done. A mark etched upon the world. That was worth something, to a mortal living amongst immortal beings. A way for me
to tell this place, *You think my life is worth nothing, but I can still leave a
stain on you that can't be washed out.*

My hands itched now to leave that mark, like an opium addict
twitching for their next fix. But dawn was too close, and the human
districts were far from the Moon Palace on foot. I couldn't risk that
journey.

Instead, I walked back the slow way, winding through deserted
back paths. I remained close to the Lituro River, one of two trib-
utaries that broke up the city and converged to form the inner city
of Sivrinaj, right where the Nightborn castle sat. I often looked
out over this view from my room. From up there, the streams were
serene and peaceful, like elegant winding streaks of paint through
the city.

Up close, it smelled like piss.

I paused at the riverbed and watched the water trickle by. A
breeze trembled my hair, and with it came a warm, familiar scent—
tobacco.

The hairs rose on the back of my neck. I wasn't alone.

I glanced to my left to see another figure standing near the water,
a cigarillo to his lips. He lifted his chin and let out a long exhale, the
smoke silver as it caught the moonlight.

The smell hit me again, stronger, and with it came a wave of familiarity that made that seeping wound in my chest ache.

I half expected to hear Ilana's cough. To see her face when I turned around. And Mother, I needed that. I craved it even more than I craved power.

"Hey."

My hand on my blade, I approached the figure.

"Can I have one of those? I'll buy it off you."

What is wrong with you? I heard Vincent's voice hiss in my ear. *Approaching a stranger? For what?*

The figure turned, cold light falling across only the lower part of his face, highlighting moon-pale skin, a narrow, angular jaw, and lips that curled slightly.

"Of course. Help yourself."

His hand, clad in a leather glove, reached from beneath his long coat, holding a little wooden box. I reached to take it from him, but his grip didn't let up.

He cocked his head, the movement allowing moonlight to creep further across his face. He was handsome, his features elegant and too sharp, like honed steel. Beneath a swoop of hair that was either silver or very fair blond—it was impossible to tell in the darkness—a set of yellow-amber eyes narrowed at me, then brightened in recognition.

"I know you."

He smiled. It was the sort of smile that no doubt loosened undergarments and opened throats all over Obitraes.

"Oh?" I said.

He released the box, and I put distance between us as I slid it open and withdrew a cigarillo. Mother, I wanted to shove my face into this box. Just inhale that familiar scent and pretend it was my friend.

"I saw you in the Full Moon Trial. Had a lot of bets hinged on you." He chuckled softly and shook his head, the light catching a single ruby dangling from one ear. "The odds against you were staggering. Lot of people lost a lot of money."

He struck a match and offered me the flame. I leaned just close enough to light my cigarillo, mumbled a thank you, and drew away.

"Sorry about your coin purse."

A different, slower smile rolled across his lips. "Sorry? Oh no, dove. I don't make bets I lose." I offered him the box, and he shook his head. "Keep it. You paid for it."

He turned away, offering one more inscrutable glance as he walked down the path. "Looking forward to tomorrow. Good luck out there."

CHAPTER SEVENTEEN

I considered not returning to the apartment, but I didn't have anywhere else to go. I was half-surprised that nobody held the door shut as I turned my key and entered. Raihn hadn't returned, and Mische swept glass from the floor. The shattered window was still wide open, a strong breeze making her short, curly hair flutter about her face like butterfly wings.

She gave me a big grin when I walked in, like she was genuinely thrilled to see me. "You're here!"

She seemed a little surprised. I was, too, frankly.

"Want me to patch that up?" I gestured to the window.

"Oh, no. I'll do something with it once Raihn comes home."

Home, she said, so casually. Like this place was a home.

I nodded and wandered closer. She had already cleaned up most of the broken glass, now just sweeping the smallest pieces into a little tray to throw in the garbage. I felt embarrassed, like a small child after throwing a temper tantrum.

"Do you need help?"

"No," she said cheerfully. "But thank you!" She waved to the table. "Sit. There's food."

I wasn't hungry, but I joined her anyway. She took a seat and sipped a goblet of blood, and though she had gestured to the chair across from hers, I still picked the one on the opposite end of the table.

Instead of reaching for the food, I pulled out the cigarillo box. "Do you mind?"

She gave me a knowing smile. "Life is too short not to indulge."

What an odd thing for a vampire to say. Vampire lives were not short by any measure. But then again . . . didn't everyone have a short life, in here?

And besides, Mische was the most unusual vampire I'd ever met.

I watched her sip her blood, looking content as she gazed out the window. Like the fight earlier hadn't even fazed her.

"Can I ask you a question, Mische?"

"Mm-hm."

"Why are you with Raihn?"

Her face snapped to me, aghast. "*With* Raihn? I'm not *with* Raihn."

"No . . . I know you're not with him like that." I'd wondered about it at first, especially since vampires fucked like rabbits, but it became quickly obvious that Mische and Raihn had a platonic relationship. They slept in separate bedrooms and treated each other far more like siblings than lovers.

Still, that only made it harder to understand. They were just so *different*. I couldn't imagine dragging someone like Mische into a tournament like this. At least if they were fucking, I could understand it even if I didn't agree with it. People did all kinds of nonsensical things when blinded by good sex.

And Raihn looked like he was probably very good at sex.

That thought shocked me the minute it crossed my mind, and I slammed my mental doors against it as hard as I could.

"He's my best friend," Mische said simply, as if that explained everything.

"But . . . *why?*"

She threw her head back and let out a high, full laugh.

"I'm going to tell him that sometime," she said when she collected herself. "Your face! *But . . . why?*" Her imitation of my voice was comically low and flat, her face twisting into an expression of exaggerated disgust.

Look, it was a fair question.

"Lots of reasons." Her insulting impression of me faded into a soft smile. "He was there for me when no one else was. He's the most loyal person I've ever met. The most trustworthy."

"Hm." I made a noncommittal noise, probably looking as unconvinced as I felt.

Other than Vincent, I'd never truly met a trustworthy vampire. Not really. All of them would skin their own children if they thought their power was under attack.

"It's just . . ." Her eyes drifted to the sky, far away in thought. "I spent a lot of time alone, before. I didn't realize how important it was to really have someone. To have someone who would just— who would kill for you. You know?"

Killing didn't especially seem to be a great favor or sacrifice for Raihn. Yet, I couldn't bring myself to challenge her point, because I knew exactly what she meant. For me, Vincent was that person. Even when I had no one else, I had him, and I knew beyond any doubt in this world or the next that he would do literally anything for me.

"A lot of people don't know how to love. Raihn has a lot of flaws, but he knows how to love. Or at least he . . ." A little wrinkle deepened between her brows, and her voice trailed off before she jerked herself out of her thought, looked back to me, and grinned.

"That, and he's a very good cook. A *very* good cook."

I wondered if my disbelief showed on my face. I couldn't imagine any of those things. The loyalty. The love. Definitely not the cooking.

Her voice went a shade more serious. "That wasn't him today."

"Oh?" I said dryly. "Then who was it?"

"The past." She gave me a sad smile. "Maybe our skin doesn't scar the same as yours, but our hearts do. Sometimes they never heal."

My scoff was not as convincingly dismissive as I wished it was.

She asked, "So . . . was that you?"

"What do you mean?"

"Today. The, uh . . . window. The magic. *Were* you hiding it this whole time?"

I didn't know why I found it hard to lie to Mische. She was just so uncomfortably genuine. I exhaled a puff of smoke instead of answering, because a lie was difficult and the truth was embarrassing.

"Ah." She nodded. "I see."

"It's unpredictable." I sounded more defensive than I meant to.

"We can work on it together."

Mother, that was a statement that should have been terrifying to me. And yet, it was strangely comforting.

"He deserved to go out the window," I said.

"He did," she agreed. Then, more seriously, she asked, "Are you going to leave?"

I took a deep drag of my cigarillo and relished the way the smoke burned my nose as I exhaled.

"No."

"That would be a stupid thing to do the day before a trial."

"It would."

"What do you think it's going to be? The trial?"

I'd spent plenty of time wondering about it, but there was nothing we could do but speculate. The Waning Moon Trial was one of the biggest wildcards in the Kejari. Year after year, it was drastically different. The first trial traditionally detailed Nyaxia's escape from the land of the White Pantheon. But the second could land at so many different places in her story—perhaps when she found the underworld, her love story with Alarus, the God of Death, or any one of the many legendary adventures that they had together.

"I don't know," I said.

"Are you nervous?"

I said nothing. I couldn't deny it, but I wouldn't admit it aloud, either.

She did not wait for an answer. "I am," she sighed, taking another drink of blood.

"It might be about her journey," I theorized. "Her journey down to the land of the dead."

Even that gave us little to go on. A journey could take so many forms, could be interpreted in limitless ways.

"Do you think she was scared back then?" Mische mused.

"Nyaxia?"

"Uh-huh."

"She was a goddess."

"Barely, in the beginning. A nobody. And so young."

I paused. Nyaxia, at this point in her story, was only one of countless powerless offspring produced by the White Pantheon; not only a lesser goddess herself, but the child of one. No one would even know if she had died alone in the wilderness, let alone mourn her. Most legends put her at only twenty, practically an infant by the standards of the deities.

People like her were born to be used and thrown away by the other gods. Fucked, feasted upon, and discarded.

Mische was probably right. She had probably been terrified.

But that was two thousand years ago, and now Nyaxia was staggeringly powerful—powerful enough to defy the White Pantheon on her own. Powerful enough to give an entire continent her gift of vampirism and create a civilization of her followers. And powerful enough that all of Obitraes now lived and died and loved and sacrificed at her feet, forever.

"Well," I said, "that changed."

"But think of all she had to give up for it."

Her husband. Murdered by the White Pantheon as punishment for marrying Nyaxia.

I considered this. Yes, maybe the Pantheon took her lover. But Nyaxia also took back her own power. I could imagine far too clearly how good that must feel after a lifetime of weakness. I was a bit ashamed to admit the things I would be willing to sacrifice for it, myself.

"At least she isn't afraid anymore," I said.

"No," Mische replied, thoughtfully. "I'd guess not. But she's probably awfully unhappy, don't you think?"

I RETURNED TO my room not long after that, but I was too nervous to sleep. Instead, I watched the color of the sky turn to ash red. I could hear Mische shuffling around down the hall, but not Raihn's return.

I was beginning to drift off when a crash made my eyes snap

open. I went to the door, listening carefully. A series of dull
*THUMP*s and the sound of rustling fabric echoed from the living
room.

"You cut it so close." Mische was trying to whisper and failing.

"I know."

"Gods, look at you."

"I know."

"Raaaaihn . . ."

"I *know*, Mische."

My curiosity got the better of me.

Very, very slowly—very, very silently—I removed the chair,
cracked my door, and slipped into the hallway. I peered around
the corner to see Mische yanking the curtains closed as Raihn sat
heavily on one of the couches. Or maybe collapsed was a better
word, like all his limbs just decided to give up at the same time.

Goddess, was he drunk?

"I thought you said after last year you weren't going to do this
again!" Mische was awful at speaking quietly. No one could even
blame me for eavesdropping.

"Fuck it. What's immortality if we don't use it to do the same
things over and over again, forever, until the end of time?"

Oh, he was *definitely* drunk.

She sighed and turned to him. He now lay against the couch,
his chin tipped back. He really was a mess—clothes stained with
I-didn't-even-know-what, hair tangled over his shoulders.

"So," she said. "Today."

She turned and I stepped back quickly to remain out of sight, so
I could no longer see them, only hear them.

He let out a low groan. "What about it?"

A silence, which was presumably filled with Mische's pointed
look.

The groan became a sigh. "Too much?"

"Definitely too much."

"She should be able to take it."

"That *was* her taking it."

"Well . . . not like *that*. Not 'taking it' by *throwing me out a fucking window.*"

"And was that *you* 'taking it,' idiot?"

Silence. I could imagine the look on his face.

Her voice grew softer. "Think about what it must have been like for her. Growing up like that."

My nose wrinkled. Growing up like *what*?

I was almost insulted that this point earned a thoughtful silence from Raihn.

Then, "Well, woe is her. So? We all have our shit."

"Yours isn't her fault."

A long pause.

I chanced a step closer so I could peer around the corner. Raihn's head was tilted back, his eyes looking straight up to the ceiling. Mische now stood behind him, leaning over the back of the chair to rest her arms around his neck, her chin on the top of his head in casual affection.

"You know that wasn't her fault," she said again. "That was your fault."

My eyebrows rose slightly. Raihn did not seem like the kind of person to suffer that kind of insult—few vampires were. I tensed, as if cringing on Mische's behalf for a sharp rebuff, verbal or physical.

But instead, to my shock, Raihn just let out a long sigh.

"I know," he said. "I know."

He patted her arm, and she pressed a chaste kiss to the top of his head.

"At least the day is over."

"Small victories."

"Drink some water. Now you're going to have to survive a trial hungover, you fool . . ."

Their whispers faded away as I backed down the hall.

CHAPTER EIGHTEEN

We didn't speak to each other much when nightfall came, and I was grateful for that. I was on edge, and I didn't trust myself not to snap at Raihn and start a whole other fight before the trial even began. After muttered good evenings, we followed our now-familiar little trail of shadow until we met with the rest of the contestants in the great room.

It was the first time I'd seen the others since the last trial. The energy had palpably changed. Gone was the excited anticipation from our first gathering, replaced with a more desperate frenetic anxiety. Several sets of eyes jumped to me the moment I walked into the room, noses twitching, the whites of their eyes bright.

I knew that look. Raihn and Mische had stolen enough blood to sustain them these last weeks, but clearly, not everyone was so lucky.

Raihn seemed to notice this too, and was surprisingly disconcerted by it, stepping a bit closer to me as he drew his sword. And equally surprisingly, I let him, my own weapons gripped tight in my hands.

No one spoke.

We knew what to expect this time. Just when the silence began to feel awkwardly long, the world fell away.

EVEN PREPARED, THE roar of the crowd momentarily stunned me, violent in contrast to the Moon Palace's silence.

I took stock of my surroundings fast.

Raihn and Mische were gone. No one stood beside me. The sand beneath my feet quivered with distant impact. I blinked into white mist, which undulated in lazy furls, illuminated by the blue light of Nightfire torches. Black stone walls surrounded me on three sides, cradling a glass ceiling, presumably to stop the winged contestants from flying above them. The ceiling wasn't smooth, but crafted into dips and valleys like an inverted topography of the earth.

I squinted into the mist. Between the smoke and the darkness, I had only a few feet of visibility in front of me. I could see no movement, nor hear anyone else nearby. I pressed my palm to the wall and felt only rock. It was rough and unfinished. The hall before me wound into the darkness.

I inhaled the harsh scent of smoke and . . . something else, something light and ominously pleasant that I couldn't place.

I took a few cautious steps. Echoes of clashes rang out in the distance, as if some of my fellow contestants had met their opponents—whoever or whatever they were.

The hallways bent to a single sharp turn to the left. Weapons ready, I followed it.

I found myself face-to-face with Ibrihim, who had just emerged from around another corner straight ahead.

We both stopped, glancing at each other, then the corridor before us. Halfway between us, another hallway veered to the right. Our path had split three ways—the route I had come from, the one Ibrihim had, and the path forward.

A maze. This was a maze. I touched the uncut stone and looked up at the strange ceiling with new insight. It was the underside of the earth—because this was intended to mimic the journey to the underworld. Nyaxia had wandered for weeks after escaping the realm of the gods before at last finding her way to Alarus's territory. She had been lost, so we would be, too.

Ibrihim and I both stilled, the realization hitting him as it had me. I could barely see his face through the layers of unearthly mist, but I knew he watched me just as closely, and I knew better than to underestimate him.

Slowly, I edged down the hall, craning my neck to peer around the corner. A massive silver door stood there, light playing off an embossed tableau of a man's stern, eyeless face—Alarus. It was firmly closed. No handle.

Ibrihim had come closer, too, and I kept one eye on him as I approached the door. Something shifted beneath my feet. I looked down. I'd stepped on a block of stone, which now sank slightly into the sand.

A dull grinding sound shook the air.

The door before us opened, leading to another hallway. In the foggy distance beyond, I could make out another turn, the sounds of distant violence closer.

Ibrihim and I peered at each other warily. He made no move for me, so I didn't move, either. Instead, I stepped closer to the door—

—and it immediately slammed down with enough force to shake the ground.

I lurched backward, nearly tripping over the slab. When I stepped back onto it, the door began to rise again.

Oh.

I stepped off. The door slammed back down.

Shit.

I looked at Ibrihim. Understanding settled over us at the same time.

The door would not remain open without weight on the stone. But it needed to be dead weight, because whoever was left here wouldn't be able to make it to the other side alone.

He gave me a weak, lopsided smile, revealing scarred gums.

"I wouldn't be here if I wasn't here to win," he said, somewhat apologetically, before he hurled a fucking star at me.

This was what Ibrihim's parents, after all, had been so worried about. He had been a quiet child, but he was also an innately talented warrior. So they did everything they could to make him a less efficient killer. They ruined his legs. They tore his wings. They took his teeth. But they couldn't take away his use of magic.

Which, unfortunately, was also very, very good.

I dropped to the ground just in time to keep my face from becoming a scalded mass of flesh. His magic, which drew upon the power of stars, wasn't as strong as Asteris, but it was still plenty deadly. He flung those streaks of light like they were nothing.

I dove around the corner, heading back to my dead end. I pressed to the wall, listening—waiting. My arm ached, the burn blistering where he had grazed my shoulder. Two minutes into this thing and I was already injured. Fabulous start.

He couldn't shoot me here without coming after me. And he would need to, because he needed my bodyweight to get that door open.

Long seconds passed. Ibrihim wasn't stupid. He knew what I was doing. Knew he was putting himself at a disadvantage, and that he had to do it anyway.

I strained over the sounds of the crowd and the distant fighting in a futile attempt to hear his footsteps—fuck, what I wouldn't give now for that vampire hearing—

The moment he approached, I leapt on him.

I had one shot. I needed to hit skin before he had time to react.

He hadn't been expecting the poison, reeling away with a gasp of pain as it ate through the first wound, a slash across his forearm. Our fight devolved into wild chaos immediately—him forcing himself not to pull away as the poison scorched his skin, me suffering through the burns of his starlight on my hands as I tried to pin his down.

Normally, I would be trying to bury my blade as deep into his chest as possible. Impossible now. I didn't have the time, distance, or leverage for a shot powerful enough to get to the heart. But I could still devour him with a hundred little bites. Let that poison do its work, slowly.

Injured or no, he was bigger than me. I got him to the ground, crawled over his body, opening mark after mark after mark in his armor. But that lasted only for a couple of minutes before he flung me away. I let out an *oof* as my back smacked the sand, knocking the breath out of me.

No time to catch it as he crawled over me. I barely managed to move my left hand down, so it was trapped between our bodies as his weight pinned me. Suffocating. I couldn't move. He grabbed my right hand and wrenched it above my head with a violent *CRACK*.

"I always liked you," he panted.

"Me too," I said, and twisted my left arm just enough to bury the blade in his gut.

His eyes widened. He opened his lips—maybe he intended to speak, but the only thing that came out was a wet, wordless grunt of pain. The poison worked fast, sizzling as it dissolved his skin. It ate at my hand, too, where his blood dripped down.

I pushed him off me. He was alive, but barely conscious, clawing at his abdomen. It had become a disgusting mess of tattered leather, pus, and blood.

I grabbed his arms and pulled. Fuck, he was heavy. I dragged him over to the slab and dropped him onto the stone.

The door opened behind me, but I stared down at Ibrihim as his head lolled, eyes slitted to meet mine.

He'd live. Miserably, and even more maimed than he was before, but he'd live. I had to put an end to that.

It shouldn't have been hard. I had killed countless times. I didn't know why I found myself hesitating as Ibrihim looked up at me. Maybe because we had always seen something familiar in each other, even if we never acknowledged it.

"I'm sorry." The words slipped from my lips without my permission as I prepared to slide my blade through his chest.

But before I could bring it down, the ground shook. A deafening groan filled my ears.

My head snapped up just in time to see the walls crumbling.

CHAPTER NINETEEN

I narrowly dodged a falling boulder as I dove through the door. The walls undulated. Not *just* collapsing, I realized—*moving*.

I almost laughed. Of course. In legend, Alarus's realm was ever-evolving. The path of morality was forever changing, and thus the path to the afterlife was, too. If this trial was meant to represent the underworld, the changing maze was just one more thing to conquer.

I ran. With the stone crumbling and floor shifting, I didn't know how long I had before my path through would be cut off completely. The mist was thicker in here. That strange smell was stronger now, too—that sweet scent.

I made decisions based on nothing but gut instinct—left, right, right, left, right, left. I skidded to a stop as I rounded a corner to see another door, this one bearing an engraving with Alarus's eyes wide open and a fistful of flowers in his hand. Beautiful—though I had no time to appreciate it, because standing before it was Kiretta, the Shadowborn.

Neither of us hesitated.

We hit each other at the same time—my body slamming against hers as her magic encircled us. I hadn't gotten the full force of it during the last trial. Green-tinted smoke enveloped me. Pain burst through the back of my head, her magic cracking open my mind.

I pushed her to the ground as she clawed at me. Squeezed my eyes shut.

Don't look at her. Don't listen to her.

Open your eyes, a singsong voice whispered within my thoughts. *Look at me, pretty girl. Look at me.*

No. If Kiretta was as good of a caster as Vincent warned, she would be able to charm me this close. The Shadowborn's gift for mind magic was just as dangerous as any weapon.

It took all my focus to hold her down while resisting her call.

Shadowborn magic was an open passage—they controlled the door, but the hallway went both ways. I pushed through her distractions, turned my mental gaze to the other end of the corridor that connected us.

Pain. Hunger. She was injured. Weak. Reckless. And I saw exactly how sloppy that desperation made her. She was a stronger magic user, but right now, I was the better fighter—and I could see all too clearly how she had underestimated me.

I let her think that she had won. Slackened my mental walls. Let my head roll back. Let my eyes open. Her stare, hypnotic and mesmerizing, was so close that even that split second was almost too much. A satisfied smile began to spread over her lips.

And then I drove my dagger into her throat.

Instantly, the poison did its work. A fleeting stab of her agony rushed through my mind before I pulled away from her, severing our mental connection. She clutched her throat on the ground, which heaved and billowed with the shifting halls. She was still fighting for breath, fighting for her feet, when I dragged her onto the stone slab. I didn't give her the opportunity to pull herself up before I dove through the door.

The scent hit me in a wall, intoxicatingly sweet.

I was now in a field of poppies. Dense white fog hung in a gentle curtain over the flowers, an expanse of bleeding red. The thunderous grind of stone echoed behind me, but here, it was eerily still. Light rippled in delicate dapples over the flower fields.

Poppies were the flowers of the dead. If the hallways behind me had been the path down, then this was the threshold of the underworld. Four arched silver doors stood before me, each revealing paths that soon faded into silver fog. The clash of steel against steel rang out ahead, as did grating rumbles that told me I wasn't done dodging falling stone.

I had to be near the back of the group. Which meant, as much as it pained me, running toward the sounds of fighting was probably my best choice. I pushed through the middle hallway. Halfway through, I passed a bloody body, which made me hesitate in confusion.

At a glance, I assumed it was a contestant. But the blood was very, very red, and the corpse wore not battle leathers but plain once-white robes, now in tatters. The red smear on the wall implied that he had been flung against it and left to slowly die on the ground.

Human. That was a human body.

I didn't understand. Why were there humans here?

A strange sound echoed in from down the hall. A sound like—like a cry. At first I thought I must have imagined it, because it didn't make any sense. Maybe it was a warped noise from the crowd or another contestant, or—

Another quake of the ground jerked me from my trance, a reminder that I didn't have time to waste. I sprinted down the rest of the hallway, until I reached another arch leading to another field of poppies—fuller now, a sea of red.

The cry echoed once more.

Not imagined. Very real.

A door stood open on the other side of the field. I stepped closer. Another lifeless—distinctly human—body lay on a stone slab. And beside her, clad in the same white robes, was a child.

My mind stopped working. Froze. Stuck on that little girl, who kneeled beside the mutilated body.

This was why my blood didn't seem to be a draw for the other contestants, even those that were hungry. Because there were many humans here.

The white robes. The white cast on their faces. The humans were not accidents. They weren't even prey. They were . . . decorations. Playing the part of the souls that occupied the underworld.

A gift. A distraction. Or simply a dramatic flair.

The little girl wept, tears streaking chalky white over her cheeks.

She looked up at me and her eyes went wide—watery blue, peering between oily tendrils of black hair.

Where did she come from? There were no human children in the inner city of Sivrinaj. Did she come from the human districts?

Why was a *child* here?

Behind me, the sound of grinding stone drew closer. I needed to go. I needed to go right now.

I took several steps toward the door.

Leave her, Vincent's voice commanded.

And with that came the echo of Raihn's, from the first night of the Kejari: *They're dead, little human. And if you go after them, so are you.*

True. And true.

And yet, I found myself turning back, crouching before the child. She scrambled away from me, terrified.

"Come with me," I said. "I won't hurt you."

She didn't move, save for terrified shaking. She was stuck, I realized—she had been pressed to the wall when the stone shifted last, leaving her ankle wedged between two slabs of black marble.

How did one interact with a child this young? What was she, four, eight? I'd never even seen a human child up close like this.

"We need to go *now*," I pressed.

No time. The floor began to quiver. I grabbed the girl's tiny body as tightly as I could and pulled.

She let out a cry of pain. Resistance, then release, as I wrenched her leg free. I tucked her against me with a silent apology, and then I wondered exactly how insane I was as I *ran*.

A mistake. A mistake on so many levels, Oraya. You can't fight like this. Can't evade like this. You're slower. You smell twice as human. You'll lose a sword arm. Leave her. She's dead anyway.

I bolted through three more doors, already open, corpses of humans or contestants mangled over their slabs. I passed several more humans cowering against the walls, clad in white. I couldn't bring myself to look at them.

The poppies grew denser, each step sluggish through the foliage. The scent was overwhelming. Carvings plastered the walls now, huge eyes that spanned from floor to ceiling, suns and stars spiraling in their depths—the symbol of Alarus, because death always watched.

Another door stood ahead, this one closed. The light had grown bright and feverish, dancing over us at the same pace as my quickening heartbeat. The girl grabbed fistfuls of my hair as she clung to me, trembling. She leaned forward, her head blocking one critical sliver of my peripheral vision.

The Bloodborn man lunged for me before I had the chance to move.

I dropped the child, cringing as I tried to push her out of the way in time for me to whirl to meet the attack. He knocked me to the ground, teeth bared. He got the first shot in, a bone-steel rapier right to my already injured thigh, which left me jerking in pain. I leapt back to my feet with everything I had, throwing myself against him to regain control—but I only made it a few inches into my attempted blow before he grabbed my wrist and sank his teeth into it.

I ripped it away, my own blood spattering over my face. Too slow. The hesitation cost me. My back cracked against stone as my opponent caught me and pushed me to the wall. He was small for a vampire, only a few inches taller than me, and I looked right into his stare as he encroached—red-rimmed pupils dilated, glistening with hunger and glee.

Time stopped. I tried to grip my blade with my injured hand. Couldn't move fast enough—

The Bloodborn lurched backward.

I sucked in a sudden gulp of air. Raihn yanked my attacker off me, nearly splitting him in two with a devastating follow-up strike from his Nightsteel sword. In return, the Bloodborn leapt on Raihn like a dying animal in their final throes. Wounds along his arms shivered, the red mist of blood magic surrounding them. Raihn was hurt. The Bloodborn would be able to manipulate his blood, too.

Raihn got in two more hits, but the Bloodborn retaliated with enough force to send him careening against the stone. Still, Raihn gripped his opponent's arms tight, not letting him pull away—and leaving his back wide open, exposed to me.

Raihn's gaze met mine over his attacker's shoulder—*now*.

I thrust my blade hard into the Bloodborn's back, sinking to the hilt. Even from behind, I knew how to pierce a heart.

The man slumped.

Raihn let the body fall as I struggled to free my weapon. He looked me up and down. "So you do know how to be helpful," he said, already turning to the door. "Let's go. I saw flames up ahead. Probably Mische. I think we're close to—where the hell are you going?"

I wasn't listening. The child had made it halfway across the poppy field. Her leg was clearly broken, more obvious than ever now as she struggled to run away from me. I grabbed her, muttering a hurried apology, and ran back to Raihn, who stared at me.

"And what is *that*?" He said it like I'd just presented him with a fluffy pink dog.

The ground rumbled. We didn't have time for this. "*Go!*" I didn't stop moving long enough to answer. Raihn dropped the Bloodborn's corpse on the slab, and we flew through the corridors.

Raihn had to be right that we were near the end of the maze. The next two doors were open, held there by the corpses of a human and a Rishan, respectively. Telltale bloodstains adorned the walls—delicate sprays of red, too fine to be from wounds. Evidence of blood magic.

We encountered only two other contestants, and between the child and my injuries, I needed to rely on Raihn's defense far more than I liked. At least he cut them down easily, just two more corpses left in the halls as we progressed.

"Raihn," I hissed as we rounded another corner, pointing to the left with my bloody blade—to a gate marked with lit Nightfire torches. This one was bigger than the others, double doors of ornate metal, one of Alarus's eyes peering from each.

The end? It could be. It had to be.

A single slab sat before us. Raihn and I looked at each other. Then looked at the child, who wept softly, barely conscious.

He'd move for me. I knew it. Me, or the child.

The minute he did, my arm swung.

My blade hit the solid leather-clad muscle of his shoulder. His jaw snapped shut, trembling. He glared at me.

"What," he hissed, between clenched teeth, "the *fuck* was that for? I was going for *that*."

He pointed his sword to a lifeless body at the far end of the hall, then muttered a string of curses and yanked my blade from his armor. Oh.

I adjusted my hold around the child and mumbled something that somewhat resembled an apology, and Raihn told me to go fuck myself. I considered telling him how lucky he was that that blade had no poison left and decided he probably wouldn't appreciate it.

He hoisted the corpse over his shoulder and was on his way back when the wave of pain hit me—acidic, all consuming, like I was being boiled from the inside out.

I had only a moment to recognize what was happening before Angelika hit me.

I barely managed to stave her off, my single free arm trembling with the strength it took to block her. Red suffused my vision. Each breath burned. The cuts over Angelika's arms quivered as the mist thickened.

She smiled. "I told you I'd kill you in the ring."

The child's body went rigid with pain as she cringed against me. Could a human child survive this?

I heard Raihn's approaching footsteps running for us. He had gone all the way down the hall. Seconds and he would be here. The smart thing would be to wait for him. I could withstand it—but the girl probably couldn't.

So I left myself unguarded for one critical moment as I evaded. The strike to my side was incapacitating.

I fell. I barely had enough awareness to push the child away from my falling weight before I hit the ground.

Angelika's clawed hand was at my throat immediately. Squeezed. I found the gates, tall and glimmering with the promise of safety as everything else blurred. I reached for my magic, and it sputtered uselessly out of reach. Always gone when I needed it most.

I groped at my side. One touch to the dagger she had embedded there made me seize with agony. But it's amazing what a body can endure to survive.

I yanked the blade out of my flesh and thrust it into Angelika's. She cursed and slammed my head against the floor.

Everything went white, then black.

I was only partially conscious when Raihn pulled Angelika away. I could not move my gaze from the ceiling. How much time passed? Seconds, minutes? The roar of the crowd swelled to a sudden crescendo. Everything spun.

Raihn leaned over me.

"It's almost over, Oraya." He looked like he was shouting but sounded so far away. "Get up. Come on. Quick. We don't have time."

I managed to turn my head. Angelika barely moved in a heap on the ground. My eyes fell to the little girl, unconscious, her leg twisted, dark hair falling over her face. So incredibly familiar. Like looking in a mirror.

I dragged myself to my hands and knees, pushing away Raihn's hand.

"Lemme go," I slurred.

"For fuck's sake, princess, I'm not going to—"

"Lemme go!"

I crawled to the girl. Gathered her in my arms. Forced myself to my feet. My gaze settled on the gate ahead, though it tilted and smeared.

What was that, ten steps? I could make it ten steps.

Raihn held my arm, perhaps in frustration, perhaps to steady me. "What are you doing?" he hissed.

I couldn't answer that even if I wanted to. It took all my energy to make it those final steps.

Still, I would not let him help me. Still, I would not let go of that child.

I crossed the threshold and fell to my knees.

The colosseum spread out before me, gold-gilded and magnificent. Thousands of spectators packed the stands, screaming for blood. And yet, even in that crowd, I found Vincent right away— right there in the front, watching me with abject horror, as if his own heart had been carved out and thrust into my hands.

It struck me, all at once, exactly how much Vincent loved me.

Was that how I had looked, I wondered, when I looked at this little girl? Just like that?

At the thought of her, sudden fear overwhelmed me. These were predators. All of them. And she was prey.

Her blood and mine ran together as I turned to Raihn.

"Don't let them take her," I choked out.

The world faded. I didn't remember falling, but suddenly, I was looking at the sky, my fingernails digging into Raihn's arm, the other hand desperately clutching the limp child to my chest. Nightborn soldiers encroached upon us.

"Don't let them take her," I begged again.

The edges of my vision grew dark.

And Raihn leaned very close to me—closer than I ever allowed anyone—as he murmured, solemn as a vow, "I won't."

CHAPTER TWENTY

My arms were empty when I awoke.

I stared at the ceiling for several long seconds. My stomach churned. The mural on the ceiling—a night sky—streaked as the world spun. I lifted my hand to my chest and felt only the slow rise and fall of my own breath.

No child.

The trial came to me in bits and pieces, assembled in a fractured mosaic. The end of it was just a blurry, poorly rendered suggestion.

The girl. I remembered how limp she had been. How hard we'd hit the ground together. Remembered the guards closing in on me—on her. She was just a small, helpless human.

My hand slid down my body. Yes, I had some nicks and cuts, but the worst of my injuries had been healed. I had survived the second trial.

And I felt nothing.

Raihn was nowhere to be found when I awoke, but Mische was excited to see me conscious. A little too excited, actually, her grin tinged with a manic hint of concern. I had been in rough shape, and unconscious for days.

"It was mostly the blood magic that got you," she told me.

As a human, I was especially susceptible to it. My blood was weak, easy to manipulate, easy to turn against my mortal flesh. If a body withstood it, recovery could be quick, but the line between survival and death, especially for a human, was very thin.

I thought of that child. How tiny she was, nestled against my chest. Surely too tiny to survive what I barely had.

I listened, numb, as Mische told me of the end of the trial—that eleven contestants had died, leaving twenty-nine of us. Even Ibrihim, miraculously, had managed to drag himself through at the last possible moment.

I sipped the water Mische gave me, but my mouth was still too dry to bring myself to ask the only question I cared about. I let her talk for a full half hour before I scraped up the courage to choke out, "The girl?"

She looked confused. "The what?"

"There was a little girl."

She gave me a weak smile and a pitying shake of her head. "I don't know."

I wanted to press, wanted to demand that we find out, but the words were thick in my throat.

Why did I care so much? I shouldn't care so much. And yet I couldn't ignore it. Couldn't escape it. I swallowed down what I could of the food Mische gave me, but the minutes ticked by and I grew antsy, as if everything I was trying to suppress just roiled and thrashed beneath my skin.

Eventually, I rose. Every muscle ached, but at least I could move. I grabbed my jacket from the coat hook.

"Where are you going?" Mische asked, alarmed, as I threw it over my shoulders.

"Just need some air."

"But you should—"

I threw open the door.

"—rest," she finished as I slammed it behind me.

IT HAD BEEN a while since I'd done three in a single night. My body railed against me for it—and I deserved that, I suppose—but even tired, the fuckers weren't difficult to kill. They were lazy, and there were too many of them. It had been weeks since I'd walked these streets. Enough time, apparently, to lull these fools into a false sense of security.

I wasn't surprised.

They were entitled. Selfish, gluttonous, entitled pieces of shit, who saw the people who lived here as nothing more than livestock. I hated them so much that watching them die—watching them watch me, a human, kill them—did nothing to ease my rage. It just made it feel like more of an injustice.

Over the years, I had learned to stitch up that wound, tuck it carefully away with all my other human weaknesses. Now, the bandage I so carefully maintained had been torn off, grasped in the little fingers of an innocent dead child.

I didn't know how to make it stop. I had been taught young that bleeding was dangerous. And though my wounds had closed, the one deep in my chest bled more than ever. It made me just as vulnerable.

When I left the Moon Palace, I thought I was going to meet Vincent. I was sure that he would be waiting for me. I'd seen the way he looked at me in there. I needed to talk to him, to ask him about my magic, ask him about the humans—*where had they come from? How did they get humans that should have been protected? Why* children?

He'd have answers.

And yet, maybe that was exactly why I found myself walking in the opposite direction, to the human districts.

Words were complicated. Questions were difficult. And that wound inside of me was bleeding so much that I knew Vincent would smell it. The blood would seep out between my fingers if he ripped it open with an answer I didn't like.

This was easier. More satisfying. At least it was fucking *doing* something.

My third victim looked at me like I was Nyaxia herself as the light left his eyes. I pinned him against the wall, here in the shit-stinking, piss-coated alleyway where he had been stalking young women in the pub across the street. I wasn't the young woman he wanted, but I was certainly the one he deserved.

He opened his mouth, a waft of his rotting breath floating over my face as he slackened.

I yanked my blade free and let him slump to the ground.

Animal. Fucking rot there with the shit and the piss and the trash, just like all the other rat carcasses.

He had opened a cut on my wrist with his fingernails. I stopped and watched the blood bubble to the surface, and with it came another unbearable wave of rage.

My skin, human skin, was so delicate and easily torn. In this moment, I hated it just as much as I hated the vampire I'd just killed. More, even. Maybe that fragility was responsible for just as much death.

"And here I was thinking that you were visiting with our great and powerful Nightborn King when you ran away in the early hours."

I spun around, blade out, to see a familiar winged form standing on the rooftop. At the sight, my heart clenched—I didn't like when they flew above me. I may be the serpent, but even snakes run for cover when hawks soar overhead.

Raihn, I was sure, would not take kindly to me killing vampires. No vampire would. They would kill each other any day, but none of them liked it when a human did it.

Not that I was in the mood to give a damn, now.

"Go away."

"That's an uncharacteristically boring retort."

It was. Almost embarrassing.

I ignored him and wiped the blood from my blade.

Raihn's smirk faltered slightly.

"I saw you kill two more in the last hour," he said, his voice a touch softer than I would have expected. "You're doing this when you were just on the edge of death? Not a wise use of your time, some might say."

That wound in my heart bled and bled. His words salted it, and I lashed out at him like an animal.

"Not a good use of my time?" I snarled, jabbing my weapon at him. "Four humans would be dead if I didn't do this today. But of course, you don't think their lives are worth an hour and a half of my time."

His smirk disappeared. "That wasn't what I meant."

"*Fuck* you."

I hoped he couldn't see my face. It probably revealed too much.

Be careful with those colorful expressions of yours, little serpent, Vincent whispered.

Fuck you, too, I thought, then, moments later, uttered a silent apology in my head.

Behind me, I heard Raihn land on the ground—surprisingly lightly for someone of his size.

"Get out." I didn't turn. "These pricks don't need you defending their honor."

He scoffed in disgust. "I'm doing no such thing. As far as I'm concerned, you're doing an important public service."

My hand stopped mid-movement.

I didn't turn, didn't reveal my face, but he chuckled. "What?"

What did he mean, *what?* Like he didn't know what. Like he wasn't *perfectly fucking aware* exactly how any vampire—even ones who looked down upon these rats, even ones who disagreed with their actions—would take a human taking it upon herself to kill them. An insult on principle alone.

I didn't bother saying this to him. We both knew.

Instead, a question swelled in my throat. It was exactly the kind of question I'd come here to avoid, the kind with an ugly answer I didn't want to hear.

I resumed cleaning my blade.

"The girl?" I choked out.

My voice came out higher and weaker than I'd intended.

A long, long silence passed. With each second, my chest tightened.

I heard footsteps approach, but I didn't move until his hand touched my shoulder. I twitched away, ready to snap at him, but something about the look on his face—oddly gentle—made me pause.

"Come with me," he said.

CHAPTER TWENTY-ONE

Raihn brought me across the city. It took us nearly a half an hour to travel there on foot—he offered to fly us, but I refused so vehemently that he put his hands up in an apparent plea for mercy—and we walked in silence. I still needed to keep my teeth gritted against everything that might escape if I opened my mouth.

This end of the district was more spread out, patches of dirt and even a few gardens spacing out the clay buildings. There was no part of the human district that didn't reek of poverty, but this area, at least, felt a bit more like people were trying to build lives here. Poor, yes. Run-down, of course. But . . . full of warmth, in some strange way.

Bittersweet grief twinged in my chest. I'd never noticed before that maybe something existed here that did not exist in the inner city. Things that lived and moved and reminded me so much of Ilana.

It was night, which meant it was quiet here, residents remaining dutifully indoors. Still, Raihn and I were careful to cling to the shadows, traveling in alleyways rather than the main streets. He peered around the corner between two buildings, then spread his wings and leapt up to the flat roof. He offered me his hand, but I ignored it and climbed up on my own, earning a light scoff and a shake of the head.

He led me to the edge of the roof, then sat, swinging his legs over and spiriting his wings away. "Look."

I didn't know what he was trying to show me. Before us were buildings that looked like all the other buildings we'd passed, and deserted streets that looked just like all the other streets we'd walked.

"What?"

"Sit. Get lower."

I crouched down. Even with my legs under me, I was still shorter than Raihn was seated. He pointed, and I craned my head to follow his gesture.

"Through that window. Over there."

The next building over had large glass windows split into many reinforced panes. Lanterns had been lit within, drenching the interior in soft, warm light. Moving bodies cast shadows inside—there were many people in that room, at least six that I could see through the window, most of them children.

"Right in the middle," Raihn said softly.

A little girl with dark hair. She sat on the floor, alone, ignoring the other children. Her head was bowed, and even if it hadn't been, she was too far away for me to see her face, anyway.

But it was her. It was *her*.

A shaky breath escaped me without my permission. The wave of sheer relief left me dizzy. I pressed my hands to the clay roof just so I wouldn't topple over the edge.

"How?" I choked out.

"I have my ways." I could hear the smirk in Raihn's voice. "Very dangerous, very clever, very impressive ways."

I wasn't about to validate his preening, but . . . it *was* impressive. I couldn't even fathom how he had managed to pull it off. Just getting the child out of the colosseum alive was practically a miracle.

"Who—who are these people? Where is this?"

"A home for children who don't have anyone else. Took me a while to find the right place. I couldn't locate her family. I thought maybe they could."

I swallowed thickly. They would not find this girl's family. She didn't have a family anymore.

"That's a fairy tale," I said.

He let out a sour, humorless chuckle. "You really just . . . don't ever let up, do you? You never accept a win?"

Did he think I didn't want it to be a win? Did he think I didn't *want* to believe that it could happen?

But before I could speak, he added gently, "Maybe you're right. But she's alive. That's something."

And I was grateful for that—I truly was. If I tried to tell him so, I would reveal too much. Yet, I wanted it to feel more like a victory. I wanted her life to be worth more than it was. Instead, she would grow up here, in a place where she would be constantly hunted, alone.

I wished saving her was as simple as keeping her heart beating. Mother, I wanted that. But would she remember that someone tried? That someone thought her life should be worth something more?

Without thinking, I rubbed the ring on my little finger.

"She should never have been there," I muttered.

"No," Raihn agreed.

The sheer hatred in his voice caught me off guard, unexpected enough to jerk me from my thoughts.

My gaze snapped to him. "Why were you following me?"

He raised his hands. "Easy, viper."

"That isn't an answer."

"You were coming into the districts as I was leaving. I was curious. Maybe even a bit concerned, if you won't take too much offense to my saying that." His voice turned more serious. "But I'm glad I did. I'm pleasantly surprised by this turn of events, actually. I—" He shook his head. "I didn't think you had it in you."

"Why? Because I'm Vincent's princess?"

He winced but didn't disagree.

I stared at him for a long moment, eyes narrowed. "I don't understand."

"What?"

"Pleasantly surprised. You said you were pleasantly surprised."

"And I meant it."

"It doesn't make sense."

"Why? Because I'm Rishan trash?"

If he expected me to wince like he had, I didn't. I just stared, unblinking, unapologetic.

He sighed. "The ones you're killing? They deserve it. They'll never stop otherwise."

"But they're vampires."

"Yes."

"And these are humans."

"I can see that."

A pause as I tried and failed to articulate my disbelief.

He sighed again, as if this discussion was exhausting him. "Is that *so* incomprehensible?"

Yes. Incomprehensible. It just . . . defied a certain world order in the House of Night. Hell, in all of Obitraes.

"Of course it is," I said.

This response seemed to irritate him. "It's that unbelievable that I have respect for human life?" he snapped. "I used to fucking *be* one of them."

My mouth had been half-open with some snippy retort that I immediately forgot. I closed it, stunned into silence.

Raihn's rust-red eyes crinkled with amusement. "It's satisfying to shock you, princess."

"You're Turned."

"I am."

Turned vampires were very rare, especially in Sivrinaj. The few that managed to survive the process usually didn't adjust well to their new existence. And the vampires of the House of Night— notoriously territorial—were never all that inclined to turn their food into their peers to begin with.

It had never even occurred to me that Raihn could be Turned. And yet, so much now made sense. The unusual ragged edge to his appearance. His decidedly un-vampiric sense of humor. And the performances—the constant performances, like he had something to prove. Like he'd had to learn how to wear different faces.

That little amused smile faded, leaving behind something rawer

and more rueful. "Centuries, and it never gets any less repulsive.
Never fucking fades."

I wanted to say, *Good.*

I hoped I still found it repulsive when I became like them. That
I never abandoned that piece of myself. And yet, so many times I'd
thought it seemed like a small price to pay, to shed my humanity
like the discarded skin of a snake.

Even if here and now, the idea sickened me.

I was quiet. I would never give voice to any of those thoughts.

"How long have you been doing this?" Raihn asked, at last.

"I don't know," I lied. "A few years."

Six years, two months, and fourteen days.

"And I have to assume our great Nightborn savior doesn't know."

I shot him a warning glance.

He laughed just enough to reveal a glimpse of pointed teeth.

"You know, part of the reason why I wanted to ally with you
was because of *that* look. That fucking face. It's just so . . . so . . ."
He clamped his lips shut, and his features twitched as if he was
getting ready to mimic me and then—wisely—thought better of it.
"Forget it."

I could have let it lie there. Yet, I found myself replying, curtly,
"No. Vincent doesn't know."

Why did I say that? Did I want to prove something to him?
Prove that I was more than Vincent's obedient pet?

"It would cause political problems," I went on. "It's better for
everyone this way."

Absolutely true. Vincent couldn't condone, even tacitly, my ac-
tivities here. Just like he couldn't condone any official action in
Rishan territory on my behalf. I would be free to act on my own
when I was strong enough to do so without being killed.

I refrained from adding that Vincent would also probably lock
me up in my room indefinitely if he knew about my little hobbies.

"Right." Raihn sounded unconvinced.

The breeze captured loose strands of both of our hair—mine
raven black, his dark red. It was welcome in this heat. I lifted my

chin to it, relishing the cooling sweat on my cheeks as I gazed out to the horizon—the crumbling bland blocks of the human district, static and angular in contrast to the rolling dunes. The Nightborn castle dwarfed all of it. From this spot, three different worlds collided: prey, predator, and the gods.

"It is admirable, Oraya," Raihn said, after a long silence. "What you did in the ring. What you do here."

I blinked in surprise. I didn't look at him, didn't respond—waited for him to add a correction, or a diminishment. But he didn't. He just made the straightforward compliment, and let it stand.

It felt strange.

"And I'm sorry for my behavior before the trial," he went on. "It was . . . I was thinking of things that had nothing to do with you. I was having a bad day."

This stunned me even more than the compliment. Even if I could practically hear Mische feeding him the words.

Again, I waited for a *but*, a diminishment, but it did not come. I allowed myself to look at him, and silence stretched out between us.

Finally, I said, "Do you want me to say I'm sorry now? Because I'm not."

He laughed. Not a chuckle or a scoff—a laugh, full and deep and shockingly loud. I couldn't even remember the last time I had heard someone laugh like that. Myself included. Not since . . . not since Ilana.

"That fucking face," he said, shaking his head. "No, I was not waiting for you to apologize. I'd be disappointed if you did."

"I have no regrets. I'd throw you out that window again."

"Oh, I know, princess. I know."

He pushed the wayward strands of his hair away from his face, the smile still clinging to his lips and moonlight outlining the angles of his profile. The sudden, overwhelming realization hit me that he was actually very handsome. I was always surrounded by beautiful people—and learned long ago, the hard way, how important it was to numb myself to that—but in this moment, just for a split second, Raihn's beauty struck me like a blow, so unexpected and staggering my breath caught in my throat. His wasn't the refined elegance of vampires, perfect cheekbones and perfect lips and perfect, glittering eyes. No, it was rougher, more lived-in. More alive.

Suddenly all those features that had seemed like so *much*—that carried the marks of a life, unlike vampire perfection that sanded them away—were magnificently captivating.

I looked away fast, shoving this observation down.

"I have an idea," he said. "Fuck training in that apartment. Let's train here."

My brow furrowed. "Here?"

"Here. Doing this. I already learned more about your style in the last two hours than I have in the last ten days, just by watching you work tonight."

I bristled at that, every instinct rebelling against being observed. But I begrudgingly had to admit he was right. If we were going to work together, we needed to understand each other.

"Think about it," he said. "We can learn how to fight together and actually do something fucking *useful*. And . . ." The corner of his mouth curled. "It'll be more fun, don't you think?"

Every part of me wanted to say no, like a child desperate to protect her secret hideaway. But I had only barely survived two trials, and my ability to make it through the third hinged on working with Raihn.

And my ability to kill him afterward hinged on my understanding of him, too.

My gaze drifted back to that window. The lights had mostly gone out, save for a single lantern that now dimly outlined the little girl's sleeping form, now tucked into bed, barely visible.

This district had been crawling with vampires tonight. One month away from my project, and so much effort undone. How many humans had died in the last month because I wasn't here? How many more could live if I had help?

"Alright," I said. "Fine. We'll do it."

I almost took it back just because Raihn looked so smugly pleased with himself.

He leaned closer, a curious look glinting in his eye. "Do you remember when you asked me for one honest thing?"

I nodded.

"One honest thing, Oraya. We have three weeks until the Halfmoon Trial. Are we really going to work together?"

I understood what he was really asking me. Whether I would cooperate with him. Whether I would *allow* us to work together.

What have you done to earn my trust? I had spat at him.

Trust was still a precious and dangerous thing. Whatever I was giving him now wasn't quite that. But . . .

I looked down to that sleeping girl. Then to Raihn. I noticed for the first time that we were sitting quite close to each other, less than an arm's length apart.

I noticed this, and I did not move.

"Yes," I said. "I think so."

CHAPTER TWENTY-TWO

"*O raya.*"

Vincent said my name in a single exhale of relief—not so much a greeting as a desperate *thank you* to the Mother that I was here.

I wasn't expecting that.

Three syllables, and so much of my anger melted away, leaving a vulnerable affection that ached beneath a stab of guilt.

I had made him wait one more day. I couldn't bring myself to see him after witnessing what happened to that little girl. And still, as I crested the hill today, I questioned whether it was a good idea.

I thought I was ready. Working in the human districts had stilled something within me. It didn't make the image of that little girl's crying face go away, but it did make her pain feel like it was worth something.

And yet, with every step I took toward Vincent's meeting place, I felt smaller and smaller. All the parts of myself that I'd been so careful to hide from him were too close to the surface.

So I was relieved when he looked at me that way, and when it made all my anger deflate. He had been worried about me, and he loved me. That was all that mattered.

"Are you hurt?"

Vincent circled me, looking me up and down even though I wore leathers that covered my entire body, the scars of my injuries sealed away beneath armor.

"I'm fine."

"You didn't look fine. You looked . . ." His back straightened, paternal worry replaced with the rage of the King of the Nightborn. "What," he hissed, "were you *thinking*? You nearly threw that match away. You nearly forfeited your life. For what?"

That stare was cold enough to freeze my heart again.

For what?

With those words, I was in the maze again, looking at that child, the horrifying realization falling over me. I had learned over the years to carefully regulate my emotions—*anger is a series of physical responses*—but this time it hit me hard, and fast.

"Why were there humans in that trial?" I asked.

I spoke calmly, but Vincent had taught me how to line words with steel. He recognized that now, blinking in surprise.

"The trials are not under my jurisdiction."

"That isn't true."

Surprise turned to indignation. "Excuse me?"

"You do not execute them, but they are under your jurisdiction. And the humans are citizens of the House of Night. There are—there are protections. There should have been protections."

I was eternally conscious of how I stumbled over my words. In my head, they sounded strong and full of conviction. Aloud, they sounded weak and childish.

His stare grew colder. "Protections? Their lives belong to Nyaxia. Just as mine does. Just as yours does. And if this is what she wants them for—"

"Children? She wants *children* for her entertainment? For—"

I cut myself off and turned so my face was shrouded in the shadows. Useless. It would hide nothing from a vampire.

Something in him softened. I could hear the change in his voice—he had morphed from father to king, and now he was my father again.

"Let me into that mind of yours, little serpent," he murmured.

He didn't know what he was asking for. He wouldn't like what he saw there, if I did. The words that weighed heavy on my tongue tasted like treason—like they might betray me to him as someone who was too dissimilar to him. Not vampiric enough.

"A human life should not be worth so little," I said. "There's a reason why humans are protected within their districts."

"All of our lives are cheap, Oraya. Human. Vampire. Even those of the gods."

He said this somewhat pityingly, as if he was surprised to have to explain something so obvious.

It was true. Death was everywhere in the House of Night. Parents killed their children. Children killed their parents. Lovers took each other's lives in the night, gone too far in the throes of passion. Even the stories of our gods were vicious, lesser deities frequently murdered for little more than sport. The Nightborn forged their people and their blades from steel, hard and cold and unforgiving.

This was life. Maybe it was a sign that something was wrong with me that I struggled to accept it. Struggled to hammer myself into that blade. Perhaps it was because I was neither human nor vampire, and because standing on that boundary made it so clear how steep the differences were.

"At least the vampires died for something," I said.

"We all die for something. Vampire and human."

I didn't accept that answer. I didn't accept it at all. If I died in the Kejari, at least I'd be doing so of my own volition. But those humans? What did they die for? Nothing. Entertainment for our bloodthirsty goddess and bloodthirsty populace. I chose this life, but that child didn't.

Vincent was right that the House of Night didn't respect any life, but it certainly still valued some more than others.

I tried so hard to stop there. But I couldn't. The words came before I could stop myself.

"That could have been me. That girl. It could have been me. Do you ever think about that?"

Vincent's expression darkened, like storm clouds blotting out the powerful stillness of the moon. "That *never* would have been you, Oraya."

"I'm—"

Human. I so rarely spoke that word to him. Never said it aloud. Like it was some dirty term that neither of us wanted to acknowledge.

"You are not like them," he cut in, forcefully. "It *never* would have been you."

He was wrong. I knew this, just as I knew better than to say it.

He stepped closer, the shadows in his gaze growing deeper, fiercer.

"Do you want to change this world, little serpent? Then climb your cage until you are so high no one can catch you. Break its bars and make them your weapons. Nothing is sharper. I know because I did it."

I was accustomed to seeing Vincent the king, Vincent the father, but it was rare that I saw this version of him: Vincent the revolutionary. It was easy to forget, sometimes, that he'd reshaped this kingdom. He knew what it was like to crave change.

"You cannot accomplish anything in this world without power," he said. "And power requires sacrifice, focus, and ruthlessness."

His gaze drifted off into the shadows behind me, and I wondered if he was thinking about his own rise to power and everything it had taken from him. I knew he had sacrificed, too. But in exchange, he had become the most powerful king the House of Night had ever seen. He'd been able to shape this kingdom into everything he wanted it to be.

You cannot accomplish anything in this world without power.

The truth. In good ways and bad. Perhaps the only useful thing my anger could do for me was motivate me. I needed to stay focused.

I swallowed and lowered my chin. "I know."

Power. The word reminded me of all the questions I still didn't have answers to. I rubbed my fingertips together as they tingled with the memory of my confusing, brief burst of magic.

"Something strange happened," I said. "Before the trial. I . . . did something I don't understand."

I told him what had happened with my magic—selectively, of course, leaving out the specifics of my argument with Raihn. I didn't need any more of Vincent's disapproval than I already had on that front.

He listened in silence, face stoic. When I was done, I watched for some sign of surprise, of concern, and found none.

"It doesn't make sense," I said. "I have never been able to do anything like that. Not even when you were training me."

He was silent for a few seconds before answering, like he had to think about what to say next. "We always knew you had talents."

The faintest tug at the corner of his mouth. Just a hint of pride.

We? Maybe he did—*maybe*, I was a bit skeptical—but I never thought I could do anything like that.

"But I never had before."

"Magic is an unpredictable force, and your life has changed dramatically these last few weeks."

I stared flatly at him, unconvinced.

"I'm not a vampire. I'm not one of Nyaxia's children. How could I have wielded that kind of power from her arts?"

"You offered your blood to Nyaxia. You offered her your life. That offering does not go unrecognized. And many have been able to wield powers that traditional wisdom said they couldn't."

I thought of Mische and her flames—a vampire wielding the power of Atroxus.

"Perhaps some part of you knows that you need this power now more than ever. So learn it. Use it." He leaned closer, eyes cold with fervor. "Nothing matters but this, Oraya. Nothing. Step over temporary barriers. Once you win, the world is yours. That is the time for dreaming. But this? This is the time for conquering."

I, ONCE AGAIN, barely returned to the Moon Palace in time for dawn. By the time I made it back to our apartment, the sun was already peeking over the horizon. I came in just as Mische was heading back into her room, but Raihn once again stood at the window, forearm braced against it, curtains parted.

He peered over his shoulder, giving me a little smirk. "Welcome back."

"You aren't going to ask me where I was?"

"I've learned it's more fun to be surprised by you. Besides, I think I know. You ready to start tomorrow?"

I thought about the last time we'd played out this moment and just how poorly it went. Briefly, I wondered whether I was insane.

But there was a Halfmoon Trial to win.

Now is the time for conquering, Vincent whispered in my ear.

"Yes," I said. "I'll be ready."

I started to go to my room, and then succumbed to my curiosity and turned back.

"Why do you do that?" I asked.

"Hm?"

"It must hurt."

"Not too bad yet."

"But . . . why? Why do you do it?"

He was silent for a long moment, then smiled at me.

"Get some rest," he said. "We have a lot of work to do."

It struck me as completely unfair that he got to see my secret but refused to explain his own stupid self-destructive habits. I decided that refraining from pointing out this hypocrisy was my first step to being a decent ally.

"Well, don't burn yourself so badly that you're going to be use-less tomorrow," I said as I turned away. "Won't do much to convince me this is a good idea."

"You say that like you aren't desperate."

I shook my head, rolled my eyes, and went back to my room.

I did not miss Mische peering around the corner of her door, not even bothering to hide her eavesdropping nor her grin.

PART FOUR
HALFMOON

INTERLUDE

The little girl was no longer a little girl. Now she was a young woman. At sixteen years old, she now thought she understood her place in her unique world. But something strange happened in those hazy years between childhood and adulthood. The things she desired changed. The things she noticed changed.

Vampires are beautiful people.

This is almost universally true. Their flesh is smooth and soft, their features bright and striking, their voices sweet and melodic. They are often the kind of beautiful that leaves a mark on one's soul—the kind that visits you again as you lie awake in bed at night, thinking about the shape of those lips.

The young woman had learned to numb herself to this. She had been taught relentlessly to view the beings that surrounded her as deadly monsters. It was only as she grew older that she began to view them as dangerous not for all the ways they were monstrous, but for all the ways they were not.

Let us be clear: she was a smart girl. She knew how to survive.

But all living creatures desire. Is that weakness?

One night, the young woman met a young vampire man. She did not often interact with members of her father's court. But this boy, too, seemed like an outsider. He was young, only a few years older than her. He was the most stunning creature she had ever seen—his face the flawless combination of hard angles and gentle curves, rendered in shades of warmth that hinted at what he had once been.

Yes, he had been Turned.

He was a lonely young man. She was a lonely young woman. Is it anything but inevitable that something should form between them?

Perhaps he himself did not understand the weapon of the skin he wore.

Perhaps he was attracted to her because she reminded him of what he once was.

Perhaps he even thought he loved her.

The young woman had never thought much of love. She had not been fed tales of storybook princesses; she did not dream of true love's kiss saving her from her treacherous life. But the memory of this boy's mouth still visited her at night. If it was love to want someone, perhaps this was it.

She was so, so young. Hard in some ways. Softly naive in others. She did not truly understand, yet, that vampires shone as the silver teeth of traps shone. Their beauty was a beckoning hand, promising sweet caresses.

The little serpent was so very lonely. She slithered right into those lovely, elegant fingers. She did not even see the claws.

CHAPTER TWENTY-THREE

I thought that perhaps if we were very, *very* lucky, Raihn and I could manage not to kill each other, but I hadn't expected that we would work well together.

Those first few nights in the districts were far from perfect. Having a mutual goal that we actually cared about helped, but we still found ourselves tripping over each other. Raihn's wall of a body managed to get in my way whenever I needed to move fast. His strikes always took our target out of my line of attack at just the wrong moment. In one memorably painful instance, his wing hit me so hard that it flung me into a wall like a swatted fly.

But there was no shortage of targets. The vampires of the inner city had happily turned the district into their hunting ground in my absence. So we continued, breaking down the barrier between us bit by bit.

Five nights in, and I realized we'd gone an entire trip without either of us accidentally—or intentionally—hitting the other.

Six nights, and I realized we hadn't even stepped on each other's feet all day.

Seven nights, and we actually managed to complement each other, dismantling one of our targets with seamless efficiency. We'd stopped and stared at each other afterward, wide-eyed, like we had both witnessed a miracle and didn't quite want to jeopardize it by acknowledging it aloud. Of course, after that, we'd gotten in each other's way for the rest of the night, but I'd take what I could get.

On the eighth night, I fell back and simply watched him work. By then, I'd started to gain an innate understanding of how he moved, and observing him with that in mind crystalized all of my observations into conclusions.

When I first met Raihn, I'd thought that he relied on his size and strength. I had been very, very wrong. All of that was a distraction. He used magic constantly, hidden in each movement and blow, obscured by showy savagery. If someone wasn't watching closely, they would think he just went at his opponent with a giant Nightsteel sword and won by sheer brute force alone—and they would be underestimating him.

It was much more than that. Those strikes were devastating because he was using his size, his speed, *and* his magic with each one. There was nothing crude about it—it was strategic. He knew when to hit, where, and how hard. Calculated.

This dawned on me as I watched him yank his sword from the chest of a limp vampire corpse. He glanced over his shoulder at me, brow quirked.

"What? Like what you see?"

"Do you do that on purpose?"

"This?" He gestured to the body, straightened, and wiped his blade. The glowing shadows along its length shuddered as the cloth ran over it. "Yes, I'd say so."

"The performance. Your fighting style is a performance. You're making it look simpler than it is."

He paused for a moment—maybe in surprise—before turning around.

"You *have* been watching closely. I'm flattered."

"Why do you hide your use of magic?"

He sheathed his sword and declined to answer. "What's next? The southern end?"

"Do you want people to think you're a brute?"

He stopped mid-step, eyebrow twitching in an expression that I now had come to know meant, *Oraya said something amusing, probably unintentionally.* "A brute?"

I didn't know what was funny about my word choice. "Yes. Even when you used it in the feast hall that time, it was all power, no finesse."

"You think I have finesse? That's flattering. So, southern end?"

"I think you deliberately try to seem like you don't."

"Southern end it is." He started walking. "Perhaps I hide my magic for the same reason you hide yours."

I had to take three steps to keep up with two of his. "You weren't entitled to know about my magic. And you aren't entitled to know why I hid it."

"Oh, I know why you hid it."

I had to fight to keep the surprise from my face.

A slow smile spread over his lips. "You hid it because you didn't know you could do it. You threw me out of a window completely by accident."

This time—Mother damn my face—the blink of shock happened before I could stop it.

"That's not—"

"Look, you are many things, princess. But a good actress is not one of them. Now let's go. We're losing moonlight."

Goddess fucking damn him, there were so many things I wanted to say—chief of which, *You fucking knew and you still gave me* that *much shit?*—but I shut my mouth, drew my blades, and went after him.

I didn't know how I felt about that—the fact that he had been observing me just as closely as I observed him.

I DIDN'T LIKE being observed—and even less liked being understood—but even I had to admit that it had undeniable bene-fits. Soon, Raihn and I worked together as if we had known each other for years.

We had learned each other's fighting styles and learned where to leave openings to accommodate each other. It took nonstop work, from the moment the sun set to the moment the horizon bled pink with impending sunrise. It took many bruises, snapped insults, and aching muscles. And we still had a long, long way to go.

But Raihn, I begrudgingly had to admit, had been right the night he had first approached me to ally: we made a good team.

After we returned from the districts, I would spend time with Mische each day, too, practicing magic use. That went . . . less well. At least Raihn and I made measurable progress every day, even on our worst outings. My magic, though, was a volatile, unpredictable beast. Sometimes, with Mische's tutelage, I managed to coax little wisps of shadow or Nightfire to my fingertips. Other nights, even asking for sparks was too much. And not once did I come even close to summoning the kind of power I'd used to throw Raihn out the window.

I was grateful that we did this work in my bedchamber, where Raihn couldn't see. I never would have gotten over the humiliation.

"You're already defeated before you even start," Mische said, after one long night in which I failed to summon my magic at all, even weakly. "It *knows* when you have a bad attitude."

"I don't have a bad attitude," I grumbled.

"You're scared of it and it's scared of you," she chirped. "You just have to, you know . . . *seize* it! Let your heart open!" She flung out her arms wide, beaming, as if this was a triumphant and completely reasonable instruction.

I gave her a deadpan stare, sighed, and then proceeded to fail fifteen more times before I gave up in exhausted rage.

The truth was, despite my grumbling, I admired Mische. It wasn't her fault that my magic was too temperamental to be useful. She was a patient and dedicated teacher, and her grasp of magic was incredible. She manipulated flame and light as if they were an extension of her body, with carefree effortlessness. It was mind-boggling.

I'd thought I might be able to learn from Mische because she, too, drew from magic that traditionally fell beyond her domain. But all I learned was that she was apparently some kind of anomaly of nature, because she didn't seem to have to try at all.

One time, when my curiosity got the better of me, I asked her, "How did you even *start* doing this? The fire?"

"It's just . . . in me."

"Right. But . . . how? How did you know that? How did you find it?"

She looked blankly at me, brow furrowed, as if I'd just asked her to describe how she began breathing. "It's just *there*. And yours is, too."

"I don't think so."

"Oh, it is!" she insisted.

It was not.

Vincent wasn't much help, either. His advice was the opposite of Mische's—doled out in scant instruction about muscle control and form and, above all, *focus focus focus*. I saw him only a handful of times over those weeks, and less as time went on. Sometimes, I was too busy to go to our meeting spot. Other times, I would wait for him for an hour and he would never appear. With each visit, he was more distracted and distant, and the knot in my stomach grew tighter.

I wasn't stupid. I knew something was happening, something bad that he didn't want to reveal to me. Whenever I gently inquired, he told me I needed to focus on the Kejari in a tone that left no room for negotiation and that I knew better than to challenge.

So I did as he said. I focused, and I trained.

In the second week of preparation, Raihn and I forwent our nightly trip to the districts to train with Mische in the apartment instead. Developing a rhythm with Raihn had been the hard part. But once we forged the foundation of our partnership, it was easy to fit Mische in. She was fast and flexible, responding intuitively to wordless cues. After only a handful of clumsy starts, the three of us fell into a balanced team.

That night, halfway through the session, Mische stopped short. She backed against the wall and crouched down with her hands pressed together, eyes round.

I faltered mid-movement. "What's wrong?" I asked, alarmed. "Did I hurt you?"

"No, no." She shook her head, a grin spreading across her mouth. "It's just . . . gods, *look* at you two! It's amazing!"

"There's no bonding like bonding over murder," Raihn said dryly.

"I'm just so *proud*," she sighed—and I was still trying to figure out whether she was joking or not as he rolled his eyes and beckoned to her. "You're just trying to get an extra break. Let's go, Mische."

Together, we refined the teamwork we had discovered, night after night after night. Every morning, I collapsed into bed exhausted. Every night, I woke up sore and ready to do it all over again.

On the sixteenth night, in the brief seconds before sleep took me, I thought, *This might actually work.*

It might actually work.

And maybe—maybe—I even liked it.

CHAPTER TWENTY-FOUR

It had been several days since Raihn and I had gone to the human districts, so when Mische holed herself up in her room working on some new spell, we took the opportunity to return. I expected that the districts would be full of vampires treating it as a hunting ground, given our absence. But instead, Raihn and I disposed of only two very drunk vampires attempting to pick off a couple of children and then found ourselves roaming aimlessly around the empty streets.

"Hm," Raihn said, after an hour of fruitless wandering. "Maybe we've built more of a reputation for ourselves than we expected."

"Even more terrifying than we thought," I said. "We're doing our jobs too well."

My cheeks tightened. I was so satisfied that it took me an embarrassingly long time to notice Raihn staring at me.

My smile disappeared, and he laughed. "There she is."

"What?" I snapped.

"You just looked so pleased with yourself."

I shrugged.

Fine. I *was* pleased with myself.

"We could go to the western quarter," I suggested.

"Mmm." He slid his hands into his coat pockets and looked around, as if with sudden realization of where we were.

"Is that agreement?"

"I have a better idea."

He set off down a side street, leaving me in the middle of the road.

"Where are you going?" I called after him.

He glanced over his shoulder, eyes crinkled. "I'm getting a drink. You coming?"

"You MEAN TO tell me that you—a human—come to this district almost every night, stab whatever poor vampire bastards you come across, become mysterious savior to the innocent human civilians, and yet, despite spending almost half your fucking life here, you've *never* interacted with these people? Never gone to a pub? Never said a quick hello to one of your rescuees? Nothing?"

He said it like it was ridiculous, and that offended me.

"I wasn't here for that." I glowered at him. The effect of the glare was somewhat diminished by the fact that he was so much taller than me and walking so fast that I had to awkwardly half run to keep up with him. "*We're* not here for that."

"Oh, hush, princess. We've been working so hard there's no one left to kill."

"Then we should go back to the Moon Palace."

"I don't want to go back to the Moon Palace. I want the most absolutely fucking disgusting beer in town. I want foamy, sour, piss beer. And the place to get it is less than a block away. Ah ha!" His face lit up, and he jabbed his finger across the street as we rounded a corner, pointing to a rickety, half-rotted wooden sign that seemed to have once read "Sandra's," but now looked more like "Sa dr 's."

"This place," he said, striding toward it, "has been here for almost a *century*, and—"

"*Wait.*" I grabbed his arm just as he was about to open the door. The movement was much rougher than I'd intended, a weak puff of shadow unfurling from my fingertips, my nails digging into the leather of his coat.

He stopped, brow furrowed, and looked down at my white-knuckled hand. Then at my face. His expression changed . . . softened.

"What's wrong, Oraya?"

"I—"

I didn't even know how to answer that question. I let go of him, clamping my hands together in front of me so he wouldn't see that they trembled.

I leveled my voice. "This is a building full of humans."

"Yes. And?"

And you are made to kill them.

And if you lose control, I don't know if I could stop you alone.

"I'm not putting them at risk so you can drink some garbage beer," I said coldly.

He let out a short laugh. "I want beer, not blood. Besides, why would I go on a hunting rampage after spending the last week and a half with you killing everyone who did just that?"

So fucking dismissive. "It isn't that simple."

"Why the hell not?"

"Because if we put someone like *you* in a packed room of humans, it might not be a matter of you *deciding* anything," I spat. "I know what bloodlust looks like, Raihn."

A momentary wave of something I couldn't decipher—something that almost, *almost* resembled compassion—flitted across his face, quickly replaced once again with amusement.

"You're worried about my self-control? How sweet." He leaned close enough that I felt his words skitter over my cheek. I didn't know why I didn't move.

"I have *plenty* of self-control, Oraya," he murmured. "Don't you worry about me."

Goose bumps rose on the back of my neck.

Yet the shiver that rolled over my flesh wasn't the familiar shiver of fear. That, at least, was a physical response I knew how to regulate. This . . . this startled me. My instinctual desire wasn't to back away, but to pull closer. I froze. My body didn't know how to react to this, reaching for fear and finding something else entirely—something much more dangerous.

A long moment passed—or maybe it had just been a second or two—and I stepped away, shooting him a glare.

"That doesn't matter. Besides, what if they recognize what you are?"

"I won't be flashing any dazzling grins, and they'll be none the wiser."

"No," I hissed. "It's a stupid idea."

The wrinkle between his brows deepened, then disappeared as he gave me a sly smirk.

"*Oh.* I see."

I blinked at him, already offended by whatever he was about to say next.

The smirk broadened to a grin. "You're scared. You're *scared* of a bunch of humans."

"No, I'm not." I said it just too-loud and too-quickly enough to confirm his suspicions.

I wasn't scared. Scared wasn't the right word. It was just . . . wrong. I belonged out here, hidden—not in there, with them. Maybe my blood was human, but I'd abandoned that part of myself a long time ago. Raihn seemed confident that he could pass as one of them, but hell, I didn't know if *I* could.

"What are you so nervous about?" he said. "You're human too, for fuck's sake."

I scowled. "Not *really.*"

He made a face. "Ix's tits. I wish you could have seen your expression just then. I'm glad you're so proud of your heritage."

Before I could stop him, he threw open the pub door and dragged me inside.

THE PUB WAS in the basement, and wobbly stairs directly within the door led us down into the dim throng. Humans gathered at mismatched wooden tables on mismatched wooden stools, leaning close and chatting bawdily over games of cards or mugs of mead. The walls were made of stone and clay, tiny windows at the top revealing peeks of the streets. Lanterns along the walls drenched the whole room in warm orange light. At the pub's center was a square counter, where a barkeep poured drinks and slid food to waiting patrons. The air was thick with a unique scent that blended beer, sweat, and bread.

It was dark and crowded inside. I wondered whether business had picked up considerably since Raihn and I started patrolling the streets again, because it seemed unthinkable to me that this many people had felt comfortable being out after dark when such dangers loomed within those shadows. Or maybe they just no longer cared. These people didn't even seem afraid.

It was so . . . so wildly *different* than anywhere I'd ever been before. I had spent a little time in vampire pubs in the inner city, briefly and out of nothing more than stupid teenage curiosity. They were plenty grimy and depraved, but everyone was so much more restrained, even in the throes of debauchery. Vampires behaved as if every emotion, every impulse, took a bit longer to reach the surface of their skin. But humans? Humans laid it bare. They were loud and expressive and unapologetic.

This struck me, strange and confusing. My humanness had been the reason why I'd spent a lifetime dimming myself. For these people, it was the reason they burned brighter.

It was so utterly foreign that I was certain—certain—that everyone would stop to stare at us the minute we crossed the threshold.

It didn't happen.

I glanced at Raihn, hand moving to the hilt of my blade, watching for signs of bloodlust. With so many sweaty humans packed into this small a space, the scent of blood must be overwhelming. But his nose didn't so much as twitch.

I'd been skeptical when he said he could pass as human. Much more separated vampires and humans than the teeth and the wings—their entire demeanors were different. Vampires simply moved like predators, all silent grace and calculated finesse. And Raihn, though he was an unusual vampire, still had that in spades.

Until he just . . . didn't.

The moment we walked into the pub, Raihn . . . changed. The

way he stood changed, growing a little more relaxed and lopsided. The way he walked changed, his steps a little more meandering. The way he held his face changed, predatory stillness replaced with laid-back ease. Everything about the way he held himself grew a little rougher, a little less polished.

And just like that, Raihn was human. A very tall human, yes—a human that no one would want to fuck with—but *human*.

He jerked his chin toward the back of the room, took hold of my arm, and led me to an unoccupied little booth in the corner. Then he announced that he was going to get us the shittiest beer the place had and was gone before I could say anything else.

I watched him in awe as he cut through the crowd. Everything, from how he gently touched people's shoulders to move them out of the way, to the half-nod greeting he gave the keeper, to the lumbering swagger of his walk back to the table—beer in hand—was immaculate.

He placed a large, chipped glass mug full of foamy mud-brown liquid in front of me, then took his own and slid into the seat beside me. The booth was a small half circle with a wobbly table at its center. He took up roughly three-quarters of the seating space. He leaned against the wall, limbs sprawled, threw his head back, and took several long gulps of his drink.

"Fucking horrific," he said affectionately, as he slammed the mug down on the table. "It's perfect."

"Impressive," I said.

"Thank you. I've had plenty of practice drinking terrible alcohol."

"Not that." I gestured broadly to him, up and down. "*That.*"

His eyebrow twitched. "I've had a lot of practice on my physique, too. I didn't think you'd noticed."

I scoffed, then leaned closer. "You are a very good actor, is what I mean. You look very . . ."

"Human."

"Yes."

He shrugged and took another drink.

"Makes sense."

I narrowed my eyes at him. "Maybe I was right to distrust you in the beginning. You have so many different versions of yourself."

"Oh, they're all me." Now it was his turn to give me *that* look— the kind that picked me apart. "Meanwhile, you look like someone has shoved you in a pen with a bunch of lions. Do you actually have your hand on your blade right now?"

I yanked my fingers away from the hilt at my hip and placed my hands on the table. "No."

"You're safe, Oraya. Relax."

It could have sounded dismissive, but his voice was unexpectedly tender.

You are safe. I could not remember the last time those words were uttered to me. It was never true, after all. And strangely enough, even though these people were so much less dangerous than the predators that surrounded me every day, I felt more exposed here than ever.

I looked out across the room. "Did you use to come to places like this? When you were . . ."

"Human? Yes. Often." His gaze slipped out over the room. "They looked quite a bit different back then, though. A lot of time has passed."

"How much time?"

A pause. "A couple of hundred years."

He said it very casually, but I knew that pause. It was the same kind of pause I made when he asked me how long I had been coming to the human districts. He knew exactly how long it had been— years, days, minutes.

"But I still come to places like this regularly. I get a bit exhausted by vampires, sometimes."

"Do you miss it? Humanity?"

It was only after the question left my lips that I realized how oddly intimate it was. I thought he wouldn't answer. He was silent, watching the patrons laugh and drink.

"I miss the sun," he said at last.

And for a moment, he wore the same expression that he did when I would come back to the apartment at dawn to find him looking out the window, long after the light would have been eating at his skin.

I didn't know why I felt the urge to pull away from that uncomfortable question, as if I'd prodded a wound. I took a sip of my beer. Thick bitterness flooded my mouth. I made a face, and Raihn laughed.

"Ugh. That's *disgusting.*"

"Disgusting and amazing."

"Just disgusting."

"You have no taste, princess."

Despite myself, I chuckled. Maybe he had a point, because I took another sip.

"Mische probably also used to be human," I remarked.

A warm smile curled the corner of his mouth. "She makes it obvious, doesn't she?"

"I haven't met another vampire like her."

"Nor have I."

"Were you the one who—"

The warmth disappeared from Raihn's face. "No," he said, sharply enough to cut off the rest of the question and any further follow-up on that topic, then took a long drink.

I watched him closer than I allowed myself to let on.

Raihn had told me that he wanted to ally with me because he was curious about me. And I hated to admit this—even to myself—but I was curious about him, too. It had been a long time since I found myself wanting to know more about someone, even if it was only because they were so confusing.

He set down his drink—already mostly empty—and we sat in silence, observing the patrons.

Eventually I asked, "Why did you enter the Kejari?"

Such an obvious question, and yet none of us had ever asked it of each other. It was like once we entered the Moon Palace, the outside world and the circumstances that had brought us there ceased to exist.

"I have a lot of people depending on me, and Turned Rishan from the slums don't get many options." He shook his head. "Never make deathbed promises, Oraya. Always bites you in the ass."

Turned Rishan from the slums. I was often so focused on the suffering of the humans within the House of Night that it was easy to forget that vampires suffered here, too. I'd thought that most would enter the Kejari for the glory of it, but maybe it was really desperation fueling all of us.

"Family?" I asked.

"In a sense. And I exhausted all other avenues. Joining this fucking barbaric spectacle was not high up on my list of things I wanted to do with my pathetic never-ending life." His mouth twisted into a wry smile. "I wouldn't even be here if Mische didn't force me into it."

My eyebrows leapt.

He chuckled and took another drink. "Look at that face. You thought *I* was the—what was your word?—*brute* who Turned Mische, carted her around Obitraes for a few hundred years, then dragged that poor, innocent little sunshine sprite halfway across the world to the bloodthirsty Kejari tournament, is that it?"

"Yes," I said, without hesitation. "Absolutely."

"That fucking girl." He shook his head. "No, this was all her idea. And she knew I'd never let her do it alone."

I struggled to reconcile this information with the version of Mische that I knew. Tried to imagine the girl who put flowers all over the apartment and giggled uproariously whenever anyone made a sound that vaguely resembled flatulence dragging Raihn to the Kejari.

I had wondered many times over these last weeks why both of them were here. They clearly loved each other deeply—neither, I was certain, would be willing to hurt the other. But then again, it wasn't unheard of for close friends to enter together, if their interests aligned. Two chances at victory were better than one.

"Then . . . why is *she* here?" I asked.

"Because she's a manipulative little thing," he grumbled, as if to himself.

"Manipulative?"

"Right. Like someone else I know. Trying to get me drunk so you can ask all kinds of invasive questions." He took a drink and shot me a wary glare. He set down his mug, and with every second of silence, I grew more surprised.

"And now," he said, "you're waiting for me to ask you why *you're* doing this."

"A bit," I admitted.

A human in the Kejari? Anyone would be curious.

"Well, I won't. I know already."

My brows rose. "Oh, you do?"

"I'll admit that before, I was wondering. I was thinking, 'Why would this human put herself in a situation where she was surrounded by predators? Near-certain death?'" He smirked. "Or, more accurately, 'Why would *Vincent* put her in this situation?' Easy, viper." He raised his hands at the glare I shot him. "I know. But I was curious about a lot. Like, why were you here at all? You're an adult. Vincent clearly doesn't keep you literally locked up. Why did you remain in the House of Night, instead of crossing the Bone Seas to the human nations, where you could live a real life?"

A real life, he said, as if my life wasn't real.

The truth was, it had barely even occurred to me that it was an option to leave the House of Night—leave Vincent. Only once, when I was seventeen years old, did I consider it. Ilana had raised the idea. It was shortly after . . . after. Those days were a blur of grief and pain. But I could still remember exactly how she had looked that day—so uncharacteristically serious, so worried. She had taken my face in her rough hands, pulled me so close I could smell the cigar smoke on her breath, and looked directly into my eyes. "You don't have to live this way, my love," she had said. "I made this choice, but you didn't. You can choose another life, in another world, where you'd be just a person."

I had only stared at her blankly before turning away.

The thought was incomprehensible. Where else could I possibly exist but the House of Night?

"I don't want to leave," I said.

"I see that now, after watching you here. You don't see yourself as human at all, do you? So why would you leave to go live with them?"

I didn't like that tone at all. "There are problems that need to be solved *here*. I'm not running away from that. This is my home. Maybe it's a home that hates me, but it's my home."

This kingdom was a part of me, and I, whether it wanted me or not, was a part of it. I was the daughter of its king, blood or no. The bones of my parents were buried in this country. No matter how many times the House of Night bruised my skin or my heart, I would stay. Just as all the humans who lived here—who did not have a choice but to live here—would stay.

This was where I belonged. Here. Not some foreign human land half a world away.

Raihn examined me, a thoughtful expression on his face. It wasn't the first time I'd seen that look, and every time, it made me uncomfortable. Like he was letting a facade drop for just these few rare, quiet moments, and revealing just how much he analyzed the world around him, typically hidden beneath violence and swagger.

I didn't especially like being the subject of that analysis.

"You have balls, princess," he said. "I will give you that." Then he leaned across the table—so small compared to his frame that even that slight movement put him right in front of me.

"Here's the other thing I have never understood about you. Vincent."

I drew back, already defensive, every muscle tensed at the mere mention of his name.

"You're just some human girl," Raihn went on. "And the King of the Nightborn, well-known to be a cold, ruthless bastard, just . . . has a moment of compassion and decides to take you in? Why?"

His brow furrowed, and his eyes searched my face, like he was really looking for an answer to this question—and like he was already concerned on my behalf for what that answer might be. I glimpsed something in that expression, the faintest edge of something strangely familiar, gone in seconds.

"Of course," he continued, "I know some vampires have a taste for human sex, but—"

"Vincent is my *father*," I cut in, disgusted.

"Right. At least if he was fucking you, I could make sense of it. But by all accounts, including yours, he's not. So . . ."

If I wasn't so offended, I would find it a bit funny that Raihn had the exact same thought about me and Vincent that I'd had about him and Mische.

"Mische is your family, even if she isn't your blood. It shouldn't be so hard for you to understand that."

"*I* understand it. I just didn't think our oh-so-great-and-powerful divine king did."

"Because you know him so well." I scoffed. "Of course you think poorly of him. You're Rishan. He unseated your people from the throne."

"I'm sure the two dozen extended family members of his that he executed to take that throne feel somewhat strongly about his commitment to familial bonds, too."

Oh, please. As if every vampire king didn't have to kill to get that power. It wasn't pleasant, but it was reality.

"And how many people are *you* about to kill to fulfill those 'responsibilities' you talked about?" I smirked at him, gesturing to myself. "And you still took in a human stray, didn't you?"

He finished the last of his beer.

"Oraya, there is nothing stray about you. I think you know precisely where you're going, even when you don't know you do."

And I was about to ask him what, exactly, *that* was supposed to mean—

—But then the floor shook in an abrupt lurch, and the crowd drew in a sudden gasp as the explosion rang out loud enough to make the world tremble.

CHAPTER TWENTY-FIVE

A shiver tore through my entire body. The sound was distant, and yet it silenced the room immediately. The ground shook once, violently—over so fast that if plates and glasses hadn't all toppled to the ground in that moment, I might have questioned if I'd imagined it.

Maybe I had been wrong about these humans being carefree, because they all sobered right away, their hushed fear rising to the surface like it had never really left.

Raihn and I were already on our feet, running outside. When we stumbled onto the street, I stopped short.

"Fuck," I breathed.

A plume of shimmery silver smoke rose from the distant Moon Palace, floating up through the night sky and blotting out the moon. The puffs of white nearly consumed the Palace's silhouette, but when a gust of wind thinned the fog, it revealed that one of the towers was simply missing. Just . . . gone. Lightning-bright cracks radiated up through the base of the building, visible even from across the city. Bursts of light clustered around the castle's foundation.

My stomach dropped.

Mische.

Mische was in the Moon Palace.

I whirled to Raihn, who had gone pale. All his masks and performances had been abandoned, leaving only bare, gut-wrenching terror.

"We'll get her," I said. "She's going to be alright. We'll get her."

I touched him without thinking, my fingers digging into the muscle of his forearm. He had to visibly fight that fear from the surface. Still, his voice shook a little as he said, "I'm flying."

"I'm coming with you."

"You'll be a liability."

"You know damned fucking well that isn't true, and you don't know what you're about to find, Raihn."

He winced, because he knew I was right. "Fine. Then you're flying with me."

It didn't sink in what, exactly, that meant. Not until Raihn stepped closer, drew me into his arms, and scooped me up like I was nothing before I had time to react.

"Hold on," he said, voice low and so close to my ear that my skin shivered. "I'm not coming back for you if you fall."

My body seized, frozen by the sheer overwhelming proximity of him. His form enveloped mine, his arms gripping me tight to his chest, encircling me with a firm hold. I was close enough to feel his heartbeat—slower than a human's. Close enough that the heat of him surrounded me at all angles.

My pulse went rapid, every instinct screaming.

Out of the corner of my eye, I saw Raihn glance at me—did he sense the increase in my heart rate?

His expression softened. "You're safe, Oraya," he murmured in my ear. "Just hold on."

You're safe, I told myself.

We didn't have time for this. *Mische* didn't have time for this. So I tightened my arms around his neck, fighting more than a decade of training in order to put myself completely at his mercy.

And as if he knew—as if he sensed my fear—Raihn's thumb traced a circle over my back in one gentle, wordless reassurance.

It startled me, that touch. It startled me because it comforted me. I didn't think it was possible to find a touch comforting ever again.

"Ready?" he said.

I nodded against his shoulder and braced myself.

A great *whoosh* surrounded us. I peered over Raihn's shoulder just in time to see a wall of black open around us—inky, glossy feathers, even more magnificent so close, with as many variations of purple and blue and red as the night sky itself.

Then my stomach dropped, and the ground fell out beneath us. My hair flew back. Warm wind stung my cheeks, whipping with such ferocity that I had to bury my face against his shoulder again as we ascended.

We soared toward the burning Palace. He flew fast. Once we leveled out, I chanced twisting my head around. Looking down was a mistake—the sight of the buildings of Sivrinaj no bigger than wooden toy blocks made me nauseous. But up . . . Mother, the night sky was incredible. *Freeing.* In any other circumstance, I would have wanted to live up here forever. Vincent rarely flew, which now seemed unthinkable. Why would anyone choose *not* to do this? Why would anyone do anything else, when they could be here?

Then I turned ahead, and when I saw the Moon Palace, that amazement withered to horror.

An entire spire had fallen, its stone remnants now a jagged mountain of rock that partially pierced the central domed roof. Blue-white light burned in the wound and glowed from within the shattered glass windows. From this height, people were nothing but little dots in the distance, but I could see them swarming in activity near the entrances. The cold flames spread, consuming nearly half of its base, obliterating the surrounding gardens. The quarter of the city nearest to the Moon Palace had been crushed, entire buildings seemingly reduced to rubble.

This was an attack. A calculated attack.

And it was an attack conducted with *Nightborn* magic. That blue-white was unmistakable. Nightfire was a gift of the House of Night alone, never used by the Bloodborn or Shadowborn.

The hairs rose on the back of my neck.

The Rishan. It had to be. Vincent had been so preoccupied lately—so obviously concerned with issues he wouldn't share with me. I knew tensions between the two Nightborn clans had been on the verge of exploding. Vincent had held on to power for two hundred years. That was a long time for one bloodline to manage to keep it. And it wouldn't be the first time the Rishan had made a violent attempt at rebellion.

I was so tight against Raihn's chest that even with the air rushing around me, I felt him shudder.

"Our tower is standing." I had to get very close to his ear because the wind was so loud, my lips brushing the crest of it. I was so shaken by what I had seen that I almost—almost—didn't notice.

He didn't seem comforted. And the truth was, neither was I. Yes, our tower was standing, but Nightfire consumed everything. It wouldn't remain that way for long.

He glided through the still-broken window of our apartment, tearing past the cloth that Mische had put up to cover the missing pane. Immediately, our hands went up to shield our faces. Raihn set me down and I struggled to get my feet under me. My eyes slitted against the blinding white.

Nightfire. *Everywhere.*

Nightfire didn't produce *heat,* exactly, so much as it withered flesh from the inside out. It wasn't hot like flames, but it wasn't cold, either. It simply devoured—devoured more quickly, and more unforgivingly, than fire ever did. People caught in Nightfire were often found in piles of pristine bone. One of Vincent's highest-ranking generals had lost his hand to it, and now the bone jutted out from black-scarred flesh, polished and gleaming.

It had overtaken the apartment. White flames leeched the color from the floors, the walls, the curtains. The fumes made my lungs sting, as if each layer of tissue was shrieking a dying wail.

The smoke was too thick and the light too bright. It took too long for my eyes to adjust—to see the movement within the licks of death. Night-dark bodies writhed through the blaze. They were small and twisted, perched on four spindly legs bent in all the wrong directions, each of which looked as if they had been pried from separate corpses and stitched together into something moderately resembling a single beast. Demons. Even through the fire, I recognized them immediately as the product of Nightborn magic; very different than the Bloodborn beasts we saw in the first trial.

Three of them surrounded Mische's limp body.

In the fire, everything was black or white, save for the violent splatter of black red, like a bucket of spilled paint, right at the center of the room.

My mind emptied, save for the horrible certainty that Mische was dead.

The demons' faces snapped to us, their eyes round, gleaming pits.

I was moving before I had time to question whether it was a good idea. I wasn't being strategic—wasn't being smart. By the third step, I thought the demons would be upon me, but they weren't. They remained completely still, staring at us. Looking at me? Or looking at Raihn?

I see you I see you I see you.

The words came in a sense different than sound, the rhythm of them burrowing in my veins.

A strong hand grabbed my wrist and yanked me away.

"Get back," Raihn commanded in a low growl.

He kept walking past me, in quick, purposeful steps, gaze fixed upon those demons. In turn, the demons stared back at him, unblinking, unmoving.

"Get the fuck away from her," he hissed, and lifted his hands.

I was several strides behind him, but even so, the force of his Asteris nearly toppled me over. My arms flew up to shield my face—if the Nightfire was intense, the flare of his magic was unfathomable. It lasted only a split second. The demons' deaths were punctuated by a high, chilling wail that fell into weeping whimpers. When the light faded, Raihn was at Mische's side, and two of the demons were simply gone, the third a mess of black liquid and twitching limbs on the opposite side of the room.

I ran to them and fell to my knees next to Raihn. The mask of deathly rage on his face had disappeared, revealing now such raw dismay. Either it was a trick of the light, or he was on the verge of tears.

"Mische," he said. "Mische, look at me."

I leaned over her, blinking away the Nightfire smoke. Her blood soaked through the knees of my pants, even through the leather. Her eyes were half-open, but unmoving. One hand was outstretched beside her, holding a long, golden object—a candlestick? My foot hit something hard and I glanced down to see that candles surrounded her, unlit blocks of wax rolling across the marble floor.

And her abdomen . . . Mother, she was torn open. Gutted. Vampires could survive so much. But this . . . how could *any* being survive this?

A sickening *CRACK* rang out. The floor quivered, groaned. For a terrifying moment, I was certain we were about to fall to our deaths. In the distance, the screams grew louder. I couldn't tell anymore where they were coming from—in here, or out there, or both.

Raihn and I, both braced over Mische's body, exchanged an alarmed glance. No time. How long did we have before this tower collapsed?

"Come on, Mische," he murmured. "We have to go."

He gathered her in his arms. She let out a tiny whimper that made my heart leap—if she was in pain, she was alive.

A burst of light flared behind us as the Nightfire swelled. It was everywhere. Raihn abandoned his gentleness for urgency as we lurched back toward the window and away from the flames.

He turned to me. "I can take you both."

No, he couldn't. He could barely extend his hand to me with Mische in his arms.

I said, "Bring her down and come back for me."

He grimaced. "Oraya—"

"It's no use to anyone if we all fall. *Go.* Fast, because I don't feel like dying tonight."

He hesitated, then said, "Fine. I'll be back. Don't burn to death," and was gone through the window.

It was only once I was alone that I realized what a supremely stupid idea this was. The floor moaned and quaked precariously. I struggled to see anything. Surges of white and blue ballooned, walls falling to the flames.

Thirty seconds and the Nightfire would overtake this entire apartment. That, or the tower would collapse. Raihn would never get back fast enough.

That is, if he even came back at all. He could just leave me here.

BANG.

It was so loud it transcended sound and became force. I whirled around just in time to see the door burst from its hinges, the light consuming me.

I COULDN'T SEE. I couldn't hear.

I was suspended in nothing but pain.

I rolled over. Pushed myself to my hands and knees—or at least I thought I did. I could be upside down. I could be falling. I wouldn't even know.

My eyes were wide open, groping desperately for something— anything—other than blinding white, and failing. My hands slid across the floor, searching for my blades. Feeling blood-slicked tile, crumbled stone, broken glass, the ice-cold ash of Nightfire debris . . .

I would die here.

I was blind and defenseless. Injured—my body didn't move the way I expected it to, but the pain from the Nightfire was so universal, hitting every nerve at once, that I couldn't even tell what was broken. Every sound was distant and muffled, as if I was under-water.

Take stock of your senses, Oraya, Vincent commanded in my head, the only clear thing in a blurry world.

I drew in a deep breath. Let it out.

I couldn't see, couldn't hear, but I could *feel.* I pressed my palms to the ground—let the vibrations from it run through me.

And there, I found something . . . strange. A hot-cold sensation bubbling up inside of me, reaching out. All at once, I became aware not only of the floor beneath my palms, but the walls, the imprint of the window frames. I could feel *myself* here, in the center of this room. Feel the placement of my blades, one several feet to my right, the other lingering just beyond the reach of my left hand.

And I could feel . . . strength. Delirious strength. It surrounded

me, ready to be drawn upon. The Nightfire. It was energy. It was
power.

Mische's words, which not long ago had seemed totally illogical—
it's just there—suddenly made sense.

I reached for that power the way I reached for my senses, like it
was already a part of me.

My eyes still saw nothing but white. And yet, I knew the exact
moment that the demons came bursting through the door. Three of
them—no, four, the last one lingering somewhat behind, its back
leg injured.

I didn't think.

I rose, opened my hands, and let out a wordless roar.

Heat and cold flashed over my skin. A shriek pierced the numb
silence of my ears. A wave of euphoria shivered over my flesh. For
two seconds, I was the most powerful being in the world. I was
fucking untouchable.

And then I was in agony.

My knees hit the ground hard. I doubled over, covering my face.
"Oraya!"

I didn't hear Raihn until he was right next to me, grabbing me
and pulling me upright. I blinked at him, his face a blurry imprint
in a world of oppressive white. He was looking past me, to the
apartment, lips parted and brow furrowed.

Then, he pulled me into his arms and hurled us out the window.

We fell for a gut-clenching moment before his wings splayed out,
turning our freefall into a graceful arc. The darkness of the night
was a relief to my eyes, though I blinked hard, over and over again,
trying to clear my vision—now all acid spots of white against sky.

"You're alright?" Raihn said into my ear.

I choked out, "You missed your chance to get rid of me."

I didn't think he was even capable of joking right now, with
Mische in the state she was. So it seemed like some grim victory
when, where my cheek pressed against his neck, I felt his throat
vibrate with a raspy, humorless laugh. "Shame. I considered it."

I laughed, too, in a strange broken sound that was too high and
too loud.

"I thought I was going to be too late." He leaned close to me, his voice low and drawn. "What did you just do in there?"

What? I wanted to say, but the words stuck in my throat.

"The Nightfire." As if he heard it anyway. "You killed four demons."

The wave of nausea had nothing to do with motion sickness.

I didn't know how to answer him, so I didn't.

Instead, I looked down. The white spots still speckled my vision. I realized, after a moment, that they didn't fade because some of those spots were actually Nightfire, spreading through the streets.

Before us was the Nightborn castle, foreboding red against the night sky. The Guard had been deployed. Vincent's army was a wave of blue and purple falling across the city, the mass of them a singular smear of death to my broken eyes.

Still, I found Vincent immediately: right there at the front, his wings spread, the black glow of Asteris surrounding him. The red outline of his wings was visible even from the sky, as was the crimson shade of his sword—the Taker of Hearts.

Even from this distance, he emanated death.

I had witnessed Vincent's power many times before. But I had never seen him like this. A horrible feeling coiled in my stomach.

"Your father has his war," Raihn remarked. "He's been waiting for this moment for a long, long time. He was made for this."

I wanted to argue. But all I could think as we soared over the wreckage was that something had changed tonight. Something would never be the same again. I couldn't describe it, couldn't make sense of it, but I felt it in the air.

This was not just an attack. Not just a culmination of tension. Not a final death spasm.

No, this was the beginning of something horrible. A bloody birth of a bloodier monster. One that could devour us all.

CHAPTER TWENTY-SIX

It was nearly a full day before the Nightfire was extinguished and the demons disposed of. Whoever had launched the attack had been very strategic about their entry points. They came in through the southern entrance of the Moon Palace, which was the quietest and least protected. The greenhouse had been easy to breach, and the plants provided fantastic kindling for the Nightfire. Now nothing remained of it but shattered glass, all buried beneath the remnants of the tower that had collapsed above.

Four contestants had been killed in the attack—two within the lost tower when it fell, one ripped apart by a demon, one consumed by Nightfire. If I'd stayed in the greenhouse instead of going with Raihn and Mische, I would have been among them.

Mische survived, barely, though she still teetered on the edge of death. And she wasn't alone. Several others had been burned—one of them so badly that he just lay in a state of semi-consciousness and moaned in pain. He no longer had a *face*. I hoped, for his sake, that he either died or recovered enough to do the deed himself.

Those with injuries so bad they couldn't fight put in requests for withdrawal to Nyaxia. In the hushed silence of dawn, we gathered in the great room. The only sounds were the whispered prayers of the injured as they slit their hands and dripped their blood to their parchment pleas, asking the Goddess for permission to withdraw their candidacies. Raihn and I did this for Mische, too; she couldn't get the words out herself. Later, the Ministaer and his acolytes moved solemnly through the room, collecting those bloodstained pieces of parchment. They instructed us to remain in the Moon Palace, reminded us that the Kejari would go on as planned, and told us to await further instruction.

That was it. So we all settled back into what was left of the Moon Palace, and we waited.

At sundown the next night, Vincent addressed the House of Night.

He did it from the castle balcony, overlooking the inner city. He commanded attention across all of Sivrinaj. Magic painted his visage to the sky in ethereal strokes of light. The first two buttons of his jacket were undone, revealing his Heir Mark. His wings were spread. His crown peeked through tendrils of blond hair like the platinum spires of a star.

The message was clear: Vincent was the Nightborn King, and anyone who challenged him would pay dearly for it.

He didn't speak to his people, but to his enemies.

"I have only one thing to say. The Nightborn are not cowards. We do not take kindly to acts of war. And make no mistake, this attack is an act of war."

His voice rang through the sky, everywhere at once—inescapable.

"Do you wish to unseat me? *Try.* You are not the only ones who know how to kill. You have opened a door you cannot close again, and you are not prepared for the horrors that I will pour through it. Horrors that will spare nothing, as you have spared nothing. Horrors that will not spare your wives or children. Horrors that will not spare your food or your homes. And horrors that will not spare *you.*" A sneer curled the corner of his lip, revealing the lethal points of his teeth. "Not even when you beg for death."

He lifted his chin. Even rendered in ghostly silver, the Mark on his throat seemed to burn, as if he and it alike had been seared into the night itself.

"I hope it was worth it, Rishan rebels."

JESMINE CAME TO the Moon Palace later that night. She brought with her a slew of Nightborn warriors, who shadowed her like deadly ghosts.

We had found another room by then—a much smaller chamber on the first floor, at the center of the Moon Palace, which was both easier for Mische to access and more central in case other parts of the structure collapsed. It wasn't nearly as grand as our previous hideaway, but it was safe and secure. Raihn had even managed to recover some of our possessions from what remained of the eastern tower. His first priority had been Mische's bag of medical supplies. When he'd dropped the remnants of my pack before me, too, I'd been casually grateful. But later, when I was alone, I had nearly wept when I tore it open to find Ilana's scarf still intact, albeit a bit singed.

When she arrived, Jesmine pounded on the door with two booming knocks; not a request, but a demand. Raihn answered it, and she gave him a cold, critical look that started at his feet and slowly moved up his body.

"Yes?" Raihn said coldly.

"Come," she said. "The Nightborn King has summoned you."

Dread simmered in my chest as I joined them at the door.

He was made for this, Raihn's voice echoed.

I hadn't witnessed Vincent in wartime, but I'd certainly witnessed what he was like when he was protecting what was his.

Raihn didn't move.

"Why?"

"Your king commands it."

"He's not my king."

I tensed. Raihn didn't blink. Jesmine was still and silent—a predator preparing for a strike.

I knew Raihn was worried and angry and tired, but he was also being a fucking idiot. I wanted to rip him away from her and tell him so.

"His life belongs to Nyaxia as long as he remains in the Kejari," I said.

Jesmine seemed to realize I was there for the first time, her cat-like violet eyes drinking me in with a glint of piqued curiosity, like I'd just said something very interesting.

"The king is well aware," she said breezily. "Contestants will be returned to the Moon Palace with their lives."

Contestants?

I peered over her shoulder to see that warriors moved about the great room, some headed down hallways to other apartments, others returning to the entrance with prisoners in tow. Angelika was among them, her arms gripped behind her by two Nightborn guards, strong features stone-set in fury.

They were taking the Rishan and Bloodborn contestants. And yet Jesmine, my father's highest-ranking general, came here *personally* to get Raihn.

All these pieces snapped together in my mind to form a gruesome picture. I looked at Raihn just as his gaze darted to me, heavy with the same realization.

"The Rishan didn't do this," Raihn said to Jesmine.

She smiled. It was downright hypnotic. Surely that smile had brought men and women, mortals and immortals alike, to their knees.

"Oh, no one is accusing *you* of such acts. But this is wartime, understand. And the Rishan have a history of such atrocities. The Nightborn King cannot take risks."

"No," I said, before I could stop myself. "He's my ally. The Halfmoon Trial is two days away. Tell Vincent that."

"Vincent is well aware." Jesmine, again, smiled sweetly. "He will be back in plenty of time for the Halfmoon. Don't worry. Now, come." She beckoned to Raihn as if he was a dog. "You must understand the urgency."

His knuckles whitened where his hand gripped the doorframe.

"I'm not leaving my friend," he said. "If the king wants to drag me out, he can come do that himself."

"*We* can drag you out if that's how you would prefer to go."

It was no bluff. If he didn't back down, I was about to see him beaten and removed from the Palace unconscious. He was good, but he wasn't good enough to take down an entire Nightborn army by himself.

My heart had quickened—surely both of them could sense it. I pushed closer, standing beside Raihn in the doorframe. "No one here appreciates the fucking threats, Jesmine," I snapped, then turned to him and lowered my voice. "I'll get you out. And I'll take care of Mische."

He searched my face, unconvinced. I could feel Jesmine's stare, too. I realized that she was looking at my hand, which rested on Raihn's forearm. I didn't even remember putting it there.

I pulled away. Raihn said through his teeth, reluctantly, "Fine."

Jesmine smirked in satisfaction as he stepped past her into the hall.

"Oh, I almost forgot." She reached into her pocket and produced two folded pieces of parchment. She handed one to him. "The Ministaer wanted this delivered to your friend."

Skeptical, Raihn took the letter and unfolded it. His face went white.

"What is this?" he choked out. "Is this a fucking joke?"

Jesmine's mouth twisted ruefully. "From experience, I know the Ministaer does not make fucking jokes."

The parchment crinkled, quivering with his rage.

"*Look* at her." He thrust his free hand toward Mische, listless in the bed within. "She can't fucking compete. And the Ministaer *rejected* her withdrawal?"

My stomach dropped.

That was a death sentence. We couldn't even move Mische up the stairs, let alone drag her into the ring. And right before the Halfmoon Trial, when half the contestants would be killed? She wouldn't survive.

"*Nyaxia* rejected her withdrawal," Jesmine corrected.

"*Fuck Nyaxia.*"

Several of the guards drew in disapproving gasps at this statement.

But this had nothing to do with Nyaxia, and we all knew it.

Mische's withdrawal had been rejected because of her friendship with Raihn. With no clear House association of her own, she might as well be Rishan.

Jesmine's patience was wearing thin. "If you have concerns, you can bring them up with the Ministaer. Now, let's go."

Two of the guards took Raihn's arms, and it looked like he was considering fighting before he finally conceded. I watched him go, mouth dry.

Jesmine offered me the other parchment. "This one is for you. From Vincent."

I took it. It held only three words written in perfect script: *Tonight. Before dawn.*

I glanced up at Raihn. He looked back over his shoulder only once, and the sheer hopelessness on his face shocked me.

For Mische. That was for Mische.

"He's handsome." Jesmine's eyes followed mine. "You could do worse. Better if they aren't a rebel, though. Just causes all sorts of trouble."

That's not what he is, I wanted to snap. Instead, I asked, "You've confirmed the Rishan were responsible?"

"Yes."

I waited for more, and she gave a low laugh. "How much detail do you really want, Oraya? Aren't you more familiar than most with what they're capable of? I know you must not remember much of what it was like in their territory, but you want to go there once the trials are over, don't you? Well, here is your chance. Easier than ever for you to slaughter the bastards without Nyaxia looking at you sideways for it."

My jaw tightened. Why did it bother me that she knew those things, about my past, my goals for the future? Why did it bother me that Vincent had told her all of that?

"I'm serious, Oraya." Her voice lowered. "Be careful with him. He's pretty, but he's still a Rishan."

I wanted to laugh in her face. As if I didn't know better than anyone exactly how wary I had to be around pretty vampire men. No, I didn't trust Raihn. I didn't even know if I especially liked him—*Really?* a voice whispered in the back of my head, at this thought—but I knew he hadn't done this. I knew it with unshakable certainty for one reason, and one reason alone: Mische.

I saw the devastation on his face when we found her. That was love. No one could fake that.

I bit my tongue as Jesmine sauntered off and slipped Vincent's parchment into my pocket.

I REMAINED AT Mische's bedside until it was time to meet with Vincent. She hadn't spoken since we dragged her out of the apartment, though her lashes shuddered as if with constant dreams. Her skin was burning hot—especially bad news for vampires, who were usually resistant to infection. I stood over her and dabbed at her with a cold washcloth, washing seeping pus from her wounds. I pulled up her sleeves and frowned at what I saw beneath them. The fresh Nightfire burns clustered around her wrists and hands, which had been exposed that night. But the smooth brown skin of her arms was dotted, too, with old burn scars—countless, all layered over each other. Some were clearly very old, and others much fresher, though not from the attack.

How could she have gotten these?

A mumbled whimper interrupted the thought. Mische stirred, her fingers shaking. I lowered her arm and leaned closer to her. She couldn't even move her head, and her eyes twitched, like she was trying to open them and failing.

It affected me more than I would have expected it to—seeing her this way. Before, Mische had flitted about like a butterfly, and now someone had ripped her wings off and left her here to wither.

You've known her for a month and a half, Vincent's voice reminded me. *And she would have killed you in that ring the moment the Halfmoon was over.*

True. And true.

Still.

"What is it, Mische?" I asked softly. "What?"

With great effort, she rolled her head over, revealing her face. Bruises darkened the hollows of her eyes and the corners of her lips with mottled black.

"He didn't come," she moaned. "He didn't answer me."

Raihn. A strange, unexpected pain twinged in my heart. If he knew that she had awoken and he wasn't there . . .

"Raihn is coming back. Soon."

I hoped.

Her eyelids fluttered, the cracked corner of her mouth tightening in an almost-smile. "Raihn? I know. Raihn always comes back."

The smile collapsed. A tear streaked her cheek. "I called and called," she whimpered. "I called and called but he wouldn't answer. He's left me."

"He's coming back," I said again, but she just kept weeping, faster and harder until she couldn't speak—until she couldn't even breathe.

I hurried to our packs, stacked in the corner of the room, and rummaged through them. The medical bag was well stocked, but not with anything strong enough to help her. Then my gaze fell to my pack. I dropped Mische's bag, went to mine, and withdrew the last potion I had left. It was mostly empty. Not much remained. It wouldn't be enough to heal Mische—not even close—but it would keep her alive through the night, and it would sedate her.

Still, I hesitated. This medicine was one of the few that could help me, as a human. I hadn't healed my own burns yet. And the Halfmoon Trial was right around the corner.

Mische let out another agonized sob. The sound cut through me, slicing the last of my restraint.

I couldn't listen to her like that. I couldn't.

I returned to her, tilted her head back, and poured in the final drops of the medicine. And I didn't leave her side as her tear-streaked face smoothed and she fell into sleep, heavy and dreamless as a child's.

CHAPTER TWENTY-SEVEN

I had never seen Vincent like this.

He was waiting for me when I arrived. Even in the shadows, the red on his wings painted his silhouette in crimson. The top three buttons of his shirt were undone, revealing his Heir Mark. The wisps of smoke that unfurled from delicate red ink lines pulsed with his heartbeat.

It was unusual for Vincent to leave his wings and his Mark visible, but those things, intimidating as they were, were not what made my stomach clench when I saw him.

Vincent was always calm—cruel when he needed to be, yes, but always elegantly restrained. Now, one look at his face, and I saw a foreign version of him, one that let rage simmer right at the surface of his skin. Normally, his temper was a smooth black sea, a tranquil surface hiding the horrors that lurked far beneath. Now, it shivered with building waves and circling fins.

I had never seen anything but safety when I looked at Vincent. But tonight, something in me recoiled at the sight of him—as if the eight-year-old version of myself insisted, *It looks just like your father, but it isn't him.*

Then he turned to me, and his eyes softened, and when his shoulders relaxed with a long breath of relief, mine did too.

No one who looked at me like that could be anything less than my father. And Goddess, I was relieved to see him.

He looked me up and down. "You're unhurt?"

I nodded.

"You avoided the worst of the attack?"

I caught the truth in my teeth. *Sure did, because I was off killing vampires in the human districts with my Rishan partner!* That would go over well.

I said, "Yes. I got lucky."

"I never wanted you to see times like these. I knew they would come, but I never wanted you to see them."

"It's the Rishan?" I asked, quietly. "You're sure?"

For some reason, I heard Raihn's voice from earlier today, speaking with such certainty: *The Rishan didn't do this.*

"Yes."

"Have they attacked elsewhere?"

His throat bobbed. "Yes. But in some ways, it is a blessing. It has been too long since I've had an opening to wipe them out once and for all. This time, I will not waste it."

He turned fully to me, the light falling over his face. It illuminated a constellation of red-black spatters over his shirt and throat—vampire blood. Darkness smeared his wrists, too, just at the boundary of his sleeve cuffs, and lingered under his fingernails. He'd probably hastily wiped his hands and face before coming here, but if he was trying to hide from me what he'd been doing these last two days, he failed miserably.

Fear, sudden and powerful, clenched in my chest.

I had lost Ilana. I didn't know if I could survive losing Vincent, too.

If the Rishan were indeed advancing, he would be their primary target. Every Rishan rebel in the House of Night understood that winning their war meant killing either a million Hiaj vampires . . . or only one: Vincent. He had no children—he knew intimately just how dangerous powerful offspring were. This meant the Hiaj clan had no Heir without him. No one to inherit the Hiaj Nightborn clan's power. No one to wield it.

When war broke out between the clans, killing the Heir and every person who could possibly inherit their power became the ultimate goal.

This, after all, was exactly what Vincent had done two hundred years ago. He had used his gift from Nyaxia—his prize for winning the Kejari—to enhance his own power and strip the Rishan Heir line of theirs. And then Vincent had used that immense strength to kill every Rishan that had any connection to their line, and kill every Hiaj that came before him in his own. Every Nightborn King, after all, was crowned on a throne of corpses.

I watched Vincent's gaze go distant, as if he, too, was thinking about that day, and an awful thought twisted in my stomach.

The Rishan had rebelled before, but never like this. This was fighting to win.

"Do you think they have an Heir again?" I asked.

Vincent had killed the entire Heir line two centuries ago. But Nyaxia, coldhearted bitch that she was, refused to let either clan die out. She liked her children squabbling. She would gift an Heir Mark to another Rishan, one day. The last time that had happened, it had taken more than three hundred years. Still, two hundred didn't seem impossible.

If the Rishan had an Heir line again, they were much more dangerous than if they didn't. They'd been known to have small rebellions in the past—like the one that brought me to Vincent—but those were headless skirmishes, driven by nothing but anger and revenge. They couldn't have ruled even if they had won.

But if there was a Rishan Heir again? Everything changed.

A muscle feathered in Vincent's jaw in a way that told me he had been thinking a lot about that very question.

"It is possible. If there is one, we will find out."

Fuck.

"If it is the case," he went on, "I'll need you, once we are bonded. We will have the freedom and the power to invade their territories. Liberate them." He gave me a sad smile. "I know how long you've wanted that. My only regret is that it has to be under such circumstances."

The thought dizzied me. A lifetime of fear and caution, and finally, the opportunity to leave my mark on the world, not with broken fingernails but with teeth that could bite just as deep as theirs.

My parents were dead. Whatever other family I may have had probably was, too. I knew that. And maybe . . . maybe a part of me hoped they were, because by the time I made it to them, I would be less like them than ever. But at least by then, I would be able to do more than pick off individual vampires in the night.

I could *be* something. *Do* something.

I swallowed the unexpected wave of emotion and gave Vincent a weak smirk.

"If I win."

He didn't return the smile. "You will win, Oraya."

Sometimes I didn't know what I had done to earn that kind of faith. I wished I was as certain as he was.

The Halfmoon Trial was days away. The grim reminder of the present crashed down over my dreams of the future. As if Vincent realized this too, he reached into his pocket, withdrawing a small vial of silver liquid. "More poison, for your blades. I haven't been able to get more medicine for you. Next time."

I winced and tried not to show it. Giving the last of my medicine to Mische might have been a mistake. I'd have to fight with the burn. Then again, I'd fought with worse.

I watched Vincent as he looked to the sky, deep in thought.

He seemed to have softened a bit since our visit began, but I was still wary of bringing up my next request. I knew how cold Vincent's wall of ice could be if he felt challenged. It always thawed for me—eventually—but I did not want to go into the Halfmoon Trial on bad terms with him.

Still . . . I had to try.

"There is one other thing," I said carefully. "There's a girl. One of my allies for the Halfmoon. She was injured very badly in the attack, but the Ministaer rejected her withdrawal from the Kejari. She won't survive the trial."

His lips thinned. "Unfortunate. Just more blood that the Rishan will have on their hands."

"Is there something you could do? To help her withdraw?"

His eyes flicked to me, his stare suddenly sharp. "Why?"

"She's my ally, and she's too weak to fight."

"Then let her die in the ring. Abandon her when the trial begins."

I fished through my memory of hundreds of hours spent studying the Kejari. "We don't know what the trial is. It could be something that links our fates. If she dies, I die. That has happened before. The sixth Kejari. The fourteenth."

Two. Two out of twenty. Still, he hesitated at this. I knew that even those odds were far too great for him.

After a moment of thought, he said, "Kill her tonight. Then she's no longer your problem."

I tried so hard to keep my expression neutral. Still, the shock struck me hard.

Why?

Not long ago, there would have been nothing shocking about that proposition. Actually, even more shocking now was that it hadn't even crossed my mind to kill Mische.

And most shocking of all was that the very thought filled me with revulsion.

Vincent narrowed his eyes just enough to show that he had noticed my change in behavior.

"What's the objection? The Kejari allows killing between the contestants this year. If she's that injured, she is useless to you as an ally in the trial itself, and only a danger afterward if she somehow manages to survive. It's the clean, simple solution."

I tried desperately to come up with an argument against this and failed. And now Vincent was watching me closely. I couldn't push back more. It would make him question so much about me.

Even now, the fact that I was having this struggle made me question so much about myself.

"No objection," I said. "You're right. But I still have one other problem."

I was pushing. I was pushing hard. But I let the words come anyway.

"That leaves me with only one other ally. And you have him."

"I do?" Vincent looked back to the sky, as if his mind was already beginning to drift. "Questioning is Jesmine's task."

I blinked, taken aback despite myself. Vincent had always been my only pillar of certainty, the only thing in my life that earned absolute trust. And yet . . . his ignorance felt . . . disingenuous.

"He was taken with the others today," I said.

"We need to find who did this, Oraya. And our enemies among the Kejari contestants are obvious suspects. I'm sure he will be returned in one piece before the trial, just like all the others, once Jesmine is confident of his innocence."

Our enemies among the Kejari contestants. I knew what Vincent did to his enemies.

"Of course. I just . . . I need him. The Halfmoon is the deadliest of the trials, and my survival depends on him."

Vincent's gaze leapt to me. "I know full well how dangerous the Halfmoon is," he snapped. "Do you think I'm not aware? Do you think I don't think about you, and that trial, and how deadly it is, *constantly?*" His mouth curled into a sneer that eerily echoed the one he had worn during his death-drenched speech. "Do you know what would make it more dangerous, little serpent? If you were paired with an ally who was merely waiting for the right time to stab you in the back."

"He needs me to survive that trial, too."

"And after?"

"And after, I'm ready to kill him when I need to." I spoke with definitive force, but the statement settled strangely on my tongue. "But right now, I need him."

The man who stared back at me was the king, not the father. His face was cold and hard. I took another step.

"He didn't do this, Vincent."

"How can you know that?"

"Because—" Mische. I didn't know how to explain that to him. "Trust me. He didn't."

"Trust." A scoff. "Do you understand how dangerous that word is?"

It was insulting that he even asked me such a thing. I had so many reasons to distrust Raihn. And maybe . . . maybe I had allowed myself to forget that more frequently than I should have.

But this . . . that look on his face when he saw the Palace burn-ing . . . I might not trust Raihn. But I trusted that.

"Don't break him," I said. "Question him, fine. But don't break him. Please."

Vincent stared stonily at me. For one terrifying moment, I won-dered if maybe I had done the exact opposite of what I should have—if perhaps my plea made him more suspicious than even Raihn's Rishan blood ever could.

He lowered his head and sighed. "Fine." When he turned back to me and his face fell into the light, he suddenly looked exhausted, his worry etched deep into every pinched line of his expression. "But this is wartime. We are surrounded by those who would like to see us dead. Don't forget those teeth of yours, little serpent. You will need them."

NYAXIA'S TEMPLE HAD to be the grandest building in Sivrinaj, a city of grand buildings, save only for the Nightborn castle and the Moon Palace. Nyaxia, of course, had many temples through-out the three Houses—every major city and even minor townships throughout the House of Night had one. But each House, in their capital, had one great tribute to their creator and Dark Mother. I'd heard that the House of Shadow's was a single black steel spire reaching up to the night sky, twice the height of even their grandest castles.

I rarely—fine, never—went to the Nightborn temple, located in the perfect geographic center of Sivrinaj. It was the first build-ing to be constructed here. When Sivrinaj had been built, the Nightborn—young vampires, created by Nyaxia less than a year before—had been rebuilding their kingdom after it had been oblit-erated by the human nations to the east. They had nothing but the bones of a dead society, fresh immortality, and infant magic that they didn't understand.

And yet, the first thing they did was build a fucking church. Not shelter. Not hospitals. A church. What a priority.

I hated it here.

Everything seemed to echo and hush at once. Far above me, silver metalwork and enchanted stained glass painted a night sky, the platinum stars slowly drifting across it. The light in here was cool and dim—all of it Nightflame, safely contained in hundreds upon hundreds of little crystal dome lanterns, which cast lazy mandalas across the ground.

It was silent. Speaking was forbidden on the main floors of the church. Nyaxia's acolytes gathered around the curved walls, faces inches from the fresco-painted plaster, as still and soundless as statues—meditating, apparently, on their utmost adoration of their goddess.

Sometimes I thought Nyaxia must have a hell of a sense of humor. Did she word it that way, I wondered? *Go build a temple to show me how much you love me. Make it nauseatingly beautiful. And then go inside of it and stare at the wall for fifteen hours at a time.*

Of course, Nyaxia had many other fanatical devotees, and many of them were much more interesting—and dangerous—than the dark acolytes. I hoped I went my entire life without encountering the worst of them.

Boring as they might be, at least the poor bastards had excellent discipline. They didn't even turn their heads as I walked by, even though I was bleeding—and, however I might want to deny it, nervous—which meant I probably smelled mouthwatering to them.

I traveled up staircase after staircase, winding my way up the floors of the church until I reached the top. The set of double doors, crafted from ancient carved wood, loomed over me.

I looked down at my hands. They were trembling.

Fuck that. No. If I was going in there, I wouldn't let it show for a moment—not for a single damned second—that I was frightened.

Fear is a series of physical responses.

I shook away the shiver on my skin and slowed my breathing to force my heart to do the same. I touched the hilts of my blades— both freshly filled with Vincent's poison—just to remind myself how easy it was to reach them.

I knocked on the door and opened it when I was called within.

It had been nearly a year—the last equinox festival—since I had seen the Ministaer this close. It shocked me all over again. When I was younger and I first heard the Ministaer speak, I questioned whether it was possible he was really two thousand years old. One look at him up close put those doubts to rest.

No, there were no wrinkles on his face, save for a couple of harsh lines at the corners of his eyes. But all of him just looked worn—everything too sharp and smooth at once. His skin was papery-thin, veins visible where it stretched tight over his jutting cheekbones, his tight lips, the lids of his dead-white eyes. They say that vampires' blood gets darker as they age. The Ministaer's must have been pure black.

He rose as I entered.

"Oraya. Daughter of the Nightborn. Welcome."

The muscles drew taut around his mouth, but it was a twitchy, uneven movement. Fitting for someone who hadn't known humanity in two millennia.

Yet he recalled my name immediately.

I shuddered.

"What do you have to offer Nyaxia this eve?" he asked.

I kept my face carefully neutral.

"You—" I had to correct myself. "Nyaxia rejected a request for withdrawal from the Kejari. One of my allies."

The Ministaer's expression did not change. "Nyaxia has her reasons."

"I come to you, Ministaer, to see if there is anything one could do to change her mind on this matter."

The Ministaer stared at me. His eyes—solid, milky white—didn't allow me to track their movement, but I knew he was looking me up and down. Goddess fucking damn him, I hated this man. Everything about him repulsed me.

"Is there *anything*," I said, drawing out the word, "anything at all, that I can offer Nyaxia that would ease the loss of this contestant?"

The Ministaer was silent for a long moment, and I thought that maybe I'd misjudged him. Then I stepped closer, and his nostrils twitched.

There it was. Hunger.

"Perhaps an offering of blood would suffice," he said. "To compensate for the lost blood offering of the contestant."

Every part of me recoiled at the way he looked at me. Despite myself, my heartbeat quickened. He must have felt it, because I glimpsed his dry, fleshy tongue dart out to slide along his lower lip.

"A small blood offering, then." I could barely choke out the words. "Human blood."

"Human?" The Ministaer made a strange sound that sounded like a laugh from someone who had never heard one before. But that grotesque smile disappeared as I extended my wrist, veins up, over his desk.

His eyelids fluttered. Lust. Pure lust.

He cradled my hand, placing his palm beneath mine. His skin was too smooth, too cold—exactly the same temperature as the rest of the air.

"Ah, this is far better," he purred.

I could not fucking believe I was doing this. My other hand crept to my weapon. Rested there.

Just in case.

I said, "Drink."

THE MOMENT I closed the door of our chambers, I collapsed onto an armchair. My wrist stung, the pain burning up my arm. I'd offered the right one—my non-dominant hand—but it was the same hand that my Nightfire wound was on, making that entire arm now a mangled mess of pain. My head was fuzzy, senses venom-smeared.

Raihn had still not returned, which I did not like.

I slumped further into the armchair and looked across the room. Mische slept, but even unconscious, little twitches of pain spasmed across her face.

I made a pragmatic decision.

If Mische died, Raihn would never be able to compete. And

I couldn't tell Vincent that I wouldn't kill her without earning—perhaps rightfully—his doubt. I did the only thing I could do.

I told myself this as my vision faded around Mische's sleeping form.

Told myself it even though I knew, somewhere deep inside, that I wouldn't have been able to thrust that knife into her chest.

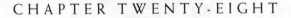

CHAPTER TWENTY-EIGHT

"... called and called and he didn't come."

I blinked away the remnants of my dream. My neck hurt fiercely, wedged at an awkward angle against the arm of the chair.

Across the room, a broad silhouette sat before Mische's bed, backlit by the lanterns.

"Why didn't he come?" she whimpered, over and over. "I can't get him to answer. I can't, I—"

Raihn murmured, "Don't worry about that right now."

"How can I worry about anything else? How can I—"

"Worry about getting better. Just rest. Can you do that?"

"I—"

But the silhouette shifted, his hand going to her face—perhaps using magic—and Mische went silent.

I struggled to fight the haze of sleep. Vampire venom was a sedative. The Ministaer's, old as he was, hit me hard.

I ignored the spinning room and pushed myself upright. Raihn rose, very slowly. Something was odd about the movement, but I couldn't place what. He turned, just enough to show me the profile of his face. He raised a finger to his lips, then nodded to the door to the next room.

When I stood, the floor tilted so sharply I was sure I'd topple over. Somehow I managed to follow Raihn into the adjoining bedroom. When I closed the door behind me, the shock was enough to jerk me from the remnants of my haze.

The back of Raihn's shirt, once white linen, was soaked through with blood. The stains bloomed over his back like flowers—some patches of dry near-black, some streaks of stiffening burgundy, some blotches of fresh dark crimson. It covered the full expanse of his form, plastering the fabric to his flesh and dousing the tips of his hair.

"Fuck," I whispered.

He let out a light scoff, then seized, as if the expression had hurt. "Yes."

"I—what—what happened?"

What a stupid fucking question. As if I didn't know exactly what would happen to the Rishan in questioning.

Raihn kept his back to me. His arms lifted, the movement stiff and stilted.

"How is Mische?" he asked.

"She's been—"

As if he hoped the answer would distract him, he yanked his shirt off over his head.

"—the same." The words deflated.

Raihn's body went rigid with pain for several long seconds.

"*Fuck*," I whispered.

"*Fu-u-u-u-ck*," he agreed, in a ragged hiss.

There was so much blood on his back that at first, I couldn't even tell what I was looking at. Only the harsh side-lighting of the lanterns cut through it, orange light defining the borders of the brutal wounds. The two gashes were symmetrical, running down each side of his back from the curve of his shoulder, over his shoulder blades, all the way to the dips at the base of his spine. They were deep, the flesh split in layer-by-layer—deep enough that I could have sworn I saw the movement of muscle as his back shifted.

Not a single strike. Nothing quick. No, the skin had been carefully flayed away, a fine network of wounds fanning out in all directions from the cuts.

Another mark ran down the center of his back, too—a large diamond-shaped patch of mottled flesh over his shoulders, which then continued down his spine. The blood covered so much that I wasn't sure if it was a part of his fresh injuries or something older.

I was speechless, even though I shouldn't have been. It wasn't the first time I had seen the results of torture. I knew that the Nightborn Guard was relentless. Trained to wield pain as just another weapon.

And yet, a dizzying bolt of rage speared me at the sight of it. Rage, and strange betrayal, and a single sentence: *I told him not to break him.*

And Vincent had looked me in the eye and agreed.

How old were the freshest of these wounds? How many had been inflicted after I had spoken to him? Did he know he was lying to me when he said it?

These questions shook me, hard, one after the other like arrows. Immediately, the voice in the back of my head smoothed over the sharpest of their accusations—*he has a million other things on his mind; he had nothing to do with it; he had to do what was right for his kingdom.*

But deep, deep inside my heart, somewhere I wouldn't look at too closely, I could feel it. A crack.

"Your wings," I choked out. "Are they—"

Raihn gave me a weak smirk over his shoulder. "This happened because I refused to reveal my wings. Made the right choice, don't you think?"

The relief at this was short-lived.

He still had his wings, yes. But conjuring them with these wounds, right where they would connect to his body . . . it would be agonizing, if not impossible, until they healed.

I swallowed thickly.

"That needs to be treated," I said. "Cleaned. Stitched up."

"Mische has a pouch of supplies in her pack." He started to turn, then winced and gave me an apologetic look. "Could you—"

I nodded and went to the next room, grabbing Mische's bag and returning. Raihn was exactly where I'd left him, like moving even slightly was too much for him.

"Could you—could you kneel in front of the bed, maybe?" I said. "You could lean on it."

"You implying I can't keep myself upright, princess?"

I wasn't *implying* anything. The minute I started stabbing, I was certain he'd double over and rip all the stitches out. Even if he had the pain tolerance of a statue. *Statues* would fucking crumble at that.

Apparently my face had changed, because he rasped a laugh. "I concede. Fine. You got me. You're right."

"I could try to find some alcohol," I offered.

"I'll be sending you off into the human districts to bring me some of that piss beer after this."

"You'll have earned it," I said, and meant it.

He chuckled again—Mother, I almost felt bad for making him do that—and slowly turned around.

The torture, it seemed, had been limited to his back. A small mercy for him. There wasn't a scratch on the front of his torso, though little scars nicked his skin, clearly much older than tonight. Warm light cascaded over the swells and valleys of his flesh— illuminating the landscape of his muscular form and highlighting every raised or pitted scar.

In any other moment, I might have wished I could freeze time there. He looked like a painting. Beautiful, but also interesting, every expanse of skin whispering of another story, another past.

The strange, irrational, overwhelming urge to step closer—to touch him—hit me in a wave, crashing and then mercifully subsiding.

I swallowed and pushed away those thoughts. "Kneel there. I'll sit behind you."

He obeyed, each movement slow and stiff. So painfully different from his typical grace. He kneeled at the edge of the bed and leaned against it, his arms crossed over the bedspread.

I sat behind him. Up close, the wounds looked even worse.

I let out a hiss through my teeth. How could I even begin to close these?

"That sounds promising," Raihn said.

"I just—I'm sorry for what I'm about to do to you."

"I'm glad your bedside manner is about as delicate as I would have expected."

I didn't even crack a smile.

I rummaged through the medical bag. Mische had everything in here—disinfectants, needles, string, bandages, even little splints. I pulled out the disinfectant and hoped that it was magically enhanced in some way.

"You want a warning?" I asked.

"Probably not—FUCK."

His hands clenched the bedspread as I poured the disinfectant over his back.

"I figured you were least expecting it then."

"You figured right," he grunted.

I strung the needle, eyeing his wounds. I felt like I was preparing for a whole other trial.

Trials. The thought of the word made my chest clench. Vampires healed much, much faster than humans. But . . . fuck, how could he compete like this?

"You've got to talk to me through this," Raihn said. "A whole conversation. Then you'll be in as much pain as I am."

I choked out a laugh at that, though I quickly tried to disguise it as a scoff.

"I have to stitch you up *and* talk to you?"

No warning, he'd said.

So I didn't give him any as I began stitching.

His entire body tensed. The bedspread shifted as he clutched it tighter.

"You alright?" I asked.

"Define 'alright.'"

"Alive."

He scoffed. "Glad you have such high standards."

I didn't want to ask. But I had to, even though I already hated the answer I knew was coming. "What did they ask you?"

"Ask. You make it sound so polite—*fff.*" He hissed as I made another stitch. "They wanted to know what I knew about the attack." His voice took on an exaggerated flat, hard edge, mimicking Jesmine's. "Was I sympathetic to the Rishan cause? Did I know

of the assailants? Had I ever summoned Nightborn demons before? Was I aware of an organized Rishan rebellion? Mostly, they
wanted to know if I destroyed the fucking Moon Palace."

Did you? I almost asked. Vincent's words echoed in my ears. I
had little reason to trust Raihn.

But I didn't say it aloud. I didn't because I already knew that the
answer was no, and already knew I believed him. Even if Vincent
thought I was a fool for it.

"You said you don't think this was Rishan work."

"No. I don't."

"Why?"

"The Rishan aren't organized anymore. Your dear father has
done a wonderful job whittling them down over the last few centuries. They couldn't get their shit together enough to do this."

They. Not *we.* But then, I hadn't seen Raihn so much as speak
to any of the other Rishan contestants here. Not that that was unusual. Vampires were territorial and unfriendly creatures. Hell,
most of the Hiaj didn't talk to each other, either.

"I told them that, too," Raihn chuckled, then seized, fingers
tightening again. "Didn't seem to believe me."

I eyed the wounds before me. No, they didn't. They didn't believe him for hours and hours and hours. They didn't believe him,
by my estimation, dozens and dozens of times.

I decided to give him good news, because he probably needed it.
"The Ministaer accepted Mische's withdrawal."

"He *what*?" He tensed, as if his instinct was to whirl around to
look at me and he had to stop himself.

"Nyaxia must have changed her mind."

He let out a long, long sigh—so relieved he didn't even flinch at
the next stitch.

"You did this," he said, finally.

I blinked. He thought better of me than I thought, for him to
come to that conclusion so quickly. It was . . . touching.

"No," I said. "Maybe they realized it just made the most sense."

"You're a terrible actress." I could hear the smile in his voice.
Warm enough to ease the sting in my right hand. Almost warm

enough to make me forget the way the Ministaer's lips felt against my skin.

"We can take her somewhere when the sun sets," I said.

"I'll figure something out. Hopefully she'll still be too groggy to argue."

Three more stitches. I had to pause to wipe my hands with Raihn's discarded shirt, leaving smears of red-black on the few clean patches left.

Raihn said softly, as if he didn't mean to speak, "I haven't seen her like this in a very, very long time."

"Her wounds are already starting to heal."

"I'm not worried about those. It's . . ."

He trailed off. In the silence, Mische's agonized words echoed in my head.

He left me. I called and called and he wouldn't come.

Only now did it occur to me that she hadn't been talking about Raihn.

"Do you know what she was trying to do, when we found her?" he said, voice full of quiet wrath. "She was trying to call upon Atroxus. Her magic failed her and she couldn't get it back. She was there with those demons and that fucking Nightfire begging her god for help. If she died there, the last thing she heard would have been his silence."

His fingers tightened around the fabric as I made another stitch.

"I told her it would happen. It hurt her every time she used that magic. And I told her, I fucking *told* her, that one day he would stop answering. That the God of the Sun wouldn't keep allowing one of *Nyaxia's children*"—he spat the term in disgust—"to draw upon his power. But she just . . ."

The burns on Mische's arms. Years' and years' worth. Suddenly so much made sad, morbid sense.

"How was she ever able to do it?" I asked. "Wield that magic?"

"She was a priestess. Before. When she was human."

My brows leapt. "A priestess of Atroxus?"

"Mhm. In Pachnai. Came here for some kind of missionary work. Isn't that something?" A short laugh, cut off with a wince.

"Missionaries coming to preach to fucking vampires. And that's when it happened. Whoever Turned her just left her there to die. Probably figured he had a nice little eternal slave if she lived, and at least got a decent meal out of it if she didn't. Decided she was too much trouble when she got sick and left. She didn't even know what he was doing to her."

I had long ago grown accustomed to the careless cruelty of the vampires. But it still sickened me to imagine what Mische, a foreigner barely older than a teenager, must have gone through.

I thought again of the Ministaer's mouth on my skin, just hours ago. Thought of a kiss on my throat, and teeth, and pain—then jerked back to reality when Raihn cursed because I jabbed him a little too hard.

"Sorry." I steadied my hand. "Who? Who was it?"

"I wish I fucking knew. I don't even know what House she is. She won't tell me. If I found out . . ."

He let out a low breath that made all sorts of wordless promises.

Fuck, I'd help.

"The thing that kills me," Raihn said, "is that the bastard didn't even know or care that he was taking literally everything from her. Didn't even give enough of a shit to drag her to civilization before leaving her to die. And now . . ."

And now the final vestige of her humanity was gone.

"They don't care," I said softly. "They never care."

"No. They never fucking care. And sometimes—" He tensed. Maybe because of the stitch. Maybe not. "Sometimes I'm ashamed to call myself one of them."

I don't want to watch you become one of them, Ilana had said to me.

And until now—until this exact moment—I hadn't even thought about it as giving something up. Not until I heard the ache in Raihn's voice that had nothing to do with the wounds on his back.

"What was it like?" I asked. "Turning?"

"Ix's tits. Your bedside manner really is awful, princess."

I could hear the expression on his face. My mouth tightened. Almost a smile.

I didn't think he would answer, but he said, "It feels like death. I don't remember most of it."

"Who—?"

"Now *that's* a question I can't answer in a moment like this." The cadence of a joke. The edge of a rebuke. Fair enough.

I finished the last two stitches, then admired my handiwork.

"How does it look?" he asked.

I answered honestly. "Fucking awful."

He sighed. "Terrific."

Blood still covered the rest of his back. I took the towel and gently wiped it away—from his shoulders, his sides, and finally, down the middle of his spine.

There, I paused, the cloth half raised. I had been right—the mark down the center of his back was a scar, a big one, far older than the marks from tonight. It carved a large triangle across his upper back, then trailed all the way down its center. A burn, maybe?

"How did you get this?"

"No, no, no. That isn't how this works." With a grunt of pain, he rose. "I don't need to be distracted anymore, which means that I don't have to answer your questions."

I stood, too, wincing as I stretched the stiff fingers of my right hand. He turned to me, the corner of his mouth quirked, clearly about to say something insulting—but then he noticed me rubbing my bandaged wrist, and his face changed.

The smirk was gone.

"What's that?"

"Nothing. A little cut."

"*What happened*, Oraya?"

The intensity of his voice struck me in places I didn't expect.

"Nothing happened," I said, tucking my hand away. "It's from the attack."

His eyes searched my face, unblinking. They looked redder than ever in the firelight, reflecting the orange of the lanterns behind me. He didn't believe me, but he didn't say so.

I reached into the medicine bag and pulled out a little glass bottle of tablets. I took his hand and placed the vial in it. "Here. They won't heal you, but at least they'll help the pain enough for you to sleep."

I didn't know why I didn't remove my hand. Nor why I didn't step back, even though he was so close—close enough his body heat surrounded me.

I swallowed. "I'm sorry. I'm sorry that he did this to you."

"It isn't your fault."

Still. I felt it, even if I didn't know why.

And I still didn't move when he said, "One honest thing, Oraya. Do you want a different partner for the Halfmoon Trial?"

I knew why he was asking. Because now it was just me and him. Because his back was destroyed. Because he couldn't use his wings.

"You could find one," he went on. "People died in the attack. They left partners behind. I would understand."

It surprised me that the answer was so clear, so immediate.

"Too late for that. You're stuck with me."

I watched his lips curl. The smile looked real. Different than the smirks.

"The one human and mangled vampire," he murmured. "The others should be trembling in pure fucking terror."

I surprised myself by returning it.

"They'd better."

My hand still lay over Raihn's calloused palm. His fingers curled around mine, as if in silent agreement.

One more day.

When the Halfmoon was over, we would be enemies. Maybe this felt something like intimacy, but soon, we would try to kill each other.

I never forgot that.

Tonight, though, my soul was heavy—with Raihn's torture and Mische's past, with Vincent's lies and the dark memories stirred by the Ministaer's mouth on my skin. Maybe I was weak. Maybe I was foolish.

But even though I knew I should pull away, I didn't.

No, I drank up Raihn's touch like one last gulp of wine. A secret, shameful vice.

MISCHE WANTED TO stay. Even in her half-conscious, delirious state, she protested as Raihn carried her from the Moon Palace. He had some friends, he told me, who would take her away from Sivrinaj and care for her until she recovered. I was secretly glad she was not only leaving the Kejari, but leaving Sivrinaj entirely. I couldn't shake the feeling that things here would get far worse before they got better.

She was conscious when I said goodbye to her. She gave my hand a weak squeeze when I approached—and I let her, even though I didn't like goodbyes.

"Take care of yourself," I told her.

"You too. Keep feeding that shy magic." Her weak smile softened. "And . . . keep an eye on him, alright?"

She didn't need to specify who.

"He acts tough, but he needs someone. And he likes you."

No, he doesn't, I wanted to say. *He shouldn't. The worst possible thing he could do is like me.*

But I just gave Mische my best attempt at a comforting smile and said, "Rest. Get better quickly."

To which she gave me an equally weak, but much brighter, wave. "I'll see you soon."

WE WERE SUMMONED only hours later. Raihn and I didn't speak to each other on the walk there—what was there to say? We only nodded at each other in grim acceptance of our task.

We all stood in awkward silence in the great room. The only sounds were the hushed whispers shared between teammates. I looked around the room, carefully memorizing who had paired with whom. Three House of Blood contestants stood together. Beside them, Angelika and her partner, a slight blood magic user by the name of Ivan. Ibrihim had managed to find a partner, a Shadow-born man, who had also been badly injured in the last trial. Apparently no one else would have them. Neither looked pleased.

They weren't the only ones who appeared to have paired up out of sheer necessity. Four other Rishan contestants now partnered with each other—presumably out of last-minute changes, dumped by their previous partners after Jesmine's torture. I eyed them and tried not to show it, a knot in my stomach.

Their backs were sealed beneath layers of armor, but they moved stiffly, and I could imagine what they looked like. Still, they didn't seem to be in as much pain as Raihn, who couldn't even get into his own armor. I had to strap the leather over his back while he gripped the edge of the bureau and cursed through teeth so tight I was sure he'd crack them. He hid it now, though, and well, tucking every wince and slow movement away. This was not the time to show weakness.

I saw it anyway.

Vampires healed fast, but his wounds had improved only a little. I was disappointed, but not surprised. Nightborn soldiers wielded all kinds of tricks—poison, magic, whatever it took—to inflict as much pain as their task warranted. Raihn's, apparently, had warranted it all.

As I watched the other Rishan, I couldn't help but wonder if his had been worse. If he had been kept longer, tortured more, because of his connection to me.

He nudged my arm, snapping me from my thoughts. "We're famous," he muttered, motioning to the other side of the room, where several Hiaj contestants stared.

We did make one of the more . . . unusual pairs.

"They're jealous," I said flatly, and he chuckled.

"We'll give them a show."

Mother, I hoped so.

We all waited in silence—prepared to be spirited away at any moment. But instead, a string of Nyaxia's acolytes filed into the room. Each bore a silver goblet. They stopped at each set of allies, offering them the cup.

They didn't say a word—ours didn't even lift his eyes—but the unspoken message was clear: *drink*.

Raihn took the goblet first, making a face of disgust as he swallowed. "Unpleasant, but not poison," he said, after a moment, and passed it to me.

The liquid was dark red, nearly black, and thick. Faint smoke rolled from its surface. It smelled slightly musty. I couldn't even begin to imagine its purpose. I'd studied every Kejari, and none included a start like this.

I drank. *Ugh*. Raihn was right. It was disgusting.

I glanced at him after handing the goblet back to the acolyte, and the corner of his mouth curled. "Good lu—"

CHAPTER TWENTY-NINE

Feathers.

Feathers everywhere. Black, smothering, so dark that all color curled up and died in them.

Everything was distant and numb. I could not get my mind to work well enough to process any of it.

The feathers shifted. Light seeped between them. Or . . . no, not light. Eyes. Gold eyes. Terrible, cruel gold eyes.

I blinked, and then the eyes became a face that glared down at me from above. A man, with severe features and a neat beard and long black hair that flew out behind him, mingling with the wings that unfolded around us both.

I had never seen this person before. And yet, the sight of him filled me with paralyzing terror.

I blinked again, and the winged man's face was replaced with another one. This one, I did know. I knew every angle of it. I pretended I didn't see it every time I closed my eyes.

My old lover leaned close to me, so close the familiar cool of his breath ghosted over my cheek. "Did you miss me?" he whispered.

I struggled but couldn't move.

Blink. The two faces merged, changing back and forth with every pulse of my panicked heartbeat.

They grabbed my hand, pressed it to their chest—pressed it to the gaping wound there, right in the center. They leaned closer. Their lips touched my ear.

"Did you miss me?"

Their blood was hot on my hand, running all the way down my forearm, as I struggled, frantic, with nowhere to go.

MY ARM WAS warm and wet. My heartbeat was out of control. Sharp pain shot up my back. I was in pitch darkness, and yet, too many sensations surrounded me—like two different worlds were colliding, each feeding me conflicting information.

Oraya.

This was wrong. Something was very, very wrong.

Oraya! Calm down. Breathe.

But even my own thoughts were lost, like my mind had become a gaping, cavernous maze I no longer knew how to navigate. Something else was here, something was—

ORAYA. CALM THE FUCK DOWN.

So loud it shocked my thoughts into silence. Raihn's voice. It was Raihn's voice booming through the back of my skull.

But . . . in my *mind*. Not my ears.

Breathe, Oraya. Both of us. We need to—we need to calm down. Alright?

For a moment I questioned my sanity.

I felt a shiver of wry amusement up my spine—a wordless, soundless chuckle—and it was such a bizarre sensation it nearly sent me spiraling again.

You aren't alone in that, princess.

I put my hands straight out in front of me. I could see nothing, but they lay flat against smooth, toothy stone. The cold unyielding firmness steadied me.

And yet, even though my palms were now pressed firmly against the wall, I felt something else, too—felt them wrapped around the hilt of a sword. Felt the way my muscles strained to lift it, and a shock of pain up my back as I did.

My hands were here.

My hands were there.

"That's you," I gasped. "I'm feeling *you*."

My physical voice felt dull and flat compared to the one in my head.

Yes, Raihn answered.

A mind bonding. The potion. It must have been a spell. It would take rare, powerful magic to forge a temporary bond like this—but I supposed Nyaxia's church had all the resources to make the impossible possible.

Ix's fucking tits.

Another uncanny vibration up my spine. I shuddered.

Don't do that.

What? Laugh?

It feels strange.

The laughter *is what feels strange? That's what goes too far for you? How fitting.*

Strange was an understatement. Every single part of me railed against the unwelcome presence in my thoughts—each nerve and muscle screamed at the additional weight of another set of senses thrust upon them.

Fuck, Oraya, do you feel this tense all the time?

I was too embarrassed to admit that too often, I did.

Special circumstances, I replied instead. *You're just as bad.*

The truth. His anxiety was just as strong as mine. Different—a rolling undercurrent rather than staggering waves—but every bit as powerful.

If it was this overwhelming in just a dark box, what was this going to be like when we were actually in battle? It almost made me sick just to think about it. I felt the echoing pang of Raihn's concern, too.

Well, we'd have to make it work. Half of the contestants would die today. We needed to get out of here.

I ran my hands along the wall, and felt Raihn doing the same, wherever he was. Smooth stone here, smooth stone there.

Cells. They were cells.

That made sense. Nyaxia and Alarus had been imprisoned by the gods of the White Pantheon as punishment for their unlawful relationship. Nyaxia might have been a lesser goddess then, and Alarus weakened to a fraction of his former power, but it still proved to be an unwise decision. The two of them fought their way out of captivity, slaughtering exactly half of the keepers of Extryn, the legendary prison of the Pantheon.

This must be our Extryn.

We'll probably have to fight through whatever's out there together, when we get out, I told Raihn as we both felt around the walls of our enclosures. *Let's get these open.*

Once we found each other, we would be nearly unstoppable. I was certain of that.

I'm touched that you think so, Raihn replied, sensing that thought. I wasn't sure what to make of the fact that he actually was, and I felt it.

Here. Look.

My fingertip hit a little patch of metal, high up in the corner of my cell. I pressed down, and stone shifted. *Click.*

The door swung open, letting in a flood of cool light—from the stars, the moon, and the hundreds of torches floating above the colosseum. It was night, but compared to the darkness of the cell, it blinded me.

I blinked into it for half a second. And when my eyes adjusted, I almost let out a laugh, just because what the fuck else was I supposed to do?

Before me was carnage. Just utter carnage. Most of the contestants hadn't even made it out of their cells yet, and the sand was already soaked with blood. Monsters tore each other apart in the arena—every kind of beast one could possibly imagine. Demons like the ones from the first trial, this time with knobby, milky-white wings. Massive cats, black with gray spots and bright red eyes—creatures I'd only ever seen in storybooks, from the House of Shadow. Hellhounds—enormous, hunched wolves with pure white fur, darkness rolling from their skin. They roamed the dunes of the House of Night in packs and had been known to slaughter entire settlements.

Far beyond all of that—past all that certain death—was a wall made of piled white stone, cutting across the center of the colosseum.

A rocky path led up to its peak. Two golden doorways stood at the top, tall and narrow, pulsing with silver smoke. The stands were packed, a sea of shrieking faces surrounding the arena, thrilled by the most dramatic of the Kejari trials.

Another vision collided with this one as Raihn's door swung open and he took in a mirror image of this sight—from, I realized, the other side of the wall.

Fuck, he murmured.

Fuck was right.

Iron boxes like the one I had just stumbled out of lined the outskirts of the sand pit. The one right beside me was still closed, and the muffled sound of wordless screaming came from within. Another door opened and one of the Shadowborn contestants stumbled from their cell, clutching their head, only to wander straight into the jaws of a hellhound.

What the hell was wrong with him?

Many can't exactly handle the weight of multiple minds, Raihn answered. *Not like this.*

Through Raihn's eyes, I watched another man fall to his knees and struggle to rise. Maybe we were lucky that Mische wasn't here, after all. I couldn't imagine trying to support both of them.

I looked back to the wall and the doorways at its peak. Our goal, clearly. Or . . . one of them was. Extryn was a place of cruel chance, after all. No doubt one would lead to freedom, and one would lead to damnation.

But between us and that threat were so many more. I steeled myself as I looked out into the sea of teeth and claws and blood before me. Across the colosseum, Raihn did the same.

You ready? I asked him.

He was already lifting his sword. *Always.*

We threw ourselves into the onslaught.

At first, it was a struggle. The weight of Raihn's mind weighed heavily on my own. I lost precious seconds to separating his senses from mine. I kept myself alive—barely—as I fought across the first stretch of the arena, but I was clumsy, allowing too many close calls.

Stop resisting it, Raihn snapped at me. *Lean into it. That's the only way we make it through.*

It went against every single instinct I had. But he was right—I couldn't fight him inside my mind and still focus on keeping myself alive.

We'd trained for this, I reminded myself. Not knowingly, but . . . we'd learned to accommodate each other, to anticipate and understand each other's unspoken cues. Our partnership had never been about brute strength. It had always been about compromise.

This? This was just a matter of giving ourselves over to it.

And once we did that, we became a source of strength to each other, another well to draw upon. We might have been separated, but it was like we were back fighting side-by-side in the slums. I felt every strike he made, and he felt every one of mine.

Still, even as we found our rhythm, every step grew more treacherous. The beasts—clearly starved—were more numerous and agitated closer to the barrier. Worse, by now, all the other contestants were out of their cells. And we all understood acutely that our primary competition wasn't the hellhounds or the demons—it was each other.

Only half of us would remain after this. We fought like it.

We were all forced together into the sands. Early in the trial, a Hiaj contestant tried to fly up above the carnage, only to immediately fall to the ground, wings shredded. A barrier. Wings or no, there was no avoiding the pit of death.

I was barely halfway across the arena, and already, I had to strike down someone every step. And perhaps Raihn's presence in my mind fueled me, but it would have been a hell of a lot more helpful if he was actually beside me.

I don't understand, I thought, frustrated. *What is the point of this? We can't actually* fight *together this way.*

But before he could respond, pain sliced across my arm. I stumbled, losing precious ground to the Shadowborn woman who had come after me. I glanced down to see smooth unbroken leather armor on my own arm, but Raihn saw a trail of blood over his.

He paid for that moment of distraction as his attacker lunged for him again, again, again. I gritted my teeth and struggled to push back my own, at last shoving her into the grip of a nearby demon. But across the arena, I felt Raihn's fight continue. He wasn't faring as well. I flinched with every blow.

The memory of the demons from the first trial hit me, and with it came sudden realization.

Just now, Raihn had been hurt . . . and *I* had stumbled.

Who is that? I asked him. His vision came in broken flashes. I couldn't see a face.

What?

Who is that you're fighting right now? Look at his face!

I felt Raihn's confusion, but he obeyed. As he countered the next blow, he showed me his attacker—a Hiaj Nightborn man with fair hair.

I knew him. Nikolai. I racked my memory. Who had he been paired with?

Ravinthe. *He has a bad right knee,* Vincent had told me at the feast.

I scanned the crowd. We were lucky. Ravinthe wasn't far from me, just a few strides across the pit. I dove for him. Didn't give him time to react—my weapon went for his right knee, a direct hit. His leg folded up beneath him, blood spurting. I plunged my blade into his chest before he had time to rise.

And just as I suspected, across the arena, Raihn's opponent fell.

Shit, he whispered, a spark of pleasure spearing us both as he seized the opportunity to finish Nikolai. *You're good.*

We were separated, but that didn't mean we couldn't still help each other. With this knowledge, we cut across the battlefield. Yes, we needed to get to those gates as quickly as possible, but each of us sacrificed small gains in speed to help the other, and that give-and-take meant that as a team, we moved swiftly.

But the contestants who still remained were strong, too. The Bloodborn, in particular, knew how to compete together. One of them was the first to broach the wall of stone, fighting her way up the winding path to the top. She had nearly made it by the time I reached the wall. It looked more like a mountain up close, a looming pile of stacked rock. The path to its crest was steep and precarious.

Two others were ahead of me, chopping through stray hellhounds and demons that had made their way up.

Three coming up on this side, I told Raihn.

Two over here.

You'd better get here quick.

Only half of us would make it. Eleven.

Almost there.

I could see the path through his eyes, just a few strides ahead. We were both so, so close.

But I made it only a few steps up the path when excruciating pain tore through my back, then my shoulder. My knees hit the ground, a gasp ripping through me.

It took a few seconds to realize it wasn't my body being slashed open, but Raihn's. His sight was just a smear of clattering weapons—a cloud of red smoke—a flash of white hair.

Angelika.

I tried to pull myself up, braced against the rocks.

Go, Raihn told me. *Keep going. I can handle her.*

No. He couldn't lie, not with our minds locked together. Not when I could feel each wound she opened on his body and how hard he struggled to keep up.

Healthy, Angelika and Raihn were almost evenly matched. But Raihn had just endured hours of torture.

Today, they were not evenly matched.

I didn't even think about the decision. I turned back.

I have this, Oraya. Go!

I ignored him.

It took me a few minutes to find Angelika's partner, Ivan, in the escalating chaos. I had to double back far—all the way down the wall. I found him in the thick of the fighting in the sands, dealing a weak finishing blow to a jaguar. He was injured, each step slow and limping.

This would be easy. It would just take me a few minutes to pick him off, and with him, Angelika.

Ivan saw me coming barely in time to react. A wave of acidic agony hit me as the red mist of his magic surrounded us. The wounds on his arms quivered with exertion—with the blood he had to use to fuel it.

I didn't even let it slow me. I hit his arm, the poison eating at his skin immediately.

In Raihn's battle, Angelika faltered. He took that opening, levied a strike—

Just as Ivan pulled back, his magic swelling. It nearly incapacitated me, unbearable paired with Raihn's wounds. But I pushed through it, rolled, lunged. My blade sliced Ivan's good leg to the bone.

It collapsed beneath him.

The two of us landed in a tangle on the ground. My battle with Ivan and Raihn's with Angelika blended together, each reduced to wild flashes of burning muscles and blood and steel and magic.

I rolled on top of Ivan, pinning him.

Pain slithered across my ribs.

Not mine—Raihn's. Running out of time.

I looked right into Ivan's eyes as I raised my blade, holding him still between my knees, his back pressed to the stone of the wall.

And I was looking so intently at him that I almost didn't notice the movement out of the corner of my vision.

Raihn looked over Angelika's shoulder—looked up, at the gates of victory. The Bloodborn woman had reached the top. She paused between the two doors, clearly hesitant. A Shadowborn man was not far behind her. He ran, not slowing, as he crested the top.

And he didn't hesitate as he shoved her through one of the arches, forcing her to test the decision.

I seized up as the ground shook beneath me. I looked up just in time to see the flash of light from the gate consume everything.

Just in time to hear, in the mind that we shared, Raihn scream my name.

Just in time to feel a wave of pain as Ivan buried his dagger in my side.

And I had no time to react as his magic seized hold of my blood, my muscles. Forced them to move without my permission.

And hurled me into the thick of the bloodthirsty beasts.

CHAPTER THIRTY

Vincent had always warned me about what it would be like to be caught in a frenzy. "They will not wait until you are dead," he said. "There is no sense. There is no thought. There is only hunger."

I had thought about those words a lot in the days after Ilana's death. What I had heard that first night in the Moon Palace sounded just as Vincent had described. She had been devoured alive, and she had been powerless to do anything about it. Her final moments haunted me.

Now, as my body flung me into a mass of starving animals, my muscles beyond my reach for pivotal seconds, only one thought stuck in my mind:

Was this how she felt when she died?

Ivan's magic paralyzed me. I couldn't move, but I was conscious as those beasts descended upon me.

The animals had been provoked into a delirium by the violence and starvation. They had formed tightly packed groups, all twitching muscles and foaming mouths, as if perhaps some part of them knew that it was their only chance at survival.

For a split second, it struck me as deeply sad. They were just animals, after all. Killers reduced to prey for entertainment. Just like all of us, really.

I felt it when the first one, a demon, grabbed ahold of my leg.

Immediately, I was surrounded by so many that they completely shadowed the sky. All I saw was teeth and claws.

I couldn't even scream.

Oraya!

Raihn's panic flooded me. It was just as intense as my own.

I didn't know what to make of that.

But something about that panic jolted through me, the burst of it sharp enough to cut through the remnants of Ivan's magic. My hands flew out, stabbing wildly.

It wasn't enough.

There were so many of them. I was bleeding too much. Blood was bad. Blood was dangerous. I lashed out with my blades, but it was futile panic in an endless sea of flesh and skin and fur and feathers.

I was going to die. Mother, I was going to die. My heartbeat was wild. Every pump of blood brought them closer.

I'm coming for you, Oraya.

I didn't like that. How *scared* Raihn sounded. He had managed to slip Angelika, and he was running, running, running, pushing through the crowd on his side of the wall.

He wouldn't be fast enough.

Use your magic, he urged. I saw flashes of his vision as he ran—sprinting up the unsteady stone of his path.

You aren't even far from the end. Use it right now.

I couldn't. I couldn't grip my own power—even when I could, I produced little more than wisps of light. I fought and thrashed and struggled to calm myself, and—

I told myself, *Fear is a collection of—*

Fear is the fucking KEY to it, Oraya! Raihn's voice, booming with fear of his own, filled both of our minds. *USE IT. Pretend that you're throwing me out the fucking window. Pretend that you're dragging Mische out of that burning apartment.*

Shameful tears pricked my eyes.

I didn't know how. Didn't know how to let go of that wall within myself. I'd built it for so long, cemented over every crack. Now I clung to it. Terrified of what would happen if I let myself fall.

I'm with you, Oraya. Right now. You don't have time. We'll go together.
Alright? I'm with you.

That should have terrified me.

The beasts overwhelmed me. My back hit the sand. A demon crawled over me, its face inches from mine. It went for my throat— right there on the side, right where I had a scar that reminded me of the boy I tried not to think about every night.

Now, I let myself. Let myself think of him for the first time in so many years.

Let myself think of my parents, crushed in a broken building in a war that had nothing to do with them.

Let myself think of a little lost girl with dark hair hunted in a maze. A little girl with dark hair left alone in a ruined city.

Let myself think of a lifetime spent here, trapped by my own fear, trapped by these fucking predators, these monsters, these things that didn't see me as anything other than livestock—

And then I realized. I realized that fear, when embraced, hardens and sharpens.

That it becomes *rage.*

That it becomes *power.*

I would not die here.

I let my fury explode.

I let it spill out through my mouth and my eyes and my fingers and the tips of my hair. I let it erupt all the way to the sky—past the stars, the moon, reaching for Nyaxia herself.

And I felt her reach back.

The Nightfire roared through me, surrounding me in a blanket of light and heat and power. It consumed everything—the demons, the hellhounds, the vampires. Consumed my skin, my eyes. Consumed, above all, my anger.

I WOULD NOT DIE HERE.

I gripped my blades but did not need to wield them as I rose. I barely remembered moving. Barely remembered stepping through a sea of white flames over Nightfire-eaten corpses that might have been animal, might have been vampire, on my way up the path, climbing and climbing.

I stopped only when I reached the top—when I looked up at the sky and saw the moon.

Suddenly I felt so, so small again. Awareness plunged back into my injured mortal body. Nausea churned in my stomach. My legs almost gave out, and I thrust my hand out to steady myself.

The flames fell away. My eyes struggled to adjust to the darkness in the wake of such blinding light.

I was at the top of the wall, in the center of the colosseum. My hand braced against the frame of the one remaining gate, the other now nothing but charred, twisted metal. I felt strange and unsteady and empty. Behind me, a tableau of devastation trailed from the sands of the arena up the crumbling wall of rock—scorched stones and piles of clean white bones.

The audience watched in silence, thousands of eyes upon me. Their faces all blended together. Vincent was out there, somewhere. I was going to look for him, but instead my gaze drifted down, just several paces away, to where the path from the other side of the arena crested the top of the wall.

Raihn.

He was on his knees, staring up at me. And that—the way he looked at me—was the first thing that felt *real.*

Real, and raw, and . . . and confusing.

Because he looked at me in sheer awe—like I was the most incredible thing he had ever seen. Like I was a fucking goddess.

I blinked and tears streamed down my cheeks. Whatever I had cracked open inside myself to access that power bled like an open wound.

Raihn rose slowly at first.

And then so fast that I didn't have time to react when he closed the space between us in several long strides—and then he was all around me at once in a firm embrace, and my feet were off the ground, and my arms were around his neck, and I was allowing him to hold me. Allowing myself to cling to him. Allowing myself to bury my tear-streaked face in the warm space between his chin and throat.

And suddenly not a single thing—not the audience, or the arena, or the arch, or the Nightfire, or Nyaxia herself—existed except for this.

"You worried me for a minute there," he murmured against my hair, his voice rough. "I should've known better."

He lowered me until my feet touched the ground again, then released me. Swaying and dizzy, I looked out over the stands.

Vincent was right in the front, halfway across the ring. He was half standing, his eyes wide and unblinking. One hand clung to the rail. The other clutched his chest—as if trying to hold in his own heart.

I must have been weak with blood loss. Because I even thought that perhaps I saw a silver streak down his cheek.

"Let's go," Raihn said softly, his hand on my back.

I turned to the door, and the ghostly silence of the Moon Palace welcomed us with open arms.

Part Five

Crescent Moon

INTERLUDE

The young woman thought she was in love, or something like it. To be young and in love is an incredible thing. It teaches one so much.

She had never had a friend her own age, and so she learned how to share little pieces of herself with another.

She had never known a romantic partner before, so she learned how to kiss and touch.

She knew her father would not approve, so she learned how to hide things from him.

Her dark world was a little brighter; cold rooms a little warmer. Her young man was shy and sweet, and he seemed to be enamored with her. She would spend long days retracing his every word.

Perhaps in another world, these two people would not have found much in common. But in this world, in which they had so little else, they became everything to each other.

They fell hard and fast, and the young woman loved the rush of it. She wanted more. They pried themselves away from each of their meetings panting and breathless and forever greedy for more of each other's skin.

The young woman had never experienced sex before.

But oh, she wanted to.

She knew that night what she wanted from him. What she wanted to give back to him in return.

They met in his room. Their kisses were messy and frantic, punctuated with gasps and moans as lips grazed sensitive flesh. Their desire for each *other fell over them in a drunken haze, more potent with every layer of cloth they ripped away.*

She was faintly nervous as he pressed her to the bed and climbed over her. Nervous as he opened her thighs and prepared to push into her. But she was nervous as all young people were when losing their virginity. And that nervousness was nothing compared to her desire.

The pain was brief and quick. She buried it in the sensation of his shaking breath against her skin, their flesh as close as it could ever be, his mouth pressed to hers.

He was gentle. At first.

When he first began to move, swells of pleasure mingled with the remnants of the pain. With each stroke, slow and deep, it built.

The young woman turned herself over to it and thought to herself that she would never—never—feel anything this good ever again.

When did the first spark of fear come? When did that little voice in the back of her head whisper, Wait, something is not right?

Perhaps it was when his thrusts got too fast, too hard, the pleasure-to-pain balance disrupted despite her muffled words of hesitation.

Perhaps it was when she tried to sit up, seize control, but he forced her back down, the sharp edge of his fingernails opening little bloody wounds on her flesh.

Perhaps it was when his nostrils flared at those little drops of blood— maybe the blood on his hands, or the blood between her legs—and his kisses to her cheek, her jaw, her throat grew deeper.

Grew harder.

Grew sharper.

His lips were loving at first. Then passionate.

And then it hurt.

It hurt, it hurt it hurt it—

The young woman cried out. She told him to stop. Perhaps he did not hear; perhaps he did not care.

Bloodlust, understand, is a terrible thing.

Fear seized her. His teeth were deep into her throat as she thrashed. He was stronger than her. Her powerlessness was a noose, ready to strangle her.

The young woman came so close to death that day.

But she grabbed the silver candelabra from the bedside table and smashed it over her lover's head. It was not enough to kill him, but she was not trying to kill her lover that day. She had never killed before.

She was shaking, her heart beating frantically. As she pushed him off of her, she caught just one glimpse of his face—dazed confusion, and then horror, as if he had not even realized what he had done.

Tears streaked her cheeks.

She thought she was in love. She had not learned yet how deadly such a thing could be.

She hid her tears, grabbed her clothing, and ran. She did not look back when he called for her. Her broken dream and her broken heart tore her flesh to pieces.

She was bleeding. She was frightened. She did not intentionally choose to run to her father's room. But where else could she go, in a home where everything was dangerous?

The king opened his door and let his weeping daughter inside. She was a reserved young woman. He had taught her how to keep her emotions carefully tethered. But tonight, she was distraught. Her lover and his betrayal had shattered her defenses.

The king wrapped his daughter in a blanket, listened to her choke out her story, and was silent as he wiped the blood from her throat.

He made a decision in that moment.

The young woman did not know it. Not yet.

CHAPTER THIRTY-ONE

Eleven of us remained.

Ivan was there when we arrived, and Angelika followed not long after Raihn and I did. The last, to everyone's shock, was Ibrihim, who dragged himself through covered in gore, his sword bloodied, eyes faraway and empty. He had killed his partner right before stepping through the arch. Half was an odd number this year. Only one of them could live.

Ibrihim didn't seem all that broken up about it.

How many people did I kill today? I wondered, numbly.

Everyone was staring at me. Not in the same way they usually did, either. Not with amused hunger, but wary curiosity.

I couldn't decide if I liked the change.

Unlike after the other trials, the Ministaer and his acolytes waited in the Moon Palace to greet us as we returned. After Ibrihim, the gate—which stood of its own accord in the center of the room—simply faded away, leaving whoever still remained beyond it to their bloody fate.

The silence was deafening. The Ministaer regarded us with a placid stare, an expression that only vaguely resembled a smile twisting his mouth.

"Congratulations," he said. "You are finalists of the Kejari. You have made it into the final two trials. Our Dark Mother is very pleased with you."

No one looked pleased with themselves. Only grimly determined.

"To celebrate your victory," the Ministaer continued, "a ceremonial feast has been held at Nyaxia's pleasure, in honor of your gift to the Mother of the Ravenous Dark. The blood that has been spilled, and for the blood you have yet to give her."

His smile broadened, as if this was the only thing that brought him genuine pleasure.

Sometimes, I thought Nyaxia was a bit depraved.

"Go," he said. "Heal yourselves. Rest. The Moon Palace, by Nyaxia's generosity, has offered you all you need. Return to the church at sundown."

THE APARTMENT WAS too quiet without Mische. Raihn and I didn't talk as we returned, and I was infinitely conscious of the silence.

He spoke first, only once the door was shut firmly behind him. "Six whole hours of rest after we nearly died for the entertainment of our benevolent goddess." He gave me a half smile. "How generous of them."

I rasped a forced chuckle, and his brow flattened.

"What?"

"Hm?"

"That sounded like a dying cat, but what concerns me even more is that you actually faked a laugh at a joke that wasn't even funny."

That, I almost would have laughed at. But my head was foggy and my body exhausted. Now that the shock of the trial was starting to wear off, what I had done—and the fact that I understood so little of it—had begun to set in.

"Hey," Raihn said softly.

I looked at him.

And out of everything that had just happened today, this moment might have been the most frightening.

Because right now, two truths careened into me at the same time:

One, that he looked at me like my well-being was actually important to him. That he must actually care, because I'd *felt* the way he cared. I'd felt his panic when I was in danger, and that meant he'd felt mine when I thought Angelika would kill him.

Two, that the Halfmoon Trial was over. We no longer needed an alliance. And that meant that either he would kill me, or I would kill him.

These two undeniable facts collided so violently that I found myself leaning back against the wall.

"Well," I said, "we did it."

My voice was hoarse.

"We sure fucking did."

He took a step closer, his eyes never leaving mine.

I should have tensed. I should have reached for my blade.

I didn't.

"You were fucking magnificent, Oraya," he murmured. "I hope you know that."

I lifted my chin and said, with as much conviction as I could muster, "I know."

He laughed. His eyes crinkled when he smiled. Had I noticed before how much I liked that?

"Get a little rest if you can," he said, "before the feast. I'll leave you alone. Get ready in a different apartment."

He spoke so casually, but I knew what he really meant. Was this how he acknowledged what had changed between us? Was this his way of saying, *Neither of us have to make any moves yet?*

Either way, I was grateful for it. Grateful that I didn't have to spend these next few hours talking myself into killing him. Whatever the Oraya of tomorrow had to do . . . that could be her problem. The Oraya of tonight could just watch him for a little longer.

I refused to let even a hint of any of this into my voice as I replied, "Fine."

He lowered his chin, went to the door, and opened it. Just before he slipped through, I said, a little too quickly, "Raihn."

He glanced back.

"I'll admit that you were a good ally," I said.

He winked at me. "You knew it from the start," he said, and closed the door behind him.

I HADN'T BEEN sure exactly what the Ministaer meant when he'd said that "the Moon Palace will provide," but it turned out he meant it very literally.

The Moon Palace gave me healing potions and dressings. It gave me a hot bath with seventeen ridiculous scents of soaps. It gave me a set of hairbrushes that I had no idea what to do with.

And it gave me a gown.

When I returned to the bedchamber after my bath to see it laid out neatly over the bedspread, as if placed there by a silent, invisible servant, I actually laughed aloud.

"This must be a fucking joke," I said, to no one in particular.

Obviously, I couldn't wear this.

But I had no other options. As if the Moon Palace had predicted my displeasure, it had taken away any alternatives. The drawers and closets were empty. Even my bloody armor was gone. So, after wandering around the room naked for a few minutes in fruitless search for something else, I put on the damned dress.

I barely recognized myself in the mirror.

The fabric was smooth and silky and a dark, rich violet—a strangely familiar shade I couldn't place. The front fell into a deep V, the top structured enough to define the curve of my breasts. It was held up by black metal chain straps, and that same glistening ebony metal encircled the bodice, adorning my rib cage in a manner reminiscent of armor. The back was low and open, the long chains crossing over my back. The skirt pooled lightly around my feet, which were encased in delicate silver sandals.

Though the dress clung to my body, it wasn't restrictive. I nearly felt naked in the light, airy fabric, and it easily moved with me, the violet rippling like water through shades of black and purple. I left my hair free and straight. It dried smooth, falling down my back like tendrils of shadow.

I stared at myself for a long, long time.

I quite literally could not remember the last time I had seen myself in clothing created to be beautiful. I never, ever wore anything designed to attract attention. And this dress . . . well, it would definitely attract attention. It highlighted all the things I normally tried to hide: my skin, my shape, and the very, very exposed column of my throat.

"I can't wear this," I muttered to myself, again, but this time I sounded less convinced.

Because the truth was . . . I liked it. It was the kind of thing I'd dreamed of wearing when I was too young to understand that doing so would be a poor survival choice.

Still, I went back to my pack one last time in a final futile attempt to find something else to wear. When I opened it, I saw why this dress looked so familiar.

That purple. Bunched up right there at the top of my belongings. I would never let anyone know how many times I pulled it out, just to hold it.

I returned to the mirror, Ilana's scarf in my hands. I let it fall open. The fabric was battered and stained. But its color and texture were exactly the same as the gown's. The two could have been cut from the same stretch of cloth.

My eyes stung.

I could practically smell the cigar smoke, hear her craggy voice in my ear: *You'd better wear that dress. You'd better show those cunts.*

Fine. I would. With one addition.

I tied Ilana's scarf around my throat—a band of bloodstained purple silk tight around my neck, leaving two fluttering, slightly scorched trails to dangle over my shoulder.

If I was going to let myself be a spectacle, at least I'd be one that fucking meant something.

. . . And I'd still find somewhere to put my daggers.

CHAPTER THIRTY-TWO

If the church was beautiful in silence, it was downright stunning in movement. I showed up late intentionally—if I was going to let myself out in vampiric society practically in my underwear, I'd do it once everyone had already eaten, thank you very much—and by then, the feast was well underway.

It put even the debauchery of Vincent's parties to shame.

It was stunning, of course. Every glass surface and window of the church had been illuminated with blue and purple lights, which hovered near the ceiling. Music reverberated from every corner and crevice. Though there was only one orchestra, magic enhanced its performance, each note echoing over and over again until the sound swelled to fill the magnificent domed roof. Ivy vines bearing red and black flowers encircled every pillar. One side of the space had been turned into a dance floor, while the other held three long tables. Upon them, a selection of food sprawled that dwarfed the feast on the first night of the Kejari—I made a note to myself to make sure I stole some of that later.

But even more gruesomely impressive than the food was the sheer amount of blood. There was so, so much blood. Bowls of it at every seat, every table. Flavored blood. Alcoholic blood. Blood in every possible presentation—baked into food, offered in carafes, presented in golden basins. Goblets were never far from reach. Drunken partygoers had already adorned the tablecloth and floor with splashes of red.

My stomach turned in a way that surprised me.

I should have been grateful—with this much available, I was as safe as I ever would be surrounded by so many vampires. And I was no stranger to what vampire feasts often looked like.

So why did this bother me? Why did I find myself thinking so much more about where it all might have come from?

I stepped into the room and passed several of my fellow contestants sprawled out in their chairs, already having gorged themselves on all manner of delicacies. I wondered if this was intentional. Perhaps this was the last blood any of them would be seeing for quite some time.

The other guests paid more attention to me than I ever would have tolerated before. I felt their eyes and had to remind myself not to shrink beneath them, acutely aware of every expanse of bare skin I now left on display. When a pack of five vampires blatantly swiveled their heads after me, staring with a terrifying mix of curiosity, hunger, and wariness, the primal part of me that had been trained my entire life to avoid this very scenario actually considered leaving.

Instead, I touched the scarf on my neck—touched the stain of my friend's blood.

You are no fucking coward, Oraya, I heard her whisper.

No. I was not.

I looked around for Raihn, but—

Light footsteps approached, and I turned to meet them before they got too close. Vincent stood before me, a tight smile at the corner of his mouth.

I hadn't seen him in this much light since the Kejari started—not up close. He wore black, his jacket open at the neck to reveal most of his Heir Mark. His wings were out, too, the red at their edges especially striking under this lighting. I wondered if he ever hid them now, or if he needed to make sure they were always visible, with his rule under attack.

It wasn't the clothing, or the Mark, or the wings that shocked me, though. It was his face. His eyes looked uncannily bright, just because the darkness beneath them was so pronounced. Every plane of his expression was sharp and pinched, as if he'd set each feature in stone. And yet, the control in it was cracking. I sensed it before. Now, it was chillingly stark.

It all softened, of course, when he saw me.

I stiffened, two impulses warring with each other.

I looked at him and saw the way he had seemed ready to hurl himself into that pit during the trial.

And . . . I looked at him and saw Raihn's back. Heard the lie he had told me.

I hadn't had the chance to wrestle my anger into something I could cage, and showing Vincent untamed emotions was a dangerous prospect.

Still, he seemed so, so relieved to see me. He took in my appearance, a faint wrinkle of confusion passing over his brow.

"What are you wearing?"

"Something different."

My words were curt. I didn't feel like explaining.

"It's unwise."

Unwise to expose so much of myself. Unwise to draw attention. Unwise to wear anything other than armor.

"I know," I said.

He didn't seem to know what to do with that. He gave me an odd look, like he was just noticing something new about me. Maybe in the same way I had just noticed something new about him.

Vincent was never the type to drop a topic, so I was mildly surprised when he let his expression smooth and instead offered me his hand. "A dance?"

"A dance?"

My nose scrunched up without my permission, and he gave a dry chuckle of amusement. "Such an outrageous prospect?"

"I—" I stopped myself before I let myself speak. Still, my face was, as always, too expressive. He glimpsed the anger I didn't want to show him, anyway.

"Something bothers you."

"I saw what your men did to Raihn."

"Raihn?"

"My ally."

His face fell. "Ah."

"You—" I had to choose my words carefully. "You told me you wouldn't break him."

"Nothing about him seemed broken," Vincent said simply. "I didn't witness Jesmine's methods, but I saw him fight well in that trial."

Fought well in spite of the relentless torture he had endured.

I said nothing, because I didn't trust myself to. Even what I'd already revealed, I thought, would be too much. But contrary to my expectations, Vincent merely seemed weary and sad.

"I am a wartime king leading my people through dark times," he said. "And Jesmine is a general who knows how to do whatever it takes to protect her kingdom. And sometimes those tasks require unpleasant actions. I won't deny that." He extended his hand to me again, a weak, soft smile at his lips. "But tonight I'm just a father who, twelve hours ago, was certain he'd just watched his daughter die. So please, little serpent. Indulge me. Let me be that man for just a few minutes."

I swallowed, hesitating.

Living this life had required me to learn how to be many contradictory things at once. It forced me to divvy my mind up into many little rooms, each containing a different part of myself. Now, the beast of my anger calmed enough for me to lock it away safely within its cage. It was not gone. It was not satisfied. But it was restrained.

"I don't know how to dance," I said, at last.

"That's fine. We can pretend I'm a better father, and that I taught you such things like I was supposed to."

I softened.

Fuck it.

I took his hand, and Vincent led me to the dance floor. We stayed off to the side—far away from the borderline-orgy that was happening in the center of the room, which would have been a very awkward place to be with my father.

"You taught me more useful things than dancing, at least," I said.

He spun me into position. Maybe I didn't know how to dance, but I did know how to move, and I certainly knew how to follow his lead. All of this resulted in far less awkward stumbling than I would have expected.

"And you learned them well," he said. "That and more, if what I saw last night was any indication."

The pride in his voice lit an echoing flicker of warmth in my chest. Despite myself, my cheeks tightened.

It still felt like a fever dream. I wasn't completely sure what I had done, or how I had done it. But I knew one thing: I had felt powerful, truly powerful, for the first time in my entire life.

Vincent laughed softly. "Don't hide that pride. It is well deserved."

"I didn't know I could do that," I admitted.

Did he know? Did he suspect I was capable of that kind of power?

"Never be ashamed of exceeding expectations," he said. "Even mine."

I had never even considered that it was possible to do such a thing. Vincent's expectations were the mold I was poured into — there was nowhere for me to go, nothing for me to be, but what he made me. I understood young that the harsh words and the strong hands were necessary. He was trying to keep me safe, and one mistake would be all it took to destroy my fragile mortal life.

Vincent would never apologize to me for what he had done to Raihn. Maybe he shouldn't. Maybe, under his circumstances, he didn't do anything wrong.

But tonight, he would pretend it hadn't happened. And maybe, for tonight, I could keep following his lead, just as I had for the last fifteen years.

Yet, I couldn't help but prod. Just a little.

"The Rishan?" I asked, very casually. "Anything new?"

"Always. I'll be traveling again soon, gone for a few weeks. But let's not talk about such dark things. For now, I'm here."

He swept me around the dance floor, and I was reminded suddenly and vividly of one time when I was still small enough for him to carry me in one arm and he showed me what it was like to fly—just a little, just from the balcony to the ground. One time and never, ever again.

I told him this, and for some reason, the smile that twitched at his lips made my heart ache.

"I recall," he said softly. "It was the first time I saw you smile since I brought you here."

"I didn't remember that part."

"I never forgot it."

I thought of what it had been like to fly with Raihn—even under such awful circumstances, still so freeing and exhilarating.

"Why didn't you ever do it again? Take me flying?"

The smile faded. "The last thing I wanted was for you to think *you* could and start throwing yourself off of balconies."

Because it was always about protecting me. Always.

As if he, too, had the same thought, he said, "It never gets . . ." His voice trailed off, like the words had grown too big or complex to fit into syllables. His eyes went far away. His steps even slowed.

A spike of concern. "Vincent?"

His eyes returned, blinked, fell to mine.

"I can't take credit for everything that you've become, Oraya. Even if sometimes I wish I could. But if I'm responsible for just one small piece of that, it will have been the greatest accomplishment of my life."

We both had stopped moving, and I was grateful for it, because I would have tripped over my feet in pure shock.

He had never, ever spoken this way to me. Not once. Not ever.

"In desperate times, one thinks about all the things they haven't said. And yesterday, when I saw you fall, I realized that perhaps I had never said that to you. It occurred to me that perhaps you didn't know—that you did not know how much I—"

Vincent, the Nightborn King, the man who had never met a threat he could not defeat, seemed to bow beneath the words he struggled to choke out. "It was important for me to tell you that. That's all."

My lips parted, but I didn't know what to say.

Sometimes people would call me Vincent's pet, as if I was some passing distraction or source of amusement. And though I never questioned that he loved me, in his own way, sometimes I would still wonder. He had lived my lifetime ten times over. He was more than three hundred years old, and I had only been a part of that for less than twenty years.

The wave of warmth I felt at his words dimmed quickly to cold fear.

"What's wrong?" I asked. "What happened?"

Because that was the only reason why he would talk like this. If something awful was about to happen or had already.

But he just shook his head and swept me back into our dance steps. "Nothing. I've just become a sentimental old man. And I look forward to the day I don't have to worry about outliving you."

A streak of brightness over his shoulder caught my eye—a familiar form I would now know anywhere, even from across the room. Raihn was leaving through the doors that led to the patio, wearing a black silk jacket with a deep violet sash that hung down his back, his hair unbound in those messy red-black waves. I only glimpsed him before he was gone.

I brought my attention back to Vincent quickly, but not quickly enough. He'd noticed my distraction. He gave me a half smile as the music faded, then swelled again.

"One more song," he said, quietly, "and then I'll let you go, my little serpent."

My chest tightened with a swell of emotion I couldn't place. Eerily similar, perhaps, to grief. The strange sensation that something existed here, in this dance, that I didn't want to relinquish—a sense that once I let this moment slip away, it would be gone forever.

It was a silly thought. I didn't know why it crossed my mind.

Still, I slid my hand back into his. This time, I took the first step. "One more song," I agreed.

THE NIGHT WAS hot. By the time I wandered to the patio, sweat slicked my skin, and the humidity outside did little to cool it. When our next dance ended, Vincent had stepped out of his role as my father and stepped back into the role of the Nightborn King, ruler of a wartime nation. He was commanding and serious as he wandered off to Jesmine, speaking with her in a hushed, hurried voice—the kind that I knew better than to eavesdrop on.

Gardens surrounded the church, sprawling even though it was in the center of the inner city, where space came at a premium—and it was doubly extravagant, because in the House of Night, water was even more rare. But what didn't our goddess deserve? Nothing was more important than Nyaxia, and Nyaxia deserved the most stunning gardens on the continent.

Well, practicality aside, she certainly got them. Silver and blue flowers spread before me in blankets of color. It was so disgustingly beautiful it just seemed excessive, all of it immaculately shaped and pruned and weeded and watered. Marble tile paths circled the clusters of greenery in functionally impractical but artistically beautiful designs. From above, they would shape the sigil of the House of Night.

Figured. They'd create something for her that only she, and they, could appreciate.

Movement to the left caught my eye. A cluster of silver stood among the bushes at a neighboring path—all dressed in deep red. I recognized Angelika immediately. It was impossible not to. She wore a draped gown of deep red fabric—sleeveless, showing off her sculpted muscles—with her silver hair falling down her back in a braid. Beside her was Ivan. Both of them had their heads bowed in serious conversation with a third figure, whose back was to me.

That figure, as if sensing my stare, turned to look over his shoulder.

Recognition speared me.

The man I'd spoken to that night by the river. The man who had given me the cigarillos. He was Bloodborn. As he stood next to the other House of Blood contestants, it seemed so wildly obvious, I couldn't believe I hadn't noticed it before.

He lifted his hand dismissively to Angelika and Ivan in a way that made it clear that not only was he Bloodborn, he was also powerful—because Angelika, the type of person who seemed like she didn't take orders from anyone, fell back to the rest of the party without another word.

"You did it yet again," the man said as he approached me. Now that I knew to listen for it, I could hear the House of Blood accent—so faint, like he'd stomped it out over the course of decades, reducing it to just the hint of a melodic lilt beneath each word. "You won me quite a lot of money. But I'm afraid after that display, the odds against you won't be quite as favorable to your few believers. Shame. Plenty of benefit in being underestimated." He lifted a shoulder and let it fall. "I should have brought you more cigarillos. I'm afraid I'm all out."

My eyes slid to him. I let them rest there for a long moment, taking him in now that I was seeing him in the light. He looked Bloodborn in every sense. His eyes, the pupils slightly slitted against the lantern light, held those telltale strings of crimson and gold. The red marks at his throat lingered just beneath the edge of his collar, which was high and stiff in burgundy fabric of the traditional House of Blood style, simple and tailored. Before I hadn't been able to tell if his hair was blond or silver, and now I realized that it was both—ashy blond-gray with shocks of near-white.

The corner of his mouth tightened.

"It's a little insulting to be stared at that way. But then, I suppose that's often your reality, isn't it?"

"Just wondering how I missed the fact that you're Bloodborn."

"Ah. You're right. We shared such a lovely moment, and yet I never properly introduced myself to you." He extended his hand. "Septimus, of the House of Blood."

I didn't take it. Instead, I stepped back to compensate for the way he had leaned closer, which he seemed to find amusing. He withdrew his hand—unshaken—and slipped it into his pocket. "I see. You don't take an empty hand. Smart. Did your father teach you that?"

The hair prickled at the back of my neck.

I didn't like this man. I didn't like the way he spoke, I didn't like the stupid little smirk on his face, and I especially did not fucking like that he seemed to think he was playing with me.

"There you are."

I chose not to think about exactly how relieved I was to hear Raihn's voice. Nor did I want to think about the fact that Raihn stopped very close to me—so close our shoulders touched—and my only impulse was to move closer.

I glanced at him and had to remind myself to look away.

He looked magnificent. His clothing was different than the style most of the other Nightborn men, Rishan or Hiaj, wore here. His jacket was cut close to his body, tailored as if it had been made for him. The lapel fastened straight up-and-down, rather than asymmetrically like most Nightborn fashion did now, the buttons bright silver moons. Dark silver embroidery lined his collar and the cuffs of his sleeves, and a sweeping sash of violet draped across his chest and hung over one shoulder.

It was . . . a lot. The Moon Palace had apparently seen fit to spoil him. Yet despite all the finery, his face and hair were as rough and unkempt as ever.

Septimus smiled. "Raihn. I was just congratulating your partner on her victory. You two were remarkable."

I had to hide my surprise. Septimus addressed him by his first name. As if they knew each other.

I could practically feel the air curdle. Raihn's expression went hard, every muscle rearranging into what I knew by now was utter distaste.

"Thanks," he said, in a tone that didn't bother to hide it.

"Now, this is an interesting thought . . ." Septimus's eyes flicked between the two of us. "Now that I can't place my bets on the two of you together, I wonder who I should put my silver on next time? Someone uneducated might think it would be easy for you to kill her, Raihn, but I think Nessanyn has a good chance of—oh, I'm sorry." Another one of those smiles. "It's Oraya, isn't it? I've always been bad with names."

Nessanyn?

I narrowed my eyes, my hands drifting to my blades, which I'd secured on my thighs. A goad, obviously, even if I didn't understand what it meant. And the strike hit its target, because Raihn's entire form went rigid, the shift in energy so abrupt I felt it without even looking at him.

"You should be paying more attention to your own dogs." He turned away, his hand on my back—my very, very bare back—as he grumbled, "Let's go."

"Have a lovely night," Septimus called after us.

We walked down the garden paths without looking back. Raihn was still visibly tense.

"Sorry you had to deal with his bullshit," he said.

"You know him?"

"Unfortunately. He's been sidling up to every contestant to see what he can wring out of them. Surprised you made it this far without getting the brunt of it, too."

"Who is he?"

"One of the princes of the House of Blood. Every Bloodborn contestant is in the Kejari at his behest."

"Why is he here?"

I had wondered why the Bloodborn bothered to enter the Kejari at all. Even Nyaxia herself was hostile to Bloodborn vampires. Two thousand years ago, the House of Blood was her favored kingdom, but when they turned against her in a squabble over the gifts she'd chosen to give them, she cursed them instead. Now, she offered the House of Blood no love whatsoever. A Bloodborn vampire had won a Kejari only one time—more than a millennium ago—and Nyaxia had been reluctant to even grant her a wish.

I wasn't sure if I imagined the beat of hesitation before Raihn answered. "The House of Blood wants power more than anything. Even small alliances go a long way."

That made sense. All Houses were welcome in the Kejari. It was probably the only time that Bloodborn royalty was ever able to freely interact with other vampire kingdoms.

"He sees a lot of opportunity with the House of Night being at war with itself, the fucking vulture," he muttered, as if to himself.

We walked a few more paces in silence as I mulled this over.

I became aware of Raihn's stare—even without looking at him, I could feel it, starting at my feet and trailing up, lingering on every expanse of bare skin.

I stopped walking. Then turned to face him. We stood close enough that I had to tilt my chin up a bit to make eye contact with him. I noticed this for the first time in weeks. When had I stopped thinking about the size discrepancy between us? When had it stopped being a threat and started being . . . oddly comforting?

"You look nice," he said, in a tone of voice that made *nice* sound like a million other promises, each of which shivered over my flesh.

I asked, "Who's Nessanyn?"

A flinch—of surprise, or maybe discomfort?—flitted across his face.

"An old friend who deserves more respect than to be used as some prick's pathetic attempt at intimidation." His eyes hardened. "Be careful with him. He's a dangerous person."

"Some would call you a dangerous person."

The corner of his mouth curled. "Not with you."

I hoped he didn't hear whatever strange thing my heart did at that—the sudden tightness in my chest.

His gaze lifted past me, to the church and the party happening within its walls.

"I hate being here," he said. "Do you want to go somewhere more fun?"

I knew it was stupid to agree.

And yet, I didn't regret it at all when I answered without hesitation, "Fuck, yes. Please."

CHAPTER THIRTY-THREE

Alright, fine. I'd admit it. The piss beer was starting to grow on me. I didn't hate it. Maybe . . . *maybe* I even enjoyed it.

But still, I didn't make the face that Raihn did when he drank it. Like he was coming as close as he'd ever get to the gods themselves.

He finished his gulp and lowered his mug. His brow furrowed as he met my eyes.

"What's that face for, princess?"

"My face? I was thinking about *your* face."

His brows notched lower. "What about it?"

I was supposed to say some cutting insult here. I had been prepared with those words on the tip of my tongue. But just in that moment, the moonlight fell over his features in just the right way, and I swallowed all of them.

Because I realized that I couldn't say anything about Raihn's face. I had memorized every single line, every twitch of expression.

That realization sat heavy in my stomach. I swallowed a gulp of beer instead of answering.

We sat on the flat rooftop of an abandoned house. Raihn had spirited me off to his favorite terrible pub with his favorite terrible beer. Even with my humanness and his excellent acting skills, we couldn't exactly sit around in there without attracting too much unwanted attention while dressed like this, so we came out here instead.

I liked it. We had a nice vantage point to watch the streets while remaining hidden from prying eyes. Maybe all our hard work had paid off, because it seemed like people were actually living their lives out here. Or maybe I had just learned to appreciate it more. Humans left little marks of their lives everywhere. Flowers in window boxes, toys left in yards, a series of shoes on the doorstep that painted the image of a family.

I had never noticed these things before, and certainly never found beauty in them. Now, I tucked each one away like little secret gifts.

Raihn let out a groan, let his head fall back against the wall, and loosened another button of his jacket. It was the third one, leaving it open down to his sternum and revealing a long triangle of muscled flesh that I tried not to look too closely at.

Just as I tried not to notice the way his eyes lingered on my skin when I lifted my beer.

Just as I tried not to notice that I enjoyed it—the weight of that gaze, heavy as a touch.

"It's a relief to be away from that stuffy place," he said. "Much more pleasant out here."

"You barely even spent any time in there."

"Only enough to wait for you."

He clamped his mouth shut right at the end of the sentence—like he didn't expect it to sound the way it did.

Once again, I carefully did-not-notice this.

"Besides," he went on, "I couldn't exactly wander around socializing wearing this ridiculous outfit."

I didn't know what that meant.

"Why?" I took a sip of beer. "Does it offend your fashionable sensibilities?"

"It's about two hundred years out of style." Raihn scoffed and shook his head, his smile souring. "The Moon Palace has a cruel sense of humor."

I didn't know what that meant, either, but before I could ask, Raihn's eyes fell back to me. They started at my face and slid down. I sat with my legs folded beneath me, the silk of my dress bunched around my upper thigh on the left side, where the skirt slit. His gaze traveled from my eyes to my mouth, down my throat, shoulder, side, all the way down the bare curl of that leg.

It lingered there, on my thigh, and I didn't so much as breathe as I watched his lips curl.

"Dangerous," he said.

Yes, I agreed, silently.

"But resourceful." His smile broadened, and I realized he was talking about my blade—strapped around my upper thigh.

I exhaled. "I had to be creative."

"I'd be disappointed if you didn't walk into that party armed to the teeth."

"You're armed, too."

I lifted my chin to his sword, which had been strapped across his back. I had to notice, now, when Raihn was armed. That sword could kill me with a single strike.

He shrugged.

"What's this?" he asked, motioning to his throat.

My own fingers mimicked the movement, and I brushed Ilana's scarf. The reminder of it made a knot of grief—and anger—tighten in my stomach.

"It belonged to a friend."

Sometimes I resented the fact that Raihn so often heard the things I didn't say. Right now, though, maybe I was a little relieved by it.

"A human friend," he said.

"Yes."

"The one from that night?"

We both knew which night he was talking about.

They're dead, little human.

I gave him a questioning look—how did he know?—and he responded with a faint, humorless smile.

"It smells like the Moon Palace."

Fuck. *Fuck,* I hated that.

Raihn's smile faded. "What's that face for, princess?"

"I just—it shouldn't smell like that place. It was . . . hers. It doesn't belong to them." I touched the end of the scarf, winding it around my fingers. Like if I clutched it tightly enough, I could feel her hands as she had tried to give it to me. Mother, I wished I had taken it from her then.

And now it seemed like one more demeaning injustice. That the place where she died had erased the final remnants of her life.

It felt ridiculous. No doubt sounded ridiculous, too. And yet his face shifted slightly—shifted in a way that said he understood. He leaned a little closer.

"That isn't all," he said. "It also smells like . . ."

His eyelashes lowered, and again, he moved a bit closer—only inches between us now.

"Like rose perfume," he murmured. "And bread. And . . . cigar smoke."

I choked a strange sound, involuntarily. So often, I had been jealous of vampires—jealous of their strength, their speed, their power. But never more than I was in this moment. I would have given anything to smell Ilana again. Smell her and that disgusting messy apartment.

"Really?" I said, my voice rougher than I'd intended. "You smell all of that?"

"It's a bit difficult, over the scent of . . ." He cleared his throat. "Well. You. But yes, I do. If I try." His eyes lifted to mine. "It's all still there, Oraya. The Palace didn't take everything."

My fingers tightened around the fabric.

"What was her name?" he asked. "Your friend?"

"Ilana."

I hadn't actually spoken her name aloud since she died. The shape of the syllables on my tongue felt like rebellion.

"I'm sorry," he said softly. "I'm sorry for what happened to her. And I'm sorry that . . . this is a hard place to grieve."

A hard place to grieve. What an understatement. There was no room for grief in a place like this. No room for softness or vulnerability. And certainly no room for the kind of anger, messy and undignified, that Ilana's death had ignited inside me.

"She was a person," I said, between my teeth. "Not prey. Not a game. She was—"

Fuck, what *wasn't* she? She was silk and cigar smoke and a short temper and a million contradictions; a full life of a thousand other thoughts and dreams and desires for the future—and someone whom I loved, deeply.

I lowered my gaze to the clay of the roof, my hands tight and knuckles white around my mug. I waited for the sting in my eyes to pass.

"Can I ask you a question, Oraya?" Raihn said. "You don't have to answer, if you don't want to."

I nodded.

"When we were bonded in the trial, I felt . . . I felt a lot of things. Your anger. Fear. The grief."

My jaw tightened. My instinct was to lash out at him just for acknowledging that he saw those things in me—I so fiercely guarded them. But then, there was no accusation of weakness in his voice. And I'd felt all of that in him, too. Just as potent in his heart as it was in mine, albeit in different ways.

"If you win the Kejari," he went on, "would you ask Nyaxia to change you?"

I understood exactly what he was asking, and considered not answering. *He is Rishan,* Vincent whispered in my ear. I couldn't tell him about binding myself to Vincent, becoming his Coriatae. Those details were far too sensitive.

But Raihn, damn him, saw the crux of my answer on my face, even when I hadn't said a word.

"Yes," he said. "You will."

He sounded oddly disappointed, which I hated.

"Why wouldn't I ask her to make me something different?" I shot back, a bit too quickly. "Do you have any idea how exhausting it is to live this way? I can't change anything, *be* anything, if I'm just stuck being prey." I clamped my teeth down on my words, then shook my head once. "No. I can't do that like this. Not how I am now."

"You can't?"

I had to force myself to meet Raihn's eyes. I half thought he was mocking me. But there was nothing feigned in his stare, nothing ungenuine. Only sadness.

In that trial, he had looked at me like I could do anything. Like

I was more powerful, more awe-inspiring, than Nyaxia herself. No one had ever looked at me that way before.

And even now, a shade of it lingered.

"Don't be so quick to throw away your humanity, Oraya," he said. "You might find you miss it once it's gone."

And maybe my human eyes were weak in the darkness compared to his, but the shadow wasn't enough to hide the twinge across his face that he pretended wasn't there.

"Those parts of yourself are never really gone," I said quietly.

"Sometimes, I'm not sure about that."

"You don't think I see how hard you've worked to hold onto your humanity? You're more human than I am, Raihn. You've kept every part of it that makes you value the things in this shitty world that no one else here does. You've kept the compassion. It doesn't matter if your blood runs black now. That hasn't changed you."

Such a raw compliment tasted strange on my lips. It was so uncomfortably earnest. But I said it because I knew he needed to hear it.

And . . . I said it because it was true.

Raihn went very still and very silent. And slowly, so slowly, his gaze lifted to me.

Before, he had looked at me like I was a goddess, and I had thought I couldn't feel more powerful than I did in that moment.

I was wrong.

Because now he looked at me like I was more than that—like I was *human*. Somehow, that meant more.

I had to force the smirk to my mouth. "What's that face for?"

I expected a dry chuckle, a verbal nudge to my ribs. But he remained stone serious, a wrinkle deepening between his brows.

My smirk faded. "What?"

"Nothing."

"Give me one honest thing, Raihn Ashraj."

After a long moment of silence, he finally spoke.

"I've lived through some injustices in the last couple of centuries. Seen some fucking travesties. But one of the biggest, Oraya, is that anyone taught you that you should become anything other than exactly what you are."

My hands went numb. My fingers were so tight around my mug that they trembled. The words split me from throat to navel, pulled me open and touched my most fragile parts.

My mind emptied of thought for several long seconds. And then only one returned:

I will need to kill this person, and I don't know if I can.

It was a mercy that Raihn didn't wait for a response. He just stood and extended his hand to me. "Let's walk for a while."

The sky was growing faintly rosy with the promise of dawn. We walked in the southern end of the district, slowly wandering closer and closer to the Moon Palace.

I hated time. I always had—it was forever a marker of the gulf between me and the vampires that surrounded me—but never more than I did right now, as this night slipped through my fingers.

Any minute now, Raihn would try to kill me. Or I would have to kill him. As our conversation grew slower, the silence between our words longer, I knew that promise was sinking into us both.

Finally, he stopped in a darkened side street. Rocky steps led down to the bank of the Lituro River. We stood exactly on the boundary between our worlds—the inner city directly across the water, the human district behind us—the sun warning of its arrival. He paused and looked out over the view—first to our left, to the skyline of Sivrinaj, and then the right, to the human district and the dunes rolling beyond them.

Then he stretched and reached for the buckle of his scabbard, which cut across his chest.

I tensed and stepped back. My hand reached for my blade, still strapped to my thigh. One thought: *This is it.*

But he just unbuckled the strap. "Here. Put this over there for me, will you? My back is still fucking killing me, and this thing is heavy."

My brow furrowed. "What? Why?"

"Just put it over there."

He spoke so casually, like there was nothing at all unusual about what he was asking me to do.

I took the scabbard from him. I didn't know how he carted this thing around all the time—it was, indeed, outrageously heavy, so much so that I had to strain all my muscles to keep from letting it slip.

I did as he asked and laid it against the wall.

Raihn wandered two steps away, leaving me closer to his weapon than he was.

It was all so nonchalant. But I knew this was a performance. I'd spent months now studying Raihn's every move. This was just like his fighting style. The magic hidden in brutish strikes.

I just didn't understand why. I watched him, waiting for the trick.

He turned to me, then loosened another two buttons of his jacket, exposing several more inches of his bare chest. He leaned against the wall, then pulled apart the fabric, looked down at himself, and frowned.

"I got a nasty cut at the trial. Even the healing didn't help it much."

"You . . . what?"

"Do you think I should be concerned?"

I didn't move.

He rolled his eyes at me. "Honestly. Just come here."

I did. He held open the lapels of his jacket, his head tilted back against the wall—a broad triangle of bare skin, and his throat, completely exposed to me.

Me, who was armed.

While his sword was over there, out of his reach.

All at once, I understood what this was. What we were doing.

He was offering himself to me. He was presenting me a perfect opening. He knew it. I knew it. We both knew the other knew it.

I could kill him right now. It would take so little. I would plunge the blade right there, right in the center of that perfect expanse of skin. His blood would probably be warmer than the others I killed—I didn't know why I thought that, only that I was almost positive it would be true. I wondered if he would clutch me as it ended. How his final breath would feel over my face.

"Well?" he said. "What do you think?"

I stepped closer.

Our bodies were nearly flush. The smell of him surrounded me. It hit me, what that element of it I hadn't been able to place was.

He smelled like the sky. He smelled the way air felt as it rushed around you, freeing and terrifying and the most beautiful fucking thing you've ever experienced.

My fingertips touched his chest. His skin was warm. He had a few scars here, too, and a smattering of dark hair that was softer than I expected it to be. The sudden urge to flatten my palm against his skin, run my hands across all those different textures, nearly overwhelmed me.

I'd envied vampires my entire life. But now, for the first time, I felt a sharp pang of sympathy for them.

Because suddenly, I understood what it was like to be hungry.

It was fucking excruciating.

"Hm," I said flatly. "Looks serious."

"I was concerned you might think so."

I dragged my stare away from his chest, up the elegant cords of muscle of his throat, up to his lips—all promise, etched into the delicate curve of a smile that communicated so many things he didn't say.

I imagined that if I killed him here, that smile would linger.

"Your heart is beating fast," he murmured. "You must be very concerned for my well-being."

I let out a shaky breath that I tried to pass off as a laugh.

And I didn't move—couldn't move—my fingers still brushing his skin, as his hand lifted to my face. I let him touch me, too. Let the immaculate rough brush of his knuckles caress my cheek, then unfold over the angle of my jaw. His thumb lingered, slowly moving over the curve of my mouth, my lower lip.

"Or are you afraid?"

The smile had faded. It was a real question.

And the answer petrified me, because I was not afraid, and that was the most terrifying thing of all.

I could open his shirt, slide my hands over the expanse of his chest, and thrust my poison blade right here—right into his heart. He could tear away this ridiculous delicate spiderweb of a dress and cut me open.

The two of us could burn each other up.

My eyes lifted to his. I had never looked at them at such a distance before. I realized they looked red because they were comprised of so many different threads of color—near black and honey gold and coffee brown and even little glints of bright crimson. So many disparate pieces that shouldn't fit together. Just like him. Just like me.

And it was there, in his eyes, that I found the truth that should have broken me.

Yes, we could kill each other here. We were offering ourselves to each other.

But neither of us would.

"No," I whispered. "I'm not afraid."

I didn't notice my lips had curled until his thumb moved, tracing the shape of that smile as if it was something worthy of reverence.

"Are you going to kill me, Oraya?"

I didn't run. Didn't move. Instead, I lay my palm flat against his chest.

I surprised even myself when I replied, "Not tonight."

His hand slid from my face and swept a stray strand of black hair from my cheek, smoothing it to the side. But instead of withdrawing, his fingers tightened around my hair—clutching it, but not pulling, as if he was trying to convince himself to let me go and failing.

"You might destroy me anyway."

I saw it here, in this moment. Want. Desire.

And I knew what it was for vampires to desire someone like me. I knew it so well that it should have sent me running.

But even more frightening than his desire was mine. I felt that call echoing in my own pulse. It was so strong that when he finally released me—when I finally backed away from him and turned away without another word—I had to resist the urge to lick his touch from my fingertips.

Maybe it would taste as metallic and hot as blood.

CHAPTER THIRTY-FOUR

After the feast, Raihn and I returned to the same apartment. It was out of habit, at first. Then we had stopped at the door and looked at each other, both clearly thinking the same thing. It was unwise for us to remain together.

"Might be safer," Raihn said, at last. "For us to stick together. If you want to."

I told myself he was right. Told myself that, for one more day, it would be good to keep him close. Protection from the others. Protection from him, where I could keep an eye on him.

All bullshit, of course. At least I was self-aware.

I threw open the door. "If you're afraid to sleep alone in an empty apartment, you can just say so," I'd said, and that was the last we spoke of it.

The truth was, I *wanted* to stay. The thought of leaving him to go be by myself made a lonely ache throb in my chest. And I saw that ache in him, too, when I watched him pack up the rest of Mische's things that night, putting away the bloodstained sheets that we hadn't had time to fold up before the Halfmoon, tucking away the bag she had left behind.

When he was done, I stayed there with him in the sitting room instead of returning to my bedchamber, remaining in wordless company.

It was worth something to know you weren't alone. And I think he felt it just as I did, because he didn't leave, either. We slept that day sprawled out over couches and armchairs, but neither of us uttered a single word of complaint when we woke up to a symphony of aches and pains.

I didn't kill him the next night, either.

Or the night after that.

I didn't kill him during any of the countless, meticulously tracked moments when he left himself unguarded.

I didn't even kill him when, the next day, I walked by his bedchamber door to find that, in a stunning display of either trust or stupidity, he had left it slightly ajar.

I peered through to see him sprawled out in bed, body illuminated by the faint flicker of lantern light from the hall and the sliver of daylight that slipped between the gaps in the curtains—distinct warm and cool shades highlighting every hollow and ripple of bare muscle. He slept with every limb sprawled in a different direction, and yet it still managed to look somewhat poetic, like a master's sculpture—albeit one that snored loudly.

I was struck by how much it reminded me of the painting in the great hall of Vincent's castle. That one Rishan, falling, reaching. More beautiful now than tragic.

It is perfect timing, Vincent whispered in my ear. If I was going to kill him, now would be the time to do it.

He was fast asleep. I could throw open the blinds. Could let all that sunlight keep him from retaliating as I crawled over that beautiful naked body, gripped his hips with my knees, and plunged my sword into his chest. The sheets would be soaked by the time we were done.

I imagined myself doing it—imagined crossing the room, pulling myself on top of him. I imagined the way his bare body would look beneath me, his torso stretched out and his hair messy around his face—imagined the way it would feel, hard and powerful, like limitless potential encased in skin, firm along the inside of my thighs, along the apex of my core.

I imagined lifting my blade—

But before I could bring it down, his eyes snapped open. His hands, rough and calloused, ran up my thigh, my waist, my breast, a familiar curve to his mouth as he murmured, "Are you going to kill me, princess?"

And he didn't wait for an answer before—

I jerked awake, my face hot, sweat plastering my hair to my skin. It took a long time for my heartbeat to slow. When I got out of bed and peered through my door to see his open, I gazed at him for a few long moments, then walked away.

No, I didn't kill him that day, either.

Three days passed, and Raihn and I didn't talk about leaving, and we didn't kill each other, and I realized that I didn't want to kill him at all.

RAIHN WAS COOKING.

I'll admit it: I had been very, very skeptical when Mische had said that Raihn was "a very good cook." The thought of Raihn, hulking and battle-scarred, leaning over a stove seemed ridiculous. Well, it looked just as ridiculous as I imagined.

But it did smell fantastic.

I didn't know what he was making, only that he'd assembled it from a collection of ingredients he'd hauled back from town in a burlap bag, and that he managed to construct the entire meal using a single dented pot in the fireplace.

"Come here." He beckoned to me from the next room, where I practiced my still woefully inconsistent magic and tried to pretend that I wasn't paying any attention to him.

I did, and he held out a wooden spoon. "I need your help. Taste."

I eyed the spoon. It looked like some kind of stew, with chunks of vegetables and liberally applied spices suspended in a thick, creamy-brown sauce. I lowered my head and tasted it.

Fuck.

My knees almost gave out. Whatever words I was about to say collapsed into a jumble on my tongue, melting beneath the—the— Mother, there weren't words for the flavors. I'd never tasted anything so good.

When I finally came back to my senses, I blinked and looked at Raihn, who was watching me with a strange, bemused expression.

"That wasn't how I'd imagined making you come for the first time," he remarked.

I stopped chewing.

Raihn didn't say anything, but the flinch over his face as he turned away told me he, too, heard that his joke implied more than he had intended.

Imagined.

First time.

The air went heavy. I wiped a bit of stew from the corner of my mouth.

"I didn't believe Mische when she told me you were a good cook." I spoke very casually. "But . . . it's not awful."

It was enough to break the tension—or at least enough to make us both pretend it had.

"It's a fucking travesty that you grew up eating vampire food. Vampires don't know how to cook."

"You do."

"Only because it's dear to my heart. None of it tastes the same anymore."

Right. Vampires never stopped eating food, but their tastes were very different than humans'. I'd never stopped to think about what that might be like for Turned vampires.

"It changed over time?" I asked, and he nodded as he removed the pot from the fire and placed it on the table.

"Slowly, over the years. This? This tastes very bland to me, now. But Mische is younger than me, so her tastes are more human. It'll be more like it was for you."

My ears perked. "Mische?" I glanced to the table—to the little covered pot waiting for the stew. "This is for Mische?"

"I figured she earned it."

"You're going to see her?"

"I am. If you don't mind me sacrificing one training day."

I didn't think about the fact that he so easily assumed we would still train together.

Instead, I was thinking about Mische—Mische, and her bright smiles and easy laughs, and the way she'd treated me like I was an actual friend. The image was so different from how she had looked when she was taken away, just a shell of herself.

I touched my wrist—the bandage from the still-not-quite-healed bite from the Ministaer—without intending to.

It took a long moment for me to recognize that the feeling I was struggling to put into words was concern.

"Can I come?"

I blurted it out before I could stop myself.

Raihn, whose back was to me again, paused long enough that a wave of uncertainty flooded through me. Of course he wouldn't want to take me, an enemy in every sense of the word that mattered, to see Mische outside the bounds of the Moon Palace. Hell, if she even wanted to see me at all.

But when Raihn turned around, he was smiling—no, grinning.

He said simply, "She'd like that."

CHAPTER THIRTY-FIVE

I was surprised that Raihn could already fly. Vampires healed very quickly, and the wounds on his back had become scabbed over and bumpy with fresh pink scar tissue. Still, I had thought he was weeks away from being able to use his wings. He insisted he was fine, but I didn't miss the wince when he conjured them, nor the way his whole body seized up when he launched us into the sky.

"You alright?" I asked, after a while.

"Perfect," he replied, like he didn't even know why I was asking.

We flew for a long, long time—hours. The first time Raihn had flown with me, the attack had overshadowed all but the faintest glimmer of the joy of it. Now, with nothing else to distract me, I couldn't help but revel in it. I loved how fast we moved, the weightlessness, the freedom. I loved the way the landscape spread out beneath us, the world that had trapped me now reduced to nothing but inconsequential miniature figurines. I loved the way the air smelled, the way it rushed around my face.

I loved everything about it.

I felt Raihn shift—felt the warmth of his breath against my cheek. I glanced back at him to see him twisting his head to look at me. It put our faces very close, his nose only a few inches from mine.

His eyes sparkled with amusement. "You're grinning like a little child."

I scowled, and he chuckled. "Oh, never mind. There she is."

I rolled my eyes and looked back to the landscape below. We had flown beyond the inner city, now out to the sprawling settlements in the dunes.

"You enjoy flying," he said.

I couldn't even try to deny it. "I do."

Understatement. Mother, if I had those wings, you'd have to drag me down.

"That's unusual," he said. "Most who can't fly hate it the first few times."

"You carry around a lot of wingless women?"

"A few. Most of them vomited on me."

"Still could happen. Don't let your guard down."

"I figured your stomach is probably as strong as your will."

I craned my neck to eye him. "And how strong is that?"

He grinned and leaned close as he said into my ear, "Pure fucking steel. Obviously."

Obviously.

WE LANDED AT a farmstead. The settlement was beyond even the farthest reaches of Sivrinaj, out beyond the dunes. We had passed a little township not far from here, but the house that Raihn brought us to was long past the nearest populated street. It was a small but fine building, crafted of sandy-gray brick. Grass spread out in all directions, creamy gold even beneath the cold moonlight. To the left, horses grazed. To the right, pastures held sheep, goats, and one mule that trotted over to inspect us with obvious trepidation.

When Raihn set me down, I nearly collapsed. My knees were wobbly and uncooperative. But I paid more attention to Raihn's wince as he spirited his wings away.

He caught me watching him.

"Stop it with that face, princess."

"I'm not making a face."

He heaved a long-suffering sigh. "Are you really not aware that you are *always* making a face?"

He strode to the door and I followed, suddenly very conscious of my facial muscles. He was wrong. I was definitely not *always* making a face.

The door opened. A tall, slender man with a mop of strawberry-gold hair stood there, revealing sharp canines with a broad grin. "Raihn! What a nice surprise. Mische will be elated. And—"

His eyes, blue as the sky, fell to me over Raihn's shoulder. The smile shifted as he stepped aside to let us in—shifted into something surprised and not altogether friendly.

"Oh. Well. This is . . . I think I know who *you* are."

What a greeting. I didn't like his tone.

Raihn shook his head and touched my back. "Terrific hospitality, as always," he grumbled, and maybe I imagined the reassuring stroke of his fingertips as he led me inside.

The interior of the house matched the exterior—simple, but clean. Well-made, but not ornate. A woman with ash-brown hair bound in a sweeping knot atop her head approached through the door to what looked like a kitchen, then stopped short.

"Oraya," Raihn said, "this is Cairis." He gestured to the blond man, who waved with a hesitant smile. Then he motioned to the brunette. "And this is Ketura."

He offered no further explanation of who they were or what his relationship was to them.

Ketura didn't move or speak. Didn't even blink.

"Where's Mische?" Raihn said. "Upstairs?"

He was already on his way up, his hand on my arm, putting me before him. All so very casual, but I knew what he was doing. Growing up with Vincent, I was very familiar with what protection looked like.

"Second room to the right," Cairis called after us, but neither followed.

The door was slightly ajar. Raihn knocked, then pushed it open. Mische was in bed, surrounded by fluffy white sheets and blankets, gazing out the window with an untouched book on her lap.

When she saw Raihn, her face lit up with an effervescent grin. She sat up quickly, like she was preparing to launch herself out of bed. Raihn took two quick steps closer, as if he saw the same thing

I did and was preparing to catch her before she accidentally hurled herself to the ground.

"Don't you dare—" he started, but the minute he was within reach, she leapt up and threw her arms around his neck so forcefully he let out an *oof*.

He grumbled something unconvincingly disapproving and didn't pull away. She finally released him, and when she turned to me, her smile somehow managed to get wider.

The last remnants of my uncertainty disappeared. She just looked so *happy*.

I rubbed my wrist without meaning to.

Mische looked like she was about to jump up to hug me, too, but that was a step too far for me. I settled instead for an awkward wave.

"Feeling better?"

"Well, I am *now*!" she breathed.

While she was clearly still in some pain, bubbly enthusiasm imbued her every word. Raihn and I sat at the edge of her bed while she told us all about her time here—about Cairis's daily card games and Ketura's lessons in gardening, about the names she had given all the chickens, about the way she was sure, *totally sure*, she was slowly winning over the heart of the cranky mule out in the pasture.

"I have no doubts," Raihn said, at that, and I tried not to be offended when he gave me a sly, pointed smirk. "You seem to be good at winning the hearts of ill-tempered creatures."

Goddess. And to think he'd actually complimented me just an hour ago.

Mische asked us a million questions about the Halfmoon Trial, too, to which I gave stilted answers that Raihn enhanced with far more animated interjections. Her eyes got wider with every sentence.

"Gods above," she gasped, when we reached the end. "That shy magic of yours came through for you! I told you! It was *in* you."

I wondered if I imagined the little twitch of sadness, hastily hidden, when she said that. My gaze lingered on the burn scars peeking beneath her sleeve.

I shrugged. "It was luck."

"No, it was incredible," Raihn said, as I avoided his gaze.

We sat with Mische for a long time, conversation wandering past the trials and to other frivolities. I didn't speak much, leaving it to Mische and Raihn, which was fine with me. Even after having lived with them, I was struck all over again by the easy warmth of their interactions. Two people who were utterly comfortable with each other.

Eventually, Raihn looked out the window to the sky. "Getting late," he said, sounding a little dejected. "We should go. It'll take a while to get back."

He rose, and this time, he didn't give Mische a chance to throw herself at him before he swept her up in an embrace, holding her tight.

"Get better, alright?"

"Alright," she said into his shoulder. "Be safe. Kick their asses."

"You know it."

I shifted awkwardly, averting my gaze. It seemed like the kind of moment I shouldn't intrude on.

Then Raihn pulled away, kissed her on the top of her head, and bid her one more goodbye before going to the door. I choked out an uncomfortable goodbye of my own and went to follow him when Mische said, "Oraya."

I turned.

"You too," she said softly. "Take care of yourself, alright? Stay safe."

Guilt twinged in my chest—because I had just watched Raihn make the same promise to her, and soon, the two of us could not both keep it. Watching him with her, it was hard not to wonder if perhaps he deserved it more.

"Of course," I said.

"Thank you for coming. It . . . really meant a lot to me." She gave a tiny smile. "It meant a lot to him, too."

She held out her hand. It wasn't a hug—maybe she knew that would be a step too far for me. Still, I found myself reaching back. Her fingers were warm for a vampire, her touch soft and gentle. She squeezed my hand.

A lump rose in my throat.

"I hope you feel better soon," I said. "I'm just . . . I'm glad you made it out."

"Me too."

She released me, gave me a little wave, and I closed her door behind me. When I reached the top of the stairs, I paused. Hushed voices rose from below. Serious voices.

I couldn't help myself. I told myself I wasn't eavesdropping, exactly. I was just . . . failing to announce myself.

I moved very, very slowly down the steps, staying near to the wall to keep them from creaking under my weight. I stopped just out of view of the door to the dining room. I could just glimpse the shape of Raihn's shoulder at the edge of the doorframe.

"Vale is on his way now," Cairis was saying. "Even bringing his *new wife,* if you can imagine that."

He sounded like a gossiping housewife.

"Wife?" Raihn seemed surprised. "From Dhera? Who—"

"Human. Or *was,* at least."

Cairis said it in a tone of voice that implied a pointed look and a long sip of tea.

A long silence. I could barely see Raihn, and yet I knew he stiffened at that. His disapproval wafted thick as smoke.

"Interesting," he said dryly.

"Interesting, indeed," Cairis chirped. "Don't you think so, Ketura?"

Silence.

Then, so quietly I barely could hear it, "*She* should not be here."

"She's a friend," Raihn said.

"No, she isn't."

"She is a friend, Ketura, and you need to remember that."

My brow twitched. That was something I'd never quite heard in Raihn's voice before—command.

"Do you know what he's doing out there right now?" Ketura hissed. "You should see it, Raihn. What he's done to Genra and Isca. You should see how many people he's killed."

My mouth went dry. Genra and Isca—Rishan cities. One was even close to the district I had been born in, Salinae. The one that might still hold some of my bloodline, if anyone from my old life had survived the night Vincent had found me.

Cairis and Ketura were Rishan, then. I didn't need to see their wings to know it from the way they spoke.

"I'm aware."

"And yet you still walk through that door with her? Bringing Vincent's human whore to—"

"*Do not*," Raihn said sharply, "speak about her that way."

Immediate silence.

"I apologize." She did not sound very sorry at all.

I took one more step, and the floorboard groaned, giving away my presence. All three sets of eyes turned to me: Raihn's pleasantly casual, Cairis's blatantly curious, and Ketura's razor-edged.

I cleared my throat and hurried down the rest of the stairs.

"We need to get back," Raihn said to me. "Make sure we don't get stuck on the wrong side of the Moon Palace when dawn comes."

Then, to Ketura and Cairis, "Give Mische the food. I'll be back sometime soon." And he offered nothing else before he ushered me out the door, scooped me up in his arms, and launched both of us into the sky.

We flew in silence for some time.

"You were listening to all of that, weren't you?" he said, at last.

Of course he knew. I didn't bother denying it. "You made it easy."

"Ketura is worried and angry. Like many people are, right now. So she's a bit . . . sensitive."

He sounded like he was choosing his words very deliberately.

"If I got all upset about being called Vincent's pet, or whore, or whatever else they want to call me, I'd have no one to blame for it but myself. Hell, *you* called me that."

Raihn was quiet for a long moment. We both knew he couldn't argue.

"Ketura's wife is in Salinae," he said. "She's scared for her. These are uncertain times."

Salinae. The mention of the name made my chest ache—sympathy, followed by something more bitter.

I, too, worried for Salinae.

"I'm from there," I said. "Salinae."

"You are?"

"That's where Vincent found me. In the human districts there. It was when he was putting down a rebellion. I'd like . . ." I paused. I'd never voiced this aloud before. Not to anyone other than Vincent. Not even Ilana got this naive, fragile little dream of mine.

I rubbed the ring on my little finger.

"I'd like to go back one day," I said. "See if anyone that knew me then is still there. Family, or . . . whoever. I don't know."

A momentary silence. I couldn't bring myself to look at him. "What?" I said. "You think it's a fairy tale?"

Fairy tale. Just like I had said about his hopes for the little girl he had saved, the one who reminded me so much of myself.

"No," he said. "I think whatever family you have left would be damned lucky to have you."

My cheeks tightened. But I shrugged away from the uncomfortable compliment.

"Who are they?" I asked, changing the subject. "Cairis and Ketura?"

"Friends," he said.

I craned my neck to give him a skeptical look, which he must have felt, because he returned it. "What?"

They weren't "friends." I knew that right away. At first I wasn't sure why, until I realized that I now knew what Raihn looked like when interacting with people he considered friends. Mische. Even . . . even, maybe, me.

At my flat stare, he chuckled.

"Alright, fine. They're . . . maybe a better term would be old colleagues. I wouldn't want to drink a beer with them, but I do trust them."

That, I believed. I couldn't imagine him sending Mische off in such a vulnerable state to anyone he didn't trust absolutely.

Still . . . colleagues. Was that the right word? Ketura had apologized so quickly, even when she clearly was begrudging it.

"Did you command them?"

Raihn seemed a bit startled by that, and I found it satisfying.

It was nice that I could still surprise him the way he continued to surprise me.

"Yes," he said. "I did. You're good, princess."

"When?"

"Long time ago. We were . . . ah . . . private guards of a sort."

Now that was an interesting thought. I knew many vampire lords who had their own personal military forces. They went everywhere trailed by a series of stone-faced, hulking warriors. I could hardly imagine Raihn as one of them. They were so blankly generic, and he was so . . . not.

"Of a sort?" I pressed.

"Closest term I have for it," he replied, in a way that shut down any further questioning.

We lapsed into silence. I watched the dunes and tiny towns roll by beneath us, glistening silver under the caress of the moon.

Eventually, Raihn said, unprompted, "I don't think that about you anymore."

"Hm?"

"That you're Vincent's pet, or whore, or whatever. Maybe I did in the beginning, but not anymore. I just . . . I want you to know that."

My throat thickened a bit.

Such a stupid thing, yet it was oddly validating—oddly comforting—to be defined by something other than my relationship to Vincent. And I knew, for better or worse, that Raihn meant what he said.

"You want me to thank you for not calling me a whore?" I said flatly.

He scoffed and shook his head. "Fuck you, too, Oraya. Ix's tits. I try to say a nice thing."

"So charming."

"I won't do it again, I promise."

I made a show of rolling my eyes. But as our conversation faded, I nestled a little deeper into Raihn's embrace.

CHAPTER THIRTY-SIX

The next night, the doors to the Moon Palace were locked from the outside.

Vincent was traveling, so in lieu of his gifts, I had intended to go out into the city to find some extra poison for my blades, just in case. But when I attempted to leave, the front door did not so much as rattle. So I tried another, and another. No door would open. No window, either.

When I returned to the apartment so soon after leaving, Raihn, who was cleaning his sword, gave me a questioning look.

"Everything's locked," I said. "Doors. Windows."

His face hardened. Then he sheathed his sword and left the apartment. He returned a few minutes later with a single carafe and a basket of fruit and bread.

"Feast hall's empty," he said, "except for this."

The bread and fruit, plus what we had stored in this apartment, would at least be enough to get me by. But the blood? The carafe held less than a single glass.

He and I exchanged a glance, clearly thinking the same thing. If the Moon Palace had locked us in, it meant that it intended to starve us. And starvation was terrifying to both of us for very different reasons.

"You have more, right?" I said, nodding to the carafe. He and Mische had been hoarding blood since the beginning of the tournament, but . . . I wasn't sure how much of it had survived the attack.

"Enough," he said tightly. "We lost some of it in the fire but . . . I have enough. If I ration."

My shoulders lowered in relief. At least if Raihn had enough blood to get him by, I wouldn't be locked up in an apartment with a predator. Still, being confined to a castle with nearly a dozen more of them didn't feel much better.

Most of the trials were held in equal intervals, exactly three weeks apart. But the Crescent Trial was sometimes—not always—an exception. Some years it was a longer trial, spanning several days, and occasionally held at a location outside the colosseum.

If Nyaxia was going to starve us until the Crescent, that could be as long as three weeks, or as little as one. Either was dangerous. Some of the vampires here had not had any blood since the feast four days ago.

Raihn moved a dresser in front of the door that night.

THE DOORS AND windows didn't unlock. The food did not replenish. There was no more blood.

On the fifth day, in growing desperation, one of the Hiaj contestants tried to fly up to the top of the tower and smash through an upper window. The glass shattered, but the moment he attempted to fly through, he was cast back to the ground with a ragged shriek of pain. His entire body had been cut up as if by a thousand minuscule razor blades, shredding his skin and his wings. Raihn and I watched from a distance, but even from across the hall it was clear he'd die, whether it be of blood loss or starvation. A breeze flowed gently through that open window. It revealed nothing but the sky, the Moon Palace hiding its deadliness in innocence.

No one tried to break the windows again.

Not even as the hunger got worse.

ANOTHER WEEK PASSED.

I stopped leaving the apartment. The vampires who hadn't been able to get any blood right before the supply disappeared would now be experiencing intense hunger—not enough to kill them, not yet, but enough to drive them to desperation.

First, we started hearing footsteps pacing the hall outside the apartment door at night. Then they continued during the daylight hours as hunger led the instinctual desire for food to outweigh aversion to burning. They probably didn't even know they were doing it. If they were starving, their legs would just take them to wherever they sensed the greatest potential to feed. And I had been careful to heal all my wounds from the last trial, but I still probably smelled delicious.

Through all of this, Raihn and I somehow managed to maintain our little bubble of normalcy. We trained together in the early nights, then he would help me practice my woefully unpredictable magic later. We spent the predawn hours curled up in the sitting room, and every day I watched him linger at the curtains, peering at the horizon until the sun left little angry claw marks on his skin.

One day, when Raihn was asleep, I had an idea. I pulled the huge mirror from my bedchamber out into the sitting room, propping it up a bit precariously against the couch. I eyed it, fussed with the curtains, checked my angles and then checked them again. When Raihn woke up at sundown and came out to see the mess I'd made of the living room, he halted.

"Oh," he said. "Well, it finally happened. You've lost your mind."

I scoffed and offered no explanation. Not until the end of the night, when the sun began to rise and Raihn went to take his usual spot near the curtains. Then, I called him back into the living room.

"Watch," I said, pointing to the mirror. And then I went into my bedchamber and threw open the drapes.

He flinched, shrinking back. But the sharp corner of the hall shielded him from the rays of sunlight—while the mirror still offered him a full view of the sky.

"I tested it," I said. "As long as you stay back here, even at high noon, the light won't flood into this room. But you can still see the sun in the mirror. It's . . . it's nice in the middle of the day. The sun reflects off the church spires."

I said it so casually, as if I hadn't spent hours perfecting the placement of that mirror, making sure it framed everything I found so beautiful about the sleeping city in daylight, the way no one but me could see it. Until now.

Raihn was quiet for a long time.

"Careful, princess," he said at last, his voice rough. "Someone might think you're actually nice."

But his words mattered so much less than the persistent tug of the smile across his lips. And every day after that, he dragged a chair to that turn of the hallway, and he watched the sun rise and fall over Sivrinaj as if it was the most precious gift in the world.

In times like that, it was too easy for me to forget the grim reality of our situation.

But the darkness of it slipped through, anyway.

ONE NIGHT, IN the third week, Raihn was on edge. He seemed tense, his usual smooth, casual demeanor replaced with perpetually tapping feet and grinding teeth and fingers that would clench, unclench, clench, unclench, over and over. Every muscle in his expression was tight.

"What's wrong with you?" I asked, eventually, when he was so distracted while training that he nearly let me take his head off with Nightfire.

"Nothing," he snapped.

"That's convincing."

He didn't even have a retort, which may have been the most worrying thing of all.

He excused himself from our training, and I didn't argue. I wasn't about to show him that I was worried about him, but I also couldn't shake the nagging knot of anxiety. When I heard footsteps in the common room, I crept silently from my room and peered at him around the corner.

He was standing at the dining table, a glass in his hand. I thought it was empty at first, then realized, as he lifted it, that it held just a tiny, tiny pool of blood—barely enough to cover the bottom.

Raihn gazed at it like he was saying goodbye to a lover before throwing it back, savoring, and then swallowing.

Everything went numb and cold. The expression on his face . . . the way he stared down at the empty glass now . . . it told me all I needed to know. I felt like a fool.

"So," I said, emerging from the hallway. "That's it, isn't it?"

"Hm?"

Mother. I was so fucking stupid. Raihn was so far gone that he didn't even have it in him to convincingly feign ignorance. I thrust my palm to the empty glass, still in his hand. "You told me you had enough."

"I—" He avoided my gaze. Swallowed. "I did have enough."

"That doesn't look like enough."

"The Crescent Trial will be happening any day now. It's fine. I'm fine."

He set down the glass a little too hard, and a crack spiderwebbed up its side. If he noticed, he didn't show it. His knuckles were white.

Something about that sound—the sound of the glass cracking—cracked something open in me, too. All at once, all those signs of hunger that I hadn't wanted to see struck me. It was everywhere. How had I not noticed? Whenever I asked if he had enough, he told me he did. And I had taken him at his word without even questioning it.

Raihn was hungry, and not only hungry, but on the verge of starving.

And I had barricaded myself in a room with him.

Why had it been so hard for me to confront the reality of those two things?

It wasn't that I was afraid of him. It was that I wasn't, and I should be. *I should be.* That was nature, and that did not change because of whatever I may have come to feel.

You have been making so many mistakes, Vincent whispered in my ear. I hadn't noticed how long it had been since I'd heard him.

"I should go somewhere else," I said. "A different apartment."

I leveled my voice, but I had to try harder than I expected. And I could tell that Raihn had to try just as hard to keep his face neutral, and didn't quite succeed. There was a slight twitch to the muscle in his jaw, like he had to dampen a flinch from a blow.

I felt that blow, too. Like I had just slapped him across the face.

"Why?" he said tightly.

"*Why?*" I motioned to the empty glass. The cracks had grown. Now Raihn's fisted grip was the only thing keeping it from shattering. "Raihn, don't be a—"

"There's no reason to."

He was not going to make me say this. He couldn't possibly be so naive.

"Yes, there is. You know there is."

"I told you that—" He paused. Took a breath. Let it out. "I hope you know by now that you don't have to worry about that."

"I always have to worry."

You are never safe, Vincent whispered.

"Not with me."

"Even with you."

Especially with you, because you make me feel at ease.

And this time, he did actually flinch. The glass shattered.

"After everything, you're still afraid of me? I'm not a fucking *animal,* Oraya," he said, words so low and rough that they did, indeed, resemble a growl. "Give me a little more credit than that."

Something hardened in my heart, prodded by the hurt I felt on his behalf.

"You aren't an animal," I said. "But you are a vampire."

"I wouldn't hurt you," he snapped.

No. That was a lie. It was a lie the last time someone had said it to me. It was a lie even if Raihn completely believed it was the truth—and if he did, maybe he was more of a fool than I realized.

Hell, maybe I was, too.

We were finalists in the Kejari. We would need to hurt each other. And that was even if we made it that far.

"What are you so offended by?" I shot back. "That I'm stating the obvious aloud? You are a vampire. I am human. Maybe we don't like to say those things, but they're true. Look at yourself. You think I don't see right fucking through you?"

I was upset. My heartbeat had quickened. A muscle feathered in his cheek. His nostrils flared. Even now, I could see it. The hunger lingering beneath the hurt.

"Our dream world is nice, but it's not *real*," I said. "And I don't want to be woken up from it by you tearing open my throat."

I regretted my words immediately. But I regretted them because they were cruel, and because the terrible, childlike hurt on Raihn's face made my soul ache.

I didn't regret them because they weren't true. They were.

Did he think he was the only one who wanted to pretend otherwise? In this moment, I wanted nothing more than to live my entire life the way we had been over these last few weeks. Building something like a home in this shitty, dark Palace.

I wanted it so much that I even . . . even considered if I might be able to help him. Even though it was a foolish thought. Even though a human offering themselves to a vampire deprived of food for this long would mean near-certain death, no matter how good their intentions were. And yet, when I saw that look on his face, that desperation, I was willing to consider it.

Stupid, naive, childish.

But Raihn had already taken several steps away, his back straight, knuckles white at his sides. It was as if, even in his anger, he recognized that I needed him to put more space between us.

"Fine," he said coldly. "You're right. We've been stupid. If you want me gone, I'm gone. You shouldn't be anywhere near that hallway. I'll go."

I already wanted to take it back. The familiar grip of fear had begun to tighten around my heart. Not fear of Raihn, but fear of being without him, and the things I might feel once he was gone.

"Alright," I said, against every instinct.

Neither of us seemed to know what else to say.

So he went to his room, gathered his belongings, pushed aside the bureau in front of the door just enough to slip through, and then turned to me.

A million words hung there.

He just said, "Push this back when I'm gone. I—"

He bit down on whatever he was about to say.

I knew that feeling, because I found myself doing it, too. Swallowing down *Don't go*s and *I'll miss you*s and *I'm sorry*s.

This is fucking silly, I told myself. *He's just going to a different room, and it's the only thing that makes sense.*

But I knew—we both knew—that once Raihn left, once he became just another contestant in the Kejari, something would change between us irreparably.

"I—" He tried again, gave up, and said, "I'll see you at the next trial."

And he was gone before I could say another word.

CHAPTER THIRTY-SEVEN

That night, for the first time in a long time, I dreamed of the moon absent from the sky.

The bed, rickety and cheap as it was, was still enormous compared to my tiny body. I nestled deep under the covers, pulling them up to my nose. Jona and Leesan were asleep, or pretending to be. Momma was whispering hurriedly—*Get that lantern off right now, you knew they'd come, you knew—*

I was scared, too. But I thought, *I should never be afraid,* and slipped from the covers. I walked very, very softly to the window. I was barely tall enough to reach the sill. I gripped the splintering wood and peered into the sky.

Once I saw a dead worm with so many ants all over it that it turned into one big wiggling mass of black. Now the sky looked like that. Just a pulsating blanket of darkness.

Except it wasn't ants in the sky. It was wings.

Oraya!

My momma said my name in that way she did when she was frightened.

Oraya, get away from—!

THE AIR HIT my lungs too hard, like a gulp of salt water. But worse, because it seemed like it was eating me from the inside out.

The coughs seized my entire body. I had barely gained consciousness before I was on the verge of losing it again, rolling over onto all fours as I convulsed. My eyes were dripping, my stomach aching, my vision so blurry I heard, more than saw, the string of vomit fall to the ground. I blinked rapidly in a poor attempt to clear my vision.

I lifted my head.

No wonder I'd dreamed about that night, because this one looked just like it. Just writhing, indistinct movement in a spine-chilling mass of darkness.

Trees surrounded me—tall, sparse, and narrow, with only a few long needle-tipped branches near their tops. The ground beneath my palms was rough and sandy. Rocks piled everywhere. All of it—the dirt, the rocks, the trees—was black, moonlit outlines rendered in shades of dark ash-gray. Plumes of smoke rose from the ground, hot and gritty. When a gust of wind rolled a puff of it over me, I gasped in pain and shrank away. It burned my skin like acid.

I grabbed my blades and had them at the ready. Movement punctured the forest—too distant for me to make out what I was seeing at first, but the sound was unmistakable. Wet, heavy breathing, high-pitched shrieks, and the nauseating sound of flesh tearing open.

My mind was addled, maybe from the smoke or from whatever magic had brought us here, but I forced myself through the haze to put together what was happening.

This was the Crescent Trial. It had to be. We weren't in the colosseum—we weren't even in Sivrinaj, at least not any part of it that I'd seen—but the timing lined up, and the Crescent Trial was often the most unique.

But what was the objective?

Footsteps. I turned, and immediately something slammed into me, knocking me back to the stones. I couldn't make out the face of my assailant—not with everything so dark and blurry and the smoke pumping up from the ground, each puff bubbling my armor. I struck wildly with my blades, hitting flesh.

Normally, the poison would be enough to at least slow them, but my attacker seemed utterly unconcerned with pain. Bloodlust?

Some of the worst I'd ever seen, if so, to be so disconnected from one's own body.

I drove my blade hard into my attacker's side, and that, finally, made him falter. He staggered, falling to the ground like his wounds had caught up to him simultaneously, and I pressed over him.

He wasn't dead yet. And soon he would wake up. I stabbed him through the chest, barely avoiding the wild flail of his limbs as I finished the job. Like a starving wolf lashing out one last time. They really did become animals when things got this bad.

I yanked my blade from his corpse with a wet crunch, just as a wave of that toxic smoke rolled toward me. I had to lurch away, leaving his limp body to be consumed by it.

I needed to figure out where I was. I needed to—

Movement rustled the brush behind me. I spun around. My eyes groped in the darkness. I could only see silhouettes in the distance. Vampires, fighting. And something four-legged. Demons? I'd been so trained to expect the worst that my mind immediately went to threats. When I crept closer and realized that they weren't predators, but prey—deer, thrashing against the shadowy figures of the vampires that pinned them—I was relieved.

Good. Deer were perfect. The ideal meal to distract the starving vampires. The starvation had gone on long enough that they wouldn't have a choice but to leap on whatever blood they smelled. And I was glad that these ones had smelled the deer first.

I needed to get away from here, and fast. Then, when I was alone, I could figure out what my objective was, find Raihn, and—

I stopped myself, swallowing a sad pang. Raihn's name had flitted through my head without my permission. But we had separated. The Halfmoon Trial was over. I certainly wouldn't go out of my way to fight him, but—

I wasn't quite out of the clearing yet when a repulsive sound rang out behind me. It was something between a groan and a gurgle—an uncanny, unnatural blend between animal and vampire.

I quickly lowered into the underbrush and watched the creatures in the distance.

My eyes had adjusted to the darkness, and the moon had

reappeared from behind a misty cloud. The cold light illuminated the scene of bloody ruin behind me—the two vampires crouched between jagged rocks, the deer carcass now open before them. One of them was trying and failing to stand, their limbs spasming wildly. The other seemed to be trying to reach for their companion and failing, as if their muscles refused to cooperate.

The first, in strange, lurching movements, jumped on the other. Feral shrieks cut through the night.

I shrank back.

This . . . this wasn't hunger. Bloodlust made vampires sloppy, but it didn't turn them into mindless beasts. These people looked like they didn't even have control over their own bodies anymore.

The two vampires wailed as they tore each other apart. Unhinged, senseless, animalistic. *Fuck.* They just went at each other, not like warriors, but like animals, the deer carcass forgotten at their—

The deer carcass.

Realization snapped into place. I looked around in horror. Looked around at this place that reeked of death, and yet held such a strange abundance of soft, easy-to-catch prey.

Poisoned, trapped prey.

Nyaxia had starved them, and now she offered them tainted gifts they would be powerless to resist.

Raihn.

My head emptied save for his name. Everything I had told myself, every lie I'd hid my concern beneath, withered away.

I didn't think anymore. I just ran.

It wasn't hard to find the vampires. We had been scattered throughout the forest, but they were loud—bloodlust made them careless, and whatever poison was in these animals turned them into something even worse.

I found Raihn not far from the clearing. I recognized him immediately, even in the dark, even from such a distance. I'd learned the shape of him so well that every angle was a native language.

Yet, for all his familiarity, something was also foreign about him right now. The way he moved wasn't the deliberate poise of the man who shared my home. It was feral, uncontrolled. Still graceful—that was the only thing that made me exhale in relief, because there was nothing of that toxic, lurching insanity—but the movement of a predator released from its cage.

His wings were out. A limp body slumped against an overturned tree trunk—a Shadowborn man, whom, apparently, Raihn had just finished killing. Now he soared through the trees and debris in hunt.

And then, a moment later, saw what he was chasing: the deer, crashing through the rocky brush.

No. I dove after him before I could talk myself out of it.

He moved impossibly fast, weaving through the trees like a leaf caught in a gust of wind. He was swifter than the deer, which darted through the sparse forest in a blind panic.

It was only the panic of the animal, which practically ran in circles, that saved us both. It came too close to an impassable pile of rocks and had to veer left. I tracked the movement to cut it off, putting myself right in Raihn's path.

I heard Vincent's voice in my head: *You're about to get yourself killed, you stupid child, throwing yourself in front of a vampire in bloodlust.*

But I moved anyway.

"Raihn!" I shrieked as I leapt in front of him, hoisting myself up on one of the rocks, arms spread. *"STOP!"*

It was a stupid plan for so many reasons. First of all, any other vampire would have gladly replaced the deer with me. And secondly, he had wings—he could have just soared over me, whether I was standing on top of a stupid rock or not.

But Raihn did neither of those things. Instead, his gaze fell to me, and he faltered. Just for a second. And for that moment, I thought I glimpsed my friend there.

But otherwise, he looked so different. His stare was hard and glassy. A streak of harsh moonlight fell across one side of his face, and his eyes were even redder than usual, the pupils narrowed to a slit.

The hairs stood on my arms. Every instinct screamed at me to run, run, *run*.

Because Raihn in bloodlust was terrifying. The kind of terrifying that made every living thing in a ten-mile radius cower.

Instead, I ran at him.

Throwing myself against Raihn was like hurling a pebble against a brick wall and expecting it to crumble. Still, I hit him with enough force to knock him off balance. We tangled in a mass of flailing limbs. He let out a wordless snarl and fought against me. Pain snaked across my cheek as I was slightly too slow dodging one of his strikes, but I slipped every other. I knew how Raihn fought, and those reflexes still remained, even when he was half out of his mind.

Just as I knew how powerful a fighter he was, I also knew his openings. I knew his left side was a little weaker. And just as he faltered between blows, I hit him right where I knew he would struggle most to counter, right to that knee, forcing him to the ground.

I climbed over him, pinning his body down with mine.

"*Raihn!* Get a fucking hold of yourself!"

Mother, he was going to kill me. I was sure of it when his hands gripped my shoulders hard enough to leave bruises. That horrible glazed-over look in his eyes hadn't faded.

Come back to me, Raihn. Come back.

"I will fucking stab you again, and you know I will!" I roared. "*Snap out of it!*"

He blinked.

His fingers loosened. His nose twitched—a movement, however small, that made me tense—but then he closed his eyes and drew in a deep inhale, and when he opened them again . . .

It was him. It was *him*.

"*Oraya.*"

He said my name like it was the answer to a crucial question. His voice was thin and hoarse.

I could have wept for it.

But no time for pleasantries. Certainly no time to show him how grateful I was that I had found him. I spoke in quick, clipped sentences. "Welcome back. We're in a trial. The animals are poisoned.

I don't know what the objective is. Everyone who drinks is going insane. We have to get the fuck out of here. Let's go."

I started to push myself up, but he still held my arms—gently, now. A wrinkle deepened between his brows as he touched my cheek. The scratch.

"Did I do this?"

"It doesn't matter, Raihn. We have to go."

His expression said it did matter, but I didn't want to think about that right now, either.

"If I get off of you," I said, "will you go run after a squirrel?"

I was grateful to see that familiar, long-suffering annoyance. "Oh, fuck you, princess."

It was a bit of a relief to hear him curse at me again.

I decided I accepted that answer and pushed myself up. Raihn got to his feet right after. He moved slowly now, jerking as his left leg threatened to collapse under him. In movement, I hadn't noticed the blood all over him.

My heart stopped. The Shadowborn he'd been fighting before had, apparently, gotten a few hits in.

"You're hurt."

"Seems that way."

I looked to the sky. Dark, but ever-so-faintly rosy. Dawn wasn't far off.

"Let's find somewhere to rest," I said as we began to walk. "Then we'll figure out what's next."

Raihn made a wordless grunt of agreement. But after three steps, it became obvious that he was struggling to move. I backtracked and tucked myself under his arm.

"I'm fine," he grumbled.

"You're clearly not fine."

His jaw clenched, like he wanted to argue this and knew he couldn't.

And it wasn't just the leg, I knew. I could hear it in the weakness of his voice. He was injured—and still starving.

No, Raihn was very, very much not fine. But he accepted my help without complaint.

CHAPTER THIRTY-EIGHT

We found shelter in a cave created by some of the collapsed stones. It certainly wasn't the opulence of the Moon Palace, but it was dark and deep, with plenty of places to hide and only one entrance to guard. I wondered how many of the contestants had already fallen victim to the poisoned prey. We didn't pass another living soul on our way to the cave—only one convulsing rabbit.

I brought us deep enough into the cave that no light reached us from the outside. We reached shelter just in time. The sky was now faintly pink with dawn. The cave was so dark that Raihn had to mutter guidance to me as we went, because I could see nothing. By then he was leaning heavily on me. When we found our place to stop, he practically collapsed against the wall.

"Give us some fire. Good thing you've been doing all that practicing."

I could hear the smirk in his voice. Could also hear the exhaustion.

Practice or no, I'd been struggling to use my magic consistently. But when I thought about the way I felt when confronted with Raihn's obvious weakness, the Nightfire came to my fingertips easily. Raihn's face, hollowed and drawn, bloomed from the darkness.

I looked away and focused very hard on sculpting my little orbs of light.

"Didn't think I'd see you again," he said.

"Mm."

I didn't even know how to explain to myself why I went after him, never mind explaining it to him.

It was a stupid decision, Vincent said in the back of my mind, and frankly, I agreed with him.

I didn't regret it, though.

"Thank you," he said.

I shifted uncomfortably and was grateful I had something to do with my hands. What was I going to say? *You're welcome?*

"I would have been . . ." He swallowed thickly. I made another little ball of Nightfire, so it was now light enough for me to see every movement of his expression.

And to see every sign of weakness.

He gave me a pained smile. "You were right, princess."

"We don't have to do this." I said it more sharply than I meant to.

"We do. I do. I just . . . I owe you that, don't I?"

"You don't owe me anything."

"Ix's tits, Oraya. Let me fucking talk."

"You can barely talk as it is."

"Never stopped me before."

I managed a laugh despite myself. It sounded more like a gasp of pain. Felt like it, too.

"I'm sorry," he said.

My hands froze mid-movement, hovering around that sphere of light.

"I'm sorry," he said again. "You were right to tell me to leave."

The apology hit me like a strike. So blunt and direct. No battle of wills or egos.

"I didn't want you to see me that way," he went on. "So I pretended that version of myself didn't exist. It does. And I'm—I don't like people to see it. I didn't want *you* to see it."

I'm not a fucking animal, he had spat at me yesterday. And suddenly the anger in his voice then sounded so similar to the shame in it now.

I didn't like feeling things. Emotions were ever-shifting and devoid of logic, and they gave me no way to sink my blade into them.

But I felt too many of them now, bubbling up under the surface of my steel exterior.

I didn't say anything. The Nightfire glowed a little brighter in erratic spurts.

"We need to do something about your injuries," I said.

He was more than hurt. He was starving. Vampires could heal extremely quickly, but he wouldn't be able to if he didn't get blood.

I glanced at him. His eyes had slipped off to the distance. I could see little in the darkness, but his superior sight was probably looking to the path leading out of the cave.

"I need to go back out there."

I scoffed. "Don't be a fucking idiot."

Healthy, he might be able to survive an hour in sunlight—perhaps more if there was cloud cover, though it would be painful. In this state, though? There was no way.

"Then . . . I might need to ask you to hunt for me." He said this as if it physically pained him to do so.

"Those animals are poisoned. You saw what they did to the others."

"Then maybe it's better to die here," he said, "than to die out there, out of my mind."

A beat of silence. And in that silence, my mind ran through our situation, tracing the paths between our options. The decision snapped into place, a new immovable truth.

I stood and faced the wall of the cave. Unbuttoned the top button of my leathers. Then the second.

I made it halfway down by the time Raihn noticed what I was doing.

"No. No, absolutely not."

"You said it yourself. You don't have a choice."

My voice sounded like it was coming from a stranger. Like I was watching myself from the outside. I couldn't believe I was doing this. My hands were clammy—my heart a beat too fast.

And yet I had no doubts about it. None at all.

I unfastened the rest of my leathers. Cool air rushed against my flesh, chilling the sweaty camisole beneath.

I turned to him. His throat bobbed, eyes darkening.

I knew that look, too. A different kind of hunger. It passed quickly, but I still felt it linger on my skin—making me suddenly self-conscious of the amount of my body that was now exposed.

He rasped, "I can't do that, Oraya."

"What are your alternatives? You die in the sun. You die a mindless beast from poisoned blood. Or you die before the sun sets here, doing nothing. And I'm not going to just sit next to you while you die, Raihn. I'm just—I'm just *not.*"

Neither of us acknowledged the slight crack to my voice.

I approached him. I felt every step—every increase in our proximity. He leaned against the wall. I knelt before him, so our gazes aligned, and his eyes searched my face.

"You think I don't know?" he choked. "You think I don't know what this means for you? I can't."

Maybe I should have been surprised that Raihn understood what I'd never told him—that he'd pieced together a portrait of my past from every moment of anger or fear I'd let slip through my walls.

Maybe I should have been surprised when his fingertip gently caressed my throat, not in hunger, but in sadness—at the scar there, those two little jagged white lines.

Maybe I should have been surprised that he knew me more than I wanted him to.

But I wasn't.

Words were too weak to convey what I wanted to tell him now.

Perhaps he thought that I would think less of him after seeing him in bloodlust. But I didn't. He had been terrifying then, yes. But now I understood exactly how hard he had been trying. It would have been so easy for him to succumb to it in the Moon Palace, take the easy solution. After the Halfmoon, I was nothing but a liability to him. No one would have blamed him for doing what he had to. And yet, he'd preferred to remain in that apartment, winding himself tighter and tighter, rather than leave me or hurt me. It must have been agonizing.

Offering myself to a starving vampire was more than dangerous. Practically suicide.

And yet . . . I trusted him absolutely.

I didn't know how to say any of that. So I settled on, "I'm not afraid of you, Raihn."

And I saw in his eyes how much those words meant to him. Like he had been given something he had been waiting his entire life for.

I swallowed. "So. What's—what's the best way to do this?"

He would need my throat. Sometimes wrists or arms or—I shivered at the thought—inner thighs worked well, too, but he needed a lot of blood fast, and the throat would be the best way to do it.

I thought he might still protest. But after a moment, he said, "Come here. Lean over me."

I inched closer, then swung my legs over his thighs and around his hips, straddling him.

I tried not to think about the fact that he felt beneath me exactly how I'd imagined he would. Tried not to think about how good, how right, it felt to feel the warmth of his body pressed against mine, my inner thighs, my stomach.

And I tried not to notice that he clearly noticed all these things, too. That the muscles of his throat, so close now, flexed with a swallow. That his hands fell to my waist immediately, like they had already been waiting for me.

"Like this?" I asked.

"That's perfect."

It wasn't quite perfect, actually. I was so much shorter than Raihn that even with the extra height of his lap, I needed to push myself up a bit, and he would have to crane his neck to reach mine.

His fingertips brushed the angle of my jaw, and for one terrifying moment I thought that he was going to kiss me—it would be so easy, barely a tilt of his head. But instead, his fingers moved down, grazing my shoulder, then my waist, then reaching for my dagger at my belt. He unsheathed it and wrapped my fingers around the hilt, then angled the blade so it pointed to his chest.

"You are in control of this," he murmured. "Alright?"

Now I understood. He wanted me here, in this position, because I could pull away if I wanted to.

I nodded. My grip around that dagger was sweaty. I wondered if he could hear my heartbeat.

That was a stupid thought. Of course he could hear it. Smell it.

"You can still say no," he said softly.

"Stop telling me that," I barked.

He let out a weak laugh. "There she is."

And as if he took that as his cue, he pulled me closer—his arms sliding over my back, tugging me forward until our bodies were pressed together, save for the dagger that I still gripped between us.

I'd thought I was prepared for this, but I wasn't prepared for how gentle the movement was. Like he was cradling something precious.

I tilted my head back, staring hard at the darkness of the stone. Harder still, as I felt his breath against the sensitive skin of my throat.

"It won't hurt much. But you might feel . . . ah . . ."

"I know," I said, too sharply.

Horny. That was what he was trying to explain to me.

Vampire venom had an overwhelming effect on human prey. The biological intent was to make them soft and pliable. Sometimes that presented as a muddled, intoxicated haze, as it had with the Ministaer's bite—given his age, the location of the bite, and my distaste for him. But more commonly, it manifested as intense arousal.

And especially if one already felt . . .

I didn't finish the rest of that thought.

"Just do it," I snapped.

He chuckled. "As you wish, princess."

And then his lips were on my throat.

Every muscle tensed. I braced myself for pain. Instead, though, I felt only a caress. Just the soft touch of his mouth against my flesh, the faintest brush of his tongue, as if asking permission to enter.

My cringe melted into a shiver.

"You're safe," he whispered against my skin.

And then he bit.

He was quick and forceful, his fangs striking deep once and hitting their mark immediately.

He let out an involuntary groan that vibrated through my entire body.

The venom could not possibly have worked that fast. Yet, my eyelashes fluttered. Everything—every remaining doubt—withered away beneath the warm touch of his mouth, the press of his body against mine. My breasts, suddenly sensitive, peaked beneath the too-thin fabric of my camisole—so tight against his chest that I could feel every inhale, ragged and quickening. His tongue rolled against my skin as he took his first swallow, one languid, slow movement.

I imagined that this is what he would feel like inside me, too. This deep and all-consuming.

Unmistakable hardness formed beneath me.

My palm pressed flat against the wall behind his shoulder, the one last holdout in keeping me propped up against him. And I still clutched that dagger, though I'd let it slacken, no longer braced so tightly against his chest.

My hips rolled—I couldn't help it, not with the rigid length of his desire right there—and Raihn let out a serrated hiss against my throat.

This time I echoed it, the moan escaping me in a choked exhale. We were aligned so perfectly that when I shifted my hips, I pressed against the full, thick length of him, even through the heavy fabric of his pants. And even that stroke, with so much between us, sent sparks up my spine. Sent every nerve begging, pleading, demanding, *More*.

It wasn't enough.

The venom ate away the final dregs of my self-control, unleashing a wave of desire that utterly ravaged me and left nothing behind.

I wanted every layer between us torn away. I wanted to run my hands, my lips, my tongue over every inch of his skin, taste every scar. I wanted to offer every expanse of my flesh to him, let him do this—this, *this* fucking amazing thing—to every part of me. I wanted his magnificent length inside of me, taking me so deep I couldn't remember my own name, and I wanted him to remind me of it when he came. I wanted to watch him go.

His arms gripped me tight, pulling me closer in one desperate lurch, like he'd been trying to hold himself back and failing. My camisole was gripped in a fist in one of his hands, like it was all he could do not to tear it off of me. He drank deeper, his tongue moving against my skin like he was making love to me.

I didn't know what I was doing anymore. I rolled my hips again, and now, there was nothing hidden about my moan.

And this time, he moved with me.

I let the dagger fall to the ground with a deafening clatter I didn't hear. I pressed my hand instead straight to his chest, because even through the leather of his armor I wanted to touch more of him, sense his heartbeat quickening in time with mine.

I didn't want to stop. I wanted to give all of myself to him.

And the most frightening part of all—the part that would have scared me away, if my logical mind had been at all functional in this moment—was that it wasn't the venom. No, all of this had already been there, simmering. This was only what made it bubble over.

I abandoned my hold on the wall for his shoulder, gripping him tighter.

I moved against him again—I couldn't help it anymore. My body was nothing but nerves and raw want, exposed and tender and desperate—*desperate*—for him.

The low growl in his throat echoed through all of me. And I knew I should be afraid of him, of how much I knew he wanted me. Just as much as I did. He wanted more than I was giving him now.

But I wasn't afraid.

You're safe, Oraya, he had whispered to me, and I believed him.

And even now, he didn't touch me more, not even in all the places I blindly wanted him to. I could feel him tensing like a drawn bowstring. Could feel the urgency building in the way his tongue moved against my throat.

I wanted it. I spread my thighs wider, opened the sensitive passage between us more.

I didn't mean to say his name. Didn't mean to throw myself against him, starving for as much of his body as I could get, selfishly taking every inch of that hard length between us against my core.

Stars exploded over my vision. His name fell from my lips in a gasp. Every muscle coiled, and then released.

Nothing existed but him.

Him and everything that I still wanted.

The first thing I became aware of when the sparks of my climax faded—*oh, Mother, I had actually just done that*—was his muscles trembling. His hands were drawn into fists against my back, gripping my camisole so tightly that I was certain it had ripped, but not pulling me closer.

He was being careful, I realized. Careful not to pull me so close I couldn't get away.

He was no longer drinking. Instead, his lips ghosted over my skin, over the wound he had opened there, in tiny, gentle kisses. Kisses over the fresh scar I had asked for. Kisses over the old one I had not.

I felt dizzy, boneless, my mind coated in a blur of want. My orgasm hadn't sated me. If anything, it reminded me of everything I still wanted. I wanted his skin. I wanted him inside me. I wanted—

He pulled away. His chest was rising and falling heavily beneath the press of my palm. When he met my eyes, the sight of him cut through the haze of my desire.

He looked like a man undone. Destroyed.

A trickle of red fell at the corner of his mouth. I wanted to taste it. Taste myself on him.

His lips parted, and I kissed him before words could come out.

My blood tasted like warm iron. But that was nothing compared to the way he tasted. He smelled like the sky—he tasted like falling. His lips met mine like he'd been waiting his entire life for this kiss and had known exactly what he would do when he got it. We kissed like we fought together, responding to each touch, each movement. We understood each other by now.

But he jerked back abruptly after too-few seconds. I barely recognized my own voice when a frustrated whimper left my throat.

"No." He panted the word. "No, that's enough."

That was insulting. It wasn't enough. Not for either of us. The way his cock strained beneath me was evidence of that.

I saw no reason now not to take what we wanted.

"You aren't yourself," he said.

"Don't pretend you don't want to."

Mother, I didn't even know who this version of myself was.

He made a sound between an exhale and a scoff.

"You don't even know, Oraya." The corner of his mouth, where a little smudge of my blood remained, curled as he shook his head. "The things I've thought about. 'Want' doesn't even fucking cover it. I have a *list*."

A chill ran up my spine. I'd known he desired me, even if I didn't want to acknowledge that. But it still felt strange to hear him confirm it aloud.

I liked it.

"But I want you to want those things too. *You.* Not the venom."

The rejection stung a little. I pulled away from him.

He chuckled. "That face. There she is."

"Fuck you," I managed.

"You wish I would."

His smile faded. My scowl faded. It wasn't banter anymore because we both knew it was true.

Raihn staggered to his feet—he was unsteady, but already looked so much stronger than before. Meanwhile, when I stood, I nearly fell back to my knees.

He caught me. "Easy. You've lost a lot of blood. Your body is a bit shocked."

He was right. I *had* lost a lot of blood. Given him so much. And yet . . . not too much. Even in starvation, even two steps from bloodlust, he had stopped long before he risked me.

"Sleep," he said. "Let yourself recover."

Sleep. Sleep sounded good. Not as good as sex. But good.

I allowed Raihn to lower me gently to the ground. And I allowed him to lie down beside me, the warmth of his body, big and solid, curling around mine.

My eyelids immediately began to flutter. His hand rested on my waist, offering quiet stability and nothing more.

But then his hair tickled my face. His mouth, warm and now too-familiar, brushed against my cheek. And his words shivered over the crest of my ear as he whispered, "Thank you."

"It was the practical thing," I choked, like we were just talking about the blood and not the—the—everything.

He lay back down behind me. The world started to blur. And the last thing I heard as sleep took me was Raihn's voice, so quiet it seemed like he might be speaking to himself.

"You are the most stunning thing I've ever seen, Oraya."

CHAPTER THIRTY-NINE

I woke up warm. Unusually warm. Pleasantly warm. The sort of warm I dreamed about in the crooked bed with the scratchy blanket.

Safe warm.

Except I wasn't in a bed, I was lying on hard, gritty stone. And the source of the warmth wasn't a blanket but a wall of a man, whose chest was pressed to my back and chin rested on the top of my head, arms loosely holding me.

The events of the day before came back to me slowly. Raihn's body under mine. His mouth against my throat. My hips rolling against him and—

A flush rushed to my face. I stirred, suddenly too conscious in too many different ways of Raihn's arms around me.

Apparently, he was already awake. I rolled over to see him looking down at me, hair hanging around his face in red-black tendrils, a smirk at his lips.

"Did you know that you snore?"

Spoken with the casual lilt of our usual banter on the surface, but I heard the note of awkwardness beneath it. Like he didn't quite know how to interact with me after that, either.

I cleared my throat and sat up as he stood. I was . . . disheveled. I ran my fingers through my hair, which I was certain looked as messy and undone as I felt. The effects of the venom had worn off, leaving me strangely well-rested, slightly groggy, and extremely self-conscious.

"Well." I eyed him up and down. "You seem better."

That was an understatement. He looked like himself again, rather than the shade of a person he had been the night before. His wounds had already healed dramatically, and he moved around un-encumbered.

"I feel it," he said.

I stood, and the silence stretched. Raihn looked like he was getting a little too close to giving me another "thank you" that meant too much and lingered too long.

Who knew the man was such a sap.

"I—" he started, right on cue.

"This is meant to be Nyaxia's rescue of Alarus, right?" I cut him off, curt and businesslike. "When they captured him."

The darkest part of Nyaxia's story. She and her husband had broken out of prison once, but Alarus was lured back to the White Pantheon with the promise of amnesty for Nyaxia. Instead, the other gods dragged him out to the empty plane between the divine and mortal worlds. When Nyaxia realized what had happened, she tore apart the deadlands looking for him.

But she was too late. By the time she reached him, her husband had been decapitated and left to rot.

"These are the deadlands," I said. "There must be an end point that we need to reach."

Raihn's face shifted. For a moment, I thought he was going to try yet again to talk about what had happened between us the night before.

I breathed a sigh of relief when instead, he just nodded. "Probably."

The two of us went to the mouth of the cave, our weapons drawn. Unlike last night, it was now eerily quiet—so quiet I questioned whether the poisoned contestants had all died off. There were no voices or screams, only distant wails of animals and a *hisss* that slithered through the air as smoke rolled in waves over the gray dirt. That deadly mist was worse than last night—soupy and thick, stinging my eyes even from this distance. It even pooled in the sky, a blanket covering the stars and moon completely.

A few minutes later, it dissipated just enough to reveal the ghostly silhouette of the landscape. Not that there was much to see. Only a few gnarled, broken trees dotted the land, emerging like silent, mournful sentinels. Jagged rocks dotted the empty expanse, vicious as bared teeth.

Last night, this place had seemed dead. Now? It seemed more than that—not just dead but murdered, grieving in violent death throes.

A strange sensation prickled at the back of my neck. A nagging thought that lingered just out of reach.

"There." Raihn's voice was very close to my ear. I followed his pointing hand. "There's something over there. Gold. See it?"

I couldn't. "Your eyesight is better than mine."

"It's there. It must be the end."

"How far?"

"Miles."

Fantastic.

"The smoke is . . ." I rubbed my arm, where the leather bubbled. "I don't know what it is, but it hurts."

And worse, there was now so much more of it than the night before.

"I remember," Raihn said, touching his own burnt armor.

"So we can't just walk through the center. And you can't fly above it, because it just collects up there."

I craned my neck around the opening of the cave. The cliff—if that was even what this place was; it was so hard to tell when everything was so jagged and formless—extended straight in both directions, before devolving into an unstable-looking pile of rocks. But the land was raised along its edge—as if the broken forest before us was a crater, and we had found shelter at the edge of its rim. The ridge curved in both directions, gradually climbing up, before my weak human eyes lost track of it in the darkness.

"Could we climb along that?"

Raihn followed my gaze. "It's less direct, but it would take us to the gate. And there would be less smoke."

Less, but not none. I watched the smoke billow up from the ground in puffs. Thicker for several seconds, then thinning as the breeze shifted it. Then thicker again, as a new wave rose from the earth.

I started counting silently.

"What if—" Raihn started, but I barked, "Shh!" and tried not to lose my count.

There.

Ninety seconds.

"It's predictable," I said. "The way the smoke moves. Look."

This time, Raihn watched with me.

"See?" I said, when the billow swelled again. "Ninety seconds. It's predictable. And it takes a long time for the cloud to get up there." I pointed to the crest of the rim. "We would be able to see the wave coming."

"And do what?"

"Hide?"

"Where does one hide from smoke?"

"Behind . . . a rock?"

I knew even as I said it that it was a stupid idea.

Raihn gave me a look that said, *That's a stupid idea.*

I threw my hands up. "Well, what's your brilliant suggestion, Raihn?"

He was quiet for a long moment, thinking. Then his mouth curled. "The man I killed yesterday was Shadowborn, wasn't he?"

I COULDN'T BELIEVE we were risking our lives for a fucking cloak.

The only reason I didn't object more to this was because Raihn's fight had not been far from here. Still, we had to do some strategic guessing to figure out where the body might be—if it was even still there at all—and the consequences of being wrong were dire.

We decided Raihn would go alone. He could fly faster than I could run, and the smoke would affect him less than me.

"Wait until it's thinnest," I told him. "And if you don't find him, come back right away. Don't waste time."

"I know."

All I could think about was how weak Raihn had been just hours ago—how, even now, I could see the remnants of it.

I swallowed and said, as coldly as I could manage, "Don't do anything stupid."

He looked back, narrowing his eyes at me. "If I didn't know any better, I'd think you were worried, princess."

"I don't want to have to make that climb alone on foot."

He just chuckled. "Sometimes I have my doubts, but you really *do* like me, don't you?"

And before I had time to snap at him again, he was gone. His magnificent wings spread as the smoke thinned, and he soared down into the pit.

Ten seconds passed.

Twenty. Thirty-five.

I unsheathed my blade.

If he wasn't back by sixty, I would go, I decided.

My eyes ached from not blinking as I stared into that smoke.

For some reason, my mind went to Nyaxia. How she must have felt fighting her way across the deadlands, all alone, desperate to save her husband. It struck me with sudden clarity just how terrible it must have felt to be out of reach of someone you cared for—to feel utterly powerless to protect them.

Fifty-five seconds.

That was it. I was going.

I drew in a deep breath and held it. As if that would do anything.

I started running—

—And then something knocked me away. I was ready to fight, but a low laugh and a now-familiar hold on my shoulders stopped my hand before it moved. Raihn had yanked me back away from the smoke, a smile crinkling the corners of his eyes. His wings were still out, glistening every shade of night like melted paint in the darkness.

"Were you coming to rescue me?"

"For a second time," I muttered, and sheathed my blades.

"I'm touched. No need, though. Look."

He released me and grabbed the fabric he'd bunched up in his other hand, letting it fall. It was dark silver—a favorite of the House of Shadow—and looked as light as air. It shimmered and rippled like moonlight itself.

"Avathrian silk," Raihn said. "Just like I thought. One of the Shadowborn's finest creations. Looks fragile, but this shit filters out everything. A bitch to cut through, too."

I thought of the Shadowborn man's corpse, practically split in two. Hadn't stopped Raihn last night.

"Why don't they make all their clothes out of it?"

"It's expensive and very hard to work with. So they tend to use it for simple things." Raihn affixed the cloak to his shoulders, then raised the hood. He looked as if he was covered in molten steel. Even dirty and wounded, he was a sight to behold. Fearsome and majestic.

"Will it be enough?" I asked.

He shrugged, making the silken fabric ripple. "Let's hope so."

"That inspires confidence."

"Oh, right. My idea is the stupid one. Let's hide behind a rock instead."

I pursed my lips. Fair. It was the best option we had.

So, we decided, Raihn would wear the cloak, carry me, and move us both as quickly as possible across the rocky crest for ninety seconds. Then we would stop, take cover beneath the cloak, wait the next ninety counts for the wave of smoke to dissipate, and continue. We had no idea what we would encounter up there— monsters, competition, or both—and Raihn would be unable to defend us while moving. That would be my job. He'd be the wings. I'd be the teeth.

Repeat, until we arrived at the gate.

Or until someone else attacked and killed us.

Or until the smoke penetrated the Shadowborn fabric and ate us alive.

Fabulous.

We prepared ourselves, and Raihn scooped me up in his arms again, holding me tight to his chest while I readied my blades. From the first time he held me this way, it had felt . . . different than I expected it to, even if I wasn't ready to admit it. Now, in the wake of last night, I was very conscious in a very different sort of way of all the places our bodies touched.

His lips ducked close to my ear. "Ready?"

Not really. But as close as I was going to be.

"Ready."

And then we were rushing into the deadly mist.

CHAPTER FORTY

This wasn't flying. This was just hurtling ourselves through the air, all finesse stripped away in favor of speed. My eyes burned and face stung as bugs, dust, and stray branches clawed at us. Raihn had to move erratically, not in graceful arcs but messy jerks to dodge trees and piles of rock while keeping us low enough to avoid the cloud of acidic smoke above us—and all while fighting with the flowing fabric that threatened to tangle in his wings. I struggled to keep my eyes open and weapons ready, barely blinking.

Thirty counts, forty, sixty-five, seventy—

"*Now!*" I shouted.

Raihn held me tighter, and we slammed to the ground. He pushed me down first—hard enough that I let out a strangled *oof*—and braced himself above me, throwing the cloak over us both.

"Smaller," he grunted, and I pulled my legs up tight to my torso and rolled to the side, making myself as tiny as possible beneath him.

I'd never been so grateful to be as short as I was. It was the only reason why this worked. Raihn had said that he would magic his wings away so they didn't get in the way, but he must not have had time, because he ended up pressing them down tight to our sides, the cloak coming down around us. My heartbeat quickened at the suffocating closeness—I was pinned, the ashy ground beneath me, Raihn's body above, his wings on either side.

I couldn't see anything. But I felt it, when the smoke rolled in, because Raihn tensed.

I pressed my hand to his chest in a wordless comfort.

"Shut your eyes," he commanded, just before the burning started.

I squeezed them shut tight, but I still felt it. On my flesh, too—first in the exposed skin, like my wrists and hands and neck, and then the rest of me.

Ten seconds in, I thought, *Maybe this will kill us.*

But it didn't. The pain remained unpleasant, but far from deadly.

Ninety endless seconds.

When Raihn finally lifted off me, my skin, lungs, and eyes stung, but I was otherwise unhurt. He would have gotten the worst of it. I had no time to even look at him, though, before he grabbed me and we were flying once more.

My mind emptied of everything but counting. We had to make it miles like this, in ninety-second spurts. I lost track of how many times we repeated it, my body slamming against the ground again and again.

We were lucky at first, encountering no danger other than that smoke. But then, about halfway to our destination, Raihn threw back the cloak and we were immediately attacked by three wolves, foamy-mouthed and visibly starving. Raihn didn't have time to grab his sword, instead unleashing an immediate burst of magic to force them back—far weaker than usual, considering his still-fresh injuries.

Fifteen seconds.

I had to react fast. I gutted one while it was still stunned from Raihn's blast, and the other when it exposed its throat to me as it dove.

Forty seconds.

The third refused to die. It lunged for me while I was still pulling my blade from its companion.

Fifty-five.

I fought, and I counted. Raihn leapt in to help, taking a nasty bite intended for me. The wolf clung to life, thrashing back at every wound.

Sixty seconds. Seventy.

Eighty, as I finally killed it with a strike and a burst of Nightfire—just in time to look down the steep incline of the crater and see a wave of misty black coming for us, ten seconds early.

Raihn threw me down roughly. I saw him wince as the smoke rolled over us. We were nose to nose. The fabric didn't cover all of him.

"You were too close," he whispered.

"Blame the wolf."

This time, when those ninety counts were up, Raihn didn't move quite as quickly. As he scooped me up again, I eyed his wings. The tips had been poking out of the cloak. Now the feathers there were slightly ragged, the black flecked with what I at first thought was blood, and then realized were actually spots of red coloring.

We flew again, again, again. We were getting tired. Moving a bit slower when we needed to be going faster. I knew that the burns on Raihn's wings and legs were bothering him, as was the wolf bite.

At last, the arch came into sight. My eyesight was so poor in the dark and the fog that we were surprisingly close by the time I could make out that gold gate cutting through the night. Maybe two more sprints.

"I see it now," I said, relieved.

Raihn's hands were already at my waist, preparing to carry me again. "You should be ashamed of that terrible human—"

He stopped short.

I turned. He was looking down at something. We had climbed high, the rocky ridge now looming far above our starting point, and farther still above the deepest parts of the crater below. From this distance, it looked like a cauldron of mist. It had been difficult to see the curvature of the landscape at the bottom, but up here, the shape of it was unmistakable, the circle so well-defined that it seemed as if it had been man-made.

The hairs rose at the back of my neck. Once again, an odd sensation of familiarity passed over me.

I glanced at Raihn, and his expression made me stop breathing. Anger and fear and devastation, painted over every feature.

I had only seen that once before. When he thought Mische was dead.

Something silver glinted in the dirt. He kneeled down and picked it up. Stared at it.

"This is . . ."

He sounded as if he didn't realize he was speaking aloud. The silver in his fingers glinted as his hands shook. I realized it was a street sign—or part of one.

We were running out of time.

"Raihn, we have to go before—"

He rasped, "This is *Salinae*."

Salinae?

I almost laughed at him, because it was so outlandish. Salinae was one of the biggest cities in the House of Night. When the Rishan had been in power, it had been their second capital. I'd researched it obsessively, preparing for the day I could storm it. I'd studied every drawing, every map.

"Salinae? That's . . ."

Ridiculous, I started to say.

But I'd studied every map.

And suddenly, there it was, superimposed over this desolate wasteland. Piles of smashed rock became buildings—the city hall there, the church there, the library there. Veins of packed dirt through the landscape, dismissed before as natural rivulets in the earth, became roads.

My lips parted in sickened shock.

This wasn't a wasteland. It was ruins of a city that no longer existed. The ruins of a city that had been thoroughly, systemically devastated—as if by one of the most powerful militaries in the world.

And finally, I realized why the air felt so familiar.

It smelled like the aftermath of Asteris. Asteris and explosives, power stripped directly from the stars itself, wielded by thousands of warriors.

It smelled like this very place had smelled, sixteen years ago, the night Vincent had taken me home.

I was numb as the realization fell over me.

I will spare no one, Vincent had said. *I will not spare your wives or children.*

And he hadn't. Not just the Rishan. But the humans, too.

Vincent had killed them all.

CHAPTER FORTY-ONE

My ears rang. My hands went cold and still. I didn't move. Just stared at this place. This dead, broken place, where countless people had once lived.

Any family I had left.

Gone.

I couldn't think. Raihn was saying something, but I didn't know what. I wouldn't understand the words, even if I could hear him, which I couldn't.

Salinae is gone.

Gone.

Gone.

G—

"Oraya, *get down!*" Raihn roared as he rammed against me.

We had been distracted. We'd stopped counting. Pain seared my left foot, which jutted out beyond the cloak that Raihn had hastily thrown over us both. I felt his body tense, too. It didn't cover either of us.

For ninety long seconds, we remained that way.

Everything inside of me turned to ice, and I was grateful for it. I would rather be cold and hard and feel nothing than confront this, even though I could feel my grief there, burning under the surface, far too hot to be contained by even a lifetime of frigid control.

Vincent wouldn't have done this. He couldn't.

I couldn't help but think of Nyaxia. Mother, she couldn't have set it up more perfectly. We were acting out a morbid caricature of the worst moment of her life, when she fought through the wastelands in desperate search of her husband, only to find that he was already dead.

She had been too late. And now, so were we.

Ninety seconds passed. Raihn pulled the cloak away, slowly rising. Yet he still struggled to tear his eyes from the ashy ground. It was littered, I realized now, with little glints of silver and broken metal. Skeletal remains of the city.

"Half a million people," he choked out. "Half a million people lived here."

Distantly, a voice whispered in my ear, *You need to move. You need to move right now, little serpent—*

I looked up to see a figure moving fast toward us over Raihn's shoulder. A streak of silver, coming right for us.

No time to dodge.

I pushed Raihn out of the way and collided with Ivan at full force.

My back slammed to the ground. Ivan was on top of me, every part of his face covered by torn strips of fabric except a sliver over his eyes. I'd had time to get Raihn out of the way and stop Ivan's attack, but that meant I had no good counter of my own. My blades had been knocked from my hands. Something cut across my abdomen, shock dulling the pain to a distant throb.

Ivan's eyes crinkled with a satisfied smile.

And then the pain was suddenly excruciating, like all my blood was being boiled within my veins. Little droplets of red rose into the air, hovering around Ivan's pale face—my blood, as his magic wrung it from my body.

"For the Halfmoon," he whispered, and I prepared to meet death fighting—

But then Raihn ripped him off me, hurling him to a pile of rocks with enough force to snap a spine.

"Don't fucking *touch* her," he growled as black light cracked through the air, his Asteris awoken with fresh power.

I tried to move and couldn't. My strength drained, seeping into the ground like rainwater. I only managed to turn my head—turn it enough to see, through blurring vision, Raihn on top of Ivan, sword raised, getting ready to deal the killing blow.

Behind him, another smear of silver emerged from the smoke. Angelika. Unmistakable, even in the darkness. Like Ivan, she had covered her entire body save for her eyes. Still, every line of her radiated power.

"Raihn!" I tried to scream as she raised her bow. It came out only as a strangled grunt, but even that was enough for Raihn's head to snap up.

"*Let him go!*" Angelika bellowed.

Through my blurry vision, I noticed something strange: her arrow did not point at Raihn.

It pointed at me.

"Let him go *right now* or I'll fucking kill her, Raihn! Another Nessanyn. Do you want that? *Let him go!*"

Raihn stilled.

Everything went gray and blurry. The voices distant. Vincent's seemed closer as it whispered to me, *You made it so far, little serpent. But at least your bones will lie in your homeland.*

My palm pressed to the gritty, ashy sand, fingers loosely closing around a handful of it. I wondered if the bones of my family were here in this dirt, too, ground down to nothing but dust.

I blinked enough to make out Raihn's form, gripping Ivan's limp, injured body by the collar. "Fine," he said, at last. "I'll let him go."

And then he ripped Ivan's mask off his face and hurled him down the steep incline, directly into the incoming wave of deadly smoke.

Raihn threw himself over me. My throat released a whimper as his weight fell across my injured body. A distant wail of agony cut me to the bone—Angelika's.

At first I thought perhaps she had been caught in the mist, too. Then I realized, no—it was because of Ivan. She was screaming in grief.

Raihn pulled me close to him. When he touched my wound, I let out a weak, involuntary keen, and he stiffened as if with awful realization. He murmured into my ear, "We need to run right now."

"I'm alright," I tried to say, even though he didn't ask me that. I was losing my fight to keep my hold on the world.

"Hold your breath," he said. And then I was being lifted into the air, and my face was tucked against a solid wall of warmth, and we were flying *fast fast fast*.

Everything hurt, like my exposed skin was being flayed away in little chunks. Angelika's scream echoed behind us.

We wouldn't survive this. Not even a few seconds of it. We were being consumed.

But I forced my head up just in time to see the gate rushing toward us—

—And then it was silent.

Raihn's landing was far from graceful. He'd been moving so fast that he had to stop short to avoid hurling us both against the stone barrier opposite the gate. We ended up in a heap on a packed sand ground.

I tried to push myself up while Raihn's hold steadied me. My eyes adjusted to familiar gold-and-silver lights over an endless sea of seats.

The colosseum looked so different like this—completely empty. There were no screaming crowds, no cheering voices. Not a single spectator on those countless deserted benches. Only menacing silence.

Before us, a bloody figure sat on the sands with their knees pulled up to their chest, a dark red blanket around their shoulders. They were covered in so much blood. It took me a moment to make out who they were, until their gaze lifted to meet mine.

It was Ibrihim.

And the blanket was not a blanket, but his wings—tattered and bubbling with oozing burns that matched those around his eyes. He'd covered his face as much as he could and had covered the rest of himself with his wings, now destroyed.

Perhaps the look on my face betrayed my horror, because he smiled, a humorless twist of his lips. "The most useful they've been in years."

The Ministaer stood in eerie stillness, four of his acolytes behind him with their heads bowed.

"Welcome, Oraya of the Nightborn and Raihn Ashraj," the
Ministaer said. "Our Mother of the Ravenous Dark is pleased by
your service. You have progressed to the final trial."

I had imagined that I would feel more when I heard those words.
Instead, they were met only with a numb sense of dread.

"There has been a change," the Ministaer said. "The New Moon
Trial will not take place in three weeks. It will take place tomorrow."

My brow knitted. *What?* That was unheard of.

"Tomorrow?" Raihn repeated.

"Why?" I croaked. My fingers dug into his arm. I hoped I was
hiding how heavily I was leaning on him.

"It is very important that the Kejari concludes," the Ministaer
replied, simply, as if that answered our question.

Raihn said, "Well, of course. But why—"

"Nyaxia recognizes there is no certainty that Sivrinaj will exist
in three weeks."

The Ministaer's face lifted in the faintest hint of a nod to the
distance.

We turned to follow it.

The gates of the colosseum were wide open, revealing a grand
tableau of the city. My eyes rose to the upper stretches of the colosseum walls and the skyline of Sivrinaj beyond them.

"Fuck," Raihn breathed.

I couldn't even bring myself to speak, not even to curse.

I knew what Sivrinaj looked like. I'd memorized every shape of
this landscape in a million mournful moments at my bedroom window. And though I never forgot that this was a city—a kingdom—of
brutality, I never thought that my lethally beautiful home could become . . . this.

The city of Sivrinaj had always been as sleek as a weapon, but
now, the blade had been drawn, and it was covered in death.

Bodies lined the colosseum walls, propped up on stakes. Some still twitched in their final death throes, the life draining from them for Mother knew how long. There were hundreds of them. So many they stretched into the distance, too far for me to make out the shape of their bodies. But my father did not start anything he could not finish. I knew they would continue for the entire length of the walls, even when I could not see them.

And pinned below each stake, stretched out in garlands of death, were their wings—countless feathered wings, staked through ancient stone. Red-black blood dripped down white marble in deceptively elegant rivulets, glistening in the torchlight beneath a rainbow of brown and gold and white and gray and black feathers.

We had been locked up in the Moon Palace, isolated, for weeks. More than long enough for the war against the Rishan to escalate. Still, the sheer scale of this was staggering. Sickening.

I've had three hundred years of practice, Vincent whispered in my ear. *It is always important to be decisive and efficient.*

"You may want to rest while you have the opportunity," the Ministaer said, as if nothing of note was happening here. He gestured to another door, which offered a glimpse of the Moon Palace's great room. "Much has changed."

PART SIX

NEW MOON

INTERLUDE

The wounds on the young woman's neck had not yet healed.

Two days ago, the boy who she thought loved her had tried to kill her.

Today, her father came to her room.

"I have a gift for you," he said. "Follow me."

The king often gave the young woman gifts, though he rarely called them so. Right now, she was heartbroken. She felt hurt and foolish and stupid. She was not in the mood for gifts. But she was not in the mood for arguing, either, so she went with her father.

He led her to his throne room. It was a stunning place, a sea of marble tile in red and white and black, the Nightborn throne looming over it all. The king closed the double doors behind him and ushered his daughter inside.

She froze.

The room was empty, save for a single figure at the center of that expanse of smooth red marble—a handsome young man, kneeling, his hands bound behind his back. He looked up at her with the same eyes that she had dreamed about. Uttered a frantic apology with the same mouth that had tried to tear open her throat.

The girl could not move. The mere sight of her lover seized her heart, too many feelings thrashing in too many directions.

The king strode across the room and stood behind the boy, hands resting upon his shoulders. He turned to his daughter and said, "Come here."

She did. Up close, she could see that the boy was trembling in sheer terror.

This was strange to her. She had not yet seen that vampires, too, could be just as frightened as she was.

"Look at him," the king commanded.

She did. She did not want to. Looking into those too-familiar green eyes was agonizing.

"He's afraid," the king said. "As he should be."

The boy gazed up at his lover. He tried to apologize, tried to say that he didn't know it would be that way, that he would feel that way—

The king shushed him. He reached to his belt, unsheathed a dagger, and held it out.

"Take it."

A command. The young woman could not disobey her father's orders. She had done so only once, and now look at what had happened.

So she took the dagger.

The king had trained her for years. She knew how to handle a weapon. Her fingers fell into place immediately, now second nature. But this was the first time she had held one so close to another living being. The light from the lanterns bounced on the blade, casting sparks of green in the boy's frantic eyes.

The king said calmly, "I told you the night I brought you here that I would teach you how to wield your teeth. And I have upheld that promise. But now it is time that I teach you how to bite."

The young woman kept her face still. But inside, panic seized her.

"The heart is the easiest way," the king went on. "Straight through the chest. Slightly to the left. You will need to be forceful. Quick. It will be easy right now. But other times, they will try to run or fight. Do not give them the chance."

Everything had gone numb.

The dagger was heavy in her hands.

Her lover looked up at her and begged.

"I am so sorry, Oraya. I—I'm so sorry. I didn't know, I didn't mean to, I don't even remember—"

There are moments in one's life that remain permanently distilled in memory. Some wither within minutes, and others are carved forever into our souls.

This image, of the boy she loved begging her for mercy, would follow her for the rest of her life.

Years later, when the girl was a grown woman, she would decide that the boy had not meant to hurt her that night. That he had not yet understood his newly Turned vampire impulses. It did not change what he did. It did not make it any less unforgivable. It only made vampires more dangerous. They could love you, and still kill you.

But in this moment, the girl did not know what to believe.

I can't. The words lingered on the tip of her tongue. Shameful words. She knew better than to say them to her father.

The king stared at her, unblinking. Expectant.

"One strike. That is all."

She started to shake her head, but he snapped, "Yes. You can. You will. I warned you long ago that you were never safe with anyone but me. I warned you. This is the consequence, Oraya."

He did not raise his voice. The king rarely shouted. But the edge of his words was just as cutting, just as lethal, as the edge of the blade he handed her.

Now she understood.

This was more than just a lesson. It was punishment. She had disobeyed her father's tenets. She had allowed someone else into her heart. And now, he would force her to carve it out and lay it at his feet.

"This is a dangerous world." His voice turned soft, tender. "This is what it takes to survive."

Perhaps another teenage girl would have hated her father for this moment. And perhaps this one, in some ways, did. Perhaps she would carry a little fragment of that hatred for the rest of her life.

But she also loved him for it. Because he was right. He was forging her. If she had listened to him before, none of this would have happened.

She was not yet old enough, not yet strong enough. But she could hone herself a little sharper now, even if it meant throwing herself upon the unforgiving steel of her father's command.

She swallowed.

She lifted the dagger.

The boy wore a thin cotton shirt. It was easy to see the outline of his chest. She picked her target. Slightly to the left, just as her father said.

"You have to push hard to make it through the breastbone," the king said. "Harder than you think."

"Wait—" The boy choked.

The girl struck.

The king had been right. She'd had to push harder than she thought. She felt every layer of flesh, had to fight with the blade to get it through. The blood burst forth from the boy's skin like it had been waiting for this moment.

Bile rose in her throat as her lover cried out. He lurched, but the king held his shoulders tight.

The young woman started to turn her head, but her father hissed, "No. Don't look away, little serpent. You look them in the eye."

She forced herself to obey. Forced herself to look the boy she had loved right in the eyes until the last dregs of life seeped from them.

She held tight to that hilt long after his head lolled. At last, the king stepped back, allowing the body to flop to the floor. The boy's blood, so recently Turned, was redder than it was black. The crimson bloomed over the marble like rose petals bursting from a bud.

"Good," the king said.

He strode away. He offered his daughter no comfort, no tenderness. Why would he? The world would offer her none, either. She should learn this.

So the young woman stood there, alone, for a long time.

Strange, that girls are so often told that the loss of their virginity marks a threshold between girlhood and womanhood, as if it fundamentally alters them in some way. It was not the sex that changed the girl forever. Not the blood that spilled between her thighs that shaped her.

The blood that spilled over that marble floor, though . . .

Those are the stains on one's innocence that never fade.

CHAPTER FORTY-TWO

I insisted on walking back to the apartment, even though I could barely move. We were far down the hall by the time Angelika, the fourth and final contestant, stumbled through the door to the Moon Palace. She must have turned back in an attempt to find Ivan. But she had come back alone. Her wordless scream had echoed in every crevice of the Moon Palace.

That sound was a mirror to something inside of me that I didn't know how to acknowledge.

I clutched my abdomen. Blood bubbled beneath my fingers. But I didn't feel it. I only felt the gritty ash of Salinae—or what remained of it.

I thought of thousands of humans burning in Asteris's power.

I thought of their lungs withering in that toxic smoke.

I thought of a little boy and a little girl that I only distantly remembered—that I only allowed myself to dream might still live, somewhere—and their bodies lying deep, deep beneath the bones of a war they wanted no part of.

Raihn closed the door behind us. I stumbled, nearly falling to my knees, which seemed to jerk him back to the present. He slid his arms around me. I stiffened.

"We need to patch you up," he said, before I could protest.

I didn't have it in me to fight. He picked me up, brought me to my bedroom, and lay me down on the bed. Then he went to our packs and rummaged through them.

I stared at the ceiling. Blinked. Saw the ruins on the backs of my eyelids.

Gone. Gone. Gone.

"We have enough medicine for this," Raihn said, sounding grateful to have both good news and distraction. He returned, sat beside me on the bed, and poured the potion over my abdomen. I didn't flinch as my open wound hissed and bubbled, flesh melding to flesh.

I knew Raihn's grief was everything mine was. Everything and more. I wanted to put my hand over that wound in his heart, even when my own threatened to tear me apart.

When he set aside the glass bottle, I let my hand fall over his. It now felt so familiar beneath mine, knobby joints and scars and the coarse suggestion of hair over the back of his hand.

At first he didn't move. Then he slowly flipped his palm up, closed his fingers around mine, and circled his thumb over my skin.

Just as intimate as his lips on my neck.

I wanted to tell him I was sorry. Sorry for what my father had done to both of our peoples.

This is war, Vincent whispered in my ear. *Power demands ruthlessness. What did you expect me to do? Our hearts bleed black.*

And the worst thing was, I understood it. I understood it, and still hated it.

"I almost sent Mische there," Raihn said. "Two weeks later, and she might have been there."

The thought sickened me even more.

I felt the bedspread shift, his other hand closing into a fist.

"Your father," he hissed, "is a fucking monster."

For a moment, I agreed. But just as quickly, a wave of ashamed denial rose up to combat it.

I had to be missing something. Vincent wouldn't do it unless he had no choice. Not unless the Rishan had already done something worse, or were going to.

He wouldn't do that to me. Not knowing what I was going to go do. Not knowing why I was in this damned tournament at all.

He wouldn't.

"There must be a reason. He must have had no choice."

I hated the way the words tasted. Hated myself for even saying them.

Raihn's voice was cold and hard. "Five hundred thousand people. Half a million lives. I don't give a fuck what reason he might have. What explanation could make that acceptable?"

None. There was none.

"We don't know what happened."

"I know enough," he snapped. "I saw the ruins. I could smell the bones in that dust. That's enough, Oraya. That is enough."

My fingernails were biting into Raihn's skin, my knuckles trembling. My jaw ached because I was clenching it so hard.

And when a voice in my head whispered, *He's right. Isn't that enough?*

It wasn't Vincent's voice.

It was mine.

The line between anger and sadness is so thin. I had learned that fear can become rage, but rage can so easily shatter into devastation. The fractures spiderwebbed across my heart.

"There has to be something I'm not seeing. He couldn't have—He wouldn't—"

"Why not?" Raihn spat, mouth curled into a sneer of hatred. "Rishan lives. Human lives. What the hell are those worth to him? Why is that so hard for you to believe?"

"Because I was going back for them." I didn't mean to say it aloud. But the words were too close to the surface, ready to spill forth. "Because he *knew*. When I became his Coriatae, I was going to go back, and he *knew* I—"

Raihn went still. His grip tightened around my hand, then released abruptly as he stood, rod-straight.

"Coriatae?" he said, calmly.

My jaw snapped shut.

Do not, Vincent whispered in my ear, *tell him this.*

But I had already let Raihn see too much. As I always had. As he always did. And he could not un-hear what I said, what I had just shown him this time.

"*Coriatae?*" His voice had the same danger to it as the sound of a blade being pulled from a scabbard. "You were going to ask Nyaxia for a *Coriatis bond*?"

Judgment bit into every syllable, a sharp prod to all my weeping wounds.

"I'm not strong enough to go as I am now," I snapped. "And he knew that as well as I did."

Raihn only laughed, dark and humorless. "A fucking Coriatis bond. You were going to become Vincent's Coriatae and march into Salinae to liberate your human kin. You were going to *bind yourself to him* so you could go be a hero."

Was he mocking me? Or was the dream so outlandish that the words just sounded like a mockery aloud?

I said, "We all do what we have to—"

"You're too damned smart for this, Oraya. Do you know how many humans were left in Salinae? Almost none. Because your father had been taking them, just like he took all of Salinae's resources, for the last *twenty fucking years*."

Resources. Like humans were fruit or grain.

No. That wasn't true.

"Rishan territory was protected. He couldn't—"

"Protected," Raihn spat. "Like the human districts are '*protected*'?"

The truth of his words slipped through the plates of my armor like a too-sharp blade.

When my fingers tightened, I could feel that gritty ash of what had once been Salinae against my palms.

I had never seen Raihn like this. His rage pulled taut every line of his form. It wasn't like when I'd seen him in a bloodlust—that had been unnerving, but this was petrifying. He'd just gone utterly still, every angle of his body rigid, even his breathing too steady. Like every thread of muscle needed to unite against holding back whatever wild thing thrashed within, visible only in the rising fire of his rust-red eyes.

"He sent you into the Kejari," he said, "with a promise of being a hero, all so he could fucking *use* you? *That's* what this is for?"

He's making you do this, Ilana had told me.

I was so, so angry at Vincent. More angry than I had ever been.

Yet, so quickly I jumped to his defense, like every attack against his character struck me, too.

I leapt to my feet, rewarded by a stab of pain in my freshly healed abdomen. "Use me?" I scoffed. "He's giving me his power. Giving me—"

"You cannot possibly be this naive. Giving you his power *and* taking yours. Making a deal with a goddess so you can never hurt him. Never act against him. And sending you into this depraved cesspit to do it. What a saintly, loving father—"

My weapons were out before I could even stop myself. "Enough," I hissed. *"Enough."*

Vincent had given me everything.

He had taken me in when he never had to. He had cared for me when no one else did. He had made me a stronger version of myself, even when I didn't want to be. He had turned me into something worth fearing.

And above all, he had loved me.

I knew this. There was nothing Raihn could say to convince me that he didn't. Vincent's love was truth like the moon was truth.

Raihn didn't even look at my blades. His eyes only met mine. He took one step closer. "He killed them all," he said quietly—and just for a fractured moment, the rage in his eyes shattered to grief. Grief for the Rishan, his people. Grief for the humans, mine. And grief for me. "He killed all of them. They were nothing to him but tools or obstacles. It doesn't matter what he promised you. What he told you. *That* is the truth."

The sight of Raihn's sadness hit too deep. I shook my head, the words sticking in my throat.

"You need to ask yourself some hard questions. Why is he afraid of you, Oraya? What does he get from this?"

Afraid of me. Bullshit. What could Vincent ever hope to gain from me? What could this plan be other than a gesture of his love—to make me every bit as strong and powerful as he was? I was a human. I had nothing to offer him.

Yet Raihn's concern for me, too raw to be false, hit the places I could not protect. His hand lifted, as if to brush my cheek. A part of me longed for that touch. Longed to let myself fall apart and let him keep me together.

Instead, I jerked away.

"I can't," I choked out—even though I knew he deserved more. "I—I just can't."

I threw the door open, and he let me go.

He didn't come after me as I walked down the hall, each step fast and purposeful. I kept going until I left the Moon Palace. And I kept going straight past Vincent's meeting place.

No, I was done waiting for my father to come to me. Done waiting to meet on his terms.

This time, I was going to him.

I walked, and walked, and walked, until I reached Vincent's castle.

CHAPTER FORTY-THREE

Had the castle changed, or had I?

Before, this place had always made me feel so small, like I was too weak and impermanent to live somewhere of such grand, enduring strength. But maybe I'd mistaken brutality for strength and stagnancy for agelessness.

How, exactly, had I not noticed that its elegant scent of rose was just a little rancid? How had I not noticed that it masked the sour smell of rotting blood, like the whole damned building had been soaked in it? The flowers that adorned every table were withered at the edges, the wallpaper stained with faint death-brown blooms of old blood, the plaster cracked with the stress fractures of a kingdom that had gotten too heavy.

There were many vampires here, far more than I was accustomed to seeing roaming the halls. All Vincent's warriors. It was wartime, after all. They stopped to stare at me as I passed. I didn't even notice if their nostrils twitched. Didn't even give a fuck if they did.

I'd never once gone to Vincent's office without being invited. Now, I didn't even knock as I threw open the door.

Jesmine was there, arms folded and red-tipped fingers playing thoughtfully at red-painted lips as she observed a military map pinned to the wall. Her amethyst eyes slid to me and shone with curiosity.

"Oraya. How lovely to—"

"Where is he."

A demand, not a question.

Her perfect lips closed. The only sign of surprise. "Meetings. Busy times, as you—"

"Where?"

"He'll be done—"

"I need to speak to him now, Jesmine. Tell me where or go get him for me."

Her flicker of annoyance became a flame of irritation. She looked like she was running two calculations in her head, the first being, *Should I kill Oraya today?* and the second being, *Does she, as Vincent's daughter, outrank me, as his general?*

"I don't want to fight with you," I spat. "If you want to, it won't end well for either of us, but I'll do it. So which is it?"

Apparently, she decided that the answer to the second question was too close to call, and thus decided that the answer to the first was, *Not today.* She said, "I'm the king's chief general, not his errand girl, but I'll indulge you," and left the room.

I waited. Vincent's office was usually meticulously neat, but tonight, it was a mess—open books and papers and maps everywhere, all spattered with black and red. My hands were shaking. Shaking with anger? With grief? Or maybe with fear. Not of Vincent, but of what he might say to me.

The door opened.

Vincent came alone. His clothing was more disheveled than usual, the collar of his jacket crumpled on one side, his sleeves pushed up to his elbows. A few strands of fair hair fell into his face. His Heir Mark pulsed at a slightly faster rate than before, as if his slow heartbeat had quickened a beat since I'd last seen him.

He closed the door behind him and stood before it for a long moment, just staring at me.

I knew how to read Vincent by now, and I knew that his annoyance fought with his relief—as if Vincent the king and Vincent the father waged a silent battle behind his eyes.

"What are you doing here?" he said.

That was Vincent the king.

"You made it back from the Crescent Trial."

And that—that thankful exhale—was Vincent the father. He stepped closer, a strange uncertainty flickering over his face. Maybe he saw the difference in my expression, too.

"Salinae." My voice was hard and too rough. "You destroyed Salinae."

A hint of confusion. "I—"

"I saw it. It was the location of the fourth trial."

He tried to hide his wince. I could practically hear him utter the curse: *Nyaxia and her fucking sense of humor.*

And yet that little flinch, the expression he mostly succeeded at hiding, hurt the most, because it confirmed what I didn't want to believe.

I let out a pained, ugly laugh. "You weren't going to tell me."

And why wouldn't he hide it? Just a few weeks until I was out of the Kejari, one way or another. I was isolated. He thought I didn't even spend time with the other contestants.

"I have to make difficult decisions," Vincent said. "This is war. The Rishan were a threat. They attacked our eastern outposts. I needed a strong—"

"You were going to let me believe that they were still out there. That I could still go after them."

Was it better or worse that he didn't even deny it? "There was no use in you knowing the truth."

"Just like there was no use in keeping them alive? Easier to just kill them all?"

His face hardened.

Vincent the father stepped back. Vincent the king stepped closer.

"The decisions that I make for my people and my kingdom are beyond your judgment."

"For *your* people?"

I was lucky I was drunk on my own anger and hurt, or else I never would have been able to speak to him this way. Even now, the shock on his face had a part of me shrinking back. But another part of me liked it the same way I liked it when my blade hit a mark.

"Who are *your* people, exactly?" I snapped. "Are they the ones whose ashes are in that city? Those were *my* people, Vincent. And I—"

"I did what was right for my kingdom."

"Salinae is part of your kingdom. Half a million people. I could have been one of them. It could have been me in those slums—"

"It was never going to be you."

He always said that. But how could he not understand? It was pure chance that brought me to him that night, all those years ago. The fibers of fate twist a different way, and I never make it here at all.

"I am human, Vincent. *I am human.*" I said it twice, just because he never liked to hear it, never liked to acknowledge it. "I was born in Salinae, to human parents, to a family who—"

Vincent's restraint rarely buckled. Now, it outright shattered, the wave of his temper unleashed.

"*Family.* What does that word mean? That you were yanked from between human legs? You don't even remember them. If they had lived, they would not remember you. Perhaps they'd be grateful you were gone. What would you have been to them? Another unwanted child to keep alive? Or maybe another lost one to grieve, when the world inevitably crushed you."

Each word buried deep in my chest, skewering another unspoken fear.

His lip curled with disgust. "And yet *this* is your dream? *This* is the life you long for? And what does that make me? The cruel man who ripped you away from—what, this great life of love? Is that how you see me? As a captor?"

I swallowed a writhing twist of guilt. Even through my anger, my impulse was to apologize to him—*No, I'm sorry, that isn't what I meant. I love you and I'm grateful and thank you for saving me.*

But then, he strode to the door and threw it open so hard that the silver knobs banged against the wall. "Look," he snarled.

He grabbed my wrist and dragged me down the hall to the railing that overlooked the feast hall. It was crowded, busy with men and women wearing the deep violet uniforms of Vincent's Hiaj army. Long tables were set up below, dotted with overflowing plates. Most of the plates were untouched, though. Because instead, the warriors fed on the humans.

There were a dozen in that room alone. Some lying on the table, heads lolling, barely conscious. A few, clearly drained, slumped discarded against walls. Some had been bound to the table with rope. One man, who must have struggled fiercely, was pinned to the table with daggers piercing his flesh.

My chest burned. Stomach churned. I couldn't breathe. Even swallowing would make me vomit. How long? How long had he been doing this? I wanted to deny it. Wanted to pretend I didn't see it. This brutality was so much worse than anything I had witnessed in this castle before.

But it made sense, didn't it? How does one feed one of the biggest armies in the world? How does one keep morale up when waging an endless war? How does one entice warriors who value nothing more than blood?

A nice perk of wartime, isn't it? Endless death.

And perhaps it did not happen out in the open like this before. But maybe, like so much else, it had rotted beneath the surface, and I had chosen not to see it.

"Look, Oraya." Vincent's fingernails bruised my arm. "Look at them. These aren't people. They are livestock. You never would have allowed yourself to be one of them, because you are *better* than them. *I made you better.* I gave you teeth and claws. I made your heart steel. Do not pity them. They are less than you."

I couldn't tear my gaze from the humans below. Their blood ran over the tables in rivers of crimson.

He was right. I would never be human like they were. Just as I would never be human like the people I saved in the slums, or the ones who occupied the pub I went to with Raihn.

Just as I never would be as human as Ilana.

And maybe that was a blessing in some ways. A curse in others. Maybe Vincent had stolen something precious from me as he stripped away my humanity.

And I'd fucking let him.

Not only that, but I'd done such a wonderful job deceiving him that he thought I would see what he did when he showed me this sea of savagery.

My eyes stung. I wrenched my hand from his grip, turning away from the feast and retreating down the hall. "You lied to me."

"I indulged your childhood fantasies, knowing that one day you'd grow past them."

He thought I would become like him, and I would no longer care, just as he no longer cared. But he was wrong. I thought of Raihn, who had been a vampire for more than two hundred years and yet still so clearly mourned his humanity with every heartbeat.

Suddenly, I mourned my humanity, too. I mourned it the way I mourned Ilana.

I stopped short just within Vincent's office door. I turned to him, let out a trembling breath.

"Why do you want me to be your Coriatae?" I asked.

I knew the answer. Vincent wanted me in the Kejari, wanted me to become his Coriatae, because it was the only way to turn me into something acceptable for him to love.

My father loved me. I knew this. But he loved me in spite of what I was. Loved the parts of me that he could make like him.

Vincent's jaw tightened. Again, a glimpse of the silent battle between king and father. He closed the door behind us and leaned against it. "Because I want you to fulfill your greatest potential," he said, at last. "I want you to be strong. I want you to be powerful. And I want—I want you to be my daughter. In every sense. Because you are more like me than you ever have been like them, little serpent."

He was right, and I hated it.

My voice was strangled, on the verge of breaking. "Today, I am ashamed of that."

The words hit Vincent like a blow to his heart. Hurt careened across his face for a split second, replaced immediately by ice-frigid anger.

Vincent the father disappeared.

Vincent the king approached me, rage rising in his silver eyes with every slow, predatory step.

"Ashamed?" he said quietly. "*Ashamed?* I gave you everything. I made you all that you are. I could have killed you. Many said I should have. And you . . . you say that you are *ashamed of me*?"

I was a decent fighter, but no one was as good as Vincent. When he grabbed my arm, I didn't have time to move. And I was too shocked to, anyway, when he wrenched it, hard, and slammed me against the wall. He was so close that I could see every pulsing line of his Heir Mark, every glowing wisp of magic unfurling from each stroke of ink, just as harsh as the hateful lines on his face.

"What would you rather be, then, if you don't want to be my daughter?" His fingernails bit into my skin, tighter, *tighter*—drawing blood. "Do you want to be my enemy, instead? Is that what you'd prefer?"

I had never, ever been afraid of Vincent before. I was now.

Because now, he didn't look at me like I was his daughter. He didn't even look at me like I was human. No, this was worse.

He looked at me like I was a threat.

"Let me go, Vincent." I tried to keep the waver from my voice and failed. "Let me go."

But maybe the waver saved me, because Vincent the king disappeared all at once, and Vincent the father was appalled with himself.

A flood of horror fell over his face. He looked down at his own hand, wrapped tight around my arm, red blood and purple bruises pearling at his grip.

He released me and took several steps back. He ran his hand through his hair.

He was shaking.

"Oraya, I—I—"

He wouldn't say he was sorry. The Nightborn King apologized

to no one. And if he was going to, I didn't want to hear it. I didn't want to hear anything he had to say ever again.

A part of me thought he would stop me as I threw open the door. But he didn't.

THERE WERE MORE out here than ever now. With Raihn and me unable to come to the human districts since the Halfmoon, the place was crawling with vampires. They were lazy. Easy to kill.

Before, I'd found this satisfying. At least I could ease the unpleasant thoughts in my head with the plunge of a blade into a chest over and over again. Now, it just made me angrier. They thought so fucking little of us that they didn't even think they needed to be careful. Whatever joy I found in the dying light of their eyes was fleeting, each one a weaker rush than the last.

I killed my fourth for the night in an alleyway close to the pub that Raihn and I would frequent. It had been a very long night. It was probably close to dawn.

I couldn't bring myself to care. Not about any of it.

I didn't toy with this one. I went straight for the heart. He was so afraid that he pissed himself in the end. I stepped slightly to the left to avoid the puddle at his feet.

He'd been going for a child. A little girl. He was preparing to go through the window for her. That was rare. I didn't often see them ready to crawl into houses for their prey.

The body sank to the ground. I kneeled over him as he lay limp in the dirt, ready to pull my blade out.

He thought he was entitled to these people. Their houses weren't homes, just dens to be rooted out. Chicken coops to stick his hands into and pull out whatever he wanted. Maybe the haze of death over these recent weeks had made them believe that there was no such thing as protection, no such thing as consequences.

They are livestock, Vincent had hissed at me.

Only now did it occur to me that maybe that's exactly what humans here were. The human districts weren't for protection. They were breeding grounds. Because it would be a fucking *shame* if no more humans lived in the House of Night, wouldn't it? Just think of all that blood.

My knuckles were white around the handle of my blade, which still protruded from my victim's chest.

This piece of shit felt it for five seconds. For five seconds in a lifetime of centuries, he felt that powerlessness. When it had been bred into us, tattooed into our souls, for our entire brief pitiful existences.

I was done hating myself for all my human weaknesses.

No, I hated *them* for it.

I pulled out my dagger, but instead of sheathing it, I brought it down again. Flecks of black blood spattered my face. Withdrew. Again. Again. Again. Each strike met less resistance as bones cracked and flesh parted.

I hated them, I hated them, I HATED THEM I HATED—

"Oraya! Stop!"

The moment the hands touched my shoulders, I whirled, lashing out before I could stop myself.

I came into this world fighting. I'd leave it fighting. And I'd fight to cover every soft spot or vulnerability, and right now, I felt as if my entire body—my entire soul—was a raw wound to be protected.

I wanted to fight.

But of course, Raihn knew that. And of course, he knew me well enough to counter my every move, until finally my back hit the wall, my arm in his grasp.

He bent over me, one hand to the wall over my shoulder, the other holding my arm, firmly but gently.

The relief in his gaze shook me. He jerked his head to the body, now little more than bloody pulp. "I appreciate your thoroughness, but I think he's dead."

His eyes softened as they flicked back to me.

I really did try not to notice, or care, that they drank me in the same way he drank in sunshine.

"It's almost dawn," he said. "I've been looking for you everywhere."

He didn't ask, *Are you alright?*

But I heard it in his tone, anyway.

I was not alright. I didn't want such softness. It prodded too close to everything I was trying to protect.

His fingers shifted, encroaching on the marks that Vincent's nails had left on my arm. They hurt more than a wound so small should have. I winced slightly—barely a twitch—but Raihn still saw it. His gaze fell to my arm. Hardened.

"Where did this come from?"

"What does it matter?"

"It matters. *Him?*"

I hesitated a moment too long before saying, "Some piece of shit in the slums."

"Bullshit."

His lip curled. Pure hatred. As if those few little bloody marks were just as great of a crime as the destruction of Salinae.

I hated that.

I didn't deserve to be defended that way. And still—despite everything—I hated to see the disgust on his face. I was offended on Vincent's behalf.

I yanked my arm away. "You've done worse to me yourself. I'm not a princess to be protected. No matter what you like to call me."

"I know."

Two words, and yet, so much judgment in that expressive face of his. I knew how to see through all the masks now, and beneath it, everything was always laid out bare. Too bare.

"Stop," I hissed.

"Stop what?"

"Don't look at me that way."

"How am I looking at you?"

I pushed past him. I didn't know how to answer that. Too many ways. I saw multitudes in Raihn's eyes when he looked at me.

"Like you pity me."

He scoffed. I refused to look at him, but I could hear the twist of a sneer on his lips. "You think I pity you? I don't pity you, Oraya. I just think you deserve better."

That sounded a hell of a lot like pity to me. And if it wasn't pity, it was something else—something more real—and that, I hated even more.

I whirled around. "Why are you here?"

My tone was downright vitriolic. It was undeserved. He had done nothing but be kind to me. But I only knew how to fight.

Still, the hurt on his face disarmed me. Then his jaw went tight. "I know what this is, and I'm not doing this with you. If you want to get kicked out of the Kejari because you don't make it back to the Moon Palace before dawn, fine. I'll let you."

"Good. It'll be easier for you. Maybe you deserve the win more than I do, anyway. Why do you care?"

Raihn had already started to walk away. My voice was weaker than it had been. The look of hurt on his face had sapped the venom from my bite. Now I was that little child all over again, lashing out at monsters with feeble, human teeth.

He stopped. Turned back slowly. "Why do I care?" he repeated, indignant.

The thing was, I knew it was a ridiculous question. And it shouldn't have been, because Raihn had every reason to just let me spiral and get myself disqualified or killed. I was his enemy in every sense of the word—the daughter of the king he hated, raised in the clan that destroyed his, rival to a title that only one could win.

He took a step closer, unblinking. "*Why do I care?*" he rasped, again. "Are you a fucking fool, Oraya?"

I wasn't expecting the desperation in his voice. Like he was pleading for help.

He scoffed. "Or maybe I am."

No. We both were.

Because I knew exactly why Raihn cared. And I knew that I cared in all the same ways. I didn't breathe. I let my blade slide back into its sheath.

No, a weapon couldn't protect me from this. I wasn't sure if I wanted it to, anymore, even though my heart was open and bleeding and so very pitifully, humanly delicate.

Still, as the moonlight fell over his face, I drank in every angle of it. I had come to know it so well, and yet I discovered something new and captivating in it every time I looked at him. Now, so much of it held pain and grief.

I ached for him. And I was so, so tired of loss.

I wasn't sure what I intended to do or say when I approached him.

But I threw my arms around his neck and kissed him.

CHAPTER FORTY-FOUR

Raihn met my kiss with so much fervor that I found myself questioning which of us had moved first. His arms folded around me, pulling me flush against him, and the two of us stumbled until my back hit the wall. His mouth sought mine like he wanted to learn every part of me—claiming my lips, top and then bottom, his tongue warm and soft and demanding and giving.

A groan rose from deep in his throat—it shuddered through my entire body. I was pinned between him and the wall. His hand ran down my side, and I leaned into that touch. Not enough. Still, not enough. Whatever spark we had ignited in the cave hadn't been put out, only dampened. It roared back to life hotter and deadlier than before. And right now, I wanted nothing more than to burn alive in it.

The hand that slid down my side kept going, flattening around my hip, then my backside, and then suddenly my legs were lifted, parted around his hips, and the hard press of him between my thighs made my breath hitch.

Fuck. I needed more than this, this time. Needed less between us. I needed it so badly I didn't even care that it meant exposing myself to him, too.

His kiss slowed, deepened, shifting from frantic to tender.

I pressed my hand between us, down his abdomen, down to the stiff length of him pressing at his pants.

Another groan. His lips smiled against mine.

"Careful, princess."

I kissed him—kissed that smile—because the idea of not doing so seemed sacrilegious.

"Why?"

"Because I don't want to fuck you for the first time in an alleyway three feet from a pile of entrails."

I couldn't argue with that. Even if, embarrassingly, a part of me wanted him so much that I would have done it here, just to bury myself in a different primal pleasure. First blood, then sex. Maybe I was more vampire than I thought, after all.

But then his free hand cradled my cheek. His next kiss was different—gentle. It reminded me of the way he had kissed my throat in the cave. Like he cherished me.

My chest tightened. There was nothing vampiric about that. Nothing carnal and cold.

"Oraya, look at me."

I opened my eyes. Our noses touched. The moonlight illuminated every little scar on his skin. His pupils were slightly slitted against it, the ring around them almost violet beneath the coldness of the light.

"Give me one honest thing," he murmured.

One honest thing.

The most terrible honest thing of all was that with Raihn, it was all honest—it always had been. He saw too much of me. Understood every complexity and senseless duality. I was honest even when I didn't mean to be. He did not fear my darkness, nor pity my compassion.

And the truth was, the idea of dying without knowing him completely was torturous.

How could I say any of this? Did he want that kind of honesty? Was I even capable of wrenching it from my bleeding soul without unraveling all my stitches?

"We'll probably die tomorrow," I said. "Show me something worth living for."

A momentary pause, as if something about this response had hurt. Then a faint curl to his lips.

"Pressure." He kissed me again—this time not a demand, but a promise. "I think I'm up to it, though. We'll fly. We need to beat the dawn."

RAIHN STOLE KISSES from me as we flew, as we made it into the Moon Palace just in time for the sun to crest the horizon. They were sweet and tender, punctuated with little grazes of his teeth that promised the harder edge to our morning. By the time we returned to the apartment, my heart was beating fast behind my ribs, my breath rapid. I felt oddly dizzy—every sense dulled by the intensity of my want and sharp with anticipation of what it might be like to fulfill it. I hadn't even been able to admit to myself how many times, and in what great detail, I had imagined what it might be like to taste Raihn, to touch him, to feel him inside of me.

But reality, of course, was different than fantasies. More treacherous, and more exhilarating.

The door closed. I leaned against the wall, watching Raihn as he bolted it. Even the flex of the muscles of his forearm was beautiful, each tendon working like a string in an orchestra, elegant and graceful.

It was almost embarrassing, how stunning I found him.

He finished locking the door and turned to me. For a long moment, he said nothing. I wondered if he was thinking everything that I was. Imagining what we might do with our final night with each other.

Final.

Mother, how I had avoided thinking about that word. Everything that had happened over these last few days had chased it from my mind. But the truth was unavoidable.

The last trial was tomorrow night.

Raihn and I were both finalists.

It was unheard of for more than one contestant to survive the Kejari.

Raihn was the first to break our suspended stillness. He

approached me, fingertips running down the bridge of my nose, then my mouth, then my jaw.

"What's that face for, princess?"

I could not lie to him.

So instead I said, "Kiss me."

And—Nyaxia fucking bless him—he did.

I could melt under this kiss. I wanted to wind myself around him the way ivy claims stone. I opened my lips to him, encircled my arms around his neck. His fingers clenched around my hair, pulling just a bit.

His hand paused there, thumb rubbing my hair, kiss slowing, and I wondered if he was thinking about it, too—thinking about the night of the feast, and my hair around his fingers.

I didn't want him to let me go then, either. Maybe I realized in that moment that I never would, even if I was too terrified to admit it then.

Maybe I was too terrified to admit it now, too.

My teeth closed around his lip, coaxing a satisfying hiss from his throat. His hands roamed over my body—down my back, cupping my backside, lingering at my upper thighs, like he wanted to memorize the shape of me. His hands were so large that the pressure of his fingertips ventured agonizingly close to the core of my need. Still not close enough.

His lips slowly curled, just as his fingers did, inching ever-slightly higher—deeper.

"Your armor's too thick," he said.

What was it about him that made me so bold? I kissed him, then slid my hand down, over his chest, his abdomen, down over his length. Mother, he was big. Even through the layers of his clothing, he responded to my touch as easily as I responded to his. It was the most incredible, powerful thing, feeling him twitch under my hands. Listening to that little shudder in his breath.

"Yours too," I whispered against his lips.

It should have been frightening to me, to know that he wanted me this fucking much.

It wasn't. Instead, it made my own desire maddening.

He drew me closer, his hand tightening in my hair, and claimed my mouth in a kiss so sudden and passionate that everything but him withered away. He lowered himself, released my hair in favor of cupping my backside with both hands, and lifted me. I kissed his mouth, his jaw, his throat, as he carried me into his room, and the two of us fell onto the bed. His broad form crawled over mine. I freed my hands so I could work at his jacket. It was a complicated thing, all buttons and straps, and especially difficult to navigate when I was feeling around blindly. After a few seconds, he laughed against my lips.

"Having trouble?"

He pulled away enough to look at me—and Goddess, I mourned his mouth already—but before I could complain, the beauty of him stopped me short. It was now morning, and though the curtains were drawn, the barest hint of sunshine slipped through the fabric and outlined his silhouette in a faint kiss of gold. I'd never realized before just how much red was in his hair, or in his wings, which were still out. I touched them without thinking, prompting a sharp inhale from Raihn. They were softer than I imagined they might be.

He gently pulled my hand away. "We'll save that for another time."

"Does it . . . tickle?"

He chuckled. "In a way."

If he expected this answer to dissuade me, it very much did not. But disappointingly, with a puff of smoke, his wings were gone. And he leaned down as if to kiss me again, then paused, drinking me in the way I just had him.

His hands went to the button of my armor. "May I?"

I swallowed.

I wanted this—Mother, I wanted it, the slick ache between my legs promised that. Yet something about this made me strangely nervous, my heart fluttering against the inside of my ribs like a captured bird. I didn't want to feel that way. But the memory of the one and only time I had done this still seized me, a map carved into my body that I couldn't erase.

"You first," I whispered.

Raihn sat up. And slowly, button by button, his armor fell open, sheets of battle-worn leather parting to reveal the most stunning body I had ever seen. As he shifted the coat from his shoulders, I watched the light play over the surface of his flesh, and I was fucking jealous of it—jealous of the way it got to pool in the crevices and dips, the way it kissed the raised texture of his scars, the way it shuddered over dark hair at his chest and below his navel, disappearing beneath the low-slung waistband of his trousers.

I had stopped breathing. He caught my eye and smirked in an infuriating way that told me he knew exactly what I was thinking.

Oh, fuck him.

I rolled off the bed and rose.

"And where, exactly, are you going?" he asked.

"Nowhere."

I stood with my back to him and worked at the buttons of my jacket. Then the laces of my pants. I let my jacket fall to the ground first, then peeled off my trousers.

Raihn had shut up.

I turned around.

He had gone so still. It was rare that he embodied that stillness—vampire stillness, the kind that made the world go silent. He drank me in, starting at my face and moving down. I could feel that stare as if it was his touch—caressing the scars on my throat, the curve of my clavicle. I could feel it pause at my breasts, peaked with my arousal, covered by the tips of my black hair. It slid down my stomach, traced the angry-pink slashes from the trial. Landed at the apex of my thighs. His nostrils flared and eyes went hard, and I wondered if he could sense it, smell it—how much I needed him.

When his eyes came back to mine, he looked like a man undone. "Come here," he whispered. Pleaded.

I returned to the bed. And I couldn't help it—the moment he was in reach, my hands were all over him. I touched him like the light had, tracing every line of muscle, every scar, every trail of hair. His mouth was on mine immediately, his hands on my waist, my breasts, making me gasp with every new expanse of skin.

"Beautiful isn't enough," he rasped as he pulled away from my mouth. "Fuck, Oraya, you're—I—"

He gave up on words. Instead, he lay me down and his lips moved to my throat, soft over my flesh. He lingered at the scar where he had drunk from me—and the one beneath it.

Then, slowly, he moved down. His fingers circled my breast, thumb rolling over my nipple. When he lowered his head to me and brushed his tongue over that sensitive peak, my eyes rolled back.

I didn't know it was possible to *feel* this much. Want this much. It hadn't been like this last time. But then again, we'd both been barely more than children. And it had been . . .

Different.

I didn't mean for my thoughts to wander to that night. Just as I didn't mean for my fingertips to brush my throat, and the older scar there.

Raihn raised his head, a wrinkle of concern between his brows.

"Don't stop," I breathed.

But he just looked at me, lips thin, as if a thought had just occurred to him.

"I can't believe I didn't—Oraya, is this . . . is this your first time?"

He didn't ask it with any judgment, only genuine concern. His hand fell over mine, his thumb rubbing my palm.

"No," I said.

The truth, even though in some ways it felt like a lie.

Raihn's stare slipped to my throat—to that scar, the same one he had kissed in that cave.

He knew. He understood.

His breath was warm over that mark.

"Is that when you got this?"

I squeezed my eyes shut and was rewarded with a vivid image of a different night, a different man, a different breath on my throat.

"Yes."

"How?"

"No big story. He . . . he just couldn't control himself."

Raihn didn't believe my forced indifference for a second. His lips kissed one silvery-white jagged line, then the other. He withdrew, looking into my eyes hard, like he wanted to watch to make sure I understood what he was about to say.

"You're safe, Oraya. I need you to know that."

You're safe.

"I know." And I meant it. Because from the first time he told me those words, I believed him.

"I want you to enjoy this." His lips curled, and he shook his head, immediately correcting himself. "No. More than that. I want you to—fuck, there are no words for what I want."

"I'm not some naive virgin."

Sure, my last sexual experience had ended . . . poorly. But a girl could do a remarkable amount of experimentation on herself. Still, looking at Raihn's body—looking at the way his trousers strained—I had to admit this seemed like it would be very different.

"Oh, I know. No one could call you a shrinking violet."

He kissed me, long and slow.

"I just want you to know," he murmured, against my mouth, "that you are in control. And we can take all the time we need to make sure you're ready."

His fingertips brushed the curve of my inner knee. My thighs opened, and that touch wandered higher, my breath growing shallower with every inch.

"Time?" I barely managed to speak. "We have one night, Raihn. And then we die. So you'd better be a fucking amazing lay."

"Oh, don't you worry." He ventured farther up my thigh—still not as high as I wanted it. My heartbeat quickened as his lips moved slowly over mine. When his fingertips brushed the wetness of my folds, he shuddered too, in a way that I found very satisfying. "I've . . . done a lot of thinking about this."

Did I imagine he sounded . . . a little self-conscious?

"A lot of thinking about you." Another kiss. "What I would do to you." Another. "What you might sound like." Another—and his fingers again stroked the yearning at the apex of my thighs. "I have all kinds of experiments to conduct."

He pulled away from me abruptly, his mouth moving down my body. He kissed my breast, my stomach, the crest of my hip. And then he gracefully stepped backward off the bed, kneeled before it, and turned me so that my legs hung over the edge—as he positioned himself between them.

I propped myself up on my elbows, watching. My arousal and my fear warred with each other. I found myself stiffening, suddenly very aware of how exposed I was. I was naked. My blades were across the room. And Raihn—a predator, with a bite much sharper than mine—had me spread before him, helpless.

He opened my thighs a little more, as if he wanted to observe more of me. The sight of him there, kneeling between my legs, made something primal within me flutter with desire.

His gaze dragged back up to mine, reluctantly, as if he had to force himself to look away.

"Let me taste you."

I let out an almost-laugh. "You already have."

"And even then, I was thinking about this."

His hand roamed up my stomach. Mine met it without me telling it to. His thumb swept over the back of my hand—reminding me, I knew, that even though his teeth were so close to the most vulnerable parts of me, I was still in control.

"Yes," I whispered.

I couldn't take my eyes off him as those perfect lips curled, or as his head bowed before me.

But at the stroke of his tongue, I threw my head back.

From the first touch, it was demanding, giving. I thought he might tease me just because he knew how much I wanted him. Instead, even the first stroke was firm and definitive, caressing the length of my slit, ending with a pause at my clit that had my hips bucking.

His hands tightened around my thighs, pulling me closer to his face. He let out a groan that vibrated through the most sensitive parts of me.

"Better. Better than your blood."

Better, I agreed, blindly. Better than anything. Better than everything.

I had no snarky retort to this. No sharp comeback. Only the blind, delirious desire that he never stop doing this, ever.

I opened my thighs wider, just as his lips met me again.

His tongue was thorough, deliberate. Soft where I needed it. Hard where I needed it. My body bowed against him, with each stroke the tension of my past unraveling in favor of wanton ecstasy.

I had imagined what this might be like, the night he drank from me. But he was right. This was better. His mouth moved against me with the same urgency, the same reverence. My hands clutched fistfuls of the bedspread, every muscle growing taut in anticipation of the next kiss, the next stroke. His hands were so tight around the pale flesh of my thighs that surely his fingernails were leaving marks. Good. I wanted him to.

My breath was rapid and serrated. The final vestiges of my self-control kept me from making a sound save for a few whimpering moans. But soon, my hips rolled against him in time with his tongue.

When he lingered at my most sensitive nerves, brushing his teeth against me, the shock of pleasure was so intense that his name ripped from my throat.

Oh Goddess. Oh Mother. I was on the precipice, ready to fall, and everything shattered except for—

He stopped.

I let out a frustrated gasp. I lifted my head to see him peering at me. My chest was heaving, bare breasts rising and falling.

"Say that again," he rasped, "when you come for me."

This time, when he lowered his lips to me again, he slid two fingers inside of me—giving me everything, everything, everything, with one long, forceful stroke of his tongue.

The new combination of sensations was too much.

Pleasure consumed me. My back arched violently against the bed.

And I gave him exactly what he wanted. I moaned his name again, again, again.

I was panting when the world came into focus again. The first thing I heard was Raihn chuckling, his lips against the sensitive flesh on my inner thigh.

"Fucking incredible."

Fucking incredible, I agreed.

But not as incredible as it would feel to have all of him inside me. To reduce him to the whimpering mess that he'd just made of me.

I sat up. My entire body felt soft and loose, the last of my tension erased beneath his tongue. Before Raihn could move, I threw my legs off the bed and pushed him flat to the floor.

"Oof," he grunted, as I crawled over him. "I go through all the trouble of bringing you to the bed, too."

But he wasn't complaining. Already, his hands roamed over me, tracing the curve of my thighs as they spread over his hips, up my waist, lingering at my breasts. The deeper desire for him tightened in my core, more intense than ever now that my nervousness no longer tempered it.

I lowered myself against him and drew in a deep inhale, without even meaning to. His scent hit me like a lungful of cigar smoke, and the taste of his skin—the taste of the sky—left me dizzy.

Raihn's fingers gently tangled in my hair as I trailed down, following that widening path of soft dark hair, to the waistband of his trousers. His leathers were thick, and cut close to his body, but his length still strained admirably against them. It looked a bit painful.

He stopped breathing as I worked at the buttons and laces. Hell, I did, too. And when that fabric fell open and his cock was at last liberated, I let it out at once.

I didn't know it was possible to find such a thing so stunning, like a work of art. It was as big and powerful as the rest of him— actually, the size of it made me faintly nervous. And yet, it was also so elegant, every shade of flesh exquisitely complementary, the head peeking from a graceful sweep of tan skin.

When my fingers wrapped around it—Mother, his skin was so soft compared to the unyielding hardness of his desire—it twitched, the bead of moisture at its tip swelling.

I watched it, transfixed, then lowered my head and licked that moisture away.

Raihn let out a ragged exhale, fingers tangling in my hair.

I lifted my eyes. He had propped himself up on his elbows, watching me with his lips parted, pupils dilated. He didn't blink. Didn't move.

Maybe it was in the way he looked at me right now that made me understand exactly how much he wanted me. I had him.

After a moment, his mouth twisted into a rueful smirk. He knew exactly what I was doing. Because everything with us was a game of power and vulnerability, give and take.

My mouth curled, too.

"Should I make you beg?" I brushed my lips over him again.

He made a sound somewhere between a hiss and a chuckle. "And when I've been so generous with you, too. You already had me on my knees." Then the smile faded, his eyes sharp as my tongue swept over him once more. "I need to be inside you. I'm sick of waiting."

I was, too.

I sat up, swung over him. Positioned myself so that his rigid length lay right against my core, right between my thighs. At the first touch of his silken skin to my wet folds, we both drew in gasps.

His hands gripped my hips, his eyes never leaving mine.

"I would beg," he murmured. "For you, I would. You have fucking destroyed me, Oraya. Do you know that?"

His whisper was hoarse and raw. Too raw to be anything but the truth. And my own truth swelled in my throat, too much for words.

I would beg for him, too. Break for him. Cut myself open like an animal for dissection. He held me open that way, not just my body but my soul, too.

I would let him think that this was nothing but pleasure. Nothing but a rebellious daughter's revenge against her father or a final carnal indulgence before near-certain death. I would let him think that we were just fucking.

Or at least, I would not make him acknowledge the fact that he surely saw otherwise in my face, too, just as I saw it in his.

I reached between us and aligned him with my entrance. Even the first press of his tip into me was enough to make my breath hitch. His fingers tightened at my hips—his desire, and his steadying guidance. The grip said, wordlessly, *You are in control.*

I wanted to take him hard and deep, but my body had other plans. He was so much bigger than I was used to. I had to lower myself slowly, inch by inch, allowing myself to adjust as he filled me.

Yet what little pain there was disappeared beneath a dizzying wave of lust once I finally had all of him. We were so close together, so tightly linked. I could swear I could feel every pulse of his blood, and he was buried so deep inside of me that surely he felt every throb of mine, too.

It was so much. Too much. It was—I couldn't—

"You alright?" he whispered. His hand flattened against my thigh, a comforting stroke, and I realized that I was shaking, overwhelmed as every muscle contracted and responded to his presence within me.

My only response was to circle my hips, fractured moans escaping both of us even at that small movement.

Oh, Mother. This was going to end me. It was going to fucking annihilate me.

I pressed my palm to his stomach. Felt the taut, trembling muscles of his abdomen. My eyes locked with his.

"You're holding back."

His silence was my answer. Slowly, I rose again, so that only his tip was left within me, never looking away from him—from the feral desire in his eyes, the way his teeth closed around his lip.

"Don't," I whispered, and took his entire length in one sudden thrust.

The tension, the tenderness, shattered into a million pieces. Fucking him slowly was agonizing—fucking him hard was devastating. He released a growled curse as he grabbed my waist, helping me through each stroke, his hips rising and falling in time with mine. I didn't know how it was possible that he seemed to get deeper with each one, branding every wall within me, every muscle.

I asked him not to hold back, and he didn't.

His thrusts were deep and vicious, pistoning in and out of me with a force that left me incoherent. But it wasn't enough—I wanted more. So much of my flesh still screamed for him. As if he read my mind, he sat up, seizing my mouth in a kiss just as fierce and thorough. The change of angle forced him to abandon speed for depth, moving slower, harder.

The sound that escaped my throat didn't even sound human. He rolled his hips again, mine meeting the movement on nothing but instinct, and I realized the sound was a plea, begging for I-didn't-even-know-what.

"Yes, Oraya," he growled. "Fuck, yes. Anything."

I clawed at him, my fingernails digging into his back—surely leaving marks—our kisses wild and messy and fighting for dominance. Every sensation sent me hurtling toward a pleasure beyond my control—his lips, his tongue, his skin, his chest pressed to my breasts, his hands gripping my hair, each torturous stroke of his cock.

Pleasure shot up my spine. My mouth escaped his, kissed his jaw, his ear, his neck. He gripped my hips and levied an especially powerful thrust, one that forced a curse from my lips, and I closed my teeth around the perfect flesh of his throat, tongue darting out against the iron warmth of his blood.

He groaned, his hold on me tightening. He was close—I was close. His hands roamed my back, my ass, my hips, my breasts—like he wanted all of me, and couldn't decide what he most wanted to touch as he went.

I had to force myself away from his skin to look into his eyes.

"Say my name," I gasped, echoing his words. "Say it when you come."

He covered my words with his kiss, demanding, tongue claiming my mouth. I could feel his muscles coiling in time with mine—I knew what was coming. And as his lips moved to my throat, some distant part of me balked in memory of another moment, long ago.

But I was too far gone.

He drove deep into me, hard.

"Oraya." He whispered it like a prayer against my skin. "Oraya, Oraya, Oraya."

I cried out.

I felt his cock swell, twitch, as my walls contracted around him.

Felt the warmth of him fill me, our hips wringing out the final waves of pleasure from each aftershock.

I didn't fall back to earth so much as it all simply faded back. My senses returned to me in pieces. First the air rushing in and out of me with my heaving breaths. Then the warm solid wall of Raihn's chest. His hand rubbing my back.

He had leaned back to the floor, and I had gone with him, now limp on his chest.

I was a little surprised that I was able to move at all when I lifted my hand and brought it to my throat. I felt only the raised bump of my scar, and the damp remnant of his kiss, and nothing else.

"Fuck, Oraya," he breathed. "Just . . . *fuck.*"

His words from earlier echoed in my head:

You have destroyed me.

He had destroyed me, too. Perhaps it was good that we would die tomorrow. Because I didn't know how to remake myself after this.

I pushed myself up enough to look at him. His hair fanned out around his head on the dark wood floor. A certain contentedness had overtaken the typically harsh lines of his expression—albeit, still, with a lingering shine of lust to his eyes. But there was something else there, too. Softer than lust, gentler, and yet far more dangerous.

A drip of black-red rolled down his throat. He touched it and let out a wry chuckle.

"Why am I not surprised that you were the one to draw blood?"

I licked my lips, tasting a residual drop. "Maybe I understand what you see in it."

I meant it as a joke, and he laughed, but oddly enough, I *did* see the appeal. He tasted like he smelled. All of him—his blood, his skin, his mouth.

"So." I eyed him. "How long before you can do that again?"

"Hmm." Abruptly, he rolled over, dumping me to the floor. He grinned, his nose touching mine. His cock brushed the inside of my thigh—already hardening.

"One night. I don't plan on wasting any of it. I have a list, re-member."

A list, I thought as he kissed me again, hard, and my arms fell around his neck, and I lost myself in him all over again.

A fucking list.

The most beautiful word in the Goddess-damned world.

CHAPTER FORTY-FIVE

We barely made it halfway through.

It was an impossible task. Every time I had him, I discovered a new piece of him I wanted to claim. It was the opposite of satisfaction. With each climax, I only desired more. By the time we found ourselves crawling into the bed out of sheer exhaustion, I had come up with far, far more than a single night's worth of fantasies.

Yet I found myself not minding as I drifted too easily to sleep in his arms. And now, as I lay nose-to-nose beside him, watching the heavy fall of his lashes against his cheek and the steady rhythm of his sleeping breaths, I thought, *It was worth it, to witness him this way.*

I ran my fingers over the swell of muscle of his shoulder, down his back.

Mother. I hoped he had no clue how transfixed I was by him.

His eyes opened. The moment they landed on me, the smile warmed his lips immediately, like he was relieved that none of it had been a dream.

"Don't tell me it's time to go."

"We have a few more hours."

He stretched. "Wonderful. Not ready for death just yet. Maybe after I watch you come one more time I will be."

Death.

The pit in my stomach, the one I had desperately been trying to ignore, grew larger.

Before, I could drown all those unpleasant thoughts beneath our shared mindless, carnal pleasure. But as I'd watched him sleep, alone, all those fears seeped into the silence.

We joked about death because we had to. But it wasn't a joke. It was real, and it was coming for us. And the thought of death getting anywhere near Raihn made me feel sick.

For so long, he and I had danced around each other's pasts. It didn't behoove either of us to learn too much about the other. The less we knew, the easier it would be to carve each other out of our lives with a single well-placed strike of our blades, like a cancer excised.

But in this moment, I came to the horrifying realization that I would never be able to carve Raihn from my heart. He had embedded too deep. Roots through stone.

And as I had watched him sleep, I couldn't help but see Ilana's face float through my mind. There were so many things I hadn't asked her, too. And when she died, I had to bury myself in broken, incomplete shards of her life, because it was all I had.

I wanted more of him than that. More of his body. More of his soul, too.

I said softly, "You told me before that you had a lot of people relying on you."

Raihn's smile faded. "I do."

"Who?"

"I'd rather have more sex than this conversation. Glad your pillow talk is about as pleasant as your bedside manner, princess."

I smiled weakly, a little embarrassed. But his fingers caressed my cheek in a way that said, perhaps, he understood. And maybe he felt some of what I did, this masochistic urge to hack out little pieces of our heart for each other, because he said, "Do you want the short answer? Or the long one?"

"The long one."

What I didn't add: *I want to listen to you talk for as long as possible.*

Raihn looked away, silent for a long moment, as if he had to prepare himself.

"The man who Turned me," he said, "was a very powerful person. When I was human, I was a guard, and I took a job securing a trading ship from Pachnai to Tharima. Our boat was too small to be making a journey that long. We got caught in a storm and it flung us right to the shores of the House of Night. Snared on Nyaxia's Hook."

I knew the term—it referred to a little rocky hook of land that jutted out from the southern shores of the House of Night. The currents were very strong, and though I'd never seen it, I'd heard stories that the horizon there was littered with the remnants of shattered ships.

"I had no idea where I was when it happened. We were off course. It was dark. Most of the others died. I was close to it, too. Literally dragged myself to shore."

His eyes fell straight ahead, not to the wall, but to the past.

"Luck," he said. "Luck saved me. Or damned me. I was mostly dead by the time I found him. I'd seen a lot of death, even then, but when it's breathing down your throat, it's different. When he asked me if I wanted to live . . . what kind of a question was that? I was thirty-two years old. Of course I fucking wanted to live. I had a—I had a *life*."

The dismay in that sentence. I felt it in my heart, too. *I had a life.*

"A family?" I whispered.

"A wife. A child coming. A lot of future to live for. I was willing to do anything for it."

He said this with such rueful resentment, as if he hated his former self for thinking it.

I wondered if he thought of that version of his life as often as I thought of a different version of mine.

"So I accepted. I thought he was saving me. I traded away my broken humanity in favor of immortality. Or so I thought. But then . . ." His throat bobbed. "He didn't let me leave."

"Didn't let you—?"

"At first, it was because I was sick. Turning is . . . I hope to any god that you never know, Oraya. I really do. I fought hard to live, but clawing my new self out of the old took weeks. Months. But after that, I realized—"

He bit down hard on his words, swallowed. I slid my palm to the bare skin of his chest in silent reassurance, and his hand fell over mine, pressing hard enough that I could feel his heartbeat—quick with the memory of the past, despite the careful restraint of his voice.

"I wasn't the only person he Turned. Not the only vampire he took. He chose . . ." His head tilted slightly to the opposite wall, as if he didn't want me to see his face. "He had his tastes, alright? He was very, very old. And once someone has been alive for the better part of a millennium, it gets hard to find excitement in the world. Fulfilling their various hungers gets difficult. Entertaining those they seek to influence, keeping their attention, gets *difficult*. People become . . . nothing more than sources of amusement. And when they're that powerful, when they have that much control over every living being, you don't have any choice but to let them do what they want to you."

Horror curdled in my stomach.

Oh, Mother.

When I had first met Raihn, he had seemed like an immovable pillar of strength—first physical strength, and then emotional strength. The idea that anyone had ever used him that way . . . the idea that anyone had made him feel the level of shame that I heard now in his voice, all these years later . . .

And yet, so much now made sense. That Raihn knew so implicitly all the things I didn't say. Knew what it felt like to be so powerless, to be used in ways beyond your control. Knew how to recognize the scars of a past, whether on a throat or on a heart.

It seemed patronizing to tell him I was sorry. What good did my pity do him?

Instead I said, "I am fucking furious for you."

No, I wouldn't give him my pity. But I'd give him my rage.

The hint of a smile creased the corners of his eyes. "There she is."

"I hope he's dead. Tell me he's dead."

If not, I'd hunt him down and kill him myself.

"Oh, he's dead." A wince flinched across his features. "I'm . . . ashamed of what I let myself become, back then, once the fight was stomped out of me. There was no shortage of ways to numb myself. He won, so I took them. I hated vampires. And for seventy years, I hated myself, because I had become one of them."

Fuck. I couldn't. *I* hated them, too.

"But . . . I wasn't alone, either. There were others in the same position as me. Some Turned, some Born. Some of them were shells of who they used to be, like me. Some I formed an . . . uneasy kind of kinship with. And some . . ."

I wasn't sure how I knew. Maybe it was something about the faraway mist over his eyes, and the fact that I'd only seen that expression once before.

"Nessanyn," I murmured.

"Nessanyn. His wife. Every bit as much of a prisoner of him as I was."

A lump rose in my throat. "And you fell in love with her?"

I admit there was a little twinge of jealousy at the thought— *why?*—but that aside, I *hoped* he had. Because I knew, firsthand, that having someone to love could help someone survive impossible situations.

He didn't answer for a long time, like he really had to consider this. "I did," he answered, finally. "And loving her saved me, because by that time, I didn't think there was a single gods-forsaken thing in the entire shitty world that mattered, until suddenly, Nessanyn mattered. And the difference between nothing mattering and one thing mattering is a big one."

I was grateful to her for that. That she had helped him survive.

"But she and I were very different people. If we'd met in another life . . ." He shrugged. "I don't know if we would have paid any attention to each other. The only thing we had in common was him. But he was our entire lives, so that was enough. Together we were able to craft something that was just ours. She was the first kind vampire I'd ever met. Just a good, decent person. And through her, I met others. It just . . . changed everything." He looked away, as if embarrassed. "It sounds silly. It sounds like nothing. But . . ."

"It's *not* nothing. It's *not* silly."

I spoke more sharply than I had intended.

I was so fucking angry on his behalf. Angry that this had happened to him. Angry that anyone had dared tell him that any of it, any shred, was silly or shameful or undeserving of anything other than righteous fury.

"How did you get out?" I asked.

"The world he had built was collapsing under its own weight. All that cruelty was catching up to him. I saw it happening, and I knew it was the only chance I'd have to get out. I begged Nessanyn to go, too. Begged her to save herself. But she refused."

I couldn't fathom this. "*Why?*"

"You'd be amazed what people can be loyal to."

"She would rather die with the man who tortured her than live?"

"She was a dreamer. Kind, but soft. She'd rather escape to the world she dreamed of than fight for this one." Then he winced, as if offended on her behalf by the harshness of his own words. "It isn't that simple. But in the end, she died in the rubble of his world right alongside him. I got out, and she didn't."

"Did you ever go back to find your wife? Your—your child?"

He brushed the scar on his cheekbone. The upside-down V. "I tried. It didn't go very well. Seventy years is a long time. I didn't consider myself a vampire, but I wasn't human anymore."

I disliked how familiar that felt. I had human blood and a vampire heart. He'd had a human heart and vampire blood. The world left no room for either.

"I spent a long time traveling. When I was human, I became a guard so I could see the world. That and . . . well, look at me." He gestured to himself with a half smile. "What else was I going to do with myself? I could choose between blacksmith and soldier, and only one of those didn't require me to stare at horses' asses all day."

"You could've been a chef," I countered, and when he laughed—an actual laugh—the sound of it loosened something in my chest.

"Maybe I should have. Just spent my whole life fattening up a simple, happy wife and having a simple, happy family, and I'd be long in the ground getting much more rest than I do now."

It did seem nice. It also seemed . . . smaller than him.

"But the truth is, I didn't even get to travel much when I was human," he went on. "So when I was free, I went everywhere. The whole of the House of Night. All the islands. The House of Shadow, House of Blood—"

House of Blood? *No one* went to the House of Blood.

"It was about as morbid as you'd expect," he said, at my raised eyebrows. "I even traveled the human lands. Realized I could pass, if I was careful. But . . . after a while, I think I realized I was running. They were with me everywhere. Him reminding me of everything fucked up about the world. Her reminding me of all the good I had abandoned in it. And then, when I came back to Obitraes, I found Mische."

Those words held so much more weight now that I understood his background. "Oh."

"Mische reminded me of her, in some ways. The good, and the flaws. Both of them saw so much beauty in the world. But they also both had that . . . that fucking naiveté. That willful ignorance of what it takes to actually make that kind of reality."

He paused for a long moment of thought.

"Those seventy years with him had been . . . bad. But I met a lot of good people who were suffering, too. People that Nessanyn was trying to care for, even when she was drowning. Rishan people, who were now more trapped than ever. And I should have fought for them when it all collapsed, but I didn't. I didn't know how—or maybe I did and wished I didn't."

I thought with new horror of the hundreds of wings pinned on the wall. Thought of the ashes of Salinae.

"So you came here."

"I didn't think those responsibilities were mine for a long time. Mische disagreed. She forced my hand. Entered the Kejari first. Knew I wouldn't let her do it alone."

My brows leapt. Entering the Kejari just to force him to do it . . . to call it extreme was an understatement. She very well could have been sacrificing her life.

I must have made a face, because Raihn let out a dark, humorless laugh. "I was ready to fucking kill her myself. Stupidest thing she possibly could have done. And mark my words, I would have

found a way to get her out. One way or another." His face softened. "But that's Mische. Impulsive as shit. But always, always
well-intentioned. More than she has any right to be, after all she's
seen. Sometimes foolishly so. I love Mische like a sister, but . . . I
worry about her. The world isn't flowers and sunshine. She doesn't
realize—"

"—that you have to fight hard enough to leave a mark," I finished. "That it isn't easy to clean."

His eyes fell to me. The familiarity of them, like a mirror, struck
me deep. "Exactly."

The world was not easy or straightforward. Goodness was never
pure or simple.

When I first met Raihn, I thought we would never understand
each other. But now, for the first time, I felt like someone was really
seeing me—seeing the world as I did.

I became aware of the warmth of his skin under my palm, the
thrum of his heartbeat. If I were to kill him, I would need to put my
blade right there. Replace this caress with a strike.

And maybe . . . maybe I couldn't do it. Maybe I didn't *want* to.
Raihn had people to save. Mine were gone. Who deserved this
more?

I couldn't voice this. But I had never been able to hide my darkest thoughts from him, not even when I needed to the most. He saw
right through me.

"But then," he said softly, "I met someone who still managed to
find defiance where I thought it didn't exist anymore."

My throat tightened. *Defiance.* He made it sound so noble.

"A stupid dream," I choked out. "As if gutting a few vampire
scumbags in the alleys means anything. As if it changes anything."

"*Stop.*" The word was a sharp rebuke. "You found a way to defend your world when everyone told you that you shouldn't. Do you
know how fucking hard that is? How rare? I *wish* I had fought the
way you do. That is strength."

Was it strength to lash out against a steel wall? Or did that make
me just another naive dreamer?

"I don't know why I'm doing any of this anymore." My hand

wandered to the pile of my clothes on the other end of the bed, fingertips playing at the hilt of my blade. I withdrew it, observing the dark steel in the lantern light. Orange dripped along the swirls etched into its length.

I'd been so honored to wield this weapon. But how many like it had been used to murder people with blood like mine?

How badly would I have to injure myself, I wondered, for Nyaxia to accept my withdrawal?

Raihn could defeat Angelika. He could certainly defeat Ibrihim. And he could seize that wish and use the Goddess's power to help those who needed him.

As if he could hear my thoughts, he grabbed my hand, tight.

"Look at me, Oraya."

I didn't want to—I would see too much, he would see too much— but I did anyway.

"You are more than what he made you," he said. "Do you understand? That isn't the strength. The shit he tried to carve out of you is. You have every reason to keep going. Now more than ever. And I say this knowing—knowing how stupid it is for me, of all people, to say it."

He wasn't talking about the Kejari. He was talking about something bigger. And his fingers clutched mine, trembling, as he hissed, "So don't you fucking *dare* stop fighting, princess. It would break my damned heart."

My eyes stung.

I wouldn't admit it. But it would break mine if he did, too.

"Then you'd better not, either," I said. "Swear that to me. We're in this now. We knew what we were getting into. Nothing has changed."

Everything had changed.

But Raihn paused, then inclined his chin. "Deal. If we fight, then we fight to the end. Whatever end that may be. Whoever's blood needs to spill to win it."

I thought I would feel better, like we had restored some piece of our relationship to what it was before.

I didn't. We hadn't.

I glanced to the curtain-draped windows. The light beneath them was now scarlet.

"The sun's going down," I said. "Don't you want one last look?"

And Raihn didn't hesitate—didn't look away from me once—as he answered, "No," and kissed me.

I HAD NEVER so dreaded nightfall.

It came nonetheless. I was expecting the little thread of shadow in our room, Nyaxia's beckoning hand, but the sight still made my breath burn in my lungs. When it appeared, Raihn and I rolled out of bed and put our armor back on without a word.

Before we left the room—left it for the final time—we stopped and looked at each other.

"It has been a pleasure, princess," he said.

I watched his lips curl. Mother, those perfect lips.

I thought about kissing him one last time. Thought about winding my arms around his neck and never letting go. Dragging him back to bed and refusing to leave. At least we'd die happy when Nyaxia struck us down.

I did none of those things.

I didn't know how Raihn could possibly call me brave. I was a fucking coward.

"It's been . . ." I shrugged. The smirk crinkled my eyes without my permission. "Tolerable. I guess."

He laughed. "There she is," he said, and opened the door.

ANGELIKA AND IBRIHIM were already waiting with the Ministaer. Ibrihim did not look at us. Angelika's typically hard face was even harder than usual, her eyes sharp as daggers as she watched us approach. They were rimmed with red.

The curse? Or had she spent the last day weeping over Ivan's death?

The door appeared as it always did, with little fanfare. The Ministaer wished us luck and ushered us through. Ibrihim went first. He could barely walk. His wings hung down behind him, broken dead weight.

Next, Angelika.

And then it was only us.

Everything I couldn't say threatened to drown me. Words weren't enough. Yet without my permission, just before we crossed the threshold, I grabbed Raihn's hand—squeezed it hard, hard, hard— and oh, Mother, I couldn't let him go, I couldn't do this.

Our steps slowed. No one else would have noticed it, this split-second of hesitation. But for me, a million possibilities lived in that moment.

Fantasies. Fairy tales. Useless dreams.

I smashed them on the marble ground, pulled my hand away, and walked through the threshold.

CHAPTER FORTY-SIX

The crowd's shouts were barbaric and bloodthirsty, like the hungry roar of wolves as they tore their prey apart. The stands were packed. From this distance, the audience was visible only as a wave of people, hands raised in fists, screaming for violence. Above them, the wings of the Rishan, bloody feathers pinned open, were reduced to mere dots of death.

I took this in only for a moment, before I had to roll out of the way of a streak of fire.

Not Nightfire. *Fire.*

I barely managed to move in time. Heat singed the tips of my hair. My clumsy roll slammed me against a wall—no, not a wall, a door, bolted shut. I leapt back to my feet and turned.

The arena had been divided up. I was in a smaller enclosure, the door behind me locked. No Raihn, Ibrihim, or Angelika.

Instead, three figures circled me, two men and a woman. All three of them had empty, glowing black eyes and blank faces, wearing tattered robes that seemed like an insulting parody of religious garb. The string of fire had cut directly across my arena, leaving me scrambling to avoid the blazing path.

It came from the figure on the right. Flames surrounded him, crawling up the flowing ribbons of his robes. A crooked, tarnished crown fit poorly on his head, a chipped white circle mounted upon it.

The woman beside him wore a gown of pink, spattered with black and red. A flower circlet sat upon her stringy red hair. Two wilting roses had been shoved into her eyes. In her hands was a bow, cocked with a luminescent arrow of rusted thorns.

And at last, the final man—tall and slender, shirtless to reveal a scarred body half-marred with decay. His chin lolled, mouth gaping and blackened.

Gods, I realized.

False mimicries of them.

This was the final trial. It represented Nyaxia's ultimate rise to power. In a fit of rage and grief over her husband's death, she had turned upon her former brothers and sisters. She had fought her way through all twelve gods of the White Pantheon—and she had won.

The woman raised her bow and let her shot fly. It moved faster than air should have been able to carry it. I barely managed to dodge it.

The arrow—rusted steel, shaped like the thorny stalk of a rose— buried itself in the sand two inches from my nose. The sand around it blackened and smoked.

I kept running. Behind me, steady *thunk, thunk, thunk*s trailed my steps, growing ever-closer as arrows struck the packed sand.

The one with the fire had to be Atroxus, the god of the sun and the king of the White Pantheon. And the arrows . . . that had to be Ix, goddess of sex and fertility. Her arrows were said to plant seeds in wombs, though I was fairly certain that wasn't what they were going to do to me.

These were puppets, after all. Not the real gods, but parodies intended to mock them.

The third, though . . . I racked my brain. He wore no crown, carried no weapon—

The air split in two. The high-pitched sound made my muscles seize without my permission. I tripped over my own feet and landed hard in the sand. Pain erupted through my shoulder as one of Ix's arrows grazed my flesh, opening a smoldering tear in my armor.

Fuck. That sound. It paralyzed me. Turned my mind inside out. I forced my head up to look at them—at the third figure, whose blackened lips gaped like a fish.

As if singing.

Kajmar. God of seduction, art, beauty . . . and music.

His song stopped as abruptly as it had begun. I seized the moment just in time to avoid another encroaching wave of fire. Atroxus did not move, instead hovering inches above the sand, hands open as if in prayer and flames pooling around him in expanding waves. But Kajmar and Ix both jerked and danced across the enclosure, as if dangled on strings held by some invisible puppet master, their limp feet dragging along the ground.

I called upon the Nightfire, and was grateful when, fueled by my adrenaline, it bloomed easily to life in my hands. But I struggled to use it with precision—I couldn't shoot it at Ix or Kajmar, not when they were moving so fast, and my sloppy attempt to send a surge of it to Atroxus simply withered and died beneath the strength of his far more powerful wall of fire.

Another screech of Kajmar's song nearly ended me as I took an especially ill-timed tumble. Fire nipped at my heels. I had to fight to drag myself three inches, just out of its reach.

The moment the sound released me, I was running again, pain disappearing beneath the pounding of my heart. Everything narrowed to the steps I needed to take to stay alive.

Who was I going after first?

I couldn't get close to Atroxus; he would need to come later. And Ix's arrows had been a problem, but only because Kajmar's voice stunned me.

I needed to get rid of him. It was too dangerous to allow myself anywhere near the others so long as he could freeze me at any moment.

I had nothing but blades. So that meant there was no strategy to this next part. I just had to *run*.

My gaze locked to Kajmar, who danced in erratic fits and starts across the room. I readied my blades, braced myself, and sprinted for him with everything I had.

I didn't notice the smell until I got within two strides of him, but once I did, it was impossible to ignore. It was putrid, wringing my stomach into knots and forcing bile up my throat. He was half-decomposed. Thick paint smeared his face, cracking over slackened muscles.

He was a corpse.

And not just a corpse, but one I recognized. It was the Rishan man Raihn had killed the first night of the Kejari. Our own fallen rivals, dragged back for one final fight.

Kajmar was already preparing to move away from me before I closed the distance between us. But I pushed myself harder, threw myself at him in those final seconds.

My dagger slid far too easily into his chest.

But Kajmar didn't fall.

I tumbled to the ground as he jerked away from me, then seized when another screeching song paralyzed my mind. I barely evaded an arrow, then forced myself back to my feet.

Kajmar's wound gushed thickening globs of blood down the center of his chest. Yet still, he moved.

I'd hit the heart. I was certain of it.

But of course he hadn't fallen. He wasn't alive. That heart wasn't doing anything for him anymore.

Atroxus continued to fill the arena with layers of flame. The heat was becoming unbearable. The free space I had to move around in grew smaller and smaller.

I had minutes. Less, maybe.

I threw myself at Kajmar again. And this time, instead of stabbing him, I dug my fingernails into his necrotic flesh and dragged him closer, holding back vomit at the stench.

They weren't real gods. Just puppets. I couldn't kill what wasn't alive, so I needed to dismantle him.

His mouth was only open because his jaw was slack. Up close, I could see the unnatural swell in his neck—whatever spell or enchantment had been wedged down his throat sat there, surely. Nyaxia had no sound magic. Whatever spell made this, it would be an object that had been obtained from a different god.

How grimly funny. Something that Kajmar's magic had once touched was now being used to mock him.

I hacked through his throat as hard as I could.

His body spasmed and thrashed like a fish caught on a line. The explosion of sound felt like it would rupture my eardrums. It tore through me like a bundle of razor blades.

But I couldn't stop. Not for a second.

I slashed at him again. Again. Again. Old blood spattered my face.

I let out a roar with my final strike.

The sound went suddenly silent. My blade cut clean through the corpse's spine. Glass shattered, glints of it emerging from the gored throat.

Kajmar's body fell to the ground at my feet, still twitching, while his head remained in my hand, my fingers gripping the tangle of his hair.

Too long.

Out of the corner of my eye, I saw Ix lift her bow.

In the opposite direction, the flames swelled again.

I couldn't avoid both at once.

I forced all of my muscles to work in a final burst, pushed them against all odds, and hurled the head at Ix with all of my strength as I dove.

I rolled across the sand. Dimly, above the sound of the roaring crowd, I heard a dull thump. I recovered fast, already running by the time I hit the ground.

Seconds from the fire engulfing the pit.

I'd struck my target. Ix struggled to right herself, now a collection of uncoordinated limbs that sagged against the wall, her bow tangled in broken fingers.

I didn't slow as I hit her, blade out. I went right for her hands, slicing them off at the wrist. The nice thing about month-old flesh is that it cuts easily. The bow fell with her decaying hands.

I seized it before it hit the ground.

The arrow was already prepared. I pressed myself to the wall. Aimed.

Across the ring, Atroxus floated there in his ring of fire. Whatever magic trickery fueled his flames sat in his chest, the flare of it visible beneath the paper-thin rotted skin of his rib cage.

My target.

I didn't hear the rapid screams of the crowd, or the crack of the flames, or even the pounding of my own heartbeat.

I called and called and he wouldn't come.

I only heard Mische's sobs over the abandonment of the god to whom she had given her life.

Nightfire tore over the length of my arrow. It became a shooting star of fury as I let it fly.

It buried right into Atroxus's chest, the core of his power. For a moment, his fire and mine—warm light and cold—clashed with each other.

Mine won.

The flash blinded me. I staggered against the wall. When I opened my eyes again, the fire was gone. The corpse that lay in the center of the pit didn't even remotely resemble Atroxus. Actually, it didn't look like a person at all.

The door groaned open. The shriek of the audience reached a crescendo.

I wiped my bloody hands on my bloody clothes, grabbed my blades, and walked through without looking back.

I STEPPED THROUGH the door with my weapons ready, but this part of the arena was empty. It was a semicircle against the barrier of the stands with three other doors built into the walls that divided the colosseum. Two of them remained closed.

I looked up at the audience—at the sea of blood-drunk faces. I heard some echoes of my name, here and there. I didn't know if they were cheering for my victory or for my death. Maybe both. Who cared, so long as it was a good show?

Thousands of faces, and yet my eyes fell to Vincent's as if they already knew where to find him. He was in the front row, standing alone in his box. The chair there was designated for him, but he wasn't sitting. Instead, he stood against the rail, clutching it.

The expression on his face rearranged everything inside me, like one of Ix's poison arrows to my gut.

After our fight, I'd expected to see Vincent the king here. I saw him look at me as a threat that night, even if it was only for a few seconds. And once Vincent saw a threat, he never saw anything else.

And yes, this man had all the trappings of Vincent the war-time king—the visible wings, the exposed Heir Mark, the crown perched over his brow.

But those wings were pulled in tight, as if his nerves had tied his muscles in knots. The exposed Mark seemed less of a show of strength and more like his heart was open and vulnerable. And his face—he looked at me like he felt every stab, every burn, every wound on my skin.

I was so ready to hate him. I *wanted* to hate him.

I could hate Vincent the king, who had slaughtered whatever family I had left, who had overseen the torture of my people, who had relentlessly killed and destroyed.

But how could I hate Vincent, my father, who looked at me that way?

My anger made everything certain and easy. My love made everything complicated and difficult.

I allowed myself to be distracted.

It was Vincent's eyes, flicking up a split second before I turned, that saved me.

I whirled around just in time to dodge the arrow. A breath later, and it would have been buried in my back. Instead, I let it soar over my left shoulder, a streak of black smoke—magic—trailing it. The crowd laughed and shouted as it landed in the audience, causing a flurry of activity behind me.

Ibrihim limped from the second open door.

Fuck.

I didn't know how he was alive.

He held his bow in an iron grip, but he'd let his arrow fly, and now he struggled to ready another one. His once-good leg now dragged behind him, twisted and mangled. His hands were so covered in blood that I couldn't tell how they were injured, only that they were, and badly. If there was any doubt, the fact that he couldn't even reach for his quiver put it to rest.

He lifted his head, his mouth twisted into a grim line of determination. One eye was missing, blood running down his face.

Mother, he had fought. He had fought so hard.

I approached him. He didn't take his one eye off me as he fumbled with his weapon.

Behind me, the sound of the crowd changed in a way I couldn't make out at first. It was only as I was two strides before Ibrihim that I realized . . .

Laughter.

They were laughing at him.

Ibrihim managed to ready his bow. But his hands were trembling so badly that his fingers kept slipping from the string. He would never be able to draw it.

He jerked his chin up, a sneer at his lip. He had recognized that sound before I did. But then, he probably had been hearing it his whole life.

"You pity me?" he rasped out.

I shook my head.

No. I felt no pity for Ibrihim. He had fought, and fought well.

Maybe we were the same. Both of us had been raised in a world that had hobbled us. Both of us learned to fight twice as hard to make up for everything we weren't. Both of us had everything to hate.

I was only two steps from him. Close enough to see his shoulders lower slightly, and the flicker over his face.

He was considering giving up.

"No. Don't stop." I unsheathed my other blade. "Fuck them. Don't let them mock you. Give me a fair fight, and I'll give you a fair death, Ibrihim."

His jaw tightened. After a moment, he forced open his shaking fingers and let his bow fall to the ground. When he drew his sword, he could barely support the weight of it. Still, he threw everything he had into those final strikes.

I didn't patronize him. It took me seconds.

And when I wrenched him close, when I prepared my killing blow, that one remaining eye met mine, as if looking into a mirror.

"I'm glad it was you," he said, quietly.

And I made sure my aim was true as I slid my blade right into his heart.

CHAPTER FORTY-SEVEN

The crowd shrieked. Ibrihim's eye rolled and went distant as he died. I pulled my blade from his chest and let him fall to the sand.

I saw movement out of the corner of my eye. Across the arena, another door had opened.

I turned, ready to lunge, but instead, loosed a breath of relief.

Raihn stood there, shoulders heaving. His armor had been tattered—Mother, I didn't know what kind of creature could shred leather like that—and he was soaked, his dripping hair plastered to his face and neck. Zarux, the god of the sea, perhaps?

Fuck, I didn't even care. He was alive. I'd thank whatever god I had to for that. And I saw that same silent prayer on his lips when his gaze landed on me, too.

The fourth door swung open, breaking our trance.

Angelika looked every bit a goddess herself, her braided hair torn free from its binding, a slash over her ice-pale cheek. Behind her, I glimpsed a spattered painting of blood. She had butchered her opponents.

The moment she stepped into the ring, all four of the doors slammed closed behind us, leaving us trapped here.

Raihn, Angelika, and I tensed, eyeing each other. Maybe we were waiting for another gimmick, another one of Nyaxia's displays.

Nothing. Just the swelling roar of the audience, rising to a bloodthirsty climax.

No, there was no other trick here. Just three animals in a cage with each other. But who needed a gimmick when we were already giving them this? A human, an outcast, a monster. Lovers forced to turn on each other. A heartbroken mourner rabid for vengeance.

It was already a hell of a show.

Move, little serpent. Move before they do.

It was still Vincent's voice in my head. And despite everything, I still obeyed.

I turned my attention to Angelika first.

Her slitted eyes found mine, and we both lunged.

ANGELIKA WAS RELENTLESS.

She didn't spare even a single glance to Raihn. He might as well not have been there at all. Even when he offered her clear openings— even when he was obviously trying to draw her attention—she came only for me.

I was smaller than her, faster, more agile. But that was the only advantage I had against her. Angelika was a bred killer. She was as tall as Raihn, and nearly as strong. Halting the edge of her blade was one thing—keeping my fragile human body from crumpling, *literally crumpling,* beneath the crushing force of her strikes was another.

During one particularly vicious swing, I blocked her with my blades, only to hear a distinct *CRACK* ring out through my back. Pain shot through my spine like lightning.

I struggled to hold the block. A hoarse roar scraped from my throat. I threw everything I had into my Nightfire, flecks of it tearing up the length of my blades.

But Angelika barely reacted when those white flames nipped at her. Nor did she flinch at any cut I managed to open on her flesh, not even as the poison ate away at skin.

Her eyes, red-rimmed and cold with rage, did not move from me. She ignored Raihn, swatted away his blows, and continued her unstoppable barrage.

Seconds stretched to minutes, and the minutes stretched endlessly.

This was more than strategy. She wasn't just picking me off because I was the weaker opponent. No, this was personal. I was certain of that, even if I didn't fully understand why. Did she blame me, somehow, for Ivan's death, even though Raihn had been the one to throw him into the fog?

Did it matter?

No time to think. No time to question. No time to go on the offensive, only to evade her blows the best I could.

My eyes met Raihn's over her shoulder for a split second as I blocked one of her devastating strikes. The sheer terror on his face as he tried to get her off of me—terror on my behalf—startled me. Distracted me.

I hesitated a moment too long.

Her sword opened a river of blood over my shoulder, and her lips curled in satisfaction.

Fuck.

I tried to yank away, but her fingertips lifted. She was a skilled magic user. Not as good as Ivan had been, perhaps, but more than good enough for this. A twitch of her hand, and my own body betrayed me.

I fell to my knees. My heartbeat shuddered as the blood in my veins gushed and twisted in strange, unnatural ways. Pain bubbled up inside me, a slow burn, starting at a low simmer and quickly rising to an agony that consumed everything else. I couldn't move.

Angelika smiled as she approached me.

"You did good, human," she said. "Better than I expected."

No.

I had gotten too far to die here. I forced my way through it, forced my muscles to work against the magic.

I barely managed to lift my blade.

Raihn lunged at Angelika, but she quickly deflected him, offering me only a few seconds of reprieve—enough for me to gulp down a few lungfuls of air and stagger to my feet, barely making it up before she pushed me down again, her boot clamping down on my leg.

"It's been a pleasure, Oraya."

The certainty of death rolled over me slowly, like a cold fog, the kind that's invisible until you're drowning in its depths.

My back was to the crowd. Perhaps if it wasn't, I might have looked at Vincent. Or maybe I was grateful I wouldn't have to watch him watch me die.

Instead, my gaze flicked past Angelika, to Raihn.

I didn't know what I was searching for. Yet I felt a sharp twinge of sadness to see that he wasn't looking at me at all. He was staring past me, into the crowd. At what? I couldn't make sense of that expression. Desperation and anger. As if pleading with someone and hating every second of it.

His chin lowered. Barely a nod.

Angelika had raised her sword. It would cut me in two.

I readied my weapons. Summoned every final scrap of magic I had within my veins. I would die fighting.

But then, something strange happened. The strike did not come when I expected it. Instead, Angelika faltered, her gaze lifting briefly to the stands. Watching.

She let the blood magic slip.

And my body was already moving, and my newly freed muscles were already leaping, and my blade was already buried in Angelika's chest.

The Nightfire came a moment later, engulfing us both.

You have to push hard to make it through the breastbone.

Angelika's body was muscular and lean, and she wore armor besides. But I threw myself against her with such force that my blade hit her heart on the first try.

She collapsed. No counter, no attempted block. Maybe, if I'd had the time to think, I might have found that strange. Her eyes simply slipped to mine.

And she smiled.

"Good luck," she whispered as her claw-tipped nails fell from my arms. Her body hit the sands with a heavy thump, all the weight of greatness fallen.

I stood slowly, the pain of Angelika's magic draining away. I stepped over her body as the pool of blood soaked the soles of my boots.

Raihn was on the other side of the pit, shoulders heaving.

He looked every bit the hardened warrior. Sweat plastered a few strands of deep red hair to his face. Whatever had shredded his armor in his previous trial had done good work of it, and more tattered pieces of leather had fallen away as he moved, leaving broad patches of muscled flesh visible over his chest and shoulders—the power of his body unmistakable. Even the magic of his sword seemed fiercer than ever before, the puffs of smoke unfurling from the blade in vicious licks.

But his eyes did not belong to that person.

His eyes belonged to the person who had woken up with me today. Who had kissed the scars on my throat as if my past, and all of its dark corners, was something precious to be protected.

It was just us now. One of us would walk away, and one of us would leave our soul here, in these blood-soaked sands.

For a moment, I considered throwing down my weapons.

But then Raihn lifted his chin. The muscles of his throat shifted as he swallowed. I heard everything he didn't say in the little, encouraging nod he gave me.

Promise me you'll never stop fighting.

He had one chance to gain the power he needed to help those he left behind. I had one chance to become something more than a human left to die in a world that despised her. Neither of us could afford to sacrifice those things—no matter how much we might want to.

No, we would fight.

Raihn moved first.

CHAPTER FORTY-EIGHT

Raihn and I knew how to fight each other too well. We knew each other's strengths and weaknesses and habits. I knew not only when he would move, but how he would respond when I did. Each lunge was the result of half a dozen calculations based on the innate knowledge of each other that we had accumulated over the last months.

It felt perverse. Depraved. To use that intimacy to kill each other.

I wondered if he was thinking the same thing. There was none of his usual savage joy in this. No snarky comments or half smiles. No satisfaction in his strikes. The first time I nicked his skin, I winced as if it had hit my own. And in turn, the first time he drew my blood, he jerked back as if to stop himself.

Still, our dance continued. The crowd shrieked with amusement with every clash of steel. I barely heard them. My blood pumped in my ears, roaring.

This was agonizing. *Agonizing.* I needed it to hurt more everywhere else, so it hurt less in my heart.

As I danced closer to him, I hissed, "You're holding back."

You're holding back, I had said as I took him into my body. I knew he was thinking of it, too.

"So are you," he said.

Was that what I had to do? Go after him as hard as I could, to make him do the same to me?

"You said we're doing this," I spat, drawing back my weapons. "So fucking do it."

His gaze hardened in a way that sent a chill down my spine.

"As you wish," he said.

And when he charged at me this time, it was with his Asteris.

He was tired, and that weakened his magic considerably, but it was still a deadly force. I gasped, staggering back. I blocked his sword, but the burst of black-white light tore at my skin, leaving it bleeding and scalded. It was naive of me to be surprised that he so willingly rose to my challenge.

I asked him to come after me, and he had.

Fear is a collection of physical responses, I told myself.

Fear is accelerated heartbeats and rapid breaths and sweaty palms. Fear is a doorway to anger, and anger is a doorway to power.

When I looked into Raihn's eyes and imagined his blood soaking into this cursed dirt, the fear that stole through my lungs was overwhelming. But all of that was power, too.

When I lunged this time, Nightfire surrounded me.

Something had broken between us. All those delicate little jabs, those careful dances of blocks and dodges, shattered. We went at each other for blood.

Asteris bloomed over Raihn's every blow, as Nightfire burned in mine. Every time we came together, the two magics burst and sputtered around each other, darkness and light ripping each other to pieces. His magic raked over my skin, leaving it raw and bleeding. Mine blistered over his, searing burns into his exposed flesh.

There were no more lingering stares, no more hesitations. Only brutal efficiency.

I'd always admired Raihn's skill as a warrior. He wielded a sword the way an artist wielded a paintbrush, each stroke an exercise in grace and beauty. Now, it awed me, the elegance of his instincts and movements, all these new angles of his brutality visible only as its target. Perhaps I could only appreciate every brushstroke of death once I was the canvas.

I no longer saw or heard the crowd. Nightfire spread across the sand as quietly inevitable as the slow march of death. Raihn had loosened his grip on his magic, each burst of Asteris sweeping the entire arena.

I met his eyes through the flames. They seemed so, so red here, surrounded by the cold blue-white of my magic and the purple-black of his. Within them, I saw only grim resolve. Of course. He had everything to fight for. People relying on him. People he needed to save. Whatever we'd built together had been a bump on that road.

His next strike was to kill.

Raihn was so much bigger than me, so much stronger. I was faster, but not by much—and not when his wings were out. He extended them now, using them to hurl himself at me. I couldn't react quickly enough.

Pain, as his sword sliced open my arm.

I pulled away, panting, somewhat amazed I was alive.

Raihn's jaw was set, eyes cold.

Why did it surprise me, to see him looking at me that way? Why did it hurt? It shouldn't. I had told him to fight. I was a human girl he'd known for a few months. A friend, yes. But friends didn't exist in a place like this.

He came after me hard, again.

I saw my life flash before my eyes. My short, pathetic life. Every dead human I was too late to save. Ilana's body, little more than tatters of flesh. Barely anything left to burn.

You don't have to be this, Oraya.

She had told me that once.

I saw death coming for me at the edge of Raihn's blade, in the focused determination of his stare.

She was right. I didn't. I could make myself something better.

Raihn's blow should have been my death. I was already teetering on its precipice.

But something was left inside of me. I rallied with everything I had. Let out a roar of rage. Not at Raihn, but at the world that had put both of us here.

I didn't have to think. Didn't have to see. I fought on instinct alone, strike after strike after strike, meeting hard resistance, soft resistance, meeting the pain of Asteris, the burn of Nightfire. Meeting leather armor.

And at last, meeting flesh. Raihn's flesh.

I froze with the tip of my blade at his chest, some distant instinct screaming, *STOP.*

The crowd was shrieking in utter delight.

Raihn was beneath me. Nightfire surrounded us. Blisters opened over his skin like decaying roses. I became aware of the agonizing pain of each breath, each movement.

He trembled, too. I'd opened poison-mottled wounds all over his torso, his shoulders, his arms, even one over his cheek. I was bleeding from the ones he'd inflicted on me, too, and badly. As I draped myself over him, pinning him to the ground, his blood and mine mingled—the final strokes of his painting, red and black.

My blade was at his chest. His hand gripped my wrist, hard. His lips curled into a smirk.

And he whispered, "There she is."

All at once, I realized what he had been doing.

He had been baiting me, just like he had baited the man in the feast all those months ago. He had been fighting me so hard to make me fight back with just as much strength.

I had told myself I would do it.

I had work to do. People to help. Power to gain. I could do none of that as a human constantly struggling to survive.

A trickle of blood at the tip of my blade. My hand shook.

"End it, princess," Raihn murmured.

End the danger and the fear and the violence.

End it, end it, end it—

No. I couldn't. I wouldn't.

But Raihn's hand tightened.

Look them in the eyes as you slide the blade in, Vincent's voice whispered.

No. I squeezed my eyes shut. I thought I was pulling away.

But maybe Raihn yanked my wrist. Maybe he drove that blade into his own chest.

Or perhaps my vampire heart won the battle, after all.

Because I felt the blade slip, slip, slip. Felt the breastbone part. Felt the muscle tear. I felt that blade go into my own heart as it slid into Raihn's.

The crowd erupted into wild, gleeful wails. Warmth covered my hands. The weight below me slackened.

I opened my eyes.

I had won.

Raihn was dead.

CHAPTER FORTY-NINE

No.

My Nightfire withered away.

Raihn's head had rolled back into the sand. His eyes were half-open, staring sightlessly to the crowd. That stupid little smile still clung to his lips.

I had just gotten everything I'd ever wanted. All my greatest dreams fulfilled.

And all I could think was, *No.*

No, he wasn't dead. I hadn't done that. I knew I hadn't—I hadn't pushed that blade in. My mind grasped desperately at those last few crucial seconds.

He couldn't be dead.

He couldn't.

Distantly, as if in a whole other world, the Ministaer's voice echoed through the arena.

"The twenty-first Kejari has its victor!"

The delirious cheers of a bloodthirsty populace thrilled by their blood-soaked victor filled the colosseum.

I didn't move.

I had to force my fingers to relinquish their grip on my blade. They ghosted over Raihn's lifeless face. His skin was still warm. My thumb swept that curl at the corner of his mouth.

"Raihn," I choked, half expecting him to answer me.

He didn't.

He didn't move.

I had killed him.

I had killed him.

Oh, Mother, what had I done?

I gripped his face with both hands. My breath came in deep, painful gasps. My vision blurred.

I didn't cry when Ilana died. I hadn't cried since the last time I stabbed my lover. I swore to myself—and to Vincent—that night that I never would again.

But I had been wrong. I had been wrong about so, so much. The world had just lost an incredible force. And my presence here was not enough to make up for that.

In this game, only one of us would win. And it shouldn't have been me. It shouldn't have been me.

Nothing existed except for him and the light I had just snuffed out of this world.

Not even the sounds of the crowd. Not the Ministaer's voice, reverberating through the stands, as he said, "Rise, victor. Rise to greet your goddess."

No, I heard none of that.

I only raised my gaze when it all went silent. A shiver passed over my skin. I looked up—up to the sky. It was clear and bright, stars stark against the velvet night. My sight was so blurry with tears that they flared like little supernovas.

Or . . .

My brow furrowed.

No. It wasn't my tears. The stars did indeed brighten, as if fed with fresh kindling. Silver wisps, like torn scraps of gossamer, swirled in the sky above the colosseum. The air grew very, very still, like every breeze had been stolen for the breath of a greater being.

A greater being like the Goddess of Night, of Blood, of Shadow herself. Heir to the Crown of the Dead.

Mother of vampires.

The hair rose on my arms.

"Bow," the Ministaer whispered. "Bow for our Mother of the Ravenous Dark, Nyaxia."

CHAPTER FIFTY

I did not need to bow. I was already on my knees, and I couldn't bring myself to stand.

I felt her before I saw her.

I had always been a bit of a skeptic when it came to the gods. As much as everyone in Obitraes liked to moon over Nyaxia and her incomprehensible power, I wondered if perhaps some of it was exaggeration or myth.

In this moment, those doubts disappeared.

Because the entire damned world bowed to Nyaxia. Not just the people, but the air, the sky, the earth. The sand shifted beneath my palms, as if inching to get just a little closer to her. The night writhed, as if aching to be in her lungs.

Every part of me called to her. *Turn, turn, turn,* the wind whispered.

Still, I could not tear myself away from Raihn.

"Look at me, my child."

Her voice was a million shades of a million sounds, painted over each other in exquisite layers. History, power, grief distilled.

I forced myself to let go of Raihn's face, allowing him to slump to the sand, sickeningly lifeless.

Numbly, I rose. Turned.

Nyaxia stood before me.

She was not a person. She was an event.

My mind emptied of thought, my lips parting. She floated just above the ground, delicate bare feet pointed to the sand. Her hair was long and black, tendrils of night floating around her as if carried by an ever-present breeze. Stars glinted in its darkness—no, not just stars, but every infinite shade of the sky. Dappled streaks of distant worlds. Purples and blues of galaxies. It was nearly to her knees, a curtain of night around her. Her skin was ice-white, her eyes midnight-black. Her naked body looked to have been dipped in melted silver, a thousand shades of platinum playing across every dip of her form. Shadows caressed her curves with dancing fragments of darkness.

Her mouth was bright red. As she smiled, a drop of blood dripped down her elegant pointed chin.

I ached to touch her skin. Ached to lick the drop of blood from her mouth. I had learned long ago that vampire beauty was dangerous, a trap set with silver teeth. Their allure was made to draw in prey.

Nyaxia's allure dwarfed it, and it terrified me.

I recognized this, and yet in this moment, when the full force of her presence hit me, I would have died for her. I would have killed for her. I would have shivered in ecstasy if she had offered me agony by those stunning blood-dipped fingertips.

I struggled to steady myself. The rawness of my grief had opened me, the tear it had cut in my armor too wide to patch.

Nyaxia stepped to the sands, each footfall silent. She bent down and cradled my face in her hands. Her eyes, all black, held the waning glow of a dying sunset, revealing a different shade of the sky every time she turned her head.

"Oraya."

She said my name the only way it was ever meant to be said.

A smile twisted her lips. She looked over her shoulder.

"She has your eyes," she laughed.

Vincent. She was looking at Vincent. I tore my gaze away from her. He had pressed up against the rail, unblinking. Pride and anticipation warred over his face. His eyes shone.

"My daughter, Oraya of the House of Night," Nyaxia said. "You have fought hard and fought well. Tell me, my champion. What might I grant you as your gift?"

Champion.

Fought.

Those words destroyed the temporary haze of Nyaxia's presence. The reality of where I stood—of what I had done to be here—crashed down around me.

The grief was unbearable. A million jagged edges of a million decisions I could have made differently. The burn of Raihn's blood on my hands.

Nyaxia's devastating face went thoughtful. Those night-hewn eyes fell to Raihn's lifeless body.

"You grieve, my child."

I could not tell if it was sympathy I heard in her voice.

I didn't answer aloud, but she heard my response anyway.

"I know grief," she said, voice soft. "I know what it is to lose half of one's soul."

Half of one's soul. It did feel that way. He had taken more of me than I thought he would when he went.

Storm clouds swirled in the night of Nyaxia's stare. "To have such a thing stolen from you is a great loss indeed." Lightning faded as her eyes turned back to me. "But perhaps, too, it is a blessing, my child. Such a pure love, distilled forever in its innocence. A flower frozen in bloom."

Her fingers caressed my throat, drifted down to my chest, lingering there—as if feeling for my human pulse. "A dead lover can never break your heart."

Was that how she felt about her dead husband?

If so, I envied her. Because she was wrong. My heart was already broken. It had cracked in a thousand moments over the last sixteen years. The first blow came the night my family died. Only now, by my own hand, did it shatter.

Everything I had ever wanted was within my grasp.

Power. Strength. I could never be afraid again. I could make myself the predator instead of the prey, the hunter instead of the hunted, the ruler instead of the subject. I could make myself a monster to fear. I could make myself something to remember, instead of another fading mortal life to forget.

Everything was right here.

Two hundred years ago, Vincent had made this decision. He had sacrificed everything.

And so had Nyaxia. Her grief became her power. She forged it into a weapon sharp enough to carve a whole new world.

I understood now. It always happened this way. Love was a sacrifice at the altar of power.

My gaze found Vincent's. He was not blinking, was not breathing.

My father who had taught me how to survive, how to kill, how to feel nothing. Perhaps I didn't share his blood, but I was his child in every other sense of the word, and he loved me the only way he knew how. At the edge of a blade.

I swallowed the sudden, desperate desire to know how he had felt when he stood in my place, two hundred years ago. Did he swear that he would be better than the one who came before him?

Nyaxia's smile rolled over my cheek like the cold light of the moon.

"They always have dreams," she murmured, answering the question I did not ask. "And his were the grandest of all. Tell me, what is yours, my child?"

I cradled my wish in my weak mortal heart. Perhaps I was more human than Vincent thought, after all.

My father taught me to look them in the eye as I slid the blade into their heart. And so, I did not look away from his as I told Nyaxia, "I wish that Raihn had won."

Vincent's face went white.

Nyaxia's laugh sounded like the shifting of fates.

CHAPTER FIFTY-ONE

Nyaxia did not ask me if I was sure. She knew my soul. She knew I was.

"As you wish," she said, as if I had just done something very amusing indeed.

I wasn't sure what I was expecting—maybe some dramatic flash of light or storm of darkness, or hell, maybe that I would disappear completely—but none of it happened.

No, it turns out that fate changing is a subtle beast. The air turns just a little colder, the direction of the wind just a little lost. You look down and suddenly your hands are shaking, holding the blade that, seconds and another reality ago, had been lodged in your lover's chest.

I looked up, and Raihn was alive.

He sucked in a great gulp of air, his hands clutching at his chest—at the wound that was no longer there.

The crowd murmured and gasped.

I didn't look at them. Raihn didn't, either. Instead, his gaze shot to me. Only me. He looked at me before he even looked at Nyaxia.

The tears that pricked my eyes now were of relief.

It was worth it. I already knew it. Even if I never saw him again. It would have been worth it.

Confusion tangled in his expression as he rubbed his chest.

"Hello, Raihn Ashraj, my Nightborn son," Nyaxia purred. "Victor of the Kejari."

Raihn's confusion turned to realization. Then turned to . . .

To . . .

My brow furrowed.

That wasn't relief. That was *anguish.*

"Oraya," he choked out. "What did you—"

"Rise," Nyaxia commanded. "Rise, my son. And tell me how I may reward your victory."

Raihn did not speak for a long moment. That silence seemed to stretch a million years. At last, he rose and approached Nyaxia. Her fingers stroked his cheek, leaving in their wake little paths of blood.

"My, what a long time it has been," she crooned. "Even fate did not know if I would see this face again."

"Likewise, my lady," Raihn said.

Vincent's jaw was so tight it trembled, his knuckles white at his sides, back straight. His wings quivered, as if he had to hold himself back from flying down here.

Nyaxia's eyes danced with amusement—terrifying amusement.

My stomach clenched tight. I did not like to see that level of delight. The kind of delight that promised bloodshed.

Nyaxia likes her children squabbling.

Something . . . something was not right.

"Tell me, my son, what is your prize?"

The world held its breath. Raihn bowed his head.

In the crowd, I glimpsed Septimus pushing forward through the stands, a hungry grin spreading over his lips.

Why was Septimus looking so pleased, if his champion had fallen?

Raihn said, "Two hundred years ago, you came to this place and granted the winner of the Kejari a wish. You sealed away the power of the Rishan Nightborn King."

The smirk on Nyaxia's lips had grown to a grin, and with it, my stomach sank.

"I wish for that power, my lady. I wish for it to be restored to the Rishan Heir line. I wish for it to be restored to me."

Restored?

Nyaxia laughed, low and silken. "I wondered when this might happen. Your wish is granted, Raihn Ashraj, Turned Heir of the Rishan king."

What?

My eyes went wide. I took several steps back, toward the stands. Some spectators were laughing, soaking up the drama of it all. But others, mostly Hiaj, had started to uneasily back out through the crowd.

Nyaxia cupped her hands before her.

"Congratulations on your victory."

Raihn looked only at me, dismayed apology over his face, as Nyaxia's hands opened over his chest, her lips pressing to his forehead.

The burst of power rearranged the world.

Everything went white, then black. But the real force of the shift was deeper than that. At any given moment, one could feel Vincent's power innately—the kind of power kissed by the Goddess herself. Now, two polar extremes yanked in opposite directions.

I lifted my hand to shield my eyes. When the light faded, Raihn was standing before Vincent's box. His wings burst forth—a million colors, black as night, with one notable exception:

Red, painted at their tips.

I let out a strangled noise.

Because Raihn's armor had been so badly damaged that when his wings flung out, most of the leather had ripped away, revealing the landscape of scars over his back. The scars from Vincent's torture, yes. But also the older one, the one that started at his upper back and ran down his spine.

Now light burned through that scar tissue, streaks of red piercing the mottled flesh. It formed a design—five phases of the moon over the top of his shoulders, and a spear of smoke down the center of his back.

A mark.

An Heir Mark.

It bloomed to life as if awakened by a sudden burst of power. Even if its owner had once, long ago, tried to burn it off his skin.

Fuck. *Fuck*. What had I done? Goddess, what had I done?

By now the Hiaj spectators understood what was happening. People trampled each other in the stands trying to escape, taking to the sky or to any open exits in clumsy masses.

A deafening crack sounded from beyond the colosseum. It shook the ground, followed by a deep grinding—like stone shattering. Like city walls falling. Like an empire crumbling.

Soldiers poured from the entrances of the colosseum. Soldiers wearing the red and white of the House of Blood. Septimus watched it all and smiled.

A dead lover can never break your heart, Nyaxia's voice whispered to me, taunting.

It was all I could hear as Vincent spread his wings and drew his sword.

He didn't move as Raihn approached him. No, Vincent never backed down from a threat. He'd face his challenger head-on.

No.

I didn't remember drawing my blades. I just started running. I made it halfway up the steps to Vincent's balcony before someone grabbed me. I didn't know who. Didn't care. Didn't look.

I needed to get to him.

I needed to get to him right now, right now, *right now—*

Raihn's lip curled. "You don't even know who I am, do you?"

Vincent did not dignify this with a response. Instead, he lunged.

A cry leapt to my throat.

Vincent was one of the best warriors in all of Nyaxia's kingdoms. And yet Raihn struck him down mid-movement, as if he were nothing. Power swelled and sparked at Raihn's fingertips—flashes of light and darkness, like stars themselves, dwarfing even the force of his Asteris in the ring.

I thrashed against whoever held me back—thrashed so hard that soon another set of hands joined the first—

"We met," Raihn said. "Two hundred years ago. The day you took power and opened a river of blood in this city. The day you slaughtered your own family and every Rishan man, woman, and child within these walls. The day you killed anyone you thought even had the sliver of a chance of taking the Rishan Heir line and challenging you for the House of Night." He pushed Vincent's sword away with a burst of power, sending it clattering to the floor. "Well. You missed one."

Raihn grabbed Vincent's throat. The red of Vincent's Heir Mark sputtered in fits and starts, as if repelled by the grip of its natural enemy. A sickening *CRACK* as Raihn pushed Vincent's body to the smooth stone of the wall, smearing crimson black over white marble.

Horrible certainty fell over me.

I was about to watch my father die.

I fought harder. Two sets of hands became three. Someone yelped as I stabbed at them.

Raihn yanked Vincent closer, their heads bowing. Vincent said something to him, much too quietly for me to hear.

Then his head turned—slowly, as if it took all his strength—to look at me.

Raihn looked at me, too. And for a moment, that hate on his face was replaced with profound, tortured regret. I couldn't hear anything over my frantic scream, but his lips formed the words, *Look away.*

I screamed something—perhaps a curse, a plea. I would never remember.

And I did not look away.

Not as magic flared at Raihn's touch.

Not as Vincent's body flew back against the wall with enough force to turn bones to liquid.

No, I did not look away as I watched Raihn kill my father.

CHAPTER FIFTY-TWO

Vincent's body hit the railing and fell to the sand, a long drop from the balcony.

I didn't know what sounds I was making, only that they were ragged and animalistic and violent. It was the Nightfire that made them finally let me go. In a sudden burst, it engulfed me.

Not that I noticed, or cared.

I stumbled down the steps. Crossed the sand in several long strides. I collapsed next to Vincent.

He was still alive, barely. But it was a testament to his power that he even managed to survive these few seconds. His body had been destroyed—skin replaced with scalded flesh, bones rearranged and crushed, that elegant cold face twisted and blood-smeared. His eyes, moon-silver, were brighter than ever peering through that gore.

Growing up, I had thought Vincent was untouchable. He could not bleed. He could not break. He certainly could not die.

But the man before me was broken in every way. A collection of destroyed muscle and tissue, and a heart that was just as soft as mine in the end.

His eyes glistened. One mangled hand reached for me. I grabbed it.

"I am so sorry, my little serpent." Each word was hard-fought. "I was going to—I was going to tell—"

I just kept shaking my head. Tears marked little pools of clean skin on Vincent's face. I managed one garbled word: "Stop." *Stop speaking. Stop dying. Stop leaving me.*

But he didn't.

"I love you. I loved you from the first moment." Bubbles of blood formed at the corners of his mouth. His gaze drifted past me, to the night sky. Then it dragged back to me—the movement slow, laborious, like he was working very hard to make sure I was the last thing he saw. "So many mistakes in the end," he choked out. "Never you."

For the rest of my life, I would wish I had said something to my father as he died in my arms. He was a terrible person in so many ways. And yet I loved him.

I loved him.

I told him so three seconds too late, when his eyes had gone blank.

The grief tore me apart in its jaws. So much worse than I ever thought it would be.

No.

I preferred anger.

Blue-white flames consumed my vision. Every muscle coiled. I guarded Vincent's body like a wolf over her den—a serpent over her nest.

Something had been ripped open inside of me, and whatever had been within that carefully guarded box was too much for me to control. Pain and sorrow and *fury* poured through me, poured and poured and—

In the distance, I heard shouting. It grew closer.

Someone grabbed me.

I fought them on instinct, railed against their hold. I couldn't grip my own magic—the dam of my restraint had shattered, leaving it gushing in uncontrollable waves. Flames roared at my hands, my arms, peeled from my skin.

It was Raihn who finally dragged me back.

I hated that I knew it was him right away. Knew him by scent and touch alone as he pulled me back against him, arms around my shoulders.

"He's gone, Oraya," he murmured into my ear.

They're dead, little human, he had said to me, the first time he had met me.

They're dead. They're all dead.

I'd dropped my blades somewhere. I had no weapons. Only my flames, which were so far beyond my control that I could have burned the colosseum to the ground. But if they hurt Raihn, he didn't show it. He spun me around, held me firm by my arms.

"Breathe, Oraya. Come back to me. Please."

He said this like he cared.

Like he fucking *cared*.

I hated him. I was ready to die for him and he killed my father, and he lied to me, and he—he—

And yet the sight of Raihn's pain, of the skin on his cheeks slowly scorching, made me draw in a gulp of air.

He gave me a weak smile. "You're safe."

I never wanted him to say those words to me ever again.

People surrounded us now. Rishan warriors clustered in the arena. Dimly, I recognized Cairis watching us nearby, sword in hand, and Ketura not far beyond him. When did all these people get here?

I couldn't orient myself. Something I could not name was so—so *different*. The flames slowly ebbed. Yet I still felt like I was burning from within. I struggled to breathe. My chest hurt—my neck hurt.

As the Nightfire withered, Raihn's eyes lowered to my throat. Horror fell over his face.

"Oraya, what is—"

"*Fuck.*" Cairis stepped closer, his eyes wide. "Is that—*FUCK.*"

What?

I looked down at myself.

Red ink had spread over my chest.

Cairis gasped, "She's a fucking *Heir.*"

PART SEVEN

NIGHT

CHAPTER FIFTY-THREE

My mind stopped working.

I wasn't Vincent's daughter. Not by blood. He had never even Turned me.

I couldn't be an Heir.

Yet the Mark was there, unmistakable. I could only see the edge of it, but I could feel it—feel it burning into the skin of my throat, clavicle, upper chest.

"That's not—" I choked out. "I can't be—"

Raihn still held my shoulders. His lips had parted, but words failed him.

"Kill her," Cairis said, not taking his eyes off of me, like if he did I might attack. "*Right now.*"

Chaos exploded around us. A crowd pushed closer. Ketura was already drawing her sword. And so did so many others—all those Rishan soldiers in battle-ready armor, ready to kill me. One even went so far as to lunge for me.

But then in one abrupt movement, Raihn yanked me back. He spun me around, holding me close to him, so tight I couldn't move.

"No." His voice was foreign and cold. Nothing like the man I knew. "I have better plans for her."

The Rishan hesitated, confused. In the background, Septimus's lips curled as he raised his cigarillo to his mouth.

"I took Vincent's kingdom," Raihn snarled. "I took his life. I took his title. And now, I will take his daughter. I'll make her my wife. Keep her close, where I can keep an eye on her. And I'll make sure it hurts when I fuck her, just like it did when he raped our queen two hundred years ago."

I couldn't even process what I was hearing.

So different. Mother, Raihn was so good at performances. But I didn't know which one was real anymore. Which version of him was true.

I let this man into my bed. Into my body. This man who now boasted about raping me to a gaggle of rapt soldiers.

They hesitated. I knew what they were thinking—that it was foolish. But vampires loved sex and bloodshed. Loved pain and power. When all those things were combined? They could hardly resist.

"Think of that." Raihn's face was right next to mine as he gripped me against his body. I glimpsed his wolfish, feral grin out of the corner of my eye. "How much more interesting than death for her. There can be no other Hiaj Heir as long as she lives. And I'd happily make her my little slave forever, just as Vincent was happy to make the Rishan his." He jerked his head to Vincent's body. "Maybe I'll even prop him up so he can attend his daughter's wedding."

And it was this—this final sprinkle of nauseating savagery— that won them over. The soldiers laughed. Cairis looked unconvinced, stepping back only slightly. And Ketura did not sheathe her sword, still seemingly ready to skewer me herself.

But Raihn didn't give anyone time to argue. He motioned to the distance—to the carnage within the colosseum walls and beyond it. "Go. Go reclaim your kingdom. And let me deal with her."

They obeyed him. And Raihn, as he promised, dealt with me.

I fought him. But Raihn's power had become something else altogether, and mine was exhausted by my outburst. He dragged me across the sand, ignoring my weak struggles.

Around us, the entire world burned. The moon and stars had been blotted out with smoke the color of dried blood. House of Blood and Rishan warriors poured into the colosseum, making quick work of Hiaj who resisted. The sounds of death echoed through the night.

As Raihn pulled me away, my eyes landed on Vincent's body, little more than pulp in the sand.

He did not look like a king anymore.

"I'm so sorry, Oraya," Raihn whispered, the moment we were out of earshot. "I'm—I'm just so fucking sorry."

Sorry. The word brought to mind Vincent's final apology. Final declaration of love. How many times had I longed to hear those words from him?

And did it even matter, in the end?

"I hate you," I spat at Raihn.

His fingers brushed my face. Little wisps of shadow trailed them. Darkness. Sleep. Too powerful for me to fight.

The last thing I heard was Raihn's whisper of, "There she is."

CHAPTER FIFTY-FOUR

I woke up with a start. Sweat plastered my clothing to my skin.

I knew this ceiling. Silver stars on cerulean glass. I pushed myself up. The familiarity of this place hurt so much my breath hitched.

My room. The chambers I had spent the last sixteen years of my life in. I had left here only a few short months ago, but I returned a different person.

The girl who had lived here was a child. Now I was . . .

I didn't even know anymore.

The events of the trial came back to me in flashes, each twist driving a stake deeper and deeper into my heart. I pressed my hand to my chest and squeezed my eyes shut.

I saw Vincent's bloodied face.

Saw Raihn killing him.

I let out a shaky exhale that sounded suspiciously close to a sob.

But no. I wouldn't cry. *I would not fucking cry.*

I leapt out of bed. My leathers were gone. So were my blades. I wore only loose silk pants and a light camisole, both in midnight blue.

Fine. At least I could move in it. I could find something to fight with, could find a window to smash. I could—I could—

I glimpsed myself in the mirror, and froze.

Darkness shadowed my eyes, making their silver moon-bright, just as Vincent's had been. My cheeks were bruised and hollow.

Someone had healed me, but remnants of cuts and burns still painted my bare arms.

And the Mark—

The Mark—

I had to stare at it for a long moment, because my mind couldn't reconcile what I was seeing. I'd thought there must have been some misunderstanding, some confusion.

But no. It was an Heir Mark, unmistakable, carved onto my flesh. It adorned my throat, like Vincent's had. A circle at the base of my neck, cradled by the inner curve of my clavicle. I realized after a long moment of staring at it that it depicted all phases of the moon layered on top of each other. Beneath it, smoke lines unfurled like petals cradling a rose, extending up my neck and over the width of my shoulders. The smoke came to four points on each side—like the talons of Hiaj wings.

It was dark in here. The glow of the crimson lines seemed particularly intense. It pulsed with the quickening of my heartbeat. Wisps of faint red smoke peeled from each line of ink.

I clasped my hands together. Tight, tight, *tight*—like if I could force them to stop shaking, I could force myself into composure. I could not afford to be anything but composed.

Yet my mind could form only one word:

How?

How could this be? I was human.

Click, as the doorknob unlocked.

I whirled around.

When the door opened and Raihn stepped inside, I was ready. I threw myself on him.

I had no weapons. And my magic—even in this new, awakened state—refused to come when my rage called for it. Perhaps they had drugged me, dampened it somehow.

Fine. I had my teeth and fingernails. I attacked him like an animal.

Maybe Raihn had been expecting this, because he countered me immediately. I slipped his grasp four times before finally he restrained me by brute force alone and shoved me to the bed.

He pressed his whole weight over me. His face was inches away, our noses nearly brushing.

"Calm down, Oraya. I'm not going to—"

Calm down?

Calm down?

He winced at his own words. "Just—Oraya, I—"

I turned my head and sank my teeth into his arm as hard as I could.

He hissed a curse as I spat his blood onto the bedspread. I still couldn't get free. The weight of his body, and the white-knuckled hold he had on my shoulder with his other arm, kept me from moving.

"I have so much to explain to you," he said, "if you'll let me. Oraya—*stop fighting me.*"

"Why?" I shot back. "To make it easier for you to rape me?"

Another wince.

"I said what I had to say to save your life," he hissed.

To save my life.

Like I had saved his.

I had chosen him over my own father, over my own power, and now Vincent was dead and the Hiaj had been overthrown and the fucking House of Blood was in Sivrinaj—

I had fucked up. I had fucked up so, so badly. And I wanted to claw Raihn's eyes out for that. Mother, I wanted it more than anything.

But I wanted answers more.

I gritted my teeth. Lowered my chin.

Raihn eyed me warily.

"If I let you go," he said, "will you attack me?"

I genuinely could not bring myself to promise that I wouldn't.

"I'll try not to."

"I made sure that every single thing that could possibly be used as a weapon had been removed from this room."

"I'm sure you missed something."

The smile that twisted the corner of his mouth seemed more mournful than amused. "Glad to know you're still in there, princess."

He let me go.

I scrambled to my feet, putting several strides between us. I noticed him watch the distance widen. I wondered if he was thinking of the same thing I was—how I used to move that way every time we were in the same room together.

I wondered if I imagined that he looked a little sad.

I would be lying if I said I didn't feel a pang of it, too. Because the person I had trusted was Raihn. This man . . . I didn't even know who he was.

His gaze lingered on me. Lingered on my throat.

"How?" he said softly.

It seemed almost shameful to say that I didn't know. I didn't want to admit aloud how little I knew about the two men who had become so close to me.

"You first," I said.

"I never lied to you."

He spoke so quickly, like he'd been waiting for days to say this to me.

What a fucking joke.

"What does that even mean?" I sneered. "That you chose your truths so fucking carefully? That you picked each word to shield the things you wouldn't say to me?"

He raised his palms, as if to say, *Fair enough.*

"I wasn't ready to confront any of this, either. Trust me."

"Say words that actually mean something," I snapped.

"Everything I told you was the truth," he said. "There was just . . . more."

"What does that—"

"The man who Turned me was Neculai Vasarus. King Neculai."

My jaw snapped shut.

The Rishan king. The king that Vincent had murdered and usurped.

"I betrayed him," Raihn bit out. "The day that Vincent won the Kejari. I arranged for Vincent to get the keys to the strongholds. Handed over everything he needed to destroy the entire fucking kingdom in exchange for the safety of the innocents. He never met me in person. Never knew my name. Never saw me. But I knew it was all already going to fall apart. I just thought . . . maybe I could pour some oil on the fire. Burn it faster, and keep it from taking all of us with it. I hated it all that much."

I couldn't speak.

"But I should have known better," he said. "I got the fuck out before Neculai could figure out what I'd done, thinking I'd arranged for the safety of those who needed it. I tried to get Nessanyn to come with me. She wouldn't. So I left her behind. I left all of them behind. Trusting Vincent's word." His face went hard, hateful. "We know how that worked out."

Rape her the way he raped our queen, Raihn had said.

Bile rose in my throat. Vincent was no saint. But surely he wouldn't—he couldn't have—

"Did he—"

Raihn seemed to know exactly what I was thinking. "I don't know. All I know is that Nessanyn was one of the last to die."

I was going to throw up.

By some miracle, I didn't. I kept my face perfectly still.

"I was far away by the time I saw this." He touched his back—his Mark. "It never occurred to me that it could happen. I wasn't Neculai's blood relative, of course. Not Born. Turned. I thought Heirs could only be Born, and I was content to let the entire bastard line of them die out. But in the absence of a Born Heir, apparently, a Turned one counted." His mouth twisted into a wry, disgusted smile. "How fucking poetic. The Turned nobody, handed the power of an entire kingdom by the man who enslaved him."

A chill ran up my spine.

"I wanted no part of it. The first thing I did was try to get rid of the Mark. Nearly killed myself burning it off. I didn't want to rule this place. And I certainly didn't want to take his title." He looked around, a wrinkle forming over his nose—I wondered if he was seeing a different version of this room, from two hundred years in the past. "I didn't even want to come back to this castle. Too many bad memories. So Vincent sealed away the Rishan line's power, and he ruled, and I ran." His eyes fell back to me. "*Until.*"

Until it caught up to him. His guilt over those Nessanyn had wanted him to protect. Mische, and her desire to use his power to build something better.

All this bloodshed over a fucking fairy tale.

"So the Kejari was to you what it was to Vincent," I said. A path to steal a crown.

Raihn, to his credit, did not deny it. "Yes."

"And me?" I choked out. "Is that what I was, too?"

He looked as if I had struck him. "No, Oraya. No."

"I don't believe you."

"What do you want me to tell you? That I didn't choose you as an ally because of your relationship with Vincent? Yes. I did. And everything else I told you was true, too. That I thought you would be easy to kill after. That I would learn from you, and then get rid of you after the Halfmoon, and it would all be easy. As if I shouldn't have known from the minute you stabbed me that *nothing* would be easy with you."

He let out a sound that was a shade of a laugh. "Maybe that was why I picked you, too. Because right away, I *liked* you, princess. I was curious about you. You reminded me of me. Someone different. After a few hundred years, everyone seems the same. Not you. Not from that first night. So no, no part of that was a lie, Oraya. Trust me, it would be simpler if it was."

My chest hurt so much.

I wanted him to be lying. It would be easy if he was lying. Easy to hate him if our friendship, our . . . relationship, had been nothing but a performance.

But I knew it wasn't, even before I asked. It had all been real.

"Why is the House of Blood within our walls?" I asked.

Raihn did not want to answer this question. I knew how he looked, by now, when he was ashamed of something he was about to say.

"It takes manpower to win a war," he said. "Heir or no. The Hiaj were never going to go down without a fight, even if I killed Vincent. And he knew that, too. He'd been careful to whittle down the Rishan population over the last couple of centuries. If I was going to do this, I needed warriors. Many of them. Septimus knew that."

My palms were cold and sweaty.

"I resisted," he said. "I don't even know how he found out who I was. I don't know how he knew what I was planning. I ripped apart my own inner circle looking for whoever the source was. And he was insistent that the House of Blood could help. One favor, he told me, and the full force of the House of Blood was mine. I told him to go fuck himself. I thought we would have enough. But then . . ."

Then the strike on the Moon Palace. So neatly blamed upon the Rishan. Giving Vincent full permission to kill them indiscriminately.

"The attacks."

Raihn nodded. "Once Vincent was set loose on the Rishan, it was over. Before it would have been difficult, but maybe—*maybe*—possible. After that? There was no way."

"Did Septimus—"

"Frame the Rishan?" His face hardened. "I can't prove it. But I think the bastard created a problem he would be the only solution to. I tried every other way. Everything. And even when every other option was exhausted, I still told him no. Until . . ."

Everything clicked together at once.

The final trial. Angelika coming after me—*only* me. The way Raihn had looked past me, up to the stands.

That little nod.

"You fucking idiot," I choked out.

Raihn stepped closer, and I let him.

"I was ready to let it all go for you," he murmured. "Do you know that, Oraya? I was ready to let my kingdom fall for you. You should have let me stay dead."

Because if he was gone, there was no one to honor the Bloodborn's deal.

He made a dead man's bargain to save me knowing that he would not deliver on it. I hadn't imagined it. He had pulled my wrist. He had helped usher my knife into his heart.

Until I had brought him back.

He took another step. And again, I let him.

"That is," I rasped, "the stupidest plan I have ever heard."

And again, a humorless smile flitted over his lips. "Maybe," he admitted. "Desperate men do desperate things. And I—I believed in you, Oraya. I believed if you won, you would seize power in your own way. I believed that you would use it to accomplish all the same things I wanted to do, and probably do it better, anyway. And you wouldn't even need to sell your own gods-damned kingdom to animals to do it." The smile twisted, becoming something of a grimace. "So was it really a stupid plan?"

Yes. He put far too much faith in me. Just some nobody human. Human.

The word set my world off-kilter. Of their own accord, my fingers moved to my throat.

Raihn's eyes followed them. "Did you know?"

I knew him well by this point. It was almost comforting that I could hear the hint of betrayal in the question. Betrayal! That was rich. Like *I* had deceived *him*.

"It must be a mistake. I don't know how . . . I just . . ." I shook my head. "I'm just . . . human."

As the words left my lips, I heard the echo of how I had hurled them at Vincent. *I am human!*

It was never going to be you, he had told me, so many times. *You are not like them.*

I thought of that refrain with fresh meaning, now.

"You smell me. You've—" I choked on these words. "You've *tasted* me. You would know, wouldn't you? If I wasn't?"

"I would." The wrinkle deepened between Raihn's brows. "But maybe . . . maybe *half* human. You did taste . . . different. I just thought it was because . . . well . . ."

In any other circumstance, maybe I would have enjoyed seeing him fumble over his words like this.

He settled on, "Because of how I feel about you."

Oh, for fuck's sake.

I felt dizzy. I had not intended to sit, but I found myself leaning against the windowsill.

Half human.

That would make me Vincent's biological daughter.

No. There was no way. It just . . . it didn't make any sense.

"I can't be," I forced out. "He found me. He . . . he just *found* me."

Raihn asked, quietly, "Why was he there, that night?"

"Because it was a rebellion, and he—"

"But why did he come to *that* house?"

My head hurt. My heart hurt. "I don't know. It was just . . . just . . ."

Luck.

Fate.

I hadn't realized how much I had leaned on that. That fate had brought me to Vincent's embrace. It was my blessing, because the will of Nyaxia had saved me that night. And my curse, because such a fragile thread separated me from so many more tragic futures.

I had not realized how heavy that word had weighed upon my past, and the way I looked at it, until suddenly it was gone. Suddenly fate was replaced with secrets and whispers and questions I would likely never get answers to. Because Vincent, my father—my father in spirit, *and* in blood—was dead.

"What was it that he said to you?" Raihn asked. "As he . . ."

Died.

It was the kind of question one asked when they already knew the answer. Already knew what it meant.

I was going to tell you, Vincent had said.

Ask yourself why he's afraid of you, Raihn had spat at me, before the final trial.

In a world of immortals, there was nothing more dangerous than an heir.

I felt sick.

I didn't understand. I didn't understand any of it. If I was Vincent's daughter, and he knew who I was, why would he keep me at all?

Why wouldn't he kill me?

Raihn stepped closer again, whispering, "Breathe, Oraya." And only then did I realize that I was shaking so violently I nearly fell off the windowsill.

"We will find the answers," he said. "We'll do the wedding, and—"

Wedding. Oh, Mother.

"I'm not marrying you," I spat.

"Yes, you are."

"Fuck you. *I am not.*"

A muscle feathered in his cheek.

"It's the only way I can keep you alive. If you're not my wife, you're my enemy. And I can't justify letting you go."

"What a fucking hypocrite you are," I snarled. "You, who was so fucking *appalled* by Vincent's bonding."

Raihn flinched. He knew I was right.

I turned my head enough to look out the window. I knew this view so well. I tracked the evolution of an ancient city from this window every single night, every morning.

Now, it was a kingdom wailing through its death throes. The night sky was bright with red and white—Nightfire. Little streaks of light trailed through the distant streets. Bloodborn soldiers, invading my home. I knew that if I pressed my ear to the glass, I would be able to hear the screams of those below.

"Good thing you freed us from that tyrant," I spat. "Everything looks so much more *peaceful* now, doesn't it?"

Raihn closed the gap between us in two strides. His hand pressed to the glass as he bowed over me, one palm cupping the side of my face in a touch that couldn't decide if it was a comfort or a threat.

"Think about this. Power is a bloody business. You know that as well as I do. We have teeth, you and I. Now is the time to use them. We'll rip apart the worlds that subjugated both of us, and from the ashes we'll build something new. And there is no one I would rather have beside me to do that with than you, Oraya. No one." His voice lowered to a plea. His gaze dipped—to my mouth—before flicking back to my eyes. "And when I leave this room, and come back with a priestess, you *will* marry me. You will do it because I can't kill you. I tried. I can't. A world without you would be a dark, depressing place. And I've already inflicted enough pain without committing that fucking injustice, too. So *let me save you.*"

Now it was my turn to know he was right—to know that he meant every word of what he said—and hate it.

Anger made things easy.

Love made things complicated.

"Is this you begging me to save myself? And what if I refuse, just like she did?"

In that moment, I thought maybe I would. Maybe I'd die, just like Nessanyn, solely because he wanted me to live. Sheer spite.

"You won't." His nose was inches from mine. The words warmed my mouth. Low and smooth.

"How do you know that?"

"Because you're smarter than her. You have more than a dream. You have *vision*."

The admiration in his voice hurt, because I knew it was real.

My eyes flicked up to meet his. I took in all those stunning threads of color. All those pieces of him that did not fit together.

I thought for one long moment that he might kiss me. Even worse, I thought I might kiss him back.

Instead, his lips ghosted over my forehead. Barely a touch.

Then he straightened. "I'm getting the priestess. Every second we put this off, you're in danger."

"Wait—"

Before I could protest, he was gone.

CHAPTER FIFTY-FIVE

The wedding ceremony was performed in my chamber. The priestess was one of the Ministaer's—one of those idiots who spent half their lives staring at a stone wall in the church. Her gaze was lowered as she whispered scriptures in ancient tongues.

I stood there and considered running away. Considered attacking her. Considered attacking Raihn. Considered smashing the window and hurling myself out of it.

I didn't.

I jumped when the priestess took my hand. Her touch was cool and unnaturally smooth. She took Raihn's in the other, and then flipped both over, so our palms were raised to the ceiling.

She whispered an incantation, then brushed her fingertip over my skin.

I hissed a curse, startled by the stab of pain. A river of crimson opened over my palm.

Raihn did not flinch as she did the same to him.

"The vows," the priestess said simply. As if we were supposed to know what that meant.

I had never seen a wedding. I was never allowed at such gatherings. They often turned debauched and unruly, and Vincent always said—

Vincent.

The casual thought of his name stole the breath from my lungs, the pain unbearable.

Raihn's touch was warm and rough. The opposite of the priestess's in every way—the opposite of every vampire's.

Maybe he knew I didn't know what to say. He lifted my palm. I tensed as he brought it to his mouth. His tongue moved slowly over the wound. I hadn't been expecting the tenderness of it. Soft, and gentle. An apology, and a promise.

He lowered my hand. Swallowed my blood.

I wanted to look away. I couldn't.

"Oraya of the Nightborn," he murmured. "I give you my body. I give you my blood. I give you my soul. I give you my heart. From this night until the end of nights. From daybreak until our days are broken. Your soul is my soul. Your heart is my heart. Your pain is my pain. I bind myself to you."

I wanted it to all be a lie. But it was not a lie.

In this moment I recognized, with unmistakable clarity, that Raihn was in love with me.

He offered his hand to me. Red-black liquid pooled in his palm, seeping into the lines and scars of a life well-lived. My mouth was dry as I raised it to my lips. I thought maybe I'd throw it up once it hit my stomach.

Instead, the taste of him was the most exquisite thing I had ever experienced. His blood was warm and smooth over my tongue, sweet and metallic and deep as the night itself.

It tasted like the sky. It tasted like falling.

I lowered his hand. My fingers trembled around his skin.

"Raihn Ashraj."

Mother, my voice did not sound like it belonged to me.

"I give you my body. I give you my blood. I give you—I give you my soul. I give you . . ."

My heart.

I couldn't make myself say the words.

My heart.

My weak, human heart. Scarred and broken and bleeding. The one thing I had always been taught to protect above all. And yet, whatever thing struggled along within my rib cage now, far beneath the Mark that my dead father left on me, was anything but protected. It had been torn apart and ripped open.

How had I ever thought Vincent had given me a vampire heart? This was human.

"My . . ."

I couldn't say it.

"You must complete the vow, my lady," the priestess said.

I blinked back tears and shook my head. "No."

"But my lady—"

"It's fine," Raihn barked.

"But—"

"I said it's fine. She doesn't have to."

I allowed myself to look up at him.

I hated that he looked at me like he cared. His thumb swept over the back of my hand. I could hear his voice in that gesture: *You're safe.*

But I was not safe. Even if I felt it, just for a moment. *Especially* because I felt it.

The priestess led me through the rest of my vows. When it was done, I was married to the King of the Nightborn. I had lost my autonomy, my name, my blood. I had lost my country.

But at least I had kept my heart.

Raihn remained only briefly after the priestess left. I went to the window and watched the carnage in Sivrinaj beyond. I wouldn't look at him. I felt too much, and I felt his stare strongest of all.

"If you're waiting for me to invite you to our wedding bed," I said, after long seconds passed, "it isn't going to happen."

My voice wasn't as ruthless as I wanted it to be. The word "wedding" reminded me of how his mouth felt against my palm. The word "bed" reminded me of how it felt against my flesh. Both were equally confusing.

He said nothing. I wondered, in the silence, if he felt those things, too.

Eventually, I peered over my shoulder. He stood at the center of the room, hands at his sides, looking as if he had too many things to say and not enough words for them.

My husband.

Mother, what had I just done?

His lips parted. I didn't want to hear any of it. I couldn't.

"I'd like to be alone," I said, before he could speak.

His mouth closed. He stared at me for what felt like an endless moment—felt like it because I struggled to keep myself together with every agonizing second, and I refused to allow him to see me break.

Finally, he lowered his chin. I turned my back to him, sat on the bed, and listened to his footsteps leave. He locked the door behind him.

THE RAP ON the glass came near dawn. I had been lying on the bed, staring at the ceiling, trying very hard to feel nothing.

I thought I was hallucinating when I rose to see the figure in the window.

I drew closer, and the face that peered back at me—perfect, sculpted, dangerous—was not a reflection.

Jesmine knocked on the glass again, more urgently. I never thought I would be so grateful to see her.

I tried to open the window. It was locked, of course, but when I twisted the handle, it broke apart in my hands, a snapped bolt shooting halfway across the room. Was I stronger now than I was before? Maybe it was my newly acknowledged vampire blood. Or maybe it was just all that repressed rage.

I threw the window open. Jesmine clung to the side of the castle. Her ashy hair was braided, a few strands of it whipping about her face. She was bloody and bruised, a cut slicing her cheek. She looked as if she hadn't slept in days.

Still stunning, of course.

"Come in," I said, and it was only after the words were out of my mouth that I realized maybe I didn't necessarily want her to. It was impossible to tell who was an enemy and who was an ally.

Her gaze flicked over the window frame.

"There's a barrier here," she said. "I don't feel like getting shredded today."

Like the ones in the Moon Palace. She was right—if I squinted, I could see the faint blue-white sheen across the window. It would've been too easy.

"I can't stay," she said. "But I couldn't leave without seeing you first." She looked me up and down. "You look like shit."

I felt like shit. "Thanks."

"How are you? Are you alright?"

I blinked. It was strange. She asked the question like it really mattered to her.

No. No, I was not alright.

I said, "Yes."

Her eyes softened. "He's gone."

I swallowed. Nodded.

Jesmine bowed her head. Genuine sorrow flitted over that flawless face.

"May the Mother guide him home."

The Mother was the one who put us all in this shit situation. I wasn't sure if I was ready to ask her for anything at all.

"I don't have time for much, so excuse my bluntness," Jesmine went on. "They're waiting for me, beyond the walls."

"They?"

"The military." She said this as if to say, *Who else?*

And . . . who else, indeed? She was the Head of War. A damned good one.

"Whoever is left, anyway. The Bloodborn bastards are . . ." She hissed through her teeth. "Efficient killers. We weren't expecting them."

"How many?"

I'd made a mistake, I realized. I had been thinking like a grieving daughter. Like a prisoner. I had not been thinking like a leader.

I didn't even know what was happening beyond these walls.

"I don't know yet," she said. "I need to assess. But it's . . . it is not good, Highness."

Highness.

I physically jolted at that word. Jesmine saw it. Her eyes narrowed.

"Let me make one thing very clear. I respected Vincent as my king and my leader. But he does not hold my loyalty. The Hiaj clan holds my loyalty. Until the day I die." She jabbed a finger at me—at my chest. "I don't know how you got that. I'm as surprised as any other that you have it. But it's not my place to question that. You are the Hiaj Heir. That makes you my queen. And that means my loyalty is yours."

Maybe I had misjudged Jesmine. I had never trusted her before. I wasn't sure what it said about me that I trusted her right now.

I didn't know what to say. Thanking her didn't seem appropriate.

So I was grateful when she surveyed me again and moved on to another topic. "Did he do it? The marriage?"

"Yes."

She hissed. "Our queen married to a Turned Rishan slave. Vincent would have—" She shook her head.

"Better this than dead," I said.

She shrugged, as if this was a small consolation.

"I told you he was trouble. Pretty trouble. But trouble."

Fair enough, I thought, begrudgingly.

"What is your plan?" I asked.

"What are your orders?"

I was not at all prepared to give orders.

I tried to speak as Vincent would have. "I would like to hear your recommendation."

"We are losing men, and rapidly. We're outnumbered. We need to regroup." She peered into the room. "If you wish, Highness, I can send warriors here to—"

"No."

The last thing I needed was for Hiaj soldiers to get caught trying to rescue me. Tortured. Killed. Who knew what else.

I had to think like a leader.

"I don't want any more bloodshed than there already has been," I said. "Not until we know what we're dealing with. Retreat."

Jesmine's lip curled. "So we let him take it. Let him take the House of Night."

We could build something better, Raihn had whispered to me.

But this did not seem better.

"And let the Bloodborn—"

"I know," I cut in. "I know."

It was one thing to hand this country to Raihn.

Another to hand it to Septimus.

This country hated me. I hated it, in some ways. But it was still my home.

"I need time," I said. "Time to learn. Time to gather information. Keep yourself safe until then."

"And you?"

"He won't hurt me."

Jesmine gave me a cold stare. "That marriage is to protect him. Not you. Your doors are locked from the outside. Your windows are cursed."

"He won't hurt me," I said again, because I didn't know how to explain to her how certain I was of this.

"This is bigger than him," she said. "If I may speak frankly, Highness—you are not a prisoner. You are a queen. I have broken the unbreakable before."

She pulled open her shirt—revealing her scar. "I was bound to a man who sought to control me too, once. I nearly gave my life to break that bond. But I'm free now. I could free you, too."

Yes. I had underestimated Jesmine.

And maybe that was why I was more honest with her now than I ever intended to be.

"I don't intend to lead anyone into a war we can't win. I don't intend to fight for the sake of fighting. And maybe I have a Mark on my skin, but I don't know what that means. The world knows me as human. The Hiaj know me as human."

I knew *myself* as human.

"If you want to fight for this House, we are ready," she said. "I won't pretend it will be easy. I won't pretend that some—maybe many—won't want to accept your rule." Her lip curled. "But Raihn Ashraj's people don't want to follow him, either. He was a slave to their king. Turned. Abandoned his clan for centuries. Do you think his people don't remember those things? They'll be reluctant to go on their knees for him when they feel it should be the other way around."

Despite everything, my heart ached to know that they thought of Raihn that way.

"They are waiting to usurp him, too," she went on. "And that's only if the House of Blood doesn't slide a knife into his back first, and then we are all fucked before his own people even have the chance to turn on him."

A bang rang out in the distance, a puff of smoke rolling from the distant eastern walls. Jesmine's face snapped to the sound.

"Go," I said. "I'll be fine for now."

"You can find me when you need me," she said urgently. "Don't rely on him to protect you, Highness. He has his own threats and weaknesses. You have teeth, too. Yours are sharper than his. Just tell us when to bite, and we fight for you, and you alone."

Another bang. Another flash of light in the distance.

And Jesmine gave me no time to tell her anything else before she disappeared into the night, scaling the castle walls with the ease of someone who had centuries of experience slipping through the locked windows of powerful men.

CHAPTER FIFTY-SIX

I was escorted to the throne room at nightfall the next day. I listened to the door click four times before it swung open. Raihn stood there, Cairis at his side.

"Four locks?" I said as we walked through the halls. Cairis trailed far behind. I wondered if I should expect him to always be lingering near us, now. "How flattering."

"I know better than to underestimate you."

"Where are we going?"

He gave me an odd look, like this was an obvious question. "To work, of course."

"Why? Aren't I your prisoner?"

Another strange look—this one I couldn't quite decipher.

"You aren't my prisoner," he said. "You're my queen."

I had grown up in this Palace. I knew every crevice. I had slipped through each secret hallway in the bright hours of day, when no one could disturb me. But everything was different now. New faces in the hall. Paintings torn from the walls. The face of my father shredded and disfigured, just as it had been in life.

Raihn led me to the throne room. There were so many people here. All Rishan. All of them looked at me with utter disgust. I knew what it was to walk into a room and know that everyone there wanted to kill me. What it was to be prey in a world of predators.

This was different.

These people wanted to kill me not because I was weak, but because I was powerful.

Raihn excused himself to go speak to Ketuia, who shot me a wary glare when his back was turned. I walked through this familiar-unfamiliar room. I crossed it until I reached the double doors that overlooked the ballroom.

All the paintings—paintings of Hiaj legend and royalty—had been destroyed, smashed to pieces over the marble floor.

Only one still remained, that small painting I had always so admired: the Rishan man, falling, reaching for a savior that would not reach back.

"I am so glad we have the opportunity to work together once again."

The hairs rose on the back of my neck. The smell of tobacco smoke wafted over me. I turned to see Septimus leaning on the opposite doorframe.

I didn't feel like playing today.

"Work together," I said. "What a polite way of talking about slaughtering a kingdom."

"Slaughter? That's harsh."

"It's what you want, isn't it? Looks like it, from what I've seen."

He exhaled a puff of smoke. "Then you're not looking at much of anything, are you? Perhaps the same impulses that drive my people are the ones that drive you to murder in your human slums. After all, your people weren't the only ones used as pawns in our goddess's little games."

I didn't know what to say to that, because something about the pointed stare, full of anger he mostly managed to hide, reminded me of that first trial—of the look of horror on the Bloodborn contestant's face as he realized that he was fighting monsters that had once been his people. Both the humans and the Bloodborn had been used and discarded.

"You didn't hesitate to use Angelika as a pawn, either."

"Angelika was a good friend of mine, and the sacrifice she made for her kingdom will live on far longer than she did."

I asked bluntly, "How did you know this would work?"

"I don't know what you mean."

"Raihn made your deal"—*caved to your blackmail*—"to save me. Yet for him to hold up his end, he had to win the Kejari. Why would you think he would kill me after he had saved me?"

Septimus smirked. Exhaled smoke. "I didn't. He's clearly a romantic."

I kept my face blank, but did not understand this answer.

He chuckled and straightened. "I told you I don't make bets that I can lose. And every bet I've made on you has been a winning one, dove."

He offered me the box of cigarillos. I shook my head.

"I hope you can find it in your heart to call me a friend," he said, as he slipped the box into his pocket. "You may find we have more in common than you think. We're the only ones here who know what it's like to fight against time. Counts for a lot in this world, doesn't it?"

He sauntered away without another word, just in time for Raihn to return to my side. He eyed Septimus's departing form warily.

"What was that about?"

"Nothing."

Raihn looked unconvinced. He took my arm. I stiffened and pulled away, but followed him as he walked.

"What now?" I said.

He led me into the ballroom. To our right, floor-to-ceiling windows displayed a tableau of Sivrinaj, domes and spires gleaming beneath the star-dusted sky. The night was still hazy with smoke and white with fire, bright as inverted sunshine spilling across the ballroom's marble floors.

"Good question," Raihn said. "Guess we have to build a kingdom."

On the surface, his voice held the lilt of a flippant joke. It did little to mask the blatant fear beneath it.

I was afraid, too.

Afraid of the enemies beyond these walls, and within them. The enemies that surrounded Raihn, and the ones that surrounded me. The allies ready to betray us both.

Afraid of the fire consuming the kingdom that raised me, and for the countless innocent humans who would be caught within it.

Afraid of the danger of the future, and the secrets of the past.

Raihn took my hand.

And this time, I let him.

Our eyes met at the same moment, united in our mutual terror—united in all the ways we were the same, even if we weren't ready to admit it. For one moment, it was all laid bare.

My friend. My enemy. My lover. My captor.

King and slave. Human and vampire.

And perhaps the only other person who had ever really understood what it was like to have a heart that bled both red and black.

I hated him. And I loved him.

And I couldn't even try to deny how beautiful he was, with his life-marked face doused in the flickering light of our world falling to ash.

"And what about you?" he murmured. His thumb stroked my cheek, traced the line of my jaw. "Are you going to kill me, Oraya?"

He said it just as he had a lifetime ago, as dawn encroached on an alleyway in the human slums. And just like that night, I didn't pull away from his touch.

Instead, I pressed my palm flat to his chest. Behind him, my kingdom burned.

I thought, *Maybe.*

"Not tonight," I said.

END *of* BOOK I

Oraya and Raihn's story
will continue in
The Ashes & the Star-Cursed King,
coming soon.

AUTHOR'S NOTE

Thank you so much for reading *The Serpent & the Wings of Night*! I hope you loved reading it as much as I loved writing it.

After I finished my last series, the War of Lost Hearts trilogy, I was a little lost. Every book I'd ever written had been related to that world. Where could I possibly go next? I decided that I wanted this new universe to be a playground of possibilities—somewhere dark and intricate and vast and full of petty gods to pull all kinds of interesting magical strings. I'd been toying with the idea of vampires in an epic fantasy setting for a long time, and this seemed like the perfect world for it.

Still, a world isn't a story, and I need a beating heart to really get excited about a book. Oraya was that beating heart.

The emotional core of her story came to me when I started thinking about the themes of weakness and humanity—what it means to be physically vulnerable and emotionally vulnerable and how difficult it is to do either. Slowly, the characters came to life through these juxtapositions: a human who wants to be a vampire and a vampire who mourns his humanity, a daughter who can't hide her love and a father who has destroyed his ability to show it at all.

The world of Obitraes is a fantasy. None of us, after all, have experienced what it's like to be a lone human in a world of literal monsters (at least, I very much hope not). But the real crux of Oraya's story, the story that lies beneath the epic battles and the goddess-sanctioned tournaments, is much more personal, and I hope you can find some part of yourself in it. If you can, I've done my job!

If you enjoyed this book, I'd deeply appreciate it if you'd consider leaving a review on your book retailer site of choice and/or Goodreads. I can't overstate how important reviews are to authors!

If you'd like to keep up with new releases, new art, swag, and my general ramblings, you can find me on Instagram, Twitter, TikTok, and Facebook. You can also sign up for my newsletter at carissabroadbentbooks.com.

Thank you for coming on this journey with me, and I hope you join me for the next book in Oraya and Raihn's story!

GLOSSARY

ACAEJA — The goddess of spellcasting, mystery, and lost things. Member of the White Pantheon.

ALARUS — The god of death and husband of Nyaxia. Exiled by the White Pantheon as punishment for his forbidden relationship with Nyaxia. Considered to be deceased.

ASTERIS — A form of magical energy wielded by Nightborn vampires, derived from the stars. Rare and difficult to use, requiring significant skill and energy.

ATROXUS — The god of the sun and leader of the White Pantheon.

BLOODBORN — Vampires of the House of Blood.

BORN — A term used to describe vampires who are born via biological procreation. This is the most common way that vampires are created.

CORIATIS BOND — A rare and powerful bond that can be forged only by a god, in which two people share all aspects of their power, linking their lives and souls. Nyaxia is the only god known to grant Coriatis bonds, though any god is capable of doing so. Those who are bound are referred to as each other's CORIATAE. Coriatae share all aspects of each other's power, typically making both stronger. Coriatae cannot act against each other and cannot live without each other.

DHAIVINTH — A poison that temporarily paralyzes.

DHERA — A nation in the human lands. Vale is currently living there.

EXTRYN — The prison of the gods of the White Pantheon.

HEIR MARK — A permanent mark that appears on the Heir of the Hiaj and Rishan clans when the previous Heir dies, marking their position and power.

HIAJ — One of the two clans of Nightborn vampires. They have featherless wings that resemble those of bats.

THE HOUSE OF BLOOD — One of the three vampire kingdoms of Obitraes. Two thousand years ago, when Nyaxia created vampires, the House of Blood was her favorite House. She thought long and hard about which gift to give them, while the Bloodborn watched their brothers to the west and north flaunt their powers. Eventually, the Bloodborn turned on Nyaxia, certain that she had abandoned them. In punishment, Nyaxia cursed them. The House of Blood is now looked down upon by the other two houses. People from the House of Blood are called **BLOODBORN**.

THE HOUSE OF NIGHT — One of the three vampire kingdoms of Obitraes. Known for their skill in battle and for their vicious natures, and wielders of magic derived from the night sky. There are two clans of Nightborn vampires, HIAJ and RISHAN, who have fought for thousands of years over rule. Those of the House of Night are called **NIGHTBORN**.

THE HOUSE OF SHADOW — One of the three vampire kingdoms of Obitraes. Known for their commitment to knowledge; wielders of mind magic, shadow magic, and necromancy. Those of the House of Shadow are called **SHADOWBORN**.

Ix — Goddess of sex, fertility, childbirth, and procreation. Member of the White Pantheon.

KAJMAR — God of art, seduction, beauty, and deceit. Member of the White Pantheon.

THE KEJARI — A legendary, once-per-century tournament to the death held in Nyaxia's honor. The winner receives a gift from Nyaxia herself. The Kejari is open to all in Obitraes, but is hosted by the House of Night, as the Nightborn hold the greatest domain over the art of battle of the three vampire kingdoms.

LITURO RIVER — A river that runs through the center of Sivrinaj.

MOON PALACE — A Palace in Sivrinaj, the capital of the House of Night, specifically there to house contestants of the once-in-a-century Kejari tournament held in Nyaxia's honor. Said to be enchanted and to exert the will of Nyaxia herself.

NECULAI VASARUS — The former Rishan king of the House of Night. Usurped and killed by Vincent two hundred years prior to the events of this book.

NIGHTBORN — Vampires of the House of Night.

NIGHTFIRE — Like Asteris, a form of star-derived magic wielded by the vampires of the House of Night. While Asteris is dark and cold, Nightfire is bright and hot. Nightfire is commonly used in the House of Night but very difficult to wield masterfully.

NYAXIA — Exiled goddess, mother of vampires, and widow of the god of death. Nyaxia lords over the domain of night, shadow, and blood, as well as the domain of death inherited from her deceased husband. Formerly a lesser goddess, she fell in love with Alarus and married him despite the forbidden nature of their relationship.

When Alarus was murdered by the White Pantheon as punishment for his marriage to her, Nyaxia broke free from the White Pantheon in a fit of rage, and offered her supporters the gift of immortality in the form of vampirism—founding Obitraes and the vampire kingdoms. *(Also referred to as: the Mother; the Goddess; Mother of the Ravenous Dark; Mother of Night, Shadow, and Blood.)*

OBITRAES — The land of Nyaxia, consisting of three kingdoms: the House of Night, the House of Shadow, and the House of Blood.

PACHNAI — A human nation to the east of Obitraes.

RISHAN — One of the two clans of Nightborn vampires. Have feathered wings. Usurped by the Hiaj two hundred years ago.

SALINAE — A major city in the House of Night. Located in Rishan territory. When the Rishan were in power, Salinae was a thriving hub, functioning as a second capital. Oraya spent the first years of her life, before Vincent found her, in Salinae.

SHADOWBORN — Vampires of the House of Shadow.

SIVRINAJ — The capital of the House of Night. Home to the Nightborn castle and the Moon Palace, and host to the Kejari once every hundred years.

TURNING — A process to make a human into a vampire, requiring a vampire to drink from a human and offer their blood to the human in return. Vampires who underwent this process are referred to as TURNED.

WHITE PANTHEON — The twelve gods of the core canon, including Alarus, who is presumed deceased. The White Pantheon is worshipped by all humans, with certain regions potentially having favor toward specific gods within the Pantheon. Nyaxia is not a member of the White Pantheon and is actively hostile to them. The

White Pantheon imprisoned and later executed Alarus, the god of death, as punishment for his unlawful marriage with Nyaxia, then a lesser goddess.

ZARUX — The god of the sea, rain, weather, storms, and water. Member of the White Pantheon.

ACKNOWLEDGMENTS

Every single time I have to write one of these, I'm amazed by how surreal it still feels. I have so many people to thank for helping me dream this new dark, bloody world into existence. Chief among them:

Nathan (first as always), for being my best friend, my greatest love, my biggest supporter, my brainstorming buddy, my art director, my encyclopedia, and so much more. I would not be able to do any of this without you. I love you!

Monique Patterson and the team at Bramble, for seeing the potential in this world and helping this story reach more readers than ever. Thank you so much for taking this book on its next journey!

Ariella, Deanna, Elizabeth, and Rachel, for being amazing early readers and providing such helpful feedback. You are the best!

K.D. Ritchie at Story Wrappers for such a beautiful cover. Love working with you!

Noah, for being, as always, an amazing story sherpa. Thank you for lending your eyes to this manuscript many times over and for your invaluable editing pass.

Anthony, for fabulous proofreading and for eternally correcting my comma usage. I swear to god, one of these days, I'm going to actually nail it.

Rachel, for being the most eagle-eyed proofreader ever! Thanks for killing all my typos and correcting all my continuity errors!

Clare, thank you so much for listening to me whine all day every day and putting up with the notorious Carissa-Broadbent-brain-to-mouth pipeline. You are a star, and I adore you.

And to my Swords & Corsets crew, Jenn, Krystle, and Angela, you guys are the fucking best. I love you all and could not possibly ask for a better, more talented, and more awesome writer friend circle.

And finally, thank you to *you*—for coming on this adventure with me!

If you have been a reader since the War of Lost Hearts trilogy, thank you for following me to this new world. And if you're new to me, thank you so much for taking a chance on this book.

Your support, readership, fan art, reviews, messages, emails . . . all of it has been instrumental to my career, and I truly, truly cannot thank you enough. None of this would be happening without you, and I never forget it for a single second.

I'm excited to join you for the next one!

Turn the page for a sneak peek at
the next book in the Crowns of Nyaxia series

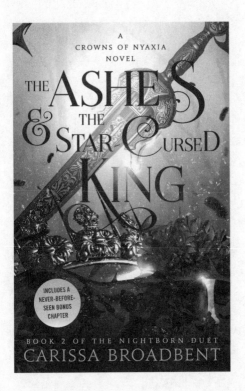

Available Summer 2024 from Bramble

The king knew, in this moment, that his greatest love would also be his ruination, and that both would come in the unlikely form of a young human woman.

He'd been putting off this realization for a long time. Longer, maybe, than he wanted to admit to himself. Clarity, strangely enough, came in a moment of utter chaos—in the raging screams of the audience, in the blood-soaked colosseum sands, in the flurry of bodies and sweat and gore as the young woman barely managed to stave off the brutal onslaught from her aggressor.

The king wasn't doing much thinking then. He was only reacting. Trying to get the Bloodborn's attention away from the human. Trying to get between them. Failing every time.

The Bloodborn contestant had one target and one target alone: the human.

One strike, and another, and another, and the young woman was on the ground, the Bloodborn towering over her, and the king couldn't feel anything but his heart in his throat as the sword rose.

And then the king looked up into the stands, and his eyes so easily fell to the Bloodborn prince, standing there with his arms crossed and a cigarillo at his lips, smirking.

He understood exactly what that smirk said: *I know what you want. You know what I want.*

It was here, in this moment, that the realization hit him.

You have fucking destroyed me, he had told the young woman the night before.

She would destroy him.

And it would be worth it.

Because the king didn't even think, didn't even hesitate, as he met the prince's eyes—and he nodded.

One little movement, and he sold away his kingdom.

One little movement, and he knew exactly what he had to do.

The next seconds blurred together. The prince's smirk becoming a satisfied smile. His signal to his Bloodborn contestant. The contestant's hesitation, so perfectly calculated, and the human woman's sword through her chest.

And then it was just him and her, and a prize that only one could live to claim.

Only one choice was left then, of course. He didn't question it. He had just made a deal to save her life—a deal that would destroy his kingdom, and that he had only one way out of.

Three hundred years was a long time to live. More time, he'd often thought, than any creature deserved.

The two of them stared at each other for several long, silent breaths, unmoving. He could read her face so easily. It was endearing that someone so prickly was also so transparent. Right now, her conflict— her pain—shone through the cracks in her walls.

She wouldn't move first, he knew.

So he did.

He knew her so well by now. He knew exactly how to push her to unleash all that ruthless, deadly, devastatingly-fucking-beautiful power. He was a good actor. He played his role well—even if beneath it, he flinched with every wound his blade opened on her flesh.

Many years later, the historians would whisper, *Why? Why did he do this?*

If they could have asked him that night, he might have said, *Is it really so hard to understand?*

Her eyes were the last thing he saw when he died.

They were beautiful eyes. Unusual. Bright silver, like the moon, though usually darkened by clouds. He found many things about the human woman beautiful, but he thought her eyes were the most stunning of all. He'd never told her so. The moment her blade came to his chest, Nightfire surrounding them both, he wondered if he should have.

Those eyes always revealed more than she ever thought they did. He saw the exact moment she caught him in his act—realized he had tricked her.

He almost laughed. Because of course she noticed. She, and those eyes, had always seen right through him.

It was too late, though. His hand gripped her wrist as he felt her balk.

His last words were not, *You have beautiful eyes*.

His last words were, "End it."

She was shaking her head, the cold fire in her face fading to dismay.

But he knew he was doing the right thing, and those eyes reassured him. Because they were strong and determined and unique, neither human nor vampire, fierce and thoughtful.

Better than his. More deserving of what would come next.

"*End it*," he said, and pulled her wrist.

And he did not look away from those eyes as he died, by the hand of the only person who deserved to kill him.

Maybe the king always knew that his greatest love would be his ruination. Maybe he knew it the moment he met her.

He'd know it the second time he died, too.

CHAPTER ONE

Oraya

My father lived in the hazy moments before I opened my eyes every day, caught between waking and dreaming.

I treasured those moments, when my nightmares had faded but they'd yet to be replaced with the grim shadow of reality. I would roll over in silk sheets and draw in a deep inhale of that familiar scent—rose and incense and stone and dust. I was in the bed I had slept in every day for fifteen years, in the room that had always been mine, in the castle I had been raised in, and my father, Vincent, the King of the Nightborn, was alive.

And then I would open my eyes, and the inevitable cruel clarity of consciousness would roll over me, and my father would die all over again.

Those seconds between sleep and waking were the best of the day.

The moment when the memory returned to me was the worst.

Still, it was worth it. I slept whenever I could, just to claw those precious seconds back. But you can't stop time. Can't stop death.

I tried not to notice that those seconds grew fewer each time I woke.

This morning, I opened my eyes, and my father was still dead.

BANG BANG BANG.

Whoever was knocking on the door did so with the impatience of someone who had been at it for longer than they'd like.

Whoever was knocking.

I knew who was fucking knocking.

I didn't move.

I *couldn't* move, actually, because the grief had seized every one of my muscles. I clenched my jaw, tighter, *tighter,* until it hurt, until I hoped my teeth cracked. My fists were white-knuckled around the sheets. I could smell the smoke—Nightfire, my magic, eating away at them.

I had been robbed of something precious. Those hazy moments where everything was as it had been.

I slipped from sleep with the image of Vincent's decimated body still seared into my mind, just as dead and just as mutilated in my sleeping moments as it was in my waking ones.

"Wake up, princess!" The voice was so loud that even with the door closed, it boomed through the room. "I know those catlike senses of yours. You think I don't know you're awake? I'd rather you let me in, but I'll barge in if I have to."

I hated that voice.

I hated that voice.

I needed ten more seconds before I could look at him. Five more—

BANG.

BA—

I threw back the covers, leapt from my bed, crossed the room in a few long strides, and threw open the door.

"Knock on that door," I breathed, *"one more fucking time."*

My husband smiled at me, lowering his raised fist, which had indeed been ready to knock one more fucking time. "There she is."

I hated that face.

I hated those words.

And I hated most of all that when he said them now, I could hear the hidden undercurrent of concern—could see the way his smirk stilled as he took me in, feet to eyes, in quick but thorough evaluation. His gaze paused at my hands, drawn into fists at my sides, and I realized I was clutching a scalded scrap of silk in one.

I wanted to use it to threaten him, remind him that the silk could be him if he wasn't careful. But something about the flicker of concern over his face, and all the things it made me feel, killed that fire in my stomach.

I liked anger. It was tangible, and strong, and it made me feel powerful.

But I felt anything but powerful when I was forced to recognize that Raihn—the man who had lied to me, imprisoned me, overthrown my kingdom, and murdered my father—genuinely cared for me.

I couldn't even look at Raihn's face without seeing it spattered with my father's blood.

Without seeing how he'd once looked at me, like I was the most precious thing in the world, the night we had spent in bed together.

Too many emotions. I stomped them down viciously, even though it physically hurt, as if swallowing razor blades. Easier to feel nothing.

"What?" I asked. It was a deflated question, not the verbal strike I wanted it to be.

I wished I didn't notice the slight disappointment on Raihn's face. Worry, even.

"I've come to tell you to get ready," he said. "We have guests."

Guests?

My stomach churned at the thought—the thought of standing in front of strangers, feeling them stare at me like a caged animal, while struggling to keep myself together.

You know how to control your emotions, little serpent, Vincent whispered in my ear. *I taught you that.*

I flinched.

Raihn's head cocked, a wrinkle deepening between his brows. "What?"

Fuck, I hated that. Every time, he saw it.

"Nothing."

I knew Raihn didn't believe me. He knew I knew it. I hated that he knew I knew it.

I stomped that down, too, until that emotion was just another numb buzz in the background, coated over with another layer of ice.

It took constant effort, keeping them that way, and I was grateful I could focus on that.

Raihn stared expectantly at me, but I said nothing.

"What?" he said. "No questions?"

I shook my head.

"No insults? No refusal? No argument?"

Do you want *me to argue?* I almost asked. But then I'd have to see that little concerned twitch on his face, and I'd have to recognize that he *did* want me to argue, and then I'd have to feel that complicated emotion, too.

So I just shook my head again.

He cleared his throat. "Alright. Well. Here. This is for you." He'd been carrying a silk bag, which he now handed to me.

I didn't ask.

"It's a dress," he said.

"Alright."

"For the meeting."

Meeting. That sounded important.

You don't care, I reminded myself.

He waited for me to ask, but I didn't.

"It's the only one I've got, so don't bother arguing with me about it if you don't like it."

So pathetically transparent. He was practically poking me with a stick to see when I'd react.

I opened the bag and glanced down to see a pile of black silk.

My chest tightened. Silk, not leather. After everything, the idea of walking through this castle in anything other than armor . . .

But I said, "It's fine."

I just wanted him to go.

But Raihn now never left a conversation without a long, lingering stare, as if he had a lot to say and it all threatened to bubble up before he left my room. Every single fucking time.

"What?" I asked, impatient.

Mother, I felt like my stitches were popping open, one by one.

"Get dressed," he said at last, to my relief. "I'll be back in an hour."

When he was gone, I closed the door and sagged against it, releasing a ragged exhale. Keeping myself together for those last few minutes was agonizing. I didn't know how I was going to do it in front of a bunch of Raihn's cronies. For longer. For fucking *hours*.

I couldn't do it.

You will, Vincent whispered in my ear. *Show them how strong you are.*

I squeezed my eyes shut. I wanted to lean into that voice.

But it faded, as it always did, and my father was dead once more.

I put on the stupid dress.

Raihn was nervous.

I wished I didn't recognize this so easily. No one else seemed to. Why would they? His act was meticulous. He embodied the role of conqueror king just as easily as he had embodied the role of human in the pub, and the role of bloodthirsty contestant, and the role of my lover, and the role of my kidnapper.

But I saw it, anyway. The single muscle tightening at the angle of his jaw. The slightly glazed-over, too-hard focus to his stare. The way he kept touching the cuff of his sleeve, like he was uncomfortable in the costume he wore.

When he returned to my room, I'd stared at him, caught off guard despite myself.

He wore a stiff, fine black jacket with blue trim and a matching sash over his shoulder, striking against the silver buttons and subtle metallic brocade. It was achingly similar to another outfit I'd seen him wear once: the outfit he had worn at the Halfmoon ball, the one that the Moon Palace had provided for him. Even then, though, he'd left his hair unkempt, his chin stubbled, as if the entire thing had been reluctant. Now, he was clean-shaven. His hair was neat and tied up to reveal the top of his Heir Mark over the back of his neck, peeking over the neck of his jacket. His wings were out, revealing the streaks of bright red at their edges and tips. And . . .

And . . .

At this, my throat grew so thick I couldn't swallow—couldn't breathe.

The sight of the crown on Raihn's head drove a spike between my ribs. The silver spires sat nestled in Raihn's red-black waves, the contrast of the two jarring when I had only ever seen that metal against my father's sleek fair hair.

The last time I had seen that crown, it had been soaked in blood, ground into the sands of the colosseum as my father died in my arms.

Had someone had to pick through what remained of Vincent's body to get that crown? Had some poor servant had to clean his blood and skin and hair from all those intricate little whorls of silver?

Raihn looked me up and down.

"You look nice," he said.

The last time he had said that word to me, at that ball, it had sent a shiver up my spine—four letters full of hidden promise.

Now, it sounded like a lie.

My dress was fine. Just fine. Plain. Flattering. It was light, finely made silk that clung to my body—it must have been made for me, to fit that well, though I had no idea how they had known my measurements. It left my arms bare, though it had a high collar with asymmetrical buttons that wrapped around my side.

I was secretly grateful that it covered my Heir Mark.

I avoided looking in the mirror when I changed, these days. Partly because I looked like shit. But also because I hated—*hated*—to see that Mark. Vincent's Mark. Every lie, seared into my skin in red ink. Every question I could never answer.

Covering the Mark was, of course, intentional. If I was going to be paraded in front of some kind of important Rishan people, I'd be expected to seem as nonthreatening as possible.

Fine.

A strange look flickered over Raihn's face.

"It's not closed."

He gestured to his throat, and I realized that he meant the dress—in addition to the clasps in the front, there were buttons in the back, too, and I'd only managed to make it halfway up.

"Do you want me to—"

"No."

I blurted it out fast, but in the seconds of silence that followed, I realized that I had no choice.

"Fine," I said, after a moment.

I turned around, showing my greatest enemy my bare back. I thought to myself, wryly, that Vincent would be ashamed that I was doing such a thing.

But Mother, I would take a dagger over Raihn's hands—would rather feel a blade than his fingertips brushing my skin, far too gently.

And what kind of a daughter did it make me, that despite everything, some part of me craved an affectionate touch?

I drew in a breath and didn't let it out until he fastened the last button. I waited for his hands to move away, but they didn't. Like he was thinking about saying something more.

"We're late."

I jumped at the sound of Cairis's voice. Raihn pulled away. Cairis leaned against the doorframe, eyes slightly narrowed, smiling. Cairis was always smiling, but he was also always watching me very, very closely. He wanted me dead. That was fine. Sometimes I wanted me dead, too.

"Right." Raihn cleared his throat. Touched the cuff of his sleeve. Nervous. So nervous.

A previous version of myself, the one now buried beneath the dozens of layers of ice I put between my emotions and the surface of my skin, would have been curious.

Raihn glanced over his shoulder at me, mouth twisting into a smirk, shoving his emotions down the same way I did.

"Let's go, princess. We'll give them a show."

THE THRONE ROOM had been cleaned up since the last time I was here—artwork and decor replaced, floors cleared of the broken pieces of Hiaj artifacts. The curtains were open, revealing the silver-shrouded silhouette of Sivrinaj. It was calmer than it had been a few weeks ago, but little sparks of light occasionally burst through the night in the distance. Raihn's men had gotten most of the inner city under control, but I could see clashes throughout the outskirts of Sivrinaj from my bedroom window. The Hiaj were not going down without a fight—not even against the House of Blood.

A twinge of something far beneath that ice—pride, maybe. Worry. I wasn't sure. It was so hard to tell.

My father's throne—Raihn's throne—sat upon the center of the dais. Cairis and Ketura took up their places behind it, against the wall, dressed in their best fineries. Ever the dutiful guards. I assumed I would be there, too, in the single chair perched there. But Raihn took one look at it, cocked his head, and then dragged it up to place it beside the throne.

Cairis looked at him like he'd just lost his mind.

"You sure about that?" he said, quietly enough that I knew I wasn't intended to hear.

"Sure am," Raihn replied, then turned to me and motioned to the chair while taking his own, not giving Cairis the chance to disagree. Still, the advisor's pursed lips said more than enough. As did Ketura's ever-present dagger glare.

If I was supposed to be moved by this show of . . . of generosity, or kindness, or whatever the fuck this was supposed to be, I wasn't. I sat and didn't look at Raihn.

A servant poked her head in through the double doors, bowing as she addressed Raihn. "They're here, Highness."

Raihn glanced at Cairis. "Where the fuck is he?"

As if on cue, the scent of cigarillo smoke drifted through the air. Septimus strode in through the hall, ascending the dais in two long, graceful strides. He was followed by his two favorite Bloodborn guards, Desdemona and Ilia, two tall, willowy women who looked so similar I was certain they must be sisters. I'd never heard either of them speak.

"Apologies," he said breezily.

"Put that out," Raihn grumbled.

Septimus chuckled. "I hope you intend to be more polite to your own nobles than that."

But he obeyed—putting out the cigarillo on his own palm. The smell of smoke was replaced by that of burning flesh. Cairis wrinkled his nose.

"That's nice," he said drily.

"The Nightborn King asked me to put it out. It would be rude not to."

Cairis rolled his eyes and looked like he was trying very hard not to say anything else.

Raihn, on the other hand, just stared across the room at those closed double doors, as if burning straight through them to what lay beyond. His face was neutral. Cocky, even.

I knew better.

"Vale?" he asked Cairis, voice low.

"He should've been here. Boat must be late."

"Mm."

That sound might as well have been a curse.

Yes, Raihn was very, very nervous.

But his voice was calm and breezy as he said, "Then I guess we're ready, aren't we? Open the doors. Let them in."

ABOUT THE AUTHOR

CARISSA BROADBENT has been concerning teachers and parents with mercilessly grim tales since she was roughly nine years old. Since then, her stories have gotten (slightly) less depressing and (hopefully a lot?) more readable. Today, she writes novels that blend epic fantasy plots with a heaping dose of romance. She lives with her husband, her son, one very poorly behaved rabbit, and one perpetually skeptical cat in Rhode Island.

carissabroadbentbooks.com
Twitter: @CarissaNasyra
Instagram: @carissabroadbentbooks
TikTok: @carissabroadbent